Praise for *Face Value*

"A fun and fantastic romp through the world of glamour as only a true insider can know. And only a true insider with the intelligence and empathy of Kathleen Baird-Murray could so entertainingly deal with the question we have been dying to ask . . . Has the world gone mad? Read it and see. I loved it."

—Poppy King, creator of Lipstick Queen

"A fascinating subject for a novel . . . It really is rare for popular fiction to handle such an incendiary, controversial subject so well." —Marian Keyes, international bestselling author of *Anybody Out There?*

D0167398

Dear Susan

face value

a novel

thank you so much!

Kathleen Baird-Murray

love

Kathleen Baird-Murray

B

BERKLEY BOOKS, NEW YORK

X

THE BERKLEY PUBLISHING GROUP
Published by the Penguin Group
Penguin Group (USA) Inc.
375 Hudson Street, New York, New York 10014, USA
Penguin Group (Canada), 90 Eglinton Avenue East, Suite 700, Toronto, Ontario M4P 2Y3, Canada
(a division of Pearson Penguin Canada Inc.)
Penguin Books Ltd., 80 Strand, London WC2R 0RL, England
Penguin Group Ireland, 25 St. Stephen's Green, Dublin 2, Ireland (a division of Penguin Books Ltd.)
Penguin Group (Australia), 250 Camberwell Road, Camberwell, Victoria 3124, Australia
(a division of Pearson Australia Group Pty. Ltd.)
Penguin Books India Pvt. Ltd., 11 Community Centre, Panchsheel Park, New Delhi—110 017, India
Penguin Group (NZ), 67 Apollo Drive, Rosedale, North Shore 0632, New Zealand
(a division of Pearson New Zealand Ltd.)
Penguin Books (South Africa) (Pty.) Ltd., 24 Sturdee Avenue, Rosebank, Johannesburg 2196,
South Africa

Penguin Books Ltd., Registered Offices: 80 Strand, London WC2R 0RL, England

This book is an original publication of The Berkley Publishing Group.

Copyright © 2008 by Kathleen Baird-Murray.
Cover design by Rita Frangie.
Text design by Tiffany Estreicher.

PRINTING HISTORY
Berkley trade paperback edition / June 2008

Library of Congress Cataloging-in-Publication Data

Baird-Murray, Kathleen.
  Face value / Kathleen Baird-Murray. —Berkley trade paperback ed.
    p. cm.
  ISBN 978-0-425-22145-7 (pbk.)
  1. Women journalists—Fiction. 2. Periodicals—Publishing—Fiction. 3. Fashion—Fiction.
4. Surgery, Plastic—Fiction. I. Title.
  PR6102.A557F33 2008
  823'.92—dc22   2008005255

PRINTED IN THE UNITED STATES OF AMERICA

10 9 8 7 6 5 4 3 2 1

In memory of Maureen Baird-Murray, 1933–2005

And for Olly, Armand, and Emmanuelle Daniaud

Acknowledgments

Olly Daniaud, my husband, has been with me and this book since the beginning and beyond, and has supported me in so many ways. My dear friends Jennifer Hochman Hamm and Madeleine Burbidge made time to read the book in its very early stages and continually encouraged me. Jon de Prudhoe helped me focus, laughed at my jokes, and gave me margaritas in Santa Monica. (He also pretty much came up with the idea for the book in the first place, so you can blame him). Holly Ross, thank you for swapping seats with me on the flight out to Sarah and Pascal's wedding when my screen was broken, then ploughing through three-hundred-odd pages of very rough first draft.

For technical information and historical research, thank you to Dr. Bernard G. Sarnat, Dr. Frank Kamer, and Dr. Raj Kanodia. A very special thank you to Irena Medavoy. Thanks also to everyone at *Tatler* magazine who worked on the very first plastic surgery supplement. Caspar Hall helped me with art references; Sahmylle Portela contributed a smattering of Portuguese. For authentic New York trivia, I have Jeffrey Miller to thank, as well as Lauren Bentley.

Fiona Wickham, my sister, helped me with details on news channels, and James Wickham, her husband, helped me decipher how the publishing industry worked. My brother, Rupert Baird-Murray, reminded me of some of the joys of a childhood in Maidstone, namely the wave machine at Larkfield Leisure Centre. His wife, my sister-in-law, Chloe Baird-Murray, has always listened, and is always helpful.

This book wouldn't be here without two fabulous agents. Ali Gunn in London and Deborah Schneider in New York have been incredibly supportive.

More readers: Nikki Tibbles, who also lent me her cottage and took my kids out for the day so I could finish an edit; Lizzie Baird-Murray, Monica Gleeson, Andrew Hodge, Kathy Katz, Tony Mason, Paul McNeil, and Marilyn Petridean.

Michael Birt, for letting me use the author picture; Sean Gleason, Lucia Pica, and Pascal and Sarah Dangin, for fuelling my vanity, a huge thank you. Rosa, for not giving birth that day!

The team at Berkley, headed up by Susan Allison, have all been wonderful, but one person has been especially nice, lovely, and brilliant. Emily Beth Rapoport is highly talented and a true joy to work with. I have been very lucky to have her.

Loads of friends suggested titles, or helped in other ways: Bryan Adams, Frederique Andreani, Sugar Ansari, Harvey Bertram-Brown, Kate Chapple, Julietta Dexter, Michael Donovan, Jenny Dyson, Mischa Eligoloff, Jo Fox-Tutchener, Amy Gardner, Maria Garcia, Elise Garland, Tina Gaudoin, John Graham, Ally Green, Victoria Grew, Nick Hamm, George Hammer, Nicola Jeal, Anil Kapil, Peter and Sophie Kemp, Marcia Kilgore, Andrew King, Andra Levinson, Craig Lynn, Henny Manley, Harriet Mays-Powell, Anna McQueen, Simon Mills, Kay Montano, Danny Moynihan, John Powell, John Prothero, Ben Read, Amanda Ross, Vicki Russell, Claudia Savino, Richard Seymour, Lynn Taylor, Christine Walker, Sharon Walker, Kaja Reiff-Musgrove, Antonia Whyatt, Richard Williams.

author's note

"Write about what you know," they say, and so I have drawn in part on my experiences traveling around the world interviewing plastic surgeons, working on magazines, even growing up in Maidstone. But I have nothing but respect for all the people I have met, and would like to state categorically that none of the characters in this book is meant to be a representation of anyone; it remains a work of fiction through and through.

Many people tell you that they're your friend . . .
Make sure that you're receiving the signals they send . . .
Better watch out for the skin deep.
    —"Skin Deep," The Stranglers

maidstone

beauty note:

Model wears faded khaki green hipster boot-cuts by Topshop, two-inch muffin-top compulsory. Cord jacket by Oxfam, Fair Trade coffee stain optional. *Eyes:* Clogged mascara, worn around eyes and not on lashes, by Rimmel (possibly Revlon, label indecipherable, worn away with time). *Lips:* Special cracked lip effect due to dehydration and loss of Chapstick, model's own. *Fragrance:* Sure Anti-Perspirant & Deodorant Roll-On, Unscented, three for two at Boots.

one

Kate Miller had a theory about celebrities. Assuming the twenty-first century survived long enough not to be wasted by global warming and global cooling (and she was one of the few who genuinely knew the difference), Kate figured it would be remembered for its obsession with the rich, famous, and wannabe rich and famous. Her best friend, Lise, and her mum, Darleen, were prime examples of a generation of women who aspired to strange badges of personal merit, which historians of the future would no doubt find themselves unable to rationalize: a haircut with the name of an actor's girlfriend, or a large bottom that no one in the Northern Hemisphere would have desired five months previously.

Kate didn't know or care about any of these so-called celebrity must-haves. At thirty-two years old, she wasn't what you might call a looker, yet neither did she have any features ugly enough to make her interesting. Her dishwasher brown hair could have been the "before" model for an antifrizz hair serum, but at least it was compensated for by her clear skin and shining brown eyes. Her skinny lips were balanced by a rounded, button nose; her cheekbones, so flat they were practically concave, almost begged to have a little fat transferred from her square-but-round bottom, which in turn was neither flat enough to be impressively androgynous nor brazen enough to be an object of desire. It was topped by a midriff that peeked out a little too bravely over her low-cut jeans and didn't seem to match her too-thin stick legs. Yet even though she was blissfully unaware of her physical flaws and plus-points (beyond knowing that she wasn't going to ride on the looks ticket to get her through life), there were mysterious things at work that made her more attractive than the sum of her parts. She didn't know it but her smile opened more doors for her than she gave it credit. Was it the gap between her teeth that had never been fixed, or the dimples that defied the not-there cheekbones as if saying, "Go on! Give it a go! *Jut* a little!"? Kate didn't care. As long as she could roll out, day after day, in her foreign correspondent–inspired uniform of khaki green hipster boot-legs and what could have been a smart-but-casual cord jacket had she ever deigned to take it to the dry cleaner's, and get on with the more important things in life, it was as if she was vaccinated against vanity. Instead she prided herself on being an anomaly in a sea of dunderheads for remaining defiantly immune to the mutual celeb-fan infatuation. But she knew, professionally speaking, that if the world was prepared to make fools of their sycophantic selves, fawning at the feet of the morally dispossessed, pandering to the lowest of the low, and worshipping at the altar of this cult of *celebrity*, then as the senior reporter for *Maidstone Bazaar* (there was no junior reporter, due to staff cuts, but they'd given her the title to make her feel better), then she would have to as well. She would have to fawn, and then write, so they could read.

And now she'd fawned, and she'd written, and they were reading, and the biggest surprise of all? It felt good. Damn good. Kate Miller stuck her feet up on her desk, leaned back in her chair, inhaled a postcelebrity cigarette, and allowed her face to stretch out in a wide, self-satisfied grin, safe in the knowledge that with the others down at the pub for lunch she was alone to indulge, to relive, reread, uninterrupted, her moment of glory, lying just a few feet away under her desk. A couple more puffs, and she sat up again, reaching down under the desk with one hand, rooting around in the recyclable carrier bag at her ankles. As she blindly negotiated her way between last month's *Green Issues* magazine and a foil-wrapped cheese sandwich her mum had made her, trying to find that day's copy she'd rolled up expressly for this moment, she could picture the blue one-hundred-and-forty-point typeface:

MAIDSTONE WEEKLY NEWS

See the image of Trisha Hillmory in the puff panel in the right-hand corner (in a red swimsuit). Delight in the right cross-ref she knew by heart: TRISHA'S BEAUTY SECRETS, MAIDSTONE BAZAAR EXCLUSIVE, SEE MAGAZINE. She retrieved the newspaper, put it on the desk in front of her, smoothing out the creases with her hands, and stared at those three magic words again: BY KATE MILLER. Her first front-page byline. Her first celebrity story.

It was hardly surprising the editor, Brian Palmers, had been so thrilled. Trisha Hillmory, BBC national newscaster, was indeed a rare and beautiful thing. A Maidstone A-lister. Celebrities had spread from international cities (London, New York, Los Angeles) to large regional towns (Newcastle, Liverpool, Manchester) thanks to football and its trappings, namely the footballer's wife. Even some northern, hitherto unnoteworthy towns (Nottingham, Shrewsbury, Blackpool) had a smattering thanks to the return visit of migrating soap stars deigning to open a cinema, appear in a play, or scratch a donkey's nose on the beach for a photo op. But strangely, Maidstone, county town of Kent, adult population 138,959 (census 2001 statistics), had not attracted them just yet, even though it had once boasted Europe's first drive-in cinema (opened by Diana Dors, no less, now sadly closed due to lack of interest) and was the home to Kimberly-Clark, one of Britain's biggest toilet paper manufacturers. And as everyone, even celebrities, needed toilet paper, that should have been enough to put the town on the map, shouldn't it?

Kate had known she was on to a winner the moment Trisha Hillmory's front door had opened that rainy afternoon ten days ago. The orange-colored manager man came out—the same one she'd seen that morning at the swimming pool opening where she'd first met Trisha. Only this time, instead of welcoming her, or facilitating the interview as she presumed was the reason for his presence, Donald Truckell—she had Googled him—flounced out of the door and brushed past her without so much as a backward glance. His face was flushed florid. He gave a petulant stamp to his feet before fandangoing his way like Rumpelstiltskin with a fake tan down Trisha's redbrick path.

"Off. Get her off," he muttered into his lapels, shaking his jacket with panicky, jerky movements, as if a tick had just landed on it. She thought she saw his hair move, slide toward his shoulder as if to give it a cheer-up pat. He clamped his flabby hand to his hair, slid it back up, and strode on, crown intact.

It left Kate in the unsatisfactory position of not really knowing what to do. With the front door still open, she had considered calling Trisha from her mobile, offering to postpone the interview. Something had happened. The interviewee needed time to reflect. To compose herself. She considered it for about two seconds, that is.

A brown court shoe with a bow at the front came hurling through the air at full force, grazing her cheek.

"Ow!" said Kate. "That was me you hit!"

"Who's that?" The voice that came from somewhere upstairs was different from the one belonging to the Trisha Kate had met before. At the Larkfield Leisure Centre pool reopening she'd been magnaminous Trisha, generous toward this scruffy local reporter who still dressed like a student. She had laughed gaily at childhood reminiscences of Larkfield Leisure Centre before the lottery money makeover. She had promised Kate an interview later that same day, all to benefit her favorite local charity, just as soon as she'd thought of one.

And now here she was. Happy, confident Trisha the newscaster was crumpled in a ball at the top of the stairs, her hair a tangled mess, her mascara making smoky trickles down her face.

There was no way Kate was going to postpone this. No way! First rule of journalism: The early bird catches the worm. And if it wriggles away, run after it. She'd made that last bit up, but it seemed apt given the circumstances.

"Oh. It's you. The local journalist." Trisha dabbed at her eyes with the back of her sleeve, then sniffed noisily. "Did I . . . ?"

"It's okay. Really, it didn't hurt."

BBC TRISHA ATTACKS LOCAL REPORTER.

Trisha stared at her with misty eyes. "I . . . we . . . just had, you know, a row. Lovers' tiff. Silly really, isn't it?" She stood up. Her pink suit was creased. The once-jaunty split of her skirt hung limp and puckered like a pair of curtains whose lining had shrunk in the wash.

What was silly? The tiff? Or the fact that Orange Man was her lover? Kate had cautiously stepped into the house, her war wounds entitling her to an all-access pass. On the wall alongside the stairs, light green wallpaper with a fleur-de-lis pattern embossed on it was broken up by four wood-framed prints of nineteenth-century women taking walks in long white skirts on deserted beaches. The frames had fake antique woodworm marks in them. She reached for her notebook to start writing notes, details, the kind of woodworm trivia her readers would lap up, then pulled back. Writing notes perhaps wasn't the most sensitive of things to do in times of crisis. There it was again, the sensitive side of her.

BBC TRISHA THROWS OUT LOVE-RAT!

"How about a cup of tea?" said Trisha, stifling a sobbing noise in an effort to regain control of the situation. "I know I'm ready for one!" Fake laughter. "I'm sorry about the, er . . . shoe thing." She limped down the stairs, thickly carpeted in cream, and sat on the bottom step, sticking her left foot out expectantly.

"Oh! I'm sorry. Your shoe!" said Kate, proffering it to her.

Over several cups of tea, perching uncomfortably on a spinning breakfast-bar chair with a shallow back and such an oversensitive axis that Kate had to balance herself every time she took a sip from her mug or risk splashing Trisha with the hot liquid, Trisha explained the cause of the shoe-throwing incident. It was the stuff a young reporter's dreams were made of. Or even a thirty-two-year-old senior reporter's dreams were made of.

Trisha had been in a deeply unhappy relationship with her manager, a svengali figure whom she'd met while still at university (she'd studied classics at Oxford, which surprised Kate as she'd always thought of Trisha as one of those new generation newscasters who looked pretty but was only just clever enough to throw in the odd impromptu question to an interview subject, the Minister of Agriculture in Mali, say). Orange Man had propelled her rapidly forward in her career, thanks mainly to his impeccable contacts and Trisha's own talent, but theirs quickly became a platonic relationship as her work took

off. Things had finally come to a fore when he found out she'd
been having an affair with her personal trainer, a former dancer
from the Ballet Rambert she'd met while doing an obituary
piece on a Royal Ballet legend. Now Trisha had finally plucked
up the courage to ditch Orange Man once and for all, and he
hadn't taken it well.

SEX-MAD TRISH IN LOVE TRIANGLE.

It was a winner.

It seemed hideously unfair that a woman in this day and age
would have to short-circuit her way to the top by having sexual
relations with a man with a toupee. But then, did she really have
to? Why couldn't she have done what every other self-respecting
young reporter did and sit it out in the suburbs until she was
ready to make her transition to a national? Kate knew the answer to that one already. They might be the same age, but you
wouldn't catch Trisha putting up with stories like "Maidstone
Mum Moonlights as Pole Dancer." Lame, lame, lame. But now
it was Kate's turn. This story was her break—her sex with her
own Orange Man. Her short-circuit to a national paper, or even
a long, convoluted, meandering, scenic route to a national.
Sure, she'd have to get a few more Trisha Hillmorys first, but
write this story and doors would open. Promotion. The making of her career. Today Maidstone. Tomorrow London. After
that, who knew?

Just as she was working out what percentage pay rise she
could negotiate, Trisha dropped the bomb.

"Of course," she said, clicking two Splenda into her
bone-china mug, "you can't write about any of this, you do
know that, don't you?" The tears had dried up, but her face was
still streaked with mascara. It did nothing to dispel the steely
narrowing of her eyes as she stirred her tea, the spoon hitting
the sides of the cup in a steady, even rhythm. "I always
sue . . . always."

Kate slipped off the spinning chair, slopping her tea onto her lap.

"You do? . . . You sue?" She couldn't let this story go, just couldn't. "But of course you know you can trust me, I mean, I'd never—"

"Never write about me in anything but a sympathetic style? Oh, sure. I know. Give me copy approval. Give me two weeks in the bleeding Bahamas. Give me a new Balenciaga. Anything. Just so long as you can break the story. . . ." She reached for her handbag, a bulging, dark brown leather thing with buckles and clasps all over, and pulled out a compact. It clicked open, extra loudly now that Kate's cozy companionship was vanquished, leaving in its place a void of bittersweet professional distance. Trisha examined her face in the mirror, dusting powder over the smudges where the tears had been, pressing it determinedly with an expert hand.

"The thing is, you might be like that, Kate, and you seem like a nice person so I suppose I could trust you. But those others . . . They'll be dreaming up the headlines the moment you tell them about all this. . . . I can see it now . . . 'Sex-Mad Trish in Love Triangle!'"

"Oh, no, you don't think . . . of course we wouldn't . . . they wouldn't . . . I mean, you really don't think that . . ." She felt her face and neck burning up, hot and red with guilt and embarrassment.

Trisha stood up squarely in front of Kate, who began swinging her chair from side to side. She stared. Kate shivered.

"Of course, there is the small matter of the graze," she said, patting a little powder onto Kate's cheek. The flesh-colored dust stung as it settled in the contours of the reddened scratch.

"Ouch!"

"So, I'll give you a different story," continued Trisha, ignoring her complaint. "It'll be positive. An 'at home with Trisha' type of thing. Plug the charity. Talk about my favorite moisturizer. And all right, you can have the end of my affair," she continued, "but we'll do it my way, okay? No shoe throwing. And I'm not seeing anyone else, you understand? Not yet, anyway. Now do we have a deal?"

AT HOME WITH TRISHA. BBC STAR REVEALS HER BEAUTY SECRETS.

It might just work.

"One more thing. Trisha Hillmory has never had Botox. Do you understand? Never ever."

She snapped the compact shut.

two

By the time Kate deigned to arrive at the office the day following her front-page debut, it was teatime. Now that the nation had apparently switched its allegiance to coffee, teatime was a somewhat redundant way of timekeeping, conjuring up obsolete images of cucumber sandwiches, Earl Grey, and dancing at the Waldorf. Four o'clock, then. It had so far been a thoroughly disappointing day, failing to live up to the previous day's promise. She had allowed herself a congratulatory late start, then attended the local planning meeting regarding the proposed new shopping mall out in Meadowparks, before skiving off for a late lunch with Lise, to which Lise hadn't shown up because she'd been sidetracked by her new boyfriend, a married bank manager. With five children.

The office reeked of the conflicting smells of oranges and burgers. *Maidstone Bazaar* shared a 1960s block with an accountancy firm, above a newsagent's and a cut-price supermarket, that was neither chic enough to be turned into some sucker's dream loft space nor ugly enough to be condemned. The main newspaper had moved two years before to a swanky new office development on the outskirts of town, but incredibly there hadn't been enough room for the magazine's staff of five despite Brian Palmers's protestations that the magazine was an integral part of the paper. He'd fired off several letters to the paper's forward-thinking development and management consultants, citing the magazine's vital role within the paper as reasons for them to find space, *damn it*, using whatever means necessary. For a while he was the paper's unwritten hero, fighting for his small yet crucial team to be recognized with all the attendant privileges and accolades of the mothership. Until that is, the powers that be took him seriously and offered *Maidstone Bazaar* an exclusive office "block" adjacent to the newspaper's executive suites, the prime site within site. Sadly, the prime site turned out to be little more than a glorified trailer, the yucca plant in the corner doing nothing to hide the condensation that misted up the windows, or the rust around the edges of the door, which rocked unsteadily on its hinges until Brian Palmers slammed it firmly behind him on his way out. On second thought, he argued, the central location of *Maidstone Bazaar*'s current home gave it unique access to its readers. Just off the high street, it would be able to keep in touch with what the people of the borough really wanted from a magazine supplement and with the main paper being so far removed, geographically speaking (he still hoped its correspondents would be able to make those crucial trips into town), perhaps it was important that he do the only proper and decent thing: stay put.

He prided himself on his democratic style of leadership. Democratic as long as everyone knew who was boss, ha-ha! But the close working conditions meant that there wasn't room for big egos or autocrats, familiarity breeding not so much contempt as a healthy tinge of sarcasm intoned into every other sentence and an overriding feeling that in career terms at least, this was it. The office was so cramped that the staff shared one table, canteen style, the heat of their computers generating enough warmth to keep winter radiators switched off permanently (so much better for asthma and allergies), and looked out onto the car park round the back of the supermarket. Brian had a separate box, with a glass screen affording some privacy, but it wasn't grand by any means. Meetings were kept blissfully short, for the simple reason that they either took place with him crouching on a spare chair by their desks, or even worse—them all perching on his desk. There had been so many spilled cups of coffee that the only beverage allowed in meetings was water. As a result most of the real decision making took place in the pub, a smoky, video game–dominated affair at the end of the block.

Kate was third in the pecking order, after Tania, the chief sub, although that was only if she confined her counting to the features department. Gavin, who was in charge of layout and design (and generally didn't have to do as many runs down to Starbucks as she did), and Lianne, a staff writer employed on a freelance basis, were both older than Kate and had been on the magazine longer than her, but if she included them in the count, then she'd be fifth out of five, which was all too depressing. Gavin's burger wrapper lay in the bin, impregnating the air with the remnants of mad cow disease. Lianne's orange peels lay on top. Everyone suspected she was anorexic as no one had ever seen her eat anything more than a satsuma washed down with coffee, but no one had actually confronted her with the dreaded truth, just in case it opened up a whole host of unwelcome problems that could dominate office politics for years and result in her taking loads of time off, and goodness knows what else. Besides, she might just be skinny and eat loads at home, like one of those people with a phobia about eating in public. She looked up as Kate walked in, and nodded a hello, tearing off more peel with her teeth and throwing it in the bin. And that, mused Kate to herself as she surveyed them all, was the true democracy of *Maidstone Bazaar*. Everyone had their own secret sin: Gavin's burger addiction, Lianne's assumed anorexia, Kate's chain-smoking (until two weeks ago, minus yesterday's totally justifiable relapse; but she still chewed her fingernails, so that could overtake smoking), Brian's un-PC jokes, and Tania's cat's hairs covering everything. Her big, fluffy, stroppy Persian cat, called Badass, was perhaps the most disgusting habit of all. Tania's obsessive love for him meant she was allowed to take him to work during the day. She called his custom of using the wastepaper basket as his own private toilet if she left the office for more than thirty minutes a symbol of the constancy of his affections.

Today Kate was working on an article for *Green Issues* magazine. She wasn't supposed to be. She was supposed to be doing eight hundred words (it felt more like "doing" than "writing") on the new cancer hospice out at Springton Banks, but she and Tania had a competition going to see who could be first to hit the one hundred mark for stories about cancer hospices; and as she was up to sixty-seven and Tania was up to eighty-nine, Kate thought it only fair that she let Tania forge ahead. If she was late with the story, Tania would have to finish it off for her, thus gaining the prize of one week's supply of cat food (the type for fussy felines). Kate had put up the prize herself, knowing that Tania was just deluded enough to see it as something worth working toward. Besides, now that the Trisha story was out she didn't want her local *Green Issues* branch to think that she was neglecting her ecological interests in favor of colluding with the devil. Fifteen hundred words on electric buses and why the local council was actively opposing them, in spite of their obvious environmental benefits, should put her back on track. She had a great quote from Councillor McQuarry—"Have you ever seen the things? They're damn ugly!"—but she suspected the councillor, a jovial, friendly man with sweaty hands, had been talking to her off the record.

Looking at the final draft, Kate still wasn't sure about the ending. Not punchy enough. She stared at her screen, waiting for the words to come. Of course, the three most important words in the piece were the three at the top: *By Kate Miller.* Mustn't be distracted by ego. That way lay the danger of celebrity. Her eyebrows furrowed downward as if in a concerted effort to drag the words out from her brain. It needed something about the bus routes that tied it back to the theme of electricity. Electric dreams become electric nightmares? Too clichéd. Anyway, she'd said it already, halfway through the piece. A strand of hair rested on what was left of the graze from where Trisha's shoe had hit her. It had healed nicely.

Brian tapped her on the shoulder.

"C'mon, love. The pub. We're all going to celebrate." She hadn't noticed Tania and the others filing out the door.

"Celebrate what?" She quickly flicked her screen to her screen saver, hoping he hadn't seen the electric bus drama unfolding there.

"Celebrate the fact that it's time for the first alcoholic unit of the day!" he laughed.

"I'll be down in a minute. There's just something I need to tweak here."

As they left, she felt the words falling. She loved this bit, where something, from somewhere, just hit her. Inspiration? She had once tried to describe the process to Lise, the excitement she felt from finding the right words, hitting on a new idea. It made her stomach spin, the satisfaction of knowing that a sentence, a paragraph, was complete, finished, couldn't be improved on, and once committed to paper was somehow permanent. Lise, thirty-one years old, frequently described as "blonde and bubbly" by her colleagues at the gym where she worked, and whose current boyfriend, Steve, was the married bank manager with five children, didn't quite get it. Had she tried sex? she'd asked, without lifting her eyes from a worn copy of *Grazia*.

There was too much noise in the office sometimes, that's why the ending had eluded her, but now it was coming, stepping out of the fog like a monster she couldn't hold back. She typed rapidly:

The question is . . . will Councillor McQuarry look beyond the aesthetics of environmentally friendly public transport and put the needs of the planet first?

Crap. It was crap. She bunched her hair up and knotted the thinning straggly ends back on themselves in some form of a chignon. She'd never been good with her hair. A yellow Post-it Note on her screen caught her eye.

Your mum called. And Lise.

Her mum. Average daily calls: three. Lise. Average daily calls: six. Well, it was only right she should call to apologize for deserting her at lunch.

The question is . . . will Councillor McQuarry turn an electric nightmare into an electric dream? Though repetitive, this was getting somewhere. Quite where exactly, she didn't know, but somewhere. She just needed to tidy it up a little. Should it be, *The question is . . . will these "ugly" buses keep our planet looking beautiful?*

The phone rang. It was probably Lise again. She'd act as though she didn't care about lunch.

She huffed into the receiver, "Kate Miller . . . *Bazaar.*"

It wasn't Lise.

three

Life had a habit of throwing the unexpected at you whenever you least expected it. At least, that's what they said in those pink-covered novels Lise was always reading. But, with the possible exception of yesterday's front-page byline, all the unexpected things that life had thrown at Kate had so far been unpleasant or uninteresting: her father dying when she was too young to remember him; finding out that Kelvin Grabbs, her second boyfriend, was using her as a "cover" to appease his homophobic parents; and her only recognizable talent an inexplicable ability to name a tune within the first two notes. These were the things, unexpected things, that life had so far thrown at Kate.

On June 10, as she answered the phone alone in the office that afternoon, life threw the unexpected once again at Kate Miller. This time, it was neither unpleasant nor uninteresting.

One minute, the calm of an empty office; the next minute, the phone call.

A woman's voice, like Cagney or Lacey or Sarah Jessica Parker—regional New York dialects aside, it was definitely American—asking was this Kate Miller, because she was calling from 'Noo-velle May-Song Editions' and had Alexis De Vere, the editor of *Darling* magazine, New York, on the line.

"You got her? It's Kate Miller? . . . Okay, put it down, I'm here." Another American voice was on the line, speaking so fast Kate could hardly understand what she was saying. "Kate, this is Alexis De Vere, two words, and may I just say, I am so pleased to have finally tracked you down! Lisette, you know Lisette, don't you? She speaks so highly of your work and she said—"

"Well . . . not personally, but . . ." Who on earth was Lisette? Who was Alexis De Vere Two Words? "I mean, I do know a Lise, but . . ." How did Lise know this woman?

"Well, we have a situation here, where we have been trying to find . . . No, forget that, how can I put it? I'm going to come straight out with it!" Kate heard the woman take a deep breath at the other end of the phone. "We love your work, Kate. Love it. Everyone loves it." She inhaled deeply again, this time as if she was smoking. "And we want you to be *Darling*'s next beauty director!"

There was another long pause, as if having thrown it out there she wanted Kate to gush back with the same exuberance, but Kate was too staggered to say anything. Whose darling?

"I mean, obviously," Two Words continued, filling a gap she didn't seem prepared for, "you're famous for your celebrity beauty stories, you do them so well, everyone's talking about them." She must have read the Trisha piece.

I've only done the one, Kate nearly said, but she wasn't quick enough, and the woman continued regardless, railroaded right over her: "Gustav—you know Gustav? Just shot Kate and this wonderful new girl from Estonia . . . forgot her name . . . Lizbet?? Lizbet?" There was a pause, as Lizbet failed to materialize. "You know who I mean, right? Amazing story, naked big sister–little sister thing, in a sauna with a bunch of Russian mafia. About antiaging. Very Helmut Newton, God bless his soul, did you ever work with him? Mind you, we can't say it's a 'tribute' or anything else. Gustav will have a fit. Likes to think he's better than Helmut, can you believe? Well, anyway, Gustav is just desperate to work with you, and you know what he's like. So, what do you think?"

"About what? I'm sorry?"

"Do you want it?"

"Well, no! I mean, yes! I mean, what exactly do I want?"

"Beauty director, *Darling* magazine, New York! What else! I just know that you're the one, Kate, just know it! Raw talent, that's what you are, plain and simple. That's why everyone's talking about you. New York needs girls like you, Kate. And we can make it very easy for you, but I must have you here in a month. One hundred fifty thousand and a relocation package suit you?"

"Well, yes . . . but . . . a hundred and fifty thousand dollars?!"

"One hundred sixty thousand, then. You strike a hard bargain. I like that. Kate! I am so thrilled! Your brilliance will shine at *Darling*, I'm sure of it!"

She was gone. In her place, the first woman, who seemed younger, identified herself as the Lizbet that Alexis had been calling for. She asked for Kate's e-mail address so she could send over a contract. They would have to install Kate in a hotel for the first couple of weeks before moving her to the company's apartment in the Meatpacking District. *Darling* wasn't usually this disorganized, but everything had happened so quickly. Would she be all right with that? And by the way, was Maidstone M-a-i-d or M-a-d-e? Was that in west London?

Kate put the phone down calmly. She looked around the office and checked that it was still only Badass, Tania's cat, staring at her. Five minutes passed.

It would come.

Ten minutes.

She could wait.

She knew what they were up to. The follow-up call, where Lise or Tania, or Gavin on the picture desk, or Lianne or Brian, or her mum, or some TV presenter would shout gleefully: "You've been framed!"

But it never came. Instead, an e-mail popped up on her screen offering flight details, then a contract to be printed out, signed, and FedExed back to Nouvelle Maison Editions, followed by another e-mail saying she should visit the US Embassy ASAP—Lizbet would take care of the necessary paperwork. Five minutes on, yet another e-mail, asking if she could fax or e-mail over one sample of her work, something she was proud of or that was recent. Purely a formality. For the publisher, who was a stickler for rules; you know how those people can be.

Kate stared at the screen, her head in her hands. She tapped her foot on the floor. Her hair had unscrunched itself from the back of her head, and itched the Trisha Hillmory graze. She scratched her neck and looked around the office again. Lisette. The Alexis woman had said Lis*ette*. But what if she'd misheard her? What if really she meant . . . Kate reached for the phone, hit the speakerphone button, and dialed Lise's number.

"I like to move it, move it" blasted out, followed by Lise's chirpy voice: *"Hi! My name's Lise! And if you like to move it, move it, come and work out with me! For personal fitness instruction leave your message after the tone, for everyone else, you can . . ."* *"Move it, move it,"* the music finished her message for her. It wasn't funny, and it wasn't clever. But what was

worrying Kate now was how someone with a *move it, move it* theme tune for their answerphone message could possibly be on nickname terms with the editor of a New York glossy magazine.

"Lise, something really weird's happened. Call me."

Standing up abruptly, she sprang her chair away from her desk and strode into Brian's office, where there was a mirror on the back of the door. All at once she felt compelled to study her reflection. *Darling* magazine had offered her a job. She had just about heard of *Darling* magazine, had seen a few copies lying around in the reception area at the gym where Lise worked. She seemed to remember it was fat and glossy, with pictures of thin girls with big breasts in expensive clothes. She didn't have big breasts. She had flat-as-pancake breasts. The crepey French ones, not the puffy American ones. It was not the kind of magazine she would ever have wanted to work at. She had hoped one day for something suitably eco-aware at *National Geographic*, or even to be the human rights correspondent at the *Observer*. Something that might change the world, which would enable her to really do something for it besides paying her Amnesty International subscription on time or writing features about electric buses that no one would ever read.

Slightly more pressing was the fact that she had no idea what a beauty director did. She knew it was a big job. With a big salary—$150,000! No wait, $160,000! She hadn't even worked out how much that was in pounds . . . a lot! Seventy-five, eighty grand! She could almost buy a flat with it!

This Alexis woman seemed to know her, know about everything she'd done, had read her work, yet how could she? Why would she? She frowned at herself, then stared into the mirror long and hard, waiting to see something, someone different, someone like the kind of person she expected would get a job at *Darling* magazine. Someone whose brilliance was shining. She mouthed at herself in the mirror,

"Hi, I'm Kate Miller, beauty director of *Darling* magazine." She looked too happy. She pursed her mouth, stuck her chin up.

"Kate Miller. *Darling* magazine."

"Magazine" spoiled the flow of the words.

"Kate Miller. *Darling.*"

That could work. She twisted her hair back up. It rested there for an instant then tumbled down again. She flicked it behind her ears. The conscious effort of trying to be someone she wasn't made her laugh. Beauty director, *Darling* magazine? What was she thinking?

It could only be a mistake.

She made her way quickly back to her desk and started typing before she'd even sat down properly.

Dear Lizbet,
I'm afraid I think you have made a mistake. Could you please call me to discuss? Or should I speak to Alexis?
Kind regards, Kate Miller

She hit Send.

She sat back in the chair and breathed deeply, hoping Lise would call back, but instead of feeling relieved at having done the right thing, doubts began to fall thick and fast. What if it wasn't a mistake? They knew her name. Her phone number. But most importantly, they knew her work. But how? Of course! The Internet! Someone there would have read the Trisha interview last night, Maidstone time, which was yesterday morning New York time. Hot off the press. Anyone in the *Darling* office could have alerted Alexis to it—maybe it was on the BBC website even! Or some Trisha Hillmory blog!

Kate's fingers rapidly typed in to Google: *Trisha Hillmory Maidstone Bazaar*. Quick as a flash, up popped the link, on top of the page of hundreds of entries on the newscaster. Those magic three words again: *By Kate Miller*. She was hot and it had taken an American to spot that—well, was that so strange? Wasn't that what Americans were good at? This was the call she had been waiting for, the door that had opened, the story that had so far evaded her, that she should now chase. She could not, should not, throw this opportunity away.

The phone rang. Lise!

"So . . . guess who turned up at the gym today to see me! Booking in for a very personal session?" Her friend giggled.

Kate hugged the phone close and spoke loudly into the mouthpiece, hoping she could be heard above the *"I like to move it, move it"* that was pumping away in the background, its rhythm accompanying every swish-swish of machinery, rowing machines, stairwalkers, and assorted pieces of equipment Kate had vowed never to set foot on.

"Lise! Stop it! This is important!"

"My lovely Steve! Isn't that great? I was so surprised—he's not exactly your average gym type, let's face it—but he'd taken time out specially to see—"

"*Lise!* Listen to me! I've been offered a job in New York!"

There was a long pause at the other end of the phone, and then:

"Oh, *my God*!" she shrieked. "Oh, my God that's . . . that's . . . weird!"

"Only I think I've just turned it down. I think it was a mistake, Lise; they said I knew Gustav and Lisette and that everyone loves my celebrity stories. I mean, that's not me, is it?"

There was a pause. Then a sigh.

"You've just turned it down? I don't understand, Kate. You've been offered a job in New York, and you've just turned it down. Are you nuts? I mean, I'm not being funny, but it's not like you've got a whole lot of other offers on the table right now, is it?"

Kate bridled at Lise's reminder of the so-far unmeteoric pace of her career. "Well, no, but the editor, Alexis, said she knew someone called Lisette and I figured that might be you."

"How would she know me? Lise is short for Lisette? I guess it could be, but—oh, my God, I bet she's like Meryl Streep in that film!"

"*Silkwood*? The one about the nuclear plant?"

"No! *The Devil Wears Prada*, you idiot!"

"Oh . . . I don't know. . . . Well, now I think they might have meant me after all, because they had my number, my name, they knew I'd done the Trisha story—they said my brilliance was shining!"

"So . . . that's great then, isn't it? I mean, what's the problem? That's great, Kate! Oh, my God! You'll get a boyfriend finally! A native New Yorker! When are you going? Can I come and stay? Do you get a flat or something?"

"Look, for the umpteenth time, I don't want a boyfriend, remember? My career comes first. Anyway, I just wrote saying they'd made a mistake."

"You did what?"

"I e-mailed saying they'd made a mistake and to call me."

"Well, can't you un-e-mail it? Isn't there some button you can just call it back on?"

"Lise . . . e-mail, computers, they don't—"

Suddenly a friendly "ping" alerted Kate to a new e-mail appearing.

"Wait . . . I'll call you back." She hung up.

So this was it, her one big chance to leave Maidstone behind, to enter the international world of journalism, to sidestep from big celebrity interviews to beauty, to write in-depth, probing articles on animal testing and the perils of a culture obsessed with antiaging, to segue effortlessly, eventually, to a healthy sideline in an eco-friendly cosmetics and skin care brand that would raise funds for global development and environmental issues, that would have Bono and Sting and every other aging rock star clamoring to front her charitable causes . . . all gone. Her knuckles felt stiff as she hit Open.

From: Lizbet@darling.com
To: Kate.miller@hotmail.com

Dear Kate,
I am so sorry, you're right, I've amended the contract address so that it now reads correctly. Apologies. Please don't tell Alexis—I assure you I will be more vigilant in the future. Let me know if there is anything I can do to ease your relocation in the meantime.
Kind regards, Lizbet

At 9:00 a.m. the following morning Kate had her resignation letter typed and on her editor's desk.

At 10:00 a.m., Brian Palmers, in a speech to the entire staff, said he was saddened, understandably, having always had a soft spot for Kate, who had been working at *Maidstone Bazaar* since she had arrived ten years ago, at age twenty-two, to make teas (why did he always have to remind her about the tea?). One of their most talented writers, she had produced some of the magazine's finest stories, including his all-time favorite, "Local Man Wins Worst DIY Husband of the Year," and now of course, the mag's biggest celebrity coup, *Trisha Hillmory*! She would be sorely missed, but he was happy she was moving on to brighter pastures, becoming a beauty consultant, imagine that! *Director*, Kate had corrected, but he'd only repeated *beauty consultant*, as if she'd be orange-faced, white-coated, and working at the cosmetics counter in the local department store. It was particularly good she was leaving now that Stacey had confirmed she would be returning after her maternity leave after all, and he wouldn't have been able to promote Kate; in fact, he'd been chatting with Tania about it yesterday afternoon at the pub, funny how fate played its cards. He knew that his training program and her experience under his directorship had no doubt in some—he coughed for effect here—small way contributed to her advancement.

"Now on your way, Kate!" he laughed, patting her bottom. Kate had winced. Tania, forty-two, single, no prospect of moving on anywhere, and nothing but a future of a basement flat shared with Badass the cat, had winced with her.

At 11:00 a.m. Tania had gone for a fag round the back of the offices. Kate had followed, eager for some passive smoking. There were more than just a few things that were troubling her. It hadn't escaped Kate's notice that, Trisha Hillmory aside, she had never written a word about beauty in her life, something she would have thought was a necessary requirement for her new job. She suspected the editor, Alexis De Vere, was either some lazy American who hadn't done her research properly or, and this increasingly seemed to be the more likely possibility, she was looking for a change of direction; something that would wake up those beauty-jaded girls of New York and give them something to get their thongs in a twist about.

"You know, what I don't understand is how they heard about me in the first place," said Kate. "I'm not being funny, but do you really think *Maidstone Bazaar* has a following in New York?"

"The Internet. Or our subscriptions department," said Tania. "You know, they get all sorts of incentives for boosting our circulation. Kimmy, my friend who works there, only needs another thousand and she qualifies for a microwave!"

"Can't you buy them for a tenner down the market?"

"Ooh, really? Maybe I should buy her one, save her doing all those extra hours." Tania stubbed her cigarette on the ground. "She works ever so hard, nearly split up with her boyfriend over it." Kate waited a respectful second or so, then picked up the butt to put in the bin later. Cigarettes took years to decompose naturally and ever since she'd given them up a few weeks ago (bar the recent relapse), she was at pains to remind the nicotine-dependent of the ills they inflicted on society.

"You can't take away her motivation," said Kate. "You know what else? If we could just talk a little bit more about me now that we've solved Kimmy's microwave dilemma . . . I don't know the first thing about beauty."

"Yes . . . well." Tania lit up another cigarette thoughtfully, casting her eyes over Kate's disheveled hair.

Over the wall Kate could see the buses queuing to get into the depot round the back of the shopping center. A group of hooded youths sat on the stone bollards by the entrance. They looked bored.

"Can there really be that much to know?"

For the following three weeks Kate went religiously round to Lise's flat every evening, where Lise's friend Yolanda, who was a beauty therapist at the gym and therefore did know about beauty (although admittedly she had only done six weeks of a course and had only covered waxing and massage, but as Lise pointed out she loved makeup, didn't she, and how hard could it be?) taught her about manicures, pedicures, hair removal, and how to blow-dry hair and cleanse skin.

"Groomed," pronounced Yolanda. "You need to look groomed." And she and Lise had frog-marched Kate to the local branch of

Topshop to stock up on acres of polyester-mix wrap dresses with added Lycra. She had to accessorize, too, Yolanda warned, with handbags, bangles, and earrings, and get highlights, because everyone in New York had highlights. Yolanda, it transpired, was learning how to do these this very week at college, and, if she wanted to, Kate could come along to a model night, where she could have her hair done for free.

"Will I have to do a catwalk show or something?"

Lise and Yolanda looked at each other, exasperated. As her New York salary hadn't yet kicked in, discounted highlights were her only option. That evening, third in a row of ten rather unwashed-looking sixteen-year-olds, Kate took her place before a mirror and submitted to the lure of the silver foil, only to emerge four hours later looking like a ginger racoon. This was all the rage, Yolanda assured her, she looked just like that TV presenter on *The Saturday Show*. She didn't want to look like a TV presenter on *The Saturday Show*, she wanted to look like a beauty editor of a New York magazine.

"Never mind," said Lise. "They have really good hairdressers out there. They'll just think you're English, and therefore eccentric. You know what? They'll expect you to be different. That's why they tracked you down!"

She had no regrets, no one she was feeling sorry to be leaving behind. Lise had been annoying her lately, chasing—obsessing over—married Steve, pretending she was in love in order to justify her affair. They'd had a little spat the last time they'd been out together, down at the Roxy. A club that had had its fifteen minutes way back in the '80s, after a brief property boom and the discovery of Lycra, it was now Kate and Lise's last resort when they'd had one too many Bacardi Breezers; it was the only place open past 2:00 a.m. They'd stood in the toilets as Lise mopped up the water from the flooding basins that had left her open-toed stilettos sodden, and Kate had told her in no uncertain terms that Lise 'n' Steve was a relationship that was going nowhere. At least she had a relationship, Lise had retorted. Two more Bacardi Breezers and some energetic shape-throwing on the dance floor had resolved the crisis. But Kate still didn't approve.

So in fact her only regret was that, well, apart from Tania at the office, and on a good day, her mum, there was no one she would miss. She wasn't sad to be going away, just nervous that she might be found out to be some kind of imposter. A local newspaper magazine journalist, not some glossy, glamorous beauty girl.

Darleen had taken the news surprisingly well. Widowed when Kate was only three, it was hard to say who was more dependent on whom. It would have been nice to have had a few tears, perhaps, considering all they had been through to-gether. Instead, she had quizzed Kate relentlessly for thirty minutes, then frog-marched her over to the neighbors' to tell them the good news.

"Of course, Kate has always been very talented, a great writer, and I suppose it was only a matter of time before she got the call."

Bob and Julie Simpson had never heard of *Darling* maga-zine. Bob, whose paper manufacturing business often took him as far away as Plymouth to renew contracts with printers, had never been to New York. Julie had been once.

"It's fantastic news, love," she'd said. "You'll love it there. All that shopping, and the policemen are ever so helpful if you get lost." Bob scratched his crotch in agreement. Kate had sipped politely on the too strong tea and stared at her feet. She didn't know how to behave, jubilant not being a look she had to do too often, her happiness suddenly overcome by an overwhelm-ing sense of guilt. It was as if with every congratulatory remark another fear came rising to the fore. She'd never been to New

York before, never been to America before. And beauty, what did she know about beauty? What *was* beauty?

"Excellent question, I know you're the right girl for the job," Alexis De Vere had said, when she'd called her one gray Maidstone afternoon to confirm the final arrangements. "Beauty is . . . something we're all striving for, quite frankly, and I'm glad the philosophical nature of this most important department at *Darling* magazine hasn't escaped you. I think it is an intrinsic part of the job, and a part that some beauty directors in the past have, I think, overlooked. . . . You have to give it to the readers, the philosophy thing, because they want, crave, and need to ask, to be asked, questions like that, in this shallow, superficial world of ours, Kate, don't you think? And I think that beauty, what is beauty . . . well, it's something we strive for, or something we are born with, or even, as I believe that great English wizard of words of yours once said, "something we have thrust upon us."

"Shakespeare?" She had called him a "wizard of words."

"Oh, you love the bard, too! I just know I've made the right decision. Kate, I'm so glad you'll be joining us!"

*   *   *

"Something's not right, is it?" her mother had asked over supper, a Marks and Spencer's oven-ready vegetarian shepherd's pie, organic, Kate's favorite.

"What do you mean?"

"You should be happier, bragging about this. You've done really well. Poached by a New York magazine!"

Scrambled, more like, Kate thought to herself. Fried, possibly. She thought New York wasn't one of the states where they still had the electric chair, but she couldn't be sure. Even her mum knew more about beauty than she did, thanks to all those late-night plastic surgery shows she watched while waiting for

Kate to return home, ready to make her a pile of Mother's Pride toast with lashings of butter.

Lise had also picked up on her anxiety.

"What's wrong with you?" she asked, the day before her departure. They had arranged good-bye drinks for her, down by the ballet school in the Old Palace, on a grassy bank overlooking the Medway. In the end what had sounded like a lavish affair, in Kate's imagination at least, populated by throngs of grateful interviewees and kicked off with a rousing speech by Trisha Hillmory, whom she would by now be on lunching terms with, had turned out to be just Kate, Lise, and Steve, whom Lise had brought along in a vain, last-ditch attempt to ingratiate himself. Steve had graciously brought along a bottle of "bubbly," as he called it, revealing a bottle of cheap bath foam as a humorous gesture toward Kate's new future as beauty director.

"Oh, that's really funny, Steve," she'd said, her face not cracking, although in fairness to Steve's abysmal sense of humor this could also be due to the remnants of last night's face mask, an egg white concoction, renowned, or so said Yolanda, for its tightening abilities. (How was she supposed to know you were meant to rinse it off after fifteen minutes? Eggs didn't come with instructions, did they?)

"Don't worry, love, the real thing's here," said Steve, hastily, and from an Oddbins carrier he produced a bottle of Pomagne, which fizzed and trickled its way into the three paper cups Lise had thoughtfully pinched from Starbucks.

Steve's bath foam was another omen. Beauty. She would be writing about lipsticks, makeup, hair products, bubble bath, all the things that Lise had probably been into since she was old enough to own her first Barbie doll. The stuff just didn't interest her.

"But you know what," Lise had helpfully pointed out, "with

that kind of salary, you might start finding it very interesting indeed. Stop thinking about yourself as some kind of fraud."

"She's right, love," said Steve. "You got the job! Got head-hunted. It happens all the time in the banking world." Anyone would think he was a director at Merrill Lynch instead of the manager of the local NatWest. A cheating love-rat type of local bank manager.

But maybe they had a point. She had been appointed on merit, and frankly, didn't she deserve it after all her hard slogging away at hospices and swimming pool openings and even interviews with Trisha Hill-bleeding-Mory? Why shouldn't she have the job? She'd always known she was a good writer, with potential—one of her journalism teachers had told her at the Bright Futures Center for Opportunities. (She'd loved the plurality of "opportunity"—you could be a chef, a personal trainer, a journalist, or all three!) Alexis must be a genius of a woman to be able to spot that burning talent and ambition, to recognize her single person status as the huge career sacrifice that it was. She could do it, and she would do it.

In the end, by the time she had packed and repacked her bag three times, packing for a destination she knew nothing about, and a world within a world she both feared and dreaded, she was relieved to be going, relieved to be getting away from a life she had outgrown, outlived, that she had somehow given thirty-two years to without it seemingly giving much back to her.

new york

beauty note:

Model wears black wrap dress, Topshop. Every day for one week. *Hair:* Orange highlights by Maidstone College of Beauty Therapists. *Lips:* Cowshed Lippy Cow Lip Balms, free sample on Virgin Airlines Upper Class. *Fragrance:* Sarah Jessica Parker Covet, parting gift from Lise.

four

The fat lady in the dark blue uniform snarled at her, apparently welcoming her to America. In deference to the stringent US entry regulations, Kate was trying hard to look cool, important, and not guilty all at once. She put her hand up to her mouth in an attempt to mask the smile of sheer euphoria that kept attempting to push its way across her face. To look too excited would only draw attention to herself. What she really wanted was to be waved through quickly to baggage collection, where the tired ugliness of her fellow aliens was already being exacerbated by the harsh, sterile lighting, and get out there, see New York! Better say that again. New York!

For now, she had to be content with the all-American threat of danger that lurked palpably in the stale conditioned air. She volunteered a finger for the imprint machine, wiping it clean first with a tissue.

"Sorry," Kate said to her new friend in Immigration. "Germs."

The woman scowled. "You got a problem with the machine?" she asked, threateningly. She flicked through Kate's passport, menace running like static through her fingertips, her eyes squinting maliciously.

Kate felt herself redden, a future in Manhattan replaced by a stint in Guantánamo.

You learn big things about countries in small places, she mused as she eventually collected her baggage. Everything in America screamed success right from the get-go. Even the luggage trolley was a SmartCart.

After clearing Customs only to find there was no one there to meet her, she'd jumped in a cab. Lizbet had given her the address of a hotel somewhere in SoHo, which, according to her *Time Out* guidebook, was a glamorous destination, once an industrial zone, and earmarked for destruction in the 1960s. She was thrilled to be in a yellow cab. Ever since she'd seen Robert De Niro in *Taxi Driver*, she'd wondered what it would be like to hail one, sink into its low leather seats, and try to strike up a conversation through the scratched plastic screen with whichever driver she got. She was no closer to fulfilling that dream, as the cabbie was not conversant in the English language. No matter, she had other sources to draw on. Whereas Lise had been glued to *Sex and the City* when it had been on TV, Kate's vision of New York had more of a literary bent to it. *Bonfire of the Vanities*; *Bright Lights, Big City*, she'd felt dizzy reading the books, and had moved from one to the other in frenzied succession. Now here she was, sundown, traversing one of the great bridges into Manhattan (unable to tell which one, and no driver to elucidate), and the reality was even more splendid. The lights of the bridge hung like diamond necklaces from pillar to pillar, all the better to highlight the city skyline as dusk fell. One by one, two by two, the city's magical, tall buildings began to self-illuminate. The lights jumped up and down like an irregular heartbeat on a hospital monitor, always beating, never flatlining; the city that never slept and refused to die. The cab swerved into a more built-up area, and gradually, the buildings closed in on her, mighty and impenetrable with their facades of steel, cast iron, sheer plated glass, green glass; industrial fabrics that seemed fitting for a nation that stood by its industrial values so determinedly. She felt like shouting for joy, a rush of adrenaline surging through the core of her being. She felt the presence of a greater power, a silent knowledge that in spite of all his shortcomings, Man had built all this, fashioned it from some vision bigger than himself! Or herself. She was glad to be alive; glad to be here. How could she ever have considered not coming?

*   *   *

The SoHo Hotel was a collection of rooms with the fashion pack's every desire in mind, or so the brochure rather grandly boasted. Lizbet had told her in Maidstone that her apartment wasn't ready, so she would have to stay at this hotel for a while, if she wouldn't mind, and to put anything she wanted on the bill. Nouvelle Maison Editions would settle all her expenses, naturally. Kate had gone straight for the minibar and, blissfully ignorant to the wages of sin that might befall her if she so much as looked at a carbohydrate, she began by devouring the numerous packets of salted potato snacks in upmarket packaging, all the while gazing at the view that dazzled from both sides, hers being a corner suite. The indomitable skyline in the distance, the hulking former warehouses across the street whose interiors now revealed homes, swish loft apartments, grandiose offices, were no doubt filled with beautiful people sipping on Cosmopolitans and listening to lounge music.

The hotel had promised to serve each and every whim of its discerning guests. From the pictorial evidence of the brochure, it seemed that whims were indeed served, providing that whim was a goldfish in a bowl, a French poodle for a fashion shoot, or organic grass-fed bison steak-frites. But they seemed to have difficulties when that whim was rather more ordinary—like passing on a message. Alexis De Vere would be picking Kate up in thirty minutes, said the bellboy at her door, just as the phone rang announcing that Alexis De Vere was in fact downstairs waiting for Kate. Now.

Kate would have preferred to crash on her king-size bed. She had never slept in a king-size bed before, although once, she'd gone round to Charlie Bell's, the one boyfriend who'd ever wanted to marry her (age twenty-one, so it didn't really count), when his parents were away. They'd been just about to christen Mr. and Mrs. Bell's bed when Charlie had chickened out, worried that they'd crumple the sheets. Theirs weren't soft Egyptian cotton sheets, inlaid with a paisley motif. Nor had they had a spray of white orchids on the pillow, or white chocolates in the shape of handbags and stiletto shoes in the place of Mrs. Bell's dentures. A pair of creamy, soft slippers rested on a silken mat at the edge of the bed. She dipped her toes in them playfully, padding about in the bedroom before leaping out of her skin in fright: *Alexis De Vere was waiting downstairs, what was she doing?!*

She looked at herself in the mirror. Her brand-new black Lycra-enriched wrap dress was crumpled and creased—a poppy bud unfurled before its time. She ran a brush through her hair, replaced the slippers with a pair of platform heels that Lise had assured her were very this season, and prepared to meet her editor.

Alexis De Vere stood slap bang in the middle of the lobby, shrouded in a soft white sheepskin gilet and nothing else bar a pair of tight white trousers and flat patent leather pumps with a buckle. The gilet had pom-pom rabbit tails hanging around the collar. Kate wasn't sure if the pom-poms were made from real rabbit tails, but she suspected her fellow local *Green Issues* members might not approve. The pom-poms pommed dramatically as Alexis spun round to greet her.

"Darling! It's my honor, my privilege to welcome you to America!" she said, loudly, not caring who saw or heard.

Kate looked Alexis squarely in the eye and gave what she hoped would come across as a full-of-confidence smile. "Thanks! I'm really pleased to be here."

She could feel eyes burning into her from the chocolate leather sofas just off the lobby. Had she been Lise, say, she could have worked this situation to her advantage, scored some major brownie points with the staff on reception, who were by now standing to attention behind the front desk, staring, obviously impressed.

"Come," Alexis purred. "I hope you don't mind, but I have to attend an art opening tonight, and I thought you could come along? Fun, no!"

And then Kate saw it. Alexis had facial hair.

She took her by the arm, and Kate, unaccustomed to the giddy heights of never-worn-before platforms, lolloped after her, down three steps and into the welcoming open door of Alexis's black Mercedes with the tinted windows. Great, she thought to herself, perhaps she'd give her a tour, point out some of the sights. She could think of nothing more exciting with which to indulge her eyes than yet more of what New York had to offer.

Alexis seemed to have small talk of a different nature on her mind. She wanted to get to know Kate a little better, she explained. She knew she was tired, but tomorrow she had such a busy schedule and she knew Kate would have one, too. Really they should have had some kind of handover period, but Diana, the previous beauty director, had left rather suddenly and when you go to another magazine, a rival at that, it's just not healthy to hang around for too long, she explained.

Kate wondered if it was rude to stare out of the window when someone was talking to you. Or really rude. The city was impossibly glamorous, each block, each burning window a world waiting to be discovered. Her skin was caressed by the dirty, balmy breath of the July night sky; her cheeks plastered into a permanent smile that she hoped radiated self-assuredness. She felt small in a nonpetite way, dwarfed by the towers that bore down on her like giant monuments to capitalism, industry, and efficiency; each rectangular soldier lining up before her like a domino. People walked so fast they looked like birds before takeoff, talked into mobiles, jostled, all in black, like an ocean at night, all the better to reflect the sparkling lights around them. Well, they had mobiles in Maidstone, too, and sometimes you walked fast, if there was a bus coming. She wasn't going to be intimidated, merely joyous, excited, curious, but she felt almost as if she couldn't breathe, she was that elated.

She positioned herself in the car as she'd once seen Lise do, that night when they'd shared a limo with two local footballers. Small-town celebrities out on the town. They'd been drunk, something she was fast realizing she wouldn't be able to admit to here, and Lise had sat with her back straight, shoulders square, and stared out of the window. Later she said it was something her mum had taught her as a child so she wouldn't throw up, but it also gave her an air of strength, capability, even indifference. She wondered what Lise was up to now. With Steve? At home in her flat? Watching TV with a bowl of Doritos?

"Now, tell me about yourself . . . ," demanded Alexis, and Kate, her face thrust like a rabbit's not so much in the headlights as way under the front wheels, attempted to change the subject.

"Actually I've heard so much about you," she said.

Alexis looked quizzically at her: "You have?"

"Well, just . . ."

"Park here, Bill, right here," barked Alexis to her driver. They'd arrived. In a hurry to extricate herself, Kate tripped over the seat belt onto the pavement. She picked herself up and tried to shake off a puddle, while Alexis glided out of the other door like a swan sailing regally off into the horizon. Cameras flashed, at whom, Kate had no idea. Alexis acted as if she hadn't seen anything, and whirled her past the security on the door and inside to the sea of black-clad bob-headed men and women chatting more reverently than animatedly, holding glasses of champagne.

The exhibition at City Art of works by Jean-Paul Suchet was exceeding everyone's expectations, but Kate knew in an instant that it would fail hers. His broad canvasses, perfect for a loft apartment's bare walls, depicted women with bare breasts, rounded bellies, their hair marcel-waved into flowing curls, juxtaposed with disconnected phallic objects, floating strangely in white spaces. Kate, her awareness of women's bodies and hairstyles heightened for the first time in her life by a sudden need to observe and draw some kind of references, however sketchy and patchy they might be, just in case they became useful to her in her new career, found them profoundly disappointing. They left her cold. Instead, she preferred to gaze at the throng of people, who seemed glossy, groomed, airbrushed, yet still with imperfections that made them fascinating to the eye: loud voices, heads that threw themselves back every time they laughed, hips that snaked through crowds, shoulders that made their presence felt when eyes were turned away from them and the owners were engaged in conversations with someone else. Theirs was a confidence she had never seen before, haughty, cold, and self-aware.

"Kate! I want you to meet Jean-Paul, the artist and a close personal friend." Alexis De Vere interrupted her from her trance. "Jean-Paul's first night, your first night!"

"Your first night . . . I don't understand," said Jean-Paul, a man neither tall nor small, nor especially handsome, who in another life could be an off-duty postman or a computer programmer, except for his French accent.

"What do you think of the show?" asked Alexis, ignoring Jean-Paul's question.

When contemplating art, there were two options. The first was to keep quiet, in an intellectual way, responding to any questions with a "Do you think so?" response in the hope that her ignorance would be cloaked by a veil of mystery. The second was to attempt to make an impression. Having arrived only that afternoon, Kate felt she had no option but the second, dangerous a game though it was. What if this was some kind of test Alexis was putting her through, a chance to make an impact on the evening? She was already aware that she could only blame jet lag for so long for her somewhat subdued demeanor. That and the fact that there were only so many times one could say "Wow!" when one was a journalist and still pretend it was a raw response, charged with unchecked emotion, and not just because she'd run out of adjectives for tall buildings.

"They look like Vargas girls," she said. (Gavin, back at *Maidstone Bazaar*, had had a copy of a Vargas book on his desk to help him design the Larkfield Leisure Centre swimming pool competition. Babes in bikinis, they'd sniggered at the time, but she was bloody glad he'd opted for that now.)

"Vargas? The illustrator!" Jean-Paul looked appalled. Was he cross-eyed? He kept looking beyond her while talking to her, which was most peculiar.

Alexis laughed. "Kate! You can't call an artist an illustrator!" She flitted off into the room as someone else in black touched her arm gently, propelling her toward some suited men with ash gray hair standing near the doorway.

"I didn't . . ." Kate started to explain to the artist, blushing as red as the lips of one of the girls in his paintings.

"You new at *Darling*, yes? I make excuses for you," said Jean-Paul. His eyes continued to scan the room curiously.

"Yes," she said. "You?"

"I bin 'ere fifteen years," he said.

"You haven't lost your accent then." She couldn't blame him for wanting to keep it. Cute.

"French people . . . zey never lose their accents. Not if they want to do well in New York, anyway," he laughed. "You want to go for a coffee one day?"

"Well . . ." All she could think about was how proud Lise would be of her.

Suddenly the Frenchman looked handsome. She was impossibly tired, desperate to fall asleep, and could curl up at any given time on one of the benches around the edge of the gallery, but at the same time, she felt energized in a way she hadn't felt for a very long time. She was in New York. With a new job. One that she might even find interesting. For a lot of money. With a Frenchman chatting her up on her first night. Anything could happen. Maybe it would.

Later, as she finally got to lie in the king-size bed, watching the moonlight cast shadows on her wall, picking out in delicate filigree the silhouette of a tree on the roof terrace outside, and reminding her of a silver Maltese cross she'd been given as a child from a father she'd never known, she allowed herself to believe for the first time, with the deepest of convictions, that her future was here, in New York. It had to be. She felt drunk on the excitement, intoxicated with the possibilities, the potential that the city was offering. And this time, there would be no hangover.

five

She was to need that same strength of conviction the following morning in her new office.

"I, like, so love your hair," said Cynthia, a twenty-something blonde with the figure of a waif and a walk like a show pony, whom Kate had just discovered was her personal assistant. An assistant! "Is that, like, the new style in England?" She seemed to be unusually interested in her hair, but then Kate remembered this was the beauty department after all, what else was she supposed to be interested in?

"You have an appointment with Lolly Bergerstein, but I can cancel it for you if you like." Cynthia chewed her lower lip, and moved her light frame over to rest on the other foot.

"Er, yes. I mean no. No, don't cancel." Who the hell was Lolly Bergerstein? Was she supposed to know? She'd have to look her up on the Internet when no one was looking.

Kate had always imagined that working in New York might

be a little stressful. She presumed all the girls on these kinds of
magazines would be complete bitches, wanting to make her
look foolish and stupid at every turn, laughing at what they
perceived as her ungainliness, her gaucheness, her mispronun-
ciation of obscure (except to the world of fashion) Mexican
photographers' names. But so far, this Cynthia girl was surprisingly friendly.

Although admittedly, there had been some consternation in
the beauty department when she had arrived at nine that morning. Her number one assistant, the deputy beauty editor (she
had *two* assistants!), Clarissa, had been comfortably ensconced,
some might say entrenched, in the beauty director's desk in the
hope that by sitting there and looking like she could do the
job, she would somehow be given the job. With Kate now
physically in the office, she was forced to admit her aspirations
had been dashed once and for all, and, wearing her best discounted Chanel suit, she set about removing pictures of her
ex-boyfriend from the wall and clearing out drawers of favorite
fluff-covered lipsticks and old business cards. Kate loitered, not
really knowing what to do with herself beyond rereading the
cards attached to the many bouquets of white orchids, white
pashminas, white candles, white handbags, all sent to her from
beauty companies keen to garner her favor. Quite why, she had
no idea.

Today's outfit, the same black wrap dress cunningly made to
look different with her new Topshop jacket, suddenly didn't
look so smart. It couldn't begin to do justice to the grandeur of
her offices. She felt she had landed somewhere truly important,
in a building whose sheer might would change things, shape
destinies, form opinions, even if it was just by imparting such
essential knowledge as how to turn a working wardrobe into a
look for the evening with the magical addition of some kohl
eyeliner and a pair of earrings (Yolanda's top tip). It was made

of stone, this building, not concrete, which was far more transient and always had the potential to be turned into a multistory car park, at least in Maidstone. Circular doors spun round, with side entrances for bulky packages being carried by bulky couriers, their helmets and shoulders making them look like American footballers in black. Receptionists, looking as old and cranky as the judges on *The Muppet Show*, lent the fashionably dressed an aura of old-fashionability. Elevators soared proudly, their elevation taking on greater social and political importance the loftier they climbed. And *Darling* magazine, she had quickly learned as she assailed the heights in the glass-walled lift, was on the fifty-second floor, which in Kate's mind made it, and her, incredibly important.

"Shall we go through the appointments?" said Cynthia. She was clearly at a loss for what to make of Kate. She was not what she expected, but then she'd read some of those weird English fashion magazines, where it was all about shocking the reader, rebelling against convention, and she wondered if Kate's black Lycra look wasn't in fact a bold avant-garde statement on the future of fashion. Her punky striped hairdo certainly seemed to testify to this.

"Appointments, yes," said Kate, wondering what the hell she was talking about. The doctor's?

"You have a ten o'clock meeting with Alexis, then—"

"What will she want to talk about?" said Kate.

Puzzled, Cynthia glanced at Clarissa for help. How would Cynthia possibly know? Since when did an editor ever discuss, let alone divulge, anything of any importance to a lowly beauty assistant?

Clarissa wasn't giving anything away.

"I guess it's probably to welcome you, talk about ideas for the next few issues, that kind of thing. . . . I can come with you if you like," Cynthia suggested.

"No, no, that's okay. Ideas. Sure." Look confident. Pretend you know what they're talking about.

"You have lunch with BeautyCorp, with Peter Skye and Marilyn Preston, the presidents. It's at Dauphinoise."

"Presidents?"

"And then that hair appointment at Lolly Bergerstein's I told you about earlier. She's changed her whole schedule so she can fit you in; she usually has a six-month waiting list."

"Oh. That's nice." So Lolly Bergerstein was a hairdresser. She was allowed to get her hair done on company time?

"There's nothing *nice* about Lolly making that appointment for you—she wants you on her side, she wants to be able to tell everyone she does your hair." Clarissa pointedly threw a large pile of files into the bin. "They're all the same."

Cynthia smiled sympathetically. "But she's very good anyway, you'll like her."

"Could you show me where the toilets are?" said Kate.

* * *

The prime site in any office was a corner on as high a floor as you could get. By these markers, Alexis was a valued member of the company. But Kate realized the moment she entered Alexis's office that over and above the floor ranking, your true status was all about window space. And Alexis loved her windows. She had pots of orchids lined up along the edge. Blinds flanked the glass walls where the office faced her staff, so she could shut herself away from them at any given time, spin her chair around, and sit and contemplate the view.

She was giving it plenty of contemplation now, seemingly tired from her night's adventures at the gallery, and evidently not in the best frame of mind to deal with a new employee, an important one at that. Today's power suit, all pink tweed with fashionably frayed edges, with big gilt buttons running down it, looked in contrast to last night's white, a bit of a mess, or so Kate thought with her uneducated eye. It transformed this legendary editor into a trussed-up turkey, frazzled and pink from a recent plucking.

She turned round to face Kate, uttered a hurried hello, and moved to the chaise longue, a black leather architectural-looking sofa that struck the right note of informality yet gravitas in her first proper meeting with her new English import.

"So, Kate, how was your first night in New York? You enjoyed Jean-Paul's opening?"

"Yes . . . he seemed nice, didn't he?"

"You English people . . . all you say is 'nice' and 'lovely' . . . and 'brilliant.' " She spoke very fast. Or was Kate speaking very slowly?

"Oh. I'm sorry."

"And 'sorry.' You're always apologizing." She got up and moved back to the chair behind the desk, checked her coffee cup for any remaining dregs of coffee, and pulled off her large gold earrings.

"Well, I suppose it's the differences that make us all interesting," Kate offered, cheerily, flicking a stray racoon-colored fringe off her face. Why was she being so gnarly this morning?

Alexis stared blankly at her. For these "differences" she was paying $160,000?

"Okay, so next three months. Fire away."

"Next three months? Is that how far ahead you're working?"

"Hold on," said Alexis impatiently. She pressed the buzzer on her intercom. "Lizbet, can you get Jane-Louise in? I need a beauty features meeting. Oh, and call in Clarissa, will you?"

Kate panicked. She knew this was the bit where she was required to come up with something good, to be the beauty director flown in at great expense and with a huge contract, bigger and better than all the local competition. But, like her neighbor's daughter Joanne, who'd spent the entire nine months of her pregnancy having reflexology and reading about birthing pools only to be stunned and surprised at the eventual and natural conclusion to this abdominal swelling-up when, guess what, a baby arrived, Kate had spent the last month thinking about getting here and not about what she would do when she actually was here.

There was an awkward silence as they waited for one of the summoned faces to appear.

"Um . . . can I borrow a pen?" asked Kate. "And some paper. I'm sorry, I left my notebook back in the office."

Alexis begrudgingly handed over her pen and a piece of paper. "Don't press too hard."

Silence again.

"Are you . . . er . . . from New York originally?" asked Kate, flicking the lid of Alexis's pen without realizing she was doing it.

Alexis glared. Kate stopped flicking.

A willowy girl with long brown hair, blow-dried immaculately, and beige makeup so flawless it looked as if it had been airbrushed on, came in and sat down.

"Hi, I'm Jane-Louise, features director," she said, shaking Kate's hand. "Pleasure to meet you."

"Hi, I'm—"

"Jane-Louise, could you bring Kate up to speed with where we are?"

"Sure, no problem. Should we wait for Clarissa?"

"What for?" said Alexis, disparagingly. Kate picked up straightaway on her disdain for her deputy. Was that a good thing, she wondered, or a bad thing? It was clear that Jane-Louise thought better of contradicting Alexis when she was in one of these moods. Tipped to be the person most likely to take over Alexis's job should she ever leave, she must be just as anxious as Alexis to see what the newcomer could come up with.

Clarissa walked in and sat down next to Jane-Louise.

"Okay," began Jane-Louise, picking up a notebook. "So we have Laetitia Mitzi on the cover for October. We were looking for something following on from autumn trends, but it can't be about film star glamour, because that's the story Fashion is doing with Laetitia."

"Kate?" Alexis waited expectantly. The phone rang.

Alexis answered, looking irritated. "Sure. Hello . . . Yes, she's right here. Kate?" She handed Kate the phone.

"Hello . . . Mum?" She put her hand over the mouthpiece and raised her eyes heavenward, mouthing, even though it was blatantly obvious, "It's my mum." Clarissa sniggered.

"Mum, I can't talk now, I'm in a meeting." Oh, God, how embarrassing. She hadn't even thought of her mum since she'd arrived, hadn't been able to, didn't even know what time it was there. "Yes, I'm fine. I'm sorry I didn't phone last night. . . . Well, the time difference. Yes, I know it's late for you. I'm sorry. Listen, I'll call you later, okay? Okay, not later, tomorrow. Yes, your time. No, it's all fine." She hissed: "All right . . . love you, too."

She put the phone down and blushed. Her bloody mother. Everyone looked at Alexis expectantly.

Alexis's face cracked into a huge grin, breaking into a loud laugh. The others, obviously surprised, dutifully followed suit.

"I love it! That's so English! Her mom calls in the middle of her first meeting! I knew I made the right decision bringing you out here, Kate. You're real! Natural! Like pure energy! Now where were we?"

Kate took a deep breath.

"October. Er . . . mothers and daughters. What we think about our . . . moms . . . as they age, and what they think about the way we look."

"Fantastic. So fresh," said Alexis. She sighed, turning her back on the assembled staff to stare out of the window at Central Park. The blaze of green, with microdot-size Rollerbladers, joggers, nannies pushing prams, soothed Kate's jet-lagged eyes. The sky was blue; it looked hot, but not sultry. Kate had a sudden urge to go outside, start exploring. She'd heard it was easy to walk Manhattan's straight up-and-down streets, to take the ferry around the Statue of Liberty, run across the Brooklyn Bridge. Get out there! She had to stop daydreaming, focus on what she was being paid to do.

"We could do it on Bianca Lazenby and her daughter, Serena," said Jane-Louise, approvingly.

"Fine. Sort it out," said Alexis, signaling the end of the meeting.

Clarissa dashed out of the office and made for the powder rooms, leaving Kate to stroll the corridors alone. Jane-Louise came running after her.

"I just wanted to say, I think that was a great idea. You'll be fine, don't worry. Alexis . . . well, her bark is so much worse than her bite, don't worry about it. And she's a huge fan, we all are! . . . If you ever want someone to lunch with, let me know."

"Oh, thank you. I can't today, but tomorrow?" They were all huge fans, imagine that.

Jane-Louise laughed, a delicate, reverberating laugh.

"Oh, no, sweetie, this week and next's all full. But we'll find a window in about three weeks, yes?" She turned, and Kate watched her enviably. She didn't walk so much as float. Why couldn't she do that?

"Oh, Kate!" Jane-Louise was turning back. Maybe she was going to cancel something for her. "I'll be seeing you later at the supplement meeting."

"Supplement?" That was cool. She could write about vita-
mins; Lise had been into those. She'd got her some of those
little fizzy sachets of vitamin C that helped with hangovers.

"The girls didn't tell you yet? I guess they haven't had a
chance. The big plastic surgery supplement. We do it every
year. It's a huge circulation booster, and you know how Alexis
is! Circulation, circulation, circulation! The meeting's at four,
so we'll get your ideas then, I guess? If they're like that last one,
it should be a breeze!"

"Sure . . . plastic surgery supplement!" For some inexplicable reason Kate clasped a strand of racoon-striped hair and
started twirling it between her fingers, a girly, nervous manner-
ism she'd seen Lise do when she was talking to boys but was
otherwise completely alien to her.

"Sure . . . no problem. See you!"

Sure. No problem. See you. What was she, some twelve-year-old
schoolgirl? And more to the point, what the hell was she going
to come up with on plastic surgery?

Back in her office, Kate's desk was clear. Finally. After
much sighing and huffing, Clarissa had moved back to her
former desk. Kate turned on her computer and opened up a
blank page. She began to write. She needed to do this, needed
to be able to think on a screen, particularly as she had no one
yet to banter with, to confide in. She had tried calling Lise
from the hotel this morning, but she wasn't answering her
mobile for some reason. Tania had been in a meeting, which
was bizarre as they hardly ever had meetings, and it had been
pointless leaving a message. She didn't think she'd be allowed
to use the office phone for international calls, and besides,
how could she talk, with Clarissa lapping up every word? She
started typing:

I have spent ten years working on a magazine. Okay, the
first three were spent making cups of tea and changing Badass's

cat litter, but no one here needs to know that. Magazines are all the same. The subject matter is different, that is all. There are deadlines. There are ideas. These things change, but the basic working order is the same. My brilliance is shining. At least, it will if I give it a bit of a polish. I can do this. I can do this. I can do this.

Clarissa and Cynthia were staring at her. She suddenly realized they were probably waiting to be told what to do. She didn't have a clue what to tell them to do. She'd never told anyone what to do before, apart from Badass, who, it hadn't escaped her attention, was a cat. And her mum, who wasn't. Start with a question.

"So . . . what are you working on right now?" she began cautiously. She went to chew her thumbnail, then stopped herself and twisted her hair instead. Be cool. Be poised. Be Jane-Louise.

Clarissa sighed. Did that girl have asthma or something? "I've just written a two-thousand-word story on backstage at the runways—autumn trends."

"And I did a news piece on the same thing. Product related—you know, which lipstick is most like the lip color used on which show," added Cynthia.

"Good . . . great . . . but it's not exactly rocket science, is it?"

"Well, Diana, your predecessor, always used to say you can't reinvent the wheel," said Clarissa. She folded her arms across her chest. So they were playing clichés now, were they?

"And I agree. But you can pump a little air into the tires now and again, no?"

Cynthia giggled.

Clarissa was stone-faced. "Air?"

"Listen, girls, this is my chance—our chance—to do something different. Sure, we give them the news pieces, the lipstick swatches, but what else can we do?" Keep asking the questions.

Keep asking the questions. Especially as the answers weren't exactly forthcoming.

"And I gather," she continued, "we're doing a plastic surgery supplement. Cynthia, could you please dig out past copies from the last ten years? I haven't seen it before, and we'll need to have ideas by four this afternoon."

Something in their expressions prompted her to throw another question out into the open. "But then you knew that, didn't you, girls?"

Cynthia turned bright red. Clarissa stared ahead, sullenly, avoiding eye contact.

"We haven't had a chance . . ."

"To talk to me, no. But an e-mail would have helped before I got here. Get me the past copies ASAP; I can read them at Lolly Steinberger's."

Cynthia giggled. Clarissa smiled a not very nice, lovely, or brilliant smile.

"It's *Bergerstein*," she said snidely.

"I knew that," said Kate, squaring her shoulders and placing her hands firmly on her hips. "I was just checking you were listening."

Six

The craggy, smoky voice creaked its way mellifluously over the thick double bass and through the speakers, waiting for a moment of silence between the late-night bar banter to make itself heard:

> He dreams of a waitress with Maxwell House eyes
> and marmalade thighs . . .

Jean-Paul Suchet, her first-night artist, leaned toward Kate and whispered breathily:

"Marmalade thighs. What is zis marmalade?"

"A type of jam, popular in England, made with orange peel," replied Kate.

She loved the *Asylum Years* album. It had a picture of a diner on the front of it, not entirely dissimilar to the one she was now sitting in. Alcohol had rendered her as some kind of ghost of

Saturday night, although probably not the one Tom Waits had envisaged when he wrote the song. So Jean-Paul was a musical philistine. At least they still had one common interest: being foreign in a city full of foreigners.

"Do you 'ave marmalade thighs? Like in ze song, Katy?" He lingered over the word "marmalade" as if he was with each syllable painting it on her legs with one of his artist's brushes and then licking it off.

"No. Jean-Pauly. But I have orange-peel skin," she replied without missing a big fat double-bass beat.

He looked confused for a second, then laughed, ostentatiously loud for such a small bar at such a small hour.

"Ah! You 'ave cellulite!" The music disappeared just as he spoke. The couple to their left looked up and—Kate could swear—looked her over.

"Yes, I 'ave cellulite, orange-peel skin, dimpled, uneven skin, bumpy contours . . . in fact I have recently collected more words for it than I have actual cellulity bumps, if you know what I mean. So what?"

It was now four weeks since Kate had arrived in New York. She had never lived by herself before, yet even without her mum to cook breakfast or pick her clothes up off the floor, she found her one-bedroom, wooden-floored, loft-style apartment in the Meatpacking District a joy. There was scarcely any furniture bar a desk, a sofa, and a bed, and the windows were always on the grimy side, but she had sunlight streaming through them and a bright blue sky as the backdrop for a skyline of water tanks, fire escape ladders, and silver air vents pumping steam. The peeling paint on her exposed brickwork had been painted for an authentic distressed look. She had a porter called Preston who teased her for her accent and cheekily commented on her lack of male visitors. She had all the takeaway numbers on speed-dial, a pretzel stall on her doorstep, and at the end of her block there was a community basketball

court, just like the ones you always saw in the movies, with crisscross fencing all around it. She woke to the sound of trucks rum-
bling down to the warehouses by the docks; she fell asleep as the
frenetic nightlife sprung into action all around her. But not tonight.
Tonight she had Jean-Paul Suchet banging on her door.

She had managed to fend off his advances successfully until
this evening, when he had not bothered phoning but just turned
up. He was clutching two tickets to see some band she'd never
heard of, but which, he promised was the next big thing.

Of course it was, she'd answered sarcastically; but, not having much else to do, bar watching one of any number of channels with a surfeit of ad breaks and crime shows, she figured
she had nothing to lose and at least it was an event she could
wear her trainers to. How wrong she was. Not only were stilettos and platform wedges the shoes in this city that moved
seamlessly from night to day, but the band was indeed the next
big thing. Or at least, it had a very cute drummer with brown,
curly, shoulder-length hair (Beauty de Bellenet's Bronzed Babe
shampoo with added extracts of birch, and Lolly Bergerstein's
antifrizzing serum would be her recommended products) and a
Roman nose (for which he needed nothing except perhaps a
sweep of Guerlain's Terracotta bronzing powder on either side
of the bridge to contour and emphasize the bump, and of
course general nasal hair maintenance—Tweezerman tweezers
were the best, or so she'd been told at the eyebrow bar she'd
visited last week). Fueled by a sudden need to quash what
would most likely remain desires of the unrequited variety,
Kate decided to drink her way through the gig. Jean-Paul, captivated by her charming grace and finesse as she pogoed up and
down for ninety minutes without a break, wholeheartedly encouraged this form of refreshment. When the band finished,
believing that some of her alcohol-fueled enthusiasm might
rub off onto him, he had steered her toward the late-night

diner, traditionally an old artists' hangout but now favored by up-and-coming six-foot-tall superthin east European models (why couldn't they send over the Hungarian shot-putters instead, Kate figured, make everyone feel a little better?).

"But seriously Kate, you 'ave cellulite?"

"Well, seriously Jean-Paul, does it make much difference? I mean, you don't honestly think you are going to see my cellulite, do you?"

"Ah . . . you mean, we keep the lights off." He looked disturbingly optimistic. "I like that . . . mystery, secrets, the dis'onest seduction of the shadows. . . ."

"No, I mean, nothing is going to happen between us," said Kate, coolly.

"Eh, I know that. . . . We are just friends!"

"Not even," she said under her breath, the alcohol wearing off now.

In a strange way, though, he was her only friend. There was something oddly familiar about him, comforting even. He had been to England before, could make jokes about the weather there, had even watched *EastEnders* a few times and understood that it was infinitely better than *Coronation Street.* Not always having to explain herself, to qualify everything, meant that he was by far the easiest of her new "friends" to be around. She put this down to their common European roots, but there were drawbacks that came with that, too. She doubted an American would make such personal remarks about cellulite so soon into a friendship. Or would he? She didn't know any American men. But at least, one thing she could say in Jean-Paul's favor was that his calls afforded her some respite from the severe workload she had—to paraphrase Alexis's love of Shakespeare—partially had thrust upon her, partially been born with. Here she was in the city of the insomniac's choice, and her social life was nonexistent. Tonight was the first evening where she hadn't felt compelled to read up on something beauty related, or sit logged on to the Internet on her office-loaned laptop at home, swotting up on whatever product launch or skin care lecture she would have to attend the following day.

She had quickly realized she could create her own agenda so long as she kept on top of the subject matter, did her research, and put the hours in. It was a policy that was paying off, starting with her relationship with her assistant and her deputy. Everything Clarissa and Cynthia had written for the forthcoming issue was fine, but just a little boring and predictable. Kate knew she was no beauty expert, but as a woman (albeit one who still couldn't walk properly in a pair of heels and who had only recently discovered waxing) and, more importantly, as a reader, she didn't feel their words on lipstick and autumn trends and moisturizers and facial hair strip wax moved or inspired her. Now, that could be because this wasn't her subject matter of choice, just as Clarissa and Cynthia might not like to read this month's essay in *Green Issues* magazine by one of the original antinuclear power protestors at Greenham Common (she'd loved that bit when the women all joined up their bras to form a big rope to tie themselves to the wire fencing—brilliant!). But why was a lipstick good just because Catherine Zeta-Jones wore it once? To her, that was a bad lipstick, because if it was any good, she would have worn it again, surely. This seemed to baffle them. She had exhorted them to rethink, and with Cynthia, she had definitely seen improvements. They'd been out for lunch a couple of times, to a small Japanese restaurant where you had to check over your shoulder before having any work-related conversation because the place swarmed with Nouvelle Maison Editions employees. Cynthia had been so thrilled to be taken out to lunch by the beauty director, she would have done anything for her after that. And Kate had enjoyed it, not just because it was the first time she'd been able to slap down a company credit card and get lunch for two as a legitimate business expense, but because she was genuinely interested in Cynthia's life. Hers was an alien world, but with striking similarities, coming as she did from a small town in Ohio, with parents who had wanted her to join the local law firm. Kate recognized in Cynthia the same hunger to carve out a career that she had—to escape. The only difference was that Cynthia was rather more knowledgeable about beauty products than Kate was. That didn't seem to make her any less intelligent; if anything she was overqualified to write "Madonna on Mole-Checking" or "Gray Eyeshadow Is the New Black Kohl."

Clarissa . . . well, Clarissa was another story, still floundering in a sea of frigid mistrust and implacable anger.

As for her own work, she had confronted Alexis head-on with her confusion as to what she was and was not allowed to do regarding the dreaded plastic surgery supplement.

"You can do whatever you want, go wherever you want, we have the budgets, we have the advertisers," Alexis had briefed her, while flicking frenziedly through a pile of uncorrected proofs. "But you have to deliver the goods. We have so many imitators, so many rivals on the surgery front, that whatever you produce has to be the best. I want luxury, I want celebrity, I want entertainment!"

"And facts, Alexis?"

Alexis looked nonplussed. "That goes without saying! That's a given! I want original stories—you have thirty pages to fill, remember. But not freaky, mind you, we are not the *National Enquirer*. Kate, it's of paramount, and I really mean paramount, importance that you get this right." She rested her cigarette in an ashtray. You weren't supposed to smoke in the offices of Nouvelle

Maison Editions, indeed you weren't supposed to smoke any-where in New York unless you were some low-ranking secretary and had time to take the elevator down fifty-two floors for a crafty puff outside with all the other low-ranking secretaries.

Kate was dying for a cigarette, dying to be a low-ranking secretary instead of an uptown, top-ranking, health-loving beauty director.

"By the way, did you know we can't use that bastard Gustav anymore? He's switched allegiances, after all I've done for him, he's just signed with *Vogue*. . . . What's wrong?" Alexis looked up, her glossy pages of color proofs for the next issue held in midflow like a dealer's cards frozen in slow motion.

"Nothing. I just gave up smoking, that's all."

"Oh, c'mon then . . ." She held out her cigarette and let Kate take a slow, satisfying draw. "Don't tell anyone."

Maybe it was the cigarette, maybe it was knowing that Nou-velle Maison Editions had a lot riding on this supplement, maybe it was the fat paycheck that had just arrived, or her new address in the city that never sleeps, but Kate wanted to do her best for Alexis. Along with Cynthia's package of the last ten years' worth of plastic surgery supplements, she had also been given a huge pile of publicity cuttings, as well as DVDs of TV interviews featuring plastic surgeons and their patients be-ing interviewed by Diana, the previous beauty editor. Diana was an impossibly glamorous blonde, with what looked like flawless skin, lips enhanced with MAC Spice lip color, and a classic root-lift blow-dry to boot. And as far as the supplement went, she seemed to have done it all already. Just when Kate was starting to agree with Cynthia and Clarissa that there re-ally was no room for air in the tires, every before-and-after "Look at me, I've had my tits done" story having been done countless times before in varying permutations, inspiration struck her at what she was quickly coming to understand was the spiritual home of every beauty director: the hairdresser's.

* * *

"You doing the surgery supplement again this year?" asked Lolly Bergerstein, while chopping haphazardly into Kate's shoulder-length tresses for the second time in a month. "Guess you'll be going to L.A. then."

Lolly had created the hairstyles of every female Oscar winner in the last five years so convincingly that an urban myth had sprung up propagating the idea that if you didn't have your hair done by her, you wouldn't win. She was brash and short, with long, wavy brown hair that belied the masculinity of her strident, booming voice.

"Chiara! Where's my fucking tail-comb?" She tugged so hard at Kate's scalp that the pile of publicity clippings tumbled from Kate's lap onto the floor.

"Can I?" Kate tried to bend down to pick up the papers, a difficult maneuver as her hair was being pulled by Lolly as if she was a Barbie with extendable tresses.

"Not yet," barked Lolly, holding the comb Chiara had rushed to get her between her teeth, while gazing in a trance at the two-inch strand of hair she was holding between her fingers. "Just finishing off this section here."

The salon was surprisingly low-key, though incredibly high-key in comparison with Yolanda's model night in Maidstone. Everywhere you looked there were trim, youthful apprentices dressed in black, bustling around in an ordered fashion like ants in a disturbed nest. Each booth was separated from the others by mirrored side panels, all the better to see what was going on at the back and sides of your hair. It also afforded some privacy for the more famous of Lolly's clientele, not that it had escaped Kate's notice that she had Sharon Stone sitting on one side and Meg Ryan on the other. (She wasn't interested, but Lise would go nuts.)

"You know, I always wondered," said Lolly, still staring fixedly at the uneven edges of hair she had just slashed. "I mean, it's so dull, all this fucking celebrity bullshit. I mean, people always ask me, what hair did you do for the fucking Oscars, and I always say, oh you know, yadda, yadda, yadda, boring, clean, straight, whatever, blah, blah, blah, natural *crap*!" She looked at herself in the mirror.

"Do they quote you on that?" Kate ventured timidly.

Lolly ignored her and continued. "And I long for a return to the age when Hollywood was fucking glamorous, y'know? Big hairstyles, pointy tits, uppity butts, slinky satin dresses. Swoosh, swoosh, swoosh, women were fucking gorgeous then! Why don't you do something on that?"

"Well, it's a surgery supplement, it's not really about the Oscars or the hair, or the dresses, but I take your point, it was a very glamorous period."

Lolly talked straight over her. "Because they all had surgery then, y'know. Kinda in a backstreet way, no one knew, and some of the doctors weren't so fucking great, but they had to get it done. The studios demanded it."

This was getting interesting.

"Go to L.A. Go to Hollywood. You'll find something cool there. Something different. I mean, it would be nice to get something fucking different, don'tcha think?" Lolly stopped, stared at herself in the mirror, her stare changing to an angry glare, then hollered, "Chiara! . . . Where is that fucking girl?! Chiara!"

Chiara reappeared, a pale creature so skinny her flesh bore an ethereal translucence.

"Honey, don't let me look like this! Check out my hair!"

It looked fine to Kate, who was more worried about the

clumps of hair that had been plundered from her own head with all the brutality of a pair of gardening shears snipping off Rapunzel's plait. Chiara dutifully flapped around Lolly with a tube of smoothing cream until the alleged ruffle was placated. Lolly rocked from hip to hip in front of the mirror, sucking her cheeks in, then shook her hair again.

"Chiara! Still not fucking right."

"Well, you shook it. . . ." Chiara ventured. Lolly picked up the hair dryer and brandished it at her as if it was a gun.

"Don't argue, sweetness, just fix it. Or be fixed."

Chiara frantically glooped on more of the cream. Lolly looked at herself again in the mirror, then said, as if surprised to see Kate still there, "You're done, honey. I hope we'll see you soon. Bye!" Chiara swooped in with her blow-dryer to finish off Kate's hair, and the star of the show moved on to her next celebrity.

Mad as the woman clearly was, Kate knew it was a great idea. The history of surgery in Hollywood. She would get back to the office and start researching straightaway. Marilyn Monroe must have had some. And if she had, they all would have. It had everything Alexis wanted: luxury, celebrity, entertainment. And it had everything Kate wanted. She had been growing increasingly nervous about the assignment. She knew it was the biggest deal-breaker in her new career, a chance to prove what she could do, boost sales, and get a reputation for herself. She didn't want to let Alexis down.

Yet there was something about plastic surgery that sat uncomfortably with her personal politics. The truth was, Kate hated plastic surgery, hated everything about it. It wasn't that she was such a big fan of the world of beauty either, but at least that was another strand of journalism to her, one that she could be objective about and find something of interest in. Her initial skepticism and mistrust had been wavering, thanks to the arrival of truckloads of expensive cosmetic products in her office, all promising to make her and every other woman look like somebody else; somebody better; somebody smoother, softer, cleaner, and wrinkle-free. This week alone she had been sent several thousand dollars' worth of cleansers, moisturizers, antiaging creams (different from your ordinary moisturizer, she was learning), perfumes, foundations (cream to powder, powder to cream, mineral, liquid—and pancake, which apparently was enjoying something of a revival thanks to new lipo-peptide-poly-hyaluronic-calafrajalistic technology she couldn't even begin to understand), lipsticks, blushers, and eyeshadows. She had a cupboard in her office the size of a small child's bedroom, full of international brands, national brands, dermatologist-led brands, chemist-led brands, little tiny niche brands, discovered-in-a-foreign-supermarket brands. When "the girls," as she'd taken to calling Cynthia and Clarissa, were out at lunch or on one of their unending appointments, she would secretly open each pot, listening out for the near-silent glide of the lid in the groove, then gently peel back the foil flap, or allow her fingers to wander over the little white plastic inner lid, find the dent, lift it up. She would smell it, dip her finger into it, try it on the back of her hand, and if she liked it, on her jaw or where tiny crevices had started to collect around the corners of her eyes. For the first time, she understood how her mother would spend half her weekly salary on a face cream, for the sheer naughtiness, self-indulgence, frivolity of it all. She was aware she was buying into a dream, but what was the harm in dreaming? She didn't know for sure whether the creams worked, and she didn't think they were still testing products on animals, but although these were things that troubled her, that she spent hours pondering over Internet sites trying to figure out, she was prepared to filter out the genuine articles over the marketing gimmicks or less scrupulous items, and believe. That was her promise to herself, to only write about the things she could investigate. In the greater scheme of things they were harmless, and in the smaller scheme of things they were hers to keep, never to be sent back, to be photographed for the magazine, or even donated to the battered women's hostel three blocks down, her idea for salvaging what was left of an increasingly fragile political sense of beauty rights and wrongs.

But plastic surgery was something else. Plastic surgery was definitely a beauty wrong.

Politically speaking, feminism wasn't right up there on her list of personal causes, because she didn't have time to save the world and fight for women's rights at the same time. So much had been achieved already by the feminists of the last few decades: equal pay; the right to vote; contraception; maternity rights; Birkenstocks as key fashion accessory. Besides, if she had been an ardent underarm-hair-growing, militant Susie Orbach–style feminist, she would never have been allowed to have someone like Lise as her friend, or to have a job like beauty director on *Darling* magazine. The feminists had all but disappeared—it had been rumored one of them had died on the operating table having a face-lift, and even Germaine Greer appeared on reality TV shows and hung out with, well, people like Lise with loud laughs, blonde hair, and big tits.

Plastic surgery was intrinsically evil, eradicating the two things men found most unpleasant about women from the face (literally) of society—age and fat—and boosting those two things they usually liked—breast one and breast two—with cancer-causing silicons and gels. And wrinkle removal on such a grand, permanent scale was nothing short of sinister. If you didn't have wrinkles, how could you remember those fun nights out? The time you fell asleep in the sun? An unhappy time of your life, even? She'd had this argument with Lise once, who had pointed out to her that the photo shop on the corner of Mayflower Street could now develop your pictures in half an hour if you really needed to remember everything, but the thought of somehow selling your soul by having it erased from your face and body with a scalpel, or a laser, still disturbed Kate. Women were no longer allowed to grow old gracefully. Age, like fat, had become a feminist issue, and it was wrong to get it cut away.

She had considered refusing to do the supplement, telling Alexis she was making a stand, like those models—*super*models—had done against fur. But then she remembered what had happened to them. The models were now virtually extinct, age having withered them. Some of the ones who had survived seemed to have relinquished their principles at the same time as they relinquished their age, embracing "age" as a movable concept more than a physiological change, one that could be deleted or denied if you used the right needle or told the right lies, all the while cloaking themselves in the warmth of the soft, downy pelts they had once rejected so vociferously.

Lolly's idea, to do something on the history of it all, was a good way round it, a compromise.

Alexis loved it. "But it's just one story. You'll need a few main stories. Something a little more commercial, more user-friendly . . . y'know, plastic surgery *lite*. You can call me from L.A. Dig around a little. The international plastic surgery conference—the Face-Off—is on at the same time. You knew that, right? You'll get another story or two there if you're lucky."

Kate nodded, although she hadn't had a clue about any conference.

"Get Cynthia to sort out your flights. Now, take your time, get it right. You can file any other work straight from your laptop. And don't forget to talk to the art department about the shoot."

Shoot. What shoot? No one had said anything about a shoot.

"Would it be possible to visit Disneyland while I'm there?"

Alexis stared stony-faced at her for a minute, then guffawed heartily. "Oh, that English sense of humor. You really are funny!"

There was an awkward silence. Kate had always wanted to see Disneyland. That castle at the beginning of every Disney film, Mickey Mouse, the Alice in Wonderland teacup thing . . .

"Was there anything else?" Alexis had moved on.

*   *   *

It was nearly closing time at the bar. Kate had long since sobered up, spurred on at the prospect of catching an early flight to L.A. the following day and feeling more than a little excited about the trip. Cynthia had booked her hotel, a glitzy little boutique hotel just off Rodeo Drive, and lined up a succession of interviews with Hollywood's finest surgeons. She was sure that would impress Alexis.

Alexis was evidently on both their minds:

"Anyway, let's go. I 'ave to see Alexis now," said Jean-Paul.

"You're seeing Alexis?"

"Well, you know . . . a man, 'e goes out, 'e has a couple of drinks, 'e wants to, you know, get a little frisky, it's late, 'e thinks, who can I call this time of night who won't mind, but who will . . . you know, 'put out,' as I believe you say in Eng-er-land?"

Kate was appalled.

"With Alexis? But I thought you wanted to, er—go out with me?"

"Ah! You're disappointed now? See, you want us to be more than just friends?"

"No, Jean-Paul, I do not. I've just got here. I have work to do. It's just that it seems a little unfair to Alexis, who, I should point out, is my new boss, for you to be calling me up and asking me out."

"Oh, she knows I see others. But it's not like we're together together, you know? I think she knows that. Oh, I can't remember what I say to her, but she's cool." He glanced downward at Kate's thighs. "She knows I don't like women with cellulite anyway."

Kate pulled her shoulders back and recoiled as far as was physically possible on a bar stool without tipping backward and off. She was angry with this impudent, idiotic Frenchman. Surely, Englishmen were not as obsessed with a woman's finer physical attributes as their French counterparts, or at least, they probably were but they had the decency to keep it to themselves. Not only was this stupid artist annoying, but he was on-off dating her boss, too. And how ridiculous to discard someone just because they had cellulite. In the last four weeks, as well as filing two main stories, having six one-hour-long meetings, and attending three perfume launches, two anticellulite product launches, three lunches in her honor, a salon opening, and a reader event, she had had her racoon stripes tamed down, her hair cut into a shoulder-length jaggedy bob-shape with the name of an up-and-coming actress she'd never heard of; three blow-drys; two manicures; and a pedicure—all to look not stunning, not attractive, not jaw-droppingly gorgeous, just plain groomed. For the first time in her life she understood what they meant when they said you had to suffer to be beautiful, a forever unattainable goal. And here he was judging her on a little thing like cellulite. Besides, had he not noticed Alexis's facial hair?

She pulled herself up stiffly, laid fifty dollars on the counter so he understood she wasn't one of "those" women, expecting for everything to be paid for, and gave him the evil eye.

"You know what, Jean-Paul? Your art sucks. And you have a saggy arse. Like two ferrets jostling to get out of a bag. And there's no cream that can change that."

She slammed the door and strode off into the night.

Jean-Paul gave a little whoop! in delight.

los angeles

beauty note:

Dress by Marchesa. The one that Scarlett Johansson wore to the Oscars, bought cut-price in a sample sale, but no one need know. *Hair:* John Frieda Sheer Blonde Highlight Activating Daily Shampoo with Light Enhancers in Honey to Caramel, smoothed with Lolly Bergerstein Styling Serum for Flyaway Ends. *Complexion:* Estée Lauder DayWear Plus Multi Protection Tinted Moisturizer SPF 15. *Eyes:* Maybelline Unstoppable Mascara in black. *Cheeks:* Bobbi Brown Shimmer Brick in Bronze. *Lips:* A dab of Nars Multiple in Malibu. *Fragrance:* Fracas by Robert Piguet.

Seven

She had lost her concentration, and she didn't want to recover it. Something to do with the peach-colored hibiscus bushes on every corner, the manicured hedgerows, the dusty, gray-green eucalyptus trees in the distance, and the suffocatingly sweet, creamy-rich gardenias in tubs scattered around her hotel that gave her a rush, a feeling of dazed exhilaration that she was gloriously unaccustomed to. Then again it could be the pure, concentrated, unadulterated sunlight, as yellow as a carton of Sunny Delight, picking out halos on every tall and tanned and young and lovely person, which was everyone who walked down the street. Even "street," she decided, was too humble a word for such broad boulevards, their low-roofed shops and houses pretty yet unassuming, giving the city a casual, low-key face unlike any she'd ever seen in any grandiose European counterpart.

"What's that noise?" she'd asked the driver who had met her

earlier at LAX. It was more than just the sound of a car going over bumps, it was a gentle, cushioned thud, reverberating through her limbs like a warm hug from a big man, a movie car noise, marking each meter's entry into the glistening city.

"What noise?"

"You know . . . kerdunk . . . kerdunk . . . there it goes!"

"Oh! I don't know. You mean the car going over the seams in the road? I guess I'm so used to it." He smiled through the mirror at her.

She resolved to make that *her* noise, the way she would remember this city and the intoxicating smells that went with it. She wrapped the noise and the smells up in the golden-hour light as it finally faded into night.

She felt as if she was on holiday. Ready to tune in, turn on, drop out, or was it the other way round? For once, it didn't really matter in which order the words came, sorry, Timothy Leary. The fact that life could be like this, could be normal for the inhabitants of Los Angeles, was insurmountable for her, made her almost angry that they had kept it a secret for so long. Except of course they hadn't, it was always on the news even if it was only as a backdrop to some celebrity gossip show on breakfast television (Lise watched them). How could the Angelinos manage to hold down jobs, run up and down beaches in red swimsuits rescuing people, or prance about on red carpets in long dresses, knowing that the sea was two blocks away, the mountains a short drive, and the possibilities—exciting, dangerous, good to know—right beneath their noses?

She had read—of course she had—of embittered, angry rap stars with bulbous guns and booty-shaking girlfriends; of impoverished Hispanics fleeing Mexico only to court low-paid jobs on street corners; of earthquakes and forest fires tearing through spoiled men's Malibu beach houses; of androgynous singers and overpaid film stars getting away with murder and molestation; of brown smog that sulked over the landscape refusing to join in the fun; but all these trials, tribulations seemed to have been forgotten time after time in the city's rush to forgive its own, to embrace the gloss of makeup, lights, cameras, action, and start over. L.A. was one big film set, from the tatty billboards with big-breasted pinups to the mirrored Dallas-type buildings that seemed to offer a token gesture of appeasement to those who wished to do business, needed that veneer of suited conformity. All of which made Kate the next best thing to the aspiring starlet just off the bus from Hicksville (Maidstone). All she had to do was smile, be her witty, charming, English self, and the city would open up its heart to her, transform her into anyone she wanted to be. The waiters, the people at the check-in desk, the driver who had ferried her from the airport into the city the night before, all had been friendly. Like one big aphrodisiac, it could all go to her head, would do if she wasn't so secure in her own skin. Which she was, wasn't she?

In spite of this rapture she was anxious tonight, as she lay on another crisp, white, king-size hotel bed, her clothes strewn on the floor around her, a room-service tray with the slurried remains of spaghetti Bolognese (made with tofu) calmly waiting outside her door to be collected by the Prada-clad waiter. Her anxiety was on a par with her first haunted, epic journey to New York, but this time her worries were more intrinsic to the very core of who she really was. She had been half able to justify the plastic surgery supplement to herself by pretending it was a factual, historical account of surgery in this most vain of cities and among that most vain of professions. She had unearthed contacts: Marilyn Monroe's last agent before she died, and an elderly, now retired surgeon whose last public appearance was to give a lecture to university students on the history of surgery in Hollywood. But what if in dressing up this story to be some kind of fabulous celebration of surgery at its celebrity best, she was losing track of the ideals and ethics she had once adhered to so closely? From the moment she'd stepped off the plane in L.A. she could barely remember what they were.

There was no doubt that in the last month, she'd changed dramatically in the physical sense. Some of those changes were to do with the fact that with more money in her pocket she could make some much-needed sartorial improvements to her wardrobe. The Topshop staples had been deposited at New York's Housing Works Thrift Shop on Seventeenth Street, where they sat uncomfortably among the designer donations, hoping the vagaries of their cheap-chic cachet might make them of interest to the fashion assistants who stalked the shop, caring not so much about raising money for the homeless as picking up their employers' castoffs. She liked her new-look bouncy hair, even if it meant she had to take the trip to Lolly's twice a week and have either Lolly or one of her assistants blow-dry it to within an inch of its life. She liked the way her skin practically squeaked it was so clean, thanks to the numerous steamings, exfoliations, extractions, serums, creams, and massages it had at least once a week. Like her new discovery of Los Angeles, she felt she had somehow tumbled into a beautiful new world, where everything was in glorious Technicolor, compared with the black-and-white world she'd been living in for so long.

But beyond the new Phillip Lim dresses and Marc Jacobs jackets that she bought in her favorite discovery, sample sales, held exclusively for those privileged few who worked in the fashion industry, with garments sold at a fraction of the price (that fraction nonetheless being approximately twice her weekly salary at *Maidstone Bazaar*), there were other changes. She had spotted a number plate on her way in from the airport with the letters OOH 36DD, and she had barely flinched. She hadn't called home for ages. And her sentences had started curling up at the ends and ending with a question mark? When they weren't really questions?

Did she need to worry about these changes? Or was this just a natural progression through life, the kind of thing everyone went through, everyone, that is, who was suddenly presented with a job in New York, a trip to L.A., and several free beauty treatments amounting to one huge makeover all in the course of one month? Which, thinking about it, was only her.

It would have been nice to have someone to share all this with. Perhaps Lise. It had been Lise and Kate for pretty much everything since meeting at the Bright Futures Center for Op-portunities. Lise had looked the part for her one-year course in personal training from day one: like an extra from a pop promo, all baggy Adidas track bottoms hanging from the hips, bare midriff, overly bronzed body. She'd been her pal in the can-teen, saving a place for her. She'd encouraged her when she'd failed her shorthand test for the third time in a row. Kate had helped her pass her driving test (four attempts). Beyond that they'd had little in common. Lise stopped attending Kate's *Green Issues* lectures once she discovered the single men there reminded her too much of her old geography teacher and the women had enough underarm hair to knit with. Kate's idea of fitness stretched to incorporating a few '80s aerobics moves when dancing to "Billie Jean" by Michael Jackson. But they laughed at and with each other, drank and danced together, and deep down . . . well, they knew they mattered more to each other than anyone else. It crossed Kate's mind that she was sometimes a little too judgmental over Lise.

She felt ever so slightly on her own. It wasn't necessarily a bad feeling, just a different feeling.

eight

It probably wasn't correct etiquette to sneak in an international phone call when you were waiting in an office that was not your own, but John Kingsley III was two hours late, so Kate figured it was entirely justifiable. Cynthia had lined up a potentially interesting interview with the thirty-four-year-old hotshot surgeon, who everyone was raving about. Everyone who needed boob jobs and nose jobs and lipo and other bits of body remodeling, that is. Kate had kept her part of the bargain, arriving at plastic surgery central at the required time. (She could tell she was in the right place by the three women exiting the elevator clutching balls of muslin and ice to their faces to quell the droplets of blood from rushed Botox injections. Although, the Jackie O impersonations in the reception area—from her much-loved scarves and shades period—were also something of a giveaway.)

JK3, as his friends referred to him, according to the press

cuttings she'd read, would often delay a whole morning's appointments if he was captivated by the beauty of the camellias in his garden. He was such a perfectionist that he liked to pick them at the first light of dawn (or so his personal assistant, Aurelie, told her), then lay them flat on specially cooled tissues, from where they would be lowered into a specially made icebox and transported ahead of him by courier to his office. Evidently the camellias were exceptionally captivating this morning. Kate's mum used to do something similar with flowers when Kate was a kid, but without the couriers and the iceboxes. She'd pick roses fresh from the garden, wrap them in tissue soaked in water, then wrap them in a final layer of foil and make Kate give them to her teacher at the end of term. All the other kids would laugh at such a homemade gift. It was a testament to the wonders of modern therapy that JK3 had clearly exorcised his no-doubt similar childhood experiences and, in the true spirit of California, turned his negative into a positive.

Not that Kate wasn't enjoying the waiting time in his office. He had an impressive catalog of before and after pictures she could flick through that weren't half as gut-wrenching as the programs she'd witnessed on TV with her mum. The afters were good: subtle, yet definite improvements on noses, chins, faces that had given in to gravity, or bodies that had caved in under the pressures of a lifetime of supersizing and crash-dieting. The press-cutting file was weighty, full of interviews mostly dating from his recent TV program, *Radical Redux: The Surgeon Who Slims Celebs*. They called him the Body Maker. Aurelie had, with just the flick of a few buttons on a remote control, summoned a plasma TV screen to magically appear from behind a wall of fake leather-bound medical journals, so that Kate could watch a DVD of interviews: JK3 and Oprah; JK3 and Letterman. He had also written his own books, not exactly DIY plastic surgery, but how to get the best from your surgeon (*Chapter 3: Always Pay Your Bills on Time! This man is operating on your face, don't make him angry!* was an especially memorable gem.) But two things—a large, leather-bound book on Michelangelo on his top shelf that didn't seem to be a disguise for a plasma TV screen, and a signed photo of JK3 standing next to Pamela Anderson on prominent display—told Kate all she needed to know: JK3 was a jerk.

Kate had researched that studying to be an aesthetic plastic surgeon in the United States took eight years. From then on, if you were any good you'd train at a public hospital putting accident victims back together, then transfer into the more lucrative private practice, usually just as your wife (archetypal Beverly Hills blonde, with torpedo tits and her first face-lift at age twenty-nine) had her first Cesarean birth and called him JK4. You'd attend the odd conference, cultivate some liaisons with distinguished older surgeons, and wait until one of them retired so you could take over their practice. To build a reputation as Hollywood surgeon of choice, you'd start frequenting movie premieres, throw lavish parties, and develop a celebrity following (current kudos was to find a celebrity politician, thereby combining gravitas and popular fame in one fell swoop). Your practice would bloom, you'd stick pictures of yourself on the walls with . . . ooh, say, Pamela Anderson, and hey, presto, you're the star surgeon of L.A. So why was he so insecure as to need a Michelangelo bible on the shelves? Was he trying to kid his clients into thinking that he was sculpting their faces in much the same way as the great Michelangelo?

Lise was in, obligingly, and able to confirm that Kate's outfit, meticulously chosen for the occasion, was neither too understated nor too brash a direction. She annoyed Kate by having already heard of JK3, reminding her that she had indeed been living in some kind of parallel universe unaffected by lipsticks, perfumes, and plastic surgery, somewhere akin to Shrek's swamp, the Grinch's mountain hovel, or Gollum's hole in *The Lord of the Rings*.

"JK3?! Oh, my God! He's the one who was on that program: *Radical Redux: The Surgeon Who Slims Celebs*."

"I know that," said Kate, brusquely. "Is that Steve with you? You're incorrigible, you know that, don't you? An old slapper with no scruples whatsoever."

"Less of the old. Luckily for you I can't really talk right now. I'm a little tied up." She could hear Steve guffawing in the background, a word she'd always hated, but there really was no other way to describe the snorting-laughing noise he made. Although there was "chortle." "I do have some news," Lise continued, a little more seriously. "I've been trying to call you all week, didn't that Clarissa girl tell you? What's it like there? Have you met anyone yet?"

"No," Kate said irritably. "And that's not the point, you know that. The work's been fantastic. Really interesting. I'm in Los Angeles now. It's brilliant. Really hot, and there's a beach. And the sun shines, everyone's lovely, the sky's really blue—"

Lise laughed. "You'd never think you were a journalist, you know. Here's a word you can use: ad-jec-tives. By the way, what's your boss like?"

"More Al Pacino than Meryl Streep," said Kate. "Facial hair . . . it's all a little nerve-wracking, to be honest."

"How come? She has a beard?"

"No, more like a mustache. She's okay, really. But this plastic surgery story I'm doing . . . I hate plastic surgery! And I have a feeling I know just what this guy's going to be like."

She looked upward to the top shelf where the Michelangelo book stared down at her.

"Listen, I have something to tell you," Lise said. The bed-clothes rustled as she got up. There was a pause as she walked somewhere else, then the flick of a kettle being switched on. "It's . . . important."

The door handle turned and Kate's heart skipped a beat.

"Gotta go," she said, just as JK3 himself entered the office. She put the phone down and jumped to her feet.

Kate's interview experience was not as great as she would have hoped it to be by this stage of her journalistic career. However, with hindsight, she would have hoped her opening greeting to JK3 might have been a little more consequential than the one that came tumbling from her mouth completely unwarranted:

"Hello, I was just booking my taxi!"

He was taller and handsomer than he appeared in his pictures, with a shock of blond hair bouncing off his tanned forehead like the crest of a wave. He grasped her by the shoulders dramatically and locked his eyes to hers. They were aquatic blue, piercing, with little tiny flecks of hazel interspersed. For a split second, Kate thought he might kiss her, which would have been embarrassing, and she would have had no option but to go ahead with the kiss as she needed an interview, and wouldn't have known how to extricate herself politely anyway. She hadn't been kissed for a long time, nor had she, New York band notwithstanding, been attracted to anyone in a while. She had to admit that a kiss would be un-likely, given that this was an ostensibly professional encounter and their first meeting. Therefore, by looking into her eyes, JK3 was obviously merely trying to determine whether she was telling the truth about the taxi.

"Look, I'm sorry, I wasn't really booking a taxi," she fired off, nervously, rapidly. "How could I have been, when you think about it, I don't even have a taxi number, and I wouldn't have known what time to book it for. But you took so long to get here I thought I'd call my friend back home, I know that's really rude, and if you like I'll give you some money for the call!"

He looked confused momentarily, then smiled and dramatically bounced his hands off her shoulders, throwing his arms in the air and laughing.

"You have a good energy. I can feel it!" He walked around her to sit down at his desk, pushing to one side a pile of books tied with a pink silk ribbon with as much of a throwaway gesture as a man who stored camellias on frozen tissues could muster. Or who used pink silk ribbon to tie books.

Kate stood there awkwardly. He said she had good energy, so why did she feel so bad?

"Please, please, sit down, my manners, what was I thinking, it is I who should be apologizing for being so late, not you! Now, gorgeous girl—because you are gorgeous, you know that, don't you, we are all gorgeous in this world, we just have to work a little on bringing it out sometimes, that's all—now, gorgeous girl, I have a question for you, for your interview." He adjusted his tie, a wide, shiny black silk tie, leaned back in his chair, then put his feet up on the desk. His shoes had leather hand-stitched soles that looked suspiciously unscratched. Maybe he flew everywhere. Or was carried by minions.

"Kate, you may put your tape recorder on now if you are using one."

He pressed his fingertips together, as if in prayer, while Kate fumbled for her Dictaphone. It wasn't very professional of her, she supposed, to have sat in his office for two hours and still not have got the tape ready.

"I'm sorry, but I have to test it. Would you mind holding it to your mouth?"

He shook his head, as if quietly enjoying her scatty performance, then opened a drawer in his desk and brought out a tripod, upon which he mounted Kate's Dictaphone, checked the sound levels, and flicked a switch with a professional air, declaring the proceedings ready to proceed. He had done this before.

"It is Kate, isn't it?"

"Yes, Kate Miller, from *Darling* magazine." She shuffled uncomfortably in her seat. "New York."

"Well, Kate, I have a question for you."

Oh, God. Here we go. What magazines had she worked on before? She'd have to launch into a lengthy explanation of *Maidstone Bazaar*, complete with sketched map showing where Maidstone was, then watch as his attention waned or his eyes glazed over, as she tried to explain there was a whole big publishing world out there, beyond New York, beyond London, just waiting to be discovered.

"Do you know the difference between *pretty* and *beautiful*?"

"Er . . ."

He cracked his knuckles loudly.

"I will tell you, Kate." He paused. For ages. For so long she wondered if he'd forgotten the answer. "Cheekbones."

Kate sensed she was in for a speech. She raised her pencil to her pad, ready to scribble as backup in case the Dictaphone tape didn't work.

"Some people, Kate, talk about the eyebrows as being the frame of the face, but my own personal obsession is the cheekbone, which I like to think represents the soul. It's like those little fleshy bits of the chicken when you turn it upside down . . . delicious, not given enough credit for the flavor they add to the dish. I used to eat chicken before I converted to macrobiotic vegetarianism, you know."

He said it wistfully, as if his dietary choice had not been without its sacrifices.

"Kate, the cheekbones are where you find the secrets of the

face. If they're hard, pointy, jutting out, they speak volumes about the character of the woman . . . is she dangerous, flighty, passionate?"

When he said the word "passionate" he gave her a funny look, as if searching for something in her eyes. She squinted uncomfortably, her discomfort making him half smile.

"Have you seen my cheekbone book? I like to fill them up, give an angle to a face, one that a woman will feel when she kisses another woman on the cheeks."

"Sounds like it would hurt, wouldn't it? Bashing your cheeks together. If they're pointed, that is."

"Hurt? No, Kate, no! It's like goats head-butting, a gentle, friendly victory as the one lets the other know who's boss. That's cheekbones for you, it's the survival of the most beautiful, and the most beautiful women in the world all have cheekbones."

The tape whirred approvingly.

"Of course, some women prefer more rounded, fleshy cheeks. It is these women for whom the expression 'the cheek of it' was invented, because, Kate, they are fun-loving . . . sexy women."

When he said the word "sexy" she felt her cheeks redden. He looked directly into her eyes again, daring her to look back. She looked away quickly.

"And it is no coincidence that if the cheekbones are the very soul of a woman, Kate, the cheeks of the bottom are the root to her fecundity, her baseness, her . . . animalistic instincts."

He was quite good-looking actually.

"I am loved in this city because I can improve the parts others dare not touch, I can enhance them, the facial cheeks and the buttock cheeks"—he moved both hands in conjoining semicircles as if outlining a bottom—"and make a woman feel . . ." He paused again. "Whole."

Arse . . . whole . . . she wrote in her notebook.

"It embarrasses you that I talk about cheeks like this, Kate?"

"No . . . no."

"You see, you have . . ." He reached across the desk and touched her face, closing his eyes to feel his way over it, tracing her cheekbones, like a blind man. His fingers were gentle, warm-tipped. She giggled, closing her eyes, too, enjoying the feeling of not knowing where on her face his fingers would touch next. He sighed, as if enraptured by what he found. Her lips parted, closed again, as she tried to envisage her face the way his fingers were now seeing it. She knew she had a flat face, undistinguished by those rounds of passion, sexiness, and the little bits of chicken that made a woman beautiful rather than pretty. But for a brief second, she wondered what it must be like to be the kind of woman who had men enraptured by her cheekbones. Perhaps this surgeon, master of faces, slimmer of celebs, could see things with his fingers that had so far eluded her friends and family. To be one of the beautiful people, even for this moment, would be some kind of revelation. It surprised her how much she wanted to join them, if only for an instant.

As if about to welcome her to this brave, new world, JK3 took his fingers away. She opened her eyes, blinking in the brightness, as he put the palms of his hands back together. He sighed.

"Fascinating. But flat. *Very* flat." He smiled, pleased with his diagnosis. "Interesting to one such as myself. I would give you cheek implants, surgically, working from the inside of the face. Or use some Juvéderm, an injectable hyaluronic acid. Both are simple procedures, but what a difference they would make to your face!"

She was flat-cheeked.

"That won't be necessary," said Kate, uptightly. She changed the subject to mask her disappointment. "And if you don't mind, I wondered if we could talk a bit about the history of plastic surgery in L.A.?"

"History?" He looked perplexed. "Oh, sure, history." He looked around his desk for something to play with. "Well, my family moved here during the war—they were of Russian-Jewish origin. My grandparents were married here." He picked up a glass paperweight with an off-white camellia flower in it, and opened and closed his hands around it, repeatedly. "The most perfect camellia I ever picked, preserved forever. If only I could do that with my work!"

He continued, "Of course, I always wanted to be a surgeon, was attracted to this amazing concept of enhancing people's faces and therefore their lives, so it came as a surprise to me that, believe it or not, my great-grandfather, who I never knew because he was killed in a prison camp in the war, had been a distinguished Russian surgeon—"

"Actually, I meant the history of surgery in L.A., as opposed to your personal history."

"Oh, you don't want to talk about me?" He looked a little disappointed. "Or *Radical Redux*? Everyone wants to talk about that. Did Aurelie not show you the DVD? I'm not sure when it's coming to England, but I know for a fact that *Darling* magazine was desperate to do a feature on me at the time. . . ." He put the paperweight down, pulled his feet off his desk, and moved his fingers nonchalantly to his platinum cuff links. "They were kinda bummed because I gave the story to *Vogue*— well, *Vogue* offered me a cover surrounded by the celebs I slimmed, so I could hardly turn it down, but hey, we can make amends, I can give you something extra-exclusive. Yeah, sure, Aurelie, what can I do for you?"

Aurelie was standing in the doorway. Kate had hardly no-ticed her before, she'd been so caught up with nosing about JK3's office, and then the phone call to Lise, but now that she came to think of it, Aurelie was something of an anomaly. For a start she was unfeasibly large for a town of predominantly size-zero proportions, with creamy, buttery skin that looked as if it had never been near the sun, and fleshy, plump limbs that by rights should be shooting golden arrows into the hearts of strapping young men. Her eyes were not warm, sexy, and flashing like JK3's, even though Kate hated herself for seeing him like that, but they were reserved, nervous, a little distant, as if she was weighing Kate up all the time.

"Your patient is here, JK. Would you like me to ask her if Kate can sit in? Purely on an anonymous basis, naturally."

"Sure thing, honey, you go ahead. Then show her in." He was the magician; she the magician's assistant.

She left the office. JK3 leaned across the desk conspiratorily and grabbed Kate's hands, reining her in, the desk jutting into her stomach uncomfortably.

"I'm having a party tonight. Wanna come?"

"Er . . . sure?" For the purposes of the story, purely. "Why not? What time is it?"

"I'll send a car for you. Nine o'clock. Aurelie will make the arrangements."

He let go of her hands, sending her reeling backward like a stretched-out sheet relinquished in a tug-of-war.

"Kate, you'll love this patient. Actress. Gorgeous girl . . . Do me a favor, don't say you're from *Darling* magazine, and keep her name a secret, okay?"

And then he did something else she really wasn't expecting. He pulled down the Michelangelo book from the top shelf, opened it up, and lifted out a miniature bottle of champagne with two glasses.

"Something to get us into the party mood, huh?"

nine

Leaving Beverly Hills for JK's home in Bel-Air, the road climbed farther and farther into green hills. The city spilled out mile after mile, its white lights flickering on and into the distance, the true stars of the town. The houses got bigger the farther they climbed, interspersed with smaller cottages, rose-entwined, as in the dimming light, Kate imagined young starlets entertaining movie moguls in the '50s; Raymond Chandler heroines receiving Philip Marlowe types.

"The price of property here is rising faster than you can say 'beach house in Malibu'!" said the driver, as if reading Kate's mind.

He was not your average chauffeur, being around Kate's age, with square-jawed superhero good looks and wearing a T-shirt emblazoned with a man on a horse waving a stick in the air. The car was not your average limo either—JK3 had sent his Mercedes Sport, "the silver one," because his other cars were out picking up couples. He hoped she wouldn't mind.

"Oh, I'm so sorry . . . I forgot," said the driver, who had introduced himself as Chuck. He reached across her over to the dashboard and pulled out a clear plastic bag with a camellia flower inside, its short stem wrapped in white paper. "Aurelie wanted me to give you this. JK3 likes his guests to wear one of these, either in their hair or on their lapel. It's one of those funny touches he has, he's so original like that."

"Thank you," said Kate, not sure what to do with it, her hair having been blow-dried by Stevie at the Rodeo Hair-Shack with two hours of precision movements worthy of the final desired result: a bed-head mess Kate Moss would have been proud of.

"Aurelie usually writes some tips . . . you know, some of the ladies don't know what to do with it. Look at the paper," said Chuck, helpfully.

Ladies. Who said "ladies" anymore?

"Have you been JK's driver for long?" Kate asked politely.

"Oh, I only do this for big occasions like tonight. The rest of the time I'm an—"

"Actor." Kate finished the sentence for him. "Don't tell me. You had a really great audition the other day, and your uncle's friends with Steven Spielberg's car washer or something—"

"Well, I am in theater, but . . ."

"Really?" Kate was embarrassed. He hadn't been so awful to her, this Chuck guy. Why had she done that to him?

"What play are you in? You must think I'm such an idiot, I'm so sorry to have assumed . . . it's just that . . ."

"I know. It's a big L.A. cliché. The model/actor/whatever thing." Chuck swerved to avoid a palm branch that had fallen in the road. The camellia tumbled to Kate's feet. She picked it up.

Chuck continued, "But there's no play. Well, not really. It's not that kind of theater. I'm JK's theater assistant. You know, 'Pass the scalpel,' that kinda thing."

Kate laughed. "I'm sure it's more important than that. You make it sound like you're an extra on *ER*."

Chuck took his eyes off the road and looked back at her, "Let's face it, everyone here is someone they're not."

Everyone here is someone they're not. Did that even make sense? Maybe the sun was getting to her. She'd spent an hour earlier that evening strolling on the beach in Santa Monica, having discovered Disneyland was way down the road toward Mexico and she didn't have enough time to go there. It was the biggest beach she'd ever seen, with white sands that went on forever, incredible considering it was in the middle of a city. It had track marks where beach cleaners had trawled the sands to keep them spotless. She had kicked off her Jimmy Choo thongs, splashed her feet in the cool, lapping waters at the edge, and picked up a caramel Frappuccino Lite at Starbucks before heading back to the hotel.

*   *   *

The actress had stayed for an hour's consultation with JK, and hadn't minded at all that Kate sat in, so long as she only made notes and didn't use the tape. Perhaps she was a voice-over artist, thought Kate, although if she was, what was the point in getting the nose job she was considering? She couldn't tell whether her getup was some kind of classic disguise mode—a head scarf, big shades, a floor-length skirt, and long-sleeved blouse—or just sun avoidance. She was about thirty years old and complained that her nose tilted up nicely—she liked that bit—but why did it have to curve over to one side? It affected her work, and seeing her nose photographed over the last ten years or so had been annoying.

Her voice whined and squeaked. "But you know, in spite of

all this, I've lived with *me* for a long time, and I don't want to look like someone else."

Except you do, thought Kate, silently scribbling down the responses she wished the actress was making as opposed to the ones she really was. You do, otherwise you wouldn't be here, and you certainly wouldn't be asking your next question:

"By the way, JK, who did Michelle Pfeiffer?"

JK3 had at this point reached across the table, grabbed the actress's hands, and reeled her in. Clearly he had some kind of technique going here.

"Honey, it doesn't matter. Because you are you, and no one is like you. You know I can't reveal the names of my celebrity clients, but you also know I won't treat them differently from you in terms of my" (he paused to make sure Kate had time to copy his words down in her notebook) "*art form*. Sure, I'll visit the big names at home, but they still have to come here for the surgery, the injectibles."

The actress looked as if she wasn't buying it. JK3 moved in for the kill.

"I'll treat you like the biggest. Celebrity. I've. Ever. Had," he said, pausing between each word as if it somehow imparted sincerity. "And what's more, I'll give you the look of celebrity."

Kate wondered if he had any celebrity clients at all. Or if Michelle Pfeiffer had ever had surgery. This confidentiality thing was all very well, and yes, she knew every surgeon signed a code of ethics that prevented them from revealing anyone's personal details, but it meant that every surgeon could whisper rumors about famous people's faces, and no one would know any better.

"Of course, there are those clients of mine who are willing to talk about my art form, and that's another thing," he said, pulling out his glossy, laminated *Vogue* cover, the one with all the famous skinny people he'd worked on.

The actress's eyes lit up. "August is a good time," she said. "I'm not busy then."

Aurelie appeared as if from nowhere with JK's diary.

The actress pulled her agenda out from her handbag. "And Venus is in retrograde."

After the actress had left, complete with a date, the promise she could change her mind anytime she wanted to, and an invitation to the party, Kate had tried to pester JK again about history, but he didn't seem to understand what she was after.

"You know who she is, I suppose?" he said.

"To be honest, JK, it's not really what my story is about. Today's celebrities. I'm looking more for those early pioneers in the film industry, the agents and film studio managers who doctored the faces of starlets to turn them into stars."

"And you don't want to hear about my Russian grandfather?"

"Um . . . not really, I mean I do, it's very interesting, but I need—"

They were interrupted by Aurelie, who warned them that a "big" studio executive was waiting in the next room for his Botox injections. She didn't mean "fat."

"You do men, too?"

"Gorgeous, simple English girl," said JK, enjoying seeing Kate blush again. "The miracle of youth is desired by men as well as women. Sometimes men chase it, sometimes they are born with it—"

"And sometimes they have it thrust upon them, squirted via a needle and a little drug called Botox. Yup. I get you."

*   *   *

Chuck turned off the road into a private gated estate. The gate itself was built like a house, big enough to house a family of ten, but used instead as a security base filled with closed-circuit TVs, spy cameras, and uniformed guards. Chuck flashed his ID and drove through, into a sparkling paradise of wedding-cake palaces, complete with mock-Georgian columns and sculpted gardens, somewhat oddly juxtaposed with vacant plots of scrubland—real estate waiting to be snapped up for a cool twenty million dollars or so, then transformed with another few million into a film-set fantasy residence for the truly rich and famous.

They pulled up outside a wedding cake, and Chuck walked round to her door, holding it open for her.

"This was scrubland this time last year," he said.

"Wait, how did they grow palm trees that quickly?" she asked.

"Nobody actually grows those," said Chuck, incredulous at the thought. "You get them full-size from the landscape gardener's."

"Oh. Of course. I knew that."

He smiled at her, took her arm, and they walked into the house.

The first thing Kate noticed inside the house was not the spiraling stone staircase descending like something from *Gone with the Wind* to the black-and-white-checkered floor, nor the floor-to-ceiling windows that led out to a decked swimming pool at the back, nor even the chandelier that was about the size of her bedroom back home that sparkled, the sole light force for the reception area. The first thing Kate noticed was the line of handsome blond Action Man look-alikes all wearing those same white T-shirts with little men on horses waving polo sticks in the air, who thronged around her with trays of what could only be peach Bellinis on them. The only time Kate had been out drinking in New York was that one night out with that Jean-Paul idiot; it was time to make amends. She quietly deposited the bottle of Cabernet Sauvignon she'd bought from the only supermarket she could find in Beverly Hills behind what in England would be called a pot-plant, but here was a towering banana tree, festooned with strings of camellia flowers and fairy lights.

"I told you there was no need to 'bring a bottle' . . . was that what you called it?" said Chuck.

"I guess he can afford his own booze, right?" she laughed.

"Here, I'll show you around. The pool's my favorite bit."

Oh, God, not the pool party. They'd all be naked, showing off their new implants, and she'd be the flat-chested, big-tummied, no-cheekboned one hiding in the corner, the one who borrowed the host's T-shirt because she was "cold," except here the T-shirts would be tight and skimpy, designed to stretch over rippling torsos rather than hang conveniently down to her knees.

"Do I have to take my clothes off?" she asked, trading her empty Bellini for a full one.

Chuck chuckled. "Only if you want to! That kinda stuff doesn't happen too much, at least not until really late. JK's guests are kinda respectable . . . governors, fund-raisers, studio executives, porn stars, coke dealers, you know!"

"Porn stars?" Kate gulped down the Bellini and reached for another one.

"That was a joke! Don't you go writing that in your magazine."

Chuck was right. No one was cavorting naked in the pool. They were draped instead over low-lying couches the size of king-size beds, wrapping themselves in furry blankets, or dangling long limbs into the black mosaicked water, all the while the hypnotic meanderings of a band like Air or Groove Armada or something equally wafting and bland trickling over them, keeping them calm, cool, chilled. Paper lanterns, all a delicate off-white color, were strung from tree to tree, trailing

off into the garden, almost begging the guests to pair off, disappear, follow the lights, and snuggle down for romantic trysts
in secret spots among the camellia bushes.

Chuck disappeared. Kate didn't know what to do with herself. Think Jane-Louise, the girl back at the office in New York,
as if she could possibly be thinking about any girl back in the
office in Maidstone, although that might be funnier. What
would Lianne do? Find a dark space and a tangerine, and wait
until it was all over. No, Jane-Louise would sidle up to the
nearest, friendliest-looking girl, introduce herself, and ask politely how she knew JK3. It would be a casual introduction, the
kind that led into a good thirty minutes' worth of chat, with
the girl no doubt inviting Kate over to her beach house in
Malibu for the weekend, seeing as Kate was new to the town
and couldn't possibly know anyone.

The blonde nymphet on the right would do.

"Hi," said Kate.

"Hi!" The blonde smiled brightly, then a puzzled look came
over her brow. Her brows could still puzzle. "Do I know
you?"

"No!" Kate laughed heartily. "No! I shouldn't think so, unless you come from Maidstone." Take the bait, take the bait.

The blonde looked blankly at her.

"Maidstone, in Kent. That's where I'm from? In England?"
Sentences going up at ends again? Invite me to your beach
house? Or at least just talk to me for five minutes?

"Oh! You're from Eng-er-land! In the United Kingdom! I
knew you had an accent!"

"That's right." Kate smiled and looked down at her gold
Jimmy Choo thongs. At least she had good shoes. Jane-Louise.
Jane-Louise. Jane-Louise. "Anyway, how do you know JK?"

The blonde laughed. "Chesney!" she shouted at a muscly
man standing a few feet away from her, talking to three

similar-looking blondes. "Hey, Chesney! Come here! This chick wants to know how I know JK!"

Was that so funny?

"Well, it's not that important. I mean, only if you want to tell me—"

Chesney walked over and grabbed the blonde from behind, squeezing her breasts playfully upward and outward. "How do you think she knows JK?" he laughed.

"Oh, I'm sorry. I didn't mean. I mean, I meant—"

"Looks like you need to get to know him a little better, too!" He put his arm around Kate's shoulders and hugged her tight. "Hey, only kidding!" He pinched her cheeks, no doubt thinking she needed cheek enhancements, too, but mercifully remembering some shred of good manners and keeping quiet about it. "Now, why don't we get you a drink? Your glass is empty. Can't have that, can we, Pancake Girl?"

The blonde, it turned out, was called Symphony, and the muscly man, Chesney, was her fiancé. Chesney was determined that Symphony was going to make it in the movies, and so had paid a fortune for her to see JK, considering him to be the top surgeon in the town. His investment in Symphony's breasts was already starting to pay off, with a couple of auditions resulting in her getting callbacks—a big deal apparently—even if they both hoped that one day the parts she was offered would be greater than Third Busty Waitress, Girl in Swimsuit, or Hooker, Sunset Boulevard. They loved Kate's accent, just loved it, and had she ever tried acting? Chesney knew a great agent who could get her fixed up with some work. Oh, she was a magazine editor! From New York! But didn't she say she was from England? They just loved England. And where did her family live? Get Pancake Girl another Bellini, someone!

And thus, for a famous-making fifteen minutes, Maidstone's collective ears burned with all the glory of the fires of ancient

Rome, or at least as if the Kimberly-Clark toilet paper factory had been set on fire. The Roxy, *Maidstone Bazaar*, even the newly reopened Larkfield Leisure Centre were described as if they were the seven wonders of the world. Kate told them stories about her mum, her best friend, Lise, the affair Lise was having with Steve ("perhaps it's true love, Kate, it can strike at any time," said Symphony); about Brian Palmers and how she'd been called out of the blue to take this job; and even about Badass the cat. Absence had made her heart grow if not fonder, then at least a little more aware that she had been away from home for well over a month and this was the first time she'd even talked about it. For some reason, Chesney and Symphony found everything hysterically funny, and not only did they find it funny, but their ten friends (Rupee, a surfing pro; Ali, some hotshot book agent; Chloe, a publicist; Fifi, somebody's girlfriend; Armand, an actor; Emmanuelle, a model; Travis, something in film; Huckle, somebody famous's tennis coach; and Flint and Glint or was it Trint and Hint . . . something else to do with film) also found her funny. She was on to her fifth peach Bellini when she was aware of a tall, blond god standing head and shoulders above the throng.

"Kate?" he called out to her. "You made it! I'm so glad, gorgeous girl!"

JK3. The throng parted and it was just her and him, him and her, and he was wearing an off-white suit, probably Gucci, with a string of wretched camellias hanging round his neck like a Hawaiian lei which he'd probably spent all week picking, laying out on frozen tissues, and sewing together because he wouldn't trust anyone else to do it for him. No wonder he'd been late for her this morning. He looked gorgeous.

"Let me show you around."

"Yes, I'd like that," she said feebly. He took her arm. The

breeze blew her hair gently across his face, catching him by surprise. He breathed in the fragrance, all that L.A.'s best hairdressers could offer, cloaked in the balmy night air, laden with jasmine. "Mmm . . ." He smiled, then moved his hand around her waist. She held her stomach in self-consciously. Thankfully she was still sober enough to walk straight up the rounded stairs without gripping too heavily on the banisters with her free hand.

Up on the first floor he led her straight to his cinema, a plush cream leather-walled square room, with one white cashmere-covered sofa bed and a huge plasma screen on the wall.

"It's a bit gay, isn't it?" she giggled. She must be drunk.

"I'm sorry?" He looked confused. Perhaps no one had told him that there was a fine line between bachelor-pad interiors and being a little too heavy-handed with the off-white leather.

"Well . . . all this . . . cream. Where I come from they'd call it a bit gay."

He laughed, a little painfully, and pulled her down onto the sofa bed. What if he kissed her now?

"Kate, I am not gay. Not that I have a problem, you understand, with being thought of as gay . . . but do you need me to prove it?"

She giggled again.

"Okay, you're not gay, but don't you think this is a little bit . . . creamy?"

"I didn't do it! My ex did. She had this obsession with this interior designer, Lopes Lopez—note the s and the z—who was most definitely creamy! And what she wanted, I wanted, so . . ."

"What happened to her?"

"No sooner had the mink throws been placed at appropriately asymmetrical angles on this sofa than she dumped me. Ran off with Lopes Lopez, who, by the way, wasn't as creamy as I thought he was. Or at least, he was creamy, but in a different way. Oh, you know what I'm saying! Anyway, all my fault. Never trust anyone with an alliterative name, that's what I've always said."

They laughed, their heads bashing together gently. It was hard to imagine this superconfident man being dumped by anyone, let alone for someone who was or was not gay.

"Oh, and I got rid of the mink throw thing. It's really not cool to be killing animals when there's perfectly good cashmere available. I'm macrobiotic vegetarian, did I tell you?"

"Yes!" They laughed again, then stopped at the same time, leaving a silence that neither was comfortable enough to have empty.

"Have you—" he said, just as she uttered the words:

"Why did—"

"You go first," he said.

"Why did you become a cosmetic surgeon?" she asked. Could he read the subtext, work out that behind her question lay a desire to understand how anyone could do what he did for a living: create Barbie doll prototypes, trout pouts, pulled-taut eyes, wind tunnel face-lifts, a homogenized, bastardized version of humanity? He was vegetarian, so clearly loved animals, although she suspected he might have problems with, say, black dog hairs on the cream chairs. He was good-looking, too. Even more so now that she'd had a couple of drinks and forgotten about not having any cheekbones. So how could someone so gorgeous, and a vegetarian at that, butcher women's faces?

A flicker of hurt flashed across his face. "You don't approve, do you?" He sighed.

"I don't want to be rude," she said, "but . . ."

"No, that's okay. It crops up occasionally." He sat more upright, suddenly older, more serious. "Let's see. I could tell you I was bullied at school. Relentlessly. Remorselessly, in fact, all for the way I looked, and that it was only when my grandfather stepped in and paid for me to get my nose fixed by a leading surgeon in L.A. that the bullying stopped."

Kate looked at his slightly squiffy nose. He should have asked for his money back.

"But that would be lying. Or I could tell you that I've always been obsessed with the ideal of beauty as outlined by Euclid in 300 BC, which says that, like it or not, there are certain measurements which universally we find pleasing to look at in others. That it is my conscious endeavor, my purpose in life, to create a beautiful figure of a man or woman that conforms at least in part to Euclid's principles."

Kate looked doubtful.

"Or I could tell you that, actually, I realized living in this town that I was never going to be famous for acting in movies or writing screenplays, so I did the next best thing. Made a ton of money at a very young age, out of helping those with fixations about certain parts of their anatomy to feel a little better about themselves."

He shrugged his shoulders, reaching out to hold her hand.

"Is that so bad?"

She didn't answer.

"Look, all that before, in my clinic, it's a bit of an act, sure, but it's not some kind of hard sell. It's how I am, as a surgeon. I know what people want to hear. I know I can make them happy. But I'm honest with them."

She shrugged her shoulders, smiling. She didn't trust herself to answer, and liked him enough not to want to upset him. His grip was firm, she felt his warm smooth skin, neat nails. A surgeon's hand, skilled, strong, dextrous.

"And the rest of the time, when I'm not being a surgeon, well, I'm me. Thirty-four years old. Single. Nice house. Nice life. But not so different from anyone else, and certainly not so different from you. . . ."

He pressed her hand firmly down onto the sofa so she couldn't move it, and started tickling her ribs until she pushed him away, giggling. Why did men always want to touch your stomach? Didn't they know that was her fat bit?

"Okay, have it your way, I'm the bad guy," he said, smiling. "But now I get to ask my question."

"What question?" She'd forgotten. Alcohol probably, or trying to work out which one of JK's answers was closest to the truth.

"My question . . . have you ever been dumped?"

"Dumped? Me?"

Her dress was riding up over her knees. She didn't pull it down. "I'm not sure if I was ever in relationships long enough for them to count as relationships. I mean, can you dump someone without officially going out with them? Because if so, well, then, yes, frequently, I have been dumped."

He paused. "I can't imagine how."

"Oh, that's sweet of you. But there are loads of reasons for dumping me."

"And I'm sure there are. But I wasn't going to say that."

She flushed. How presumptuous of her.

"I was going to say, I can't imagine how you ended up in this business. Writing about beauty. You seem too, well, intelligent, shall we say."

She was surprised at how angry she felt at this comment. What was he saying, that you had to be a bimbo to write about beauty? Yet if she was really honest with herself, hadn't she thought this, too, not just about herself and every other beauty editor, but about him?

"Well, I could say the same about you!" she retorted.

Another awkward pause. He broke it first, pulling her shoulders over to face him so that they lay even closer to each other, side by side, limbs stretched out in alcohol relaxation.

"So you could say we're two of a kind."

She knew that this was one of those instances where the witty comeback would come to her too late to have any impact. She stuttered indignantly, "You . . . you . . ."

He lifted a finger and stroked the place where her cheekbones should be. This time his finger seemed to suggest he liked what he was touching, moved slowly, appreciatively, enjoying and approving the flatness, the unbeautifulness of her face.

"We're not bad people, Kate."

Lying so close to him, feeling his breath on her face, fresh, sweet; suddenly worrying that hers was alcohol-laden made her panic, want to get up and outside, anything to avoid a conversation that was in danger of becoming heavy, intimate, or both. She was aware of his eyes looking at her freckles. Perhaps he was marveling at how anyone could still have freckles, wouldn't have bleached them off their face in a bid to get that even, retouched complexion the world seemed so obsessed with.

"Can we go outside now?"

*   *   *

Two more cocktails later, and the party was in full swing, pulsating, effervescent, fast, and glossy, just like a movie. If this were her movie, her soundtrack, she'd choose the jolly, skipping-along, cheeky-chappy beat of that song "Love Is in the Air." She could almost hear it now, enjoy its frenetic ardor, its crescendos, its *Woh! Woh! Wohs*. They walked hand in hand along the lantern-lit, moonlit path, him in his white suit, her in her Marchesa dress, as daring as she'd ever dressed, without, she hoped, looking too tarty, too much like Lise out for a Saturday night. "Love is in the air!" sang JK. So he could hear her soundtrack, too. Imagine that!

"Woh! Woh! Woh!" sang the couple on the low-lying couch nestled in the camellia bushes to her right.

So everyone could hear it. It wasn't some imaginary sound-track to the movie of her life. It was real. Time to ease up on the Bellinis.

"That was the governor of California. Bud Montefino. You've heard of him, right?"

Kate drew an appropriately sharpened intake of breath. "With Ronita Shakira, the actress?"

"His wife, yes."

She of the perfect cheekbones. "Have you done her?"

"Done her?" he joked, with a lewd twinkle in his eye. "Now, Kate, you know it would be unfair of me to say whose faces I've worked on, who's had a nose job, or a little lipo . . . unfair to my competition, that is!" JK laughed, then pulled her close to his hips and spun her around effortlessly. "I used to be a dance champion, you know. You can put that in the article."

The music switched to something a little more mellow. She could usually spot a tune instantaneously, but this one . . .

"Sufjan Stevens," said JK, beating her to it.

"How did you . . . ?"

"I have this weird talent. I can name a tune in pretty much the first two notes." He grinned at her, smugly.

"I don't believe it."

"You don't? Stick around!"

"No, I mean, it's not that I don't believe you can name it. It's just that . . . I can, too."

"We'll see about that!"

He pulled her through Sufjan Stevens and out of a camellia glade toward a large fountain. The music was more frantic here, couples spun each other around with an ease that was almost professional.

"Celia Cruz," she said, just as he said "Tito Puente" at the same time.

"A duet!" they said together.

"Dance with me!"

Kate observed the snake-hipped salsas going on around them. She felt giddy. "It's not quite the Macarena, is it?"

"Oh, don't be put off by them, they're hired for the night," said JK.

"You hire your guests?"

"Well, I hate that part of the evening when the dance floor's half empty and everyone's afraid to get up and make a fool of themselves, don't you?"

Celia Cruz reached her climactic chorus as JK spun Kate back around and neatly in front of him.

She could feel it happening.

His eyes locked hers, and this time she knew he wasn't about to quiz her about some taxi.

She stopped breathing.

He leaned in close to her face, clasped it in his hands, and brought his lips close to hers.

She went pale.

"Kate . . . I . . ."

"Excuse me!" She pushed his face away and rushed toward the fountain, where she emptied her stomach of its liquid contents. The five peach Bellinis briefly presented themselves as their very own spin-step-step-spin, a vision in swirling, orange-spangled chiffon, before being recycled away, giving their very own sepia tinge to the otherwise pristine crystal waters. Miraculously, no one seemed to have noticed. Except her host, who was holding her by the shoulders, rubbing her back, and laughing.

"Kate . . . I don't usually have this effect." He picked out a piece of peach from a strand of her hair and wiped his fingers on a white napkin on the tray of a passing waiter.

Oh, where were those huge earthquake fault lines when you needed them?

"Was it my dancing?" He was still laughing. Almost bent double.

The five peach Bellinis might have had something to do with it.

"Let me walk you to the powder room, you can freshen up. I'll wait for you outside in case you want to . . . lie down for a little afterward."

Lie down. With him.

What kind of a house had its own powder room, anyway? A plastic surgeon's house. JK's had three toilets, three separate vanity "booths" equipped with the surgeon's very own skin care line, and a white-haired octogenarian attendant, no doubt there to remind them of what would happen if they didn't submit to the surgeon's knife. A quick glance in the mirror confirmed her worst fears. The kohl smudge look she had carefully applied to her eyes while testing out Clarissa's autumn trends makeup feature to see if it actually worked had descended into Missing Member of the Ramones circa 1972. Kate was aware L.A. had had its own brief, rarely documented flirtation with new wave punk way back in the '70s, but she suspected that was all it had been, a flirtation. It was certainly not a trend about to be revived. Freshen up, she told herself. Pull yourself together. Jane-Louise. Lianne. Tania. Even Badass right now would be an improvement in the looks department. A brush, silver-plated, delicately inscribed with the words *Beauty is in the eye of the beholder*, reminded her that her bed-head should have been put to bed hours ago. She picked out the last stray piece of drying peach from the hair nearest her neck. What the hell was she playing at? He was her interviewee. She couldn't be this unprofessional!

She had to get herself together. Perhaps if she twisted her hair up and piled it on her head, it might look a little less like she'd just thrown up in a fountain. She then remembered the camellia hairpiece. Sodding camellias, but at least it was making itself useful, and she was willing to bet no one else at this party would be creating quite the same peach-infested camellia hairstyle she was. From the guts of her handbag, the clear plastic bag revealed the camellia was less battered than she might have expected it to be. No doubt Amalie or Anomaly or whatever her name was had some helpful tip or other she could use to fix her hair. She unrolled the paper around the base of the camellia.

And there it was, in black and white:

Meet me at 8 a.m., Beechwood Café, Hollywood Hills, if you want the real story. He is not all he seems. Aurelie.

ten

Pancakes or muffins. Pancakes *and* muffins. She could eat both, but she should probably choose one over the other. What was it that Chesney guy had called her? Pancake Girl. She should probably order some of those wafer-thin crepes she had seen emerge from the kitchen with a wedge of lemon on the side, French-style, as the menu had described them. On the other hand, the American penchant for light, fluffy buns with nuggets of molten chocolate secreted inside was growing more appealing by the minute.

"I'll take the muffins," Kate said to the trim waitress, who smiled patiently as she took the order, without writing a thing down. "With a side order of fried eggs, and a large mug of tea. Please."

"You have such a great accent," said the waitress, placing a napkin and some cutlery on the table before hurrying on.

She didn't have a great accent. She had an all right accent, but it wasn't what you'd call remarkable. The Queen had a great accent: cut glass, polished, and matronly. Michael Caine had a great accent: characterful, happy-go-lucky, yet sinister. Kate Miller had an average, south of London yet not as distinctive as *sarf* London accent: nondescript, clear, yet not crystal. She did, however, have the mother of all hangovers.

It was 7:30 a.m. and the Beechwood Café was already bustling with the prework activity of the well-to-do inhabitants of Hollywood Hills. Handsome men in their forties with just-so flecks of gray hair sat by themselves, tapping away lightly on their laptops, looking up every so often then tapping away again frantically as if suddenly inspired by whatever vision in baby-pink toweling jogging shorts had just walked in. Couples sat in silence, reading the *L.A. Times* and sipping coffees, the smug contentment of newlyweds radiating gently, their his and her BlackBerrys vibrating harmoniously. Kate had arrived early, partly so as not to be late, but also hoping that she could get a head start on the breakfast she knew she was going to need after last night's Bellini extravaganza. A quick examination of the premises revealed she could eat in peace, there being no sign of the mysterious Aurelie.

Her head was pounding, but her conscience hurt more. It was bound to have happened sooner or later, this mini crisis of hers. Such huge changes all at once, such a big workload—stress always got to you sooner or later, tipped you upside down and inside out and left you vomiting in a fountain at a house party in Los Angeles just before you kissed your prime interviewee, L.A.'s top plastic surgeon. *Good look, Kate.* Thank God Lise or anyone else from home for that matter hadn't been there to see what she'd got up to. In fact, she didn't think too many people at the party had seen either, which was a relief as she'd spent most of the evening prior to her *vomitus grandus* telling anyone who would listen her entire life story. She cringed at the thought of some of the things she'd told them. Had they really needed to know about the time she and Lise had . . . It didn't bear thinking about.

Unfortunately, the aftermath, the bedraggled, ashen, wrung-out, and left-to-dry detritus of Kate's big night out had been witnessed by none other than Clarissa. Kate had vanished from the party like Cinderella, without saying good-bye to Chesney or Symphony or Trint or Glint or Shint or, more importantly, John Kingsley III, plastic surgeon to the stars, as soon as she'd read Aurelie's note. She had to leave—if she hadn't she would almost certainly have shown Aurelie's note to JK3. Booze did that to her. Enabled her to confess anything to anyone whether it needed confessing or not. But more importantly, she hadn't trusted herself not to land in any more compromising positions with him. Metaphorically speaking.

She had been trying to find her key back at the hotel when a voice from beside her in the elevator made her jump.

"It's a keycard, remember, not a key you're looking for." Clarissa was the last person she had expected to see here, at this time of night.

"Ah, Clarissa, how are you?" She didn't have a clue what to say, nor any idea what Clarissa was doing here. "How's the autumn trends copy going?"

Clarissa looked blankly at her. Dud question. It was one thirty in the morning, a time when work matters might safely be discarded for greetings of a more social nature. She attempted an equally poor recovery.

"You handed it in two weeks ago, didn't you? Any luck with that, er . . . Lolly Steinberger interview?"

"It's Bergerstein," Clarissa replied coldly. "But then, you were just checking to see if I was listening, weren't you?"

"Ha. Very good. Anyway, when did you get here?" Clarissa looked as fresh as if she'd spent the last six hours in a spa having her skin steam-cleaned before the dresser arrived to put her in head-to-toe Armani.

"An hour ago." Something was wrong. Kate couldn't put her finger on it. Maybe she was a little merry, but Clarissa had no excuse to be so humorless, so prissy, so gritted-teeth and pale-faced, so . . . so . . . taupe. But of course, that was precisely what was wrong. Anyone else would have taken one look at Kate and laughed at her look-what-the-cat-brought-in appearance. Clarissa was taking it all far too seriously.

"I guess you had a late night?" Clarissa took Kate's handbag, calmly found her keycard, and inserted it into Kate's door for her.

"Correction. I was having a late night. I'm about to go to bed. And what's your excuse for being up so late?" She wasn't sure that her new, authoritative tone was having the desired effect. It sounded a little too defensive. Was she really perfectly positioned to tell Clarissa off for being up late? She couldn't be much younger than Kate. That was the trouble with not having had anyone to boss around before. It was fine when you were on safe work territory, knew your ground, and could confidently dictate the required course of action—cut this paragraph, punch up that intro, and did you check the price of the Moulin Rouge lipstick yet?—but what happened when you skidded off-piste and could no longer lead by example?

"I just flew in. They sent me out to help you with the shoot the day after tomorrow, remember?" She sighed, as if not only was she tired, but this was profoundly boring. "The hotel wouldn't let me check in without seeing my boss's credit card, and you are my boss."

"Look, come in, let's have a coffee," said Kate, grateful to have the door finally opened. A quick glance around the room revealed that it was safe to let in strangers. Room service had picked her underwear off the floor and retrieved her trainers from the window ledge, where she had left them gracelessly airing.

"No, thanks, I'm kinda beat."

"I thought you said I was your boss." Authority mixed with humor. Might just do it.

"No, *they* said you were my boss." There was now so much resentment in Clarissa's voice that even she was forced to back-track. "All right, then. But no hanky-panky, okay?"

It wasn't about to thaw an ice age, but as jokes went, it was the one Kate needed to see that not only could the girl be funny, but that she knew—almost—just how far to go before she had to stop. It showed there was potential in this relation-ship, of what kind she didn't know yet, but she was more deter-mined than ever to crack it.

"Great. Now, do they need me to call down with my credit card details?" she asked her, now they were being friendly with one another. Bosses were meant to be concerned about the wel-fare of their staff, and she couldn't let the poor girl sleep in the corridor. After all, she'd helped her with her key, which showed she cared a little.

"No, that's okay. They took one look at you as you rolled into the lobby and said in this case they'd make an exception. In fact, I really should pass on that coffee. They're taking my bags up. I just followed you to make sure you were okay."

Oh, the shame of it all. "Well, good night, then," she said, relieved that she could sidle out of the coffee without too much guilt. "And you know, thanks for helping me get into my room and everything. . . . I was okay, really I was. I was just suffer-ing from a little . . . you know, exhaustion."

Clarissa smiled sweetly. "Exhaustion. Yes. I saw a program about that once, apparently it's really big in Britain right now. Young women go out every night and drink loads and then suffer from exhaustion."

With that she turned and strode calmly off. Kate would have hated her, if she hadn't been too . . . exhausted. What a bitch. There was no other word, as much as she hated using it.

But thinking it over this morning at breakfast she couldn't help but see that Clarissa had a point. Maybe she was a bit exhausted? True, she hadn't set out to get completely drunk; hers was more about knocking back as many drinks as she could to have a good time. Everyone knew that was a completely different kind of drinking, still somewhat reprehensible now she was holding a responsible position with two members of her own staff, and perhaps she should take that into account, but definitely not binge drinking. Binge drinkers wore short skirts, never wore coats in the depths of winter, and hung out in town centers knocking back vodka shots sweetened with brightly colored cheap liqueurs. They sang football songs, tried to beat up their best mate's ex-boyfriend, then couldn't remember anything the following day. Kate had only had a few too many Bellinis on an empty stomach at a swanky house party in Bel-Air. The two were hardly compatible, were they? Comparable, she meant.

She was fortuitously interrupted from the sure and steady path to a mental posthangover telling-off by the arrival of an enormous plate of eggs, complete with a side order of pancakes and muffins. She feigned annoyance at the mistaken over-order and prepared to tuck in, only to look up and see that a brunette with dark glasses and a dodgy nose had had the nerve to sit down silently at her table, without even asking if the chair was taken. Americans just didn't have the same concept of personal space, or manners even. She would have said something, but the woman beat her to it.

"So, Pancake Girl," she whispered to Kate, "I see you have an appetite this morning."

"I'm sorry?" Kate was taken aback. Did she know her? And

then she remembered. Things like this happened in Hollywood all the time; Symphony had said so. Apparently, L.A. could be very, very small. You hung out with a small clique of people from the same world: movie actors, governors, musicians, women with surgically enhanced breasts. When that world was plastic surgery, almost anyone with money could and would get an entry visa. The only rule about this particular clique was that you'd have to pretend you'd met the surgeon at the gym, say, because to admit to knowing him as a result of having had surgery was tantamount to admitting you weren't born perfect, which in L.A. (Symphony aside) was tantamount to social suicide. This bore complications if you wanted to recommend him to anyone, but you'd get around this problem by introducing him thus: "My makeup artist knows this great surgeon . . ." (because everyone had a makeup artist, and that was okay). The presumptuous woman before her now must be a member of this strange new clique. Either that or she was Anjelica Huston—the hair was a dead giveaway. Or Cher, if you took a sideways look at the nose. Had she been at the party, too? She was much fatter in the flesh. Funny that, as she'd always thought it was the other way round, television making you look fatter than you were in real life.

"It's me." The woman raised her glasses and winked. "Aurelie."

"I . . . don't understand. Aurelie, yes . . . oh! *Aurelie! Wow!* You look so different!"

"Shh!" Aurelie's benign winking turned into a scowl. "I'm in disguise," she hissed. "Now listen. I can't stop for long. If I get caught talking to you, I'm . . . well, I'll—"

"You'll never work in this town again," said Kate. "I love it! People really do say these things! And I thought it was just a cliché!" She laughed and took a swig of her tea.

". . . I'm dead."

Kate's head ached. Did she just say "dead"? She hated to be so pedantic when death was in the offing, but she wondered whether Aurelie meant "dead" as in no pulse anymore, beaten to a pulp in an alleyway somewhere, or just "dead" as in not exactly going places, game over, take a trip back to Orange County or wherever it was Californians who fell from grace were dispatched to, without collecting your two hundred dollars or passing Rodeo Drive.

"Well, okay, not dead exactly, but I might as well be. Now listen. I have a file here. Read it. If you're interested, contact the woman in it. Her details are there." She looked at the adjacent tables to check if anyone was listening, then handed over a bulky brown envelope, its edges frayed and straining.

"What woman?" Kate was trying to concentrate, but she wanted nothing more than to be back in bed right now, hot story or no hot story. It seemed a little uncivilized to call a meeting at 8:00 a.m. after a party the night before.

"You'll see."

The waitress appeared at the table, notebook in hand. "Would you like to order something?"

Aurelie buried her wig in her hands and muttered, "No, thanks, I'm just leaving." She waited until the waitress left the table before continuing, "And by the way, you shouldn't have let those idiots laugh at you like that."

"What idiots?"

"Chesney and that floozy of his. People like that, they think that all us women should look the same."

"Oh, you mean, him calling me Pancake Girl? You saw all that?" Her boozy evening had not gone unnoticed at all. But Aurelie was right. She shouldn't have. Back in Maidstone, had Lise or Brian or Steve or Lianne, or anyone for that matter, called her Pancake Girl she probably would have slapped them. Here, in the semitropical confines of Bel-Air, a couple of Bellinis down her, she'd found it only mildly irritating, and as the evening wore on, the height of entertainment.

"In the security room. I saw everything on the closed-circuit TV cameras."

"Oh." Not good.

"That idiot, he had no right to be so derogatory about a woman's appearance. What are you supposed to do, trade your pancakes in for a couple of muffins, like this?"

She moved the two plates of food around, like a sideshow magician doing a "Now you see it, now you don't" conjuring trick. One minute the pancakes were here, the next minute the pancakes had gone and the chocolate muffins were in their place. The muffin magic didn't work as a demonstration because the pancakes were still there, just over to the left a little beyond the plate of eggs. "That's what he'd have you do. And all the other men like him. Never mind all the scars, the pain, the risks, the goddamn fakeness! And I've seen it all, believe me!"

She slammed the plate of pancakes down, violently, then, as if embarrassed by her outburst, stood up.

"I've got to go."

Kate's pancakes and muffins were now downgraded to a before and after picture that hadn't quite made JK's book of happy endings. She hoped the waitress would take them away.

"Wait!" said Kate. "Before you go . . . why are you doing this?"

More to the point, how could she tell if Aurelie was to be trusted? Up until today she'd believed she was the only one in this strange new world of the beautiful people with any doubts about the world of surgery, which was why she'd dreamed up the history in Hollywood story in the first place. (Or at least, Lolly had dreamed it up, but she'd gone along with it.) Aurelie had told her she could lose her job, so she must have some good reasons for giving Kate the inside story.

"I just am. That's all you need to know. Look, I've got to go. If anyone sees me—"

"They won't recognize you. I didn't." As soon as she'd said that, she wished she hadn't. It would be much better if Aurelie did leave sooner rather than later, for no other reason than that the eggs were starting to look a little congealed, and if they went, her entire breakfast would be ruined for her, as opposed to just the pancakes and muffins. Besides, there was always the chance that Aurelie would start spinning the eggs round to demonstrate a quick face-lift or liposuction procedure. Lucky she hadn't ordered the banana milkshake with the straw.

Aurelie sat down again.

"You're English. And you have a hangover. That's why you didn't recognize me. These others? A lot of people know me, know who I am. A lot of people who wouldn't hesitate for one second to call up JK and tell him they'd seen me out with the drunk English journalist at his party."

Okay, so she'd been drunk. Aurelie really didn't need to keep telling her. And wasn't that the point of parties, to get drunk? Besides, JK3 might actually be glad to hear the drunk English journalist was having breakfast at the Beechwood Café. For all he knew, she might be dead in a ditch, or on a plane back to Britain. She had been awful to him, nearly vomiting all over his white suit and carefully pressed camellias, then running off without saying good-bye. She was glad she had left when she did—anything could have happened—but perhaps she should have phoned to say she'd got back all right. Or was that something you only did when you still lived at home, at age thirty-two, and didn't want your mum to be worried? The difference between her and JK, nationalities, fortunes, and gender aside, was that he was a grown-up, and she was still very much a girl, one of those women who pretended to be capable and independent and in charge, but was still struggling to do what was right, follow her path, and not throw up in the fountain.

What she didn't understand was why he had seemed attracted to her in the first place, but then again, she didn't really know why Jean-Paul had been attracted to her back in New York either. She'd lived in Maidstone for years with not so much as a pip-squeak of interest, and now here they were, coming along like buses. It wasn't even as if she was that attractive. Sure, she could put the uniform together a little easier now, wear the right labels in the right combination and come out with something that vaguely resembled a "look" as opposed to just clothes to keep warm. But it hadn't escaped her notice that women here were different yet again to the efficient, streamlined New Yorkers. Here they were more tousled, more effervescent, like the fizzy sparkling aldehyde that gave Chanel No. 5 its personality. Here they were more likely to reveal toned, bronzed legs under those baby-pink toweling shorts, or a Symphony-style cleavage that popped out as if from nowhere and very often was from nowhere. Kate fell into neither camp, which led her to believe that if either man was indeed attracted to her, it could only be due to a commonly held misconception that she could, would somehow provide publicity for their careers. It was in their interests to be nice to her, to flirt with her; what she had to remember now was that their flirtation had nothing to do with their true physical feelings for her. She'd already learned a gentle lesson after she'd wrongly assumed Lolly Bergerstein's sudden appointment was down to "niceness" when in fact it was sheer opportunism. She told herself it didn't really matter, because she wasn't chasing them for friendship: she was as much after the story as they were for the publicity. Besides, as she'd always maintained to Lise: no man was going to get in the way of her career.

"Look, all I'm going to say is, you have a chance to make the world a better place. You write stuff, you have an audience. Take that chance. Don't be like me, don't get caught up in all this." Aurelie was still there.

"I'm sure it's all very, er, interesting"—Kate tapped the envelope secretively—"but I don't know if there's much I can do. I'm supposed to be writing a story about history and—"

"Don't you get it?!" Aurelie stood up. Her hissing assumed a more urgent kind of hiss, an almost nasty hiss. "This *is* history. If you don't do something to stand up to these assholes, we are all history!"

The hiss around the word "assholes" was so forceful that a droplet of saliva bounced onto Kate's plate of eggs. That did it.

"One more thing. If you see me at the surgery, not a word. We didn't have this meeting, okay?"

"Of course not. And I promise I'll read it, see what I can do."

It was awful to think of herself at a time like this, what with Aurelie putting her life on the line, and women being history, but all this talking and thinking was making Kate's headache worse. She watched Aurelie leave the café looking as conspicuous as a bloke in drag. She could vaguely make out, beyond the door, a black Mercedes pulling up, another woman at the wheel, and Aurelie getting into the passenger seat. They sped off quickly.

She was about to open the envelope when the waitress appeared.

"Wow, your friend had a heavy audition to go to today, right?"

"Something like that," said Kate, feeling really weak and pathetic and disinterested in any further intrigue. Amazing how she'd held it all together, really, despite her "exhaustion." At least she'd managed a night without cigarettes. Her first in a while. She should probably hurry back to the ever-cheerful

Clarissa and find out more about this shoot she'd been banging on about in the middle of the night.

The waitress cleared up the plates of cold-looking food. "I guess Nicole Kidman has a lot to answer for. Everyone's doing it these days."

"Nicole Kidman?"

"You know. From that film a few years ago, *The Hours*. She got the Oscar for that fake nose. Your poor friend . . . I swear, if I had a dollar for every budding actress who thinks they can get a part with a fake nose—"

"Oh, yes. Yes. That's right. The nose."

"I'll get you the check." She returned with a plate with a slip of paper on it, and two small orange sweets. "Vitamin C," she said. "It really helps, trust me. Take two, and a couple of Advil, and you'll be fine."

eleven

As soon as she arrived back at the hotel, at around 10:00 a.m., Kate had sunk under the duvet with the intention of putting aside any thoughts of work for the day until she had caught up on some much-needed beauty sleep. The maid, who, true to cultural stereotype, was of Hispanic origin, had other ideas. She banged so hard on her door when Kate had ignored the doorbell, and then burst into her room when she had ignored the banging, that Kate had no choice but to seek refuge in the bathroom and take a long, hot bath. The white noise of the Hoover energetically mowing the deep cream woolen carpet reverberated through the locked bathroom door, signifying that Mercedes (or so the pink embroidered italics on her uniform christened her) was now content with this trade-off, and that this had indeed been the right course of action. It was strangely soothing, this manic buzz of the vacuum, transforming the bathroom into a womblike sanctuary. Beige mosaic tiles with a hint of silvery green contributed to the overall Zen-like atmosphere, further enriched by Kate's discovery of a seemingly magical wet-room switch, which instantly cloaked all the Perspex cotton-wool holders, plastic hair caps, and shoe shiners with a rainlike fog. The transformation into glorified Russian bathhouse was now complete, happily without the sweating, flabby men in towels who had been in the only other Russian bath she'd visited, on East Tenth Street in New York. (Article: "Spas: The Real Deal or the Luxe Factor?")

She hoped the heat wouldn't damage the array of lotions and potions she'd brought with her from New York, items that only six or so weeks ago she wouldn't even have been able to identify, but which now she somehow found indispensable. The rose-scented moisturizer from Rosamai, a fancy French skin care company, had impinged on her life to such an extent that it was one of the first things she looked forward to as soon as she woke up. They'd explained at the launch that this was to do with the unique effect the rose oils had on the psyche due to each petal having been handpicked by a remote tribe of African women, famed for the softness of their hands. (They hadn't been country specific—"Africa" was suitably foreign and obscure enough.) Six weeks ago she would have taken her deep desire to moisturize as a sign she needed to get out more; now it was integral to the daily maintenance of her skin, an important component of any girl's grooming routine, a vital step to start each day. Her cleanser was of eastern European origin, its rather basic packaging somehow lending credibility to its more exclusive price tag, justified by the purity of the waxy ingredients and the softness of the muslin facecloth which accompanied it (made by nuns in a Romanian monastery). She was the proud owner of an eye cream called Tender'ice, which came from a Swiss laboratory and had been tested on NASA astronauts between four and six o'clock in the morning, the time when skin was apparently at its most receptive to its potent cocktail of ingredients. Kate had for the most part ignored the stories—let them pick their roses and smooth spacemen's tired eyes as much as they liked—the creams felt divine to the touch, and her skin was better than it had ever been before. Of course, before it had been lucky if it had come into contact with a bar of soap, so perhaps she wasn't the best judge, but these few things were nonetheless carefully edited down to be her favorites among the multitude of dazzling concoctions presented to her. At least for this week.

Insofar as she was wearing anything at all, she disrobed, dropping the huge fluffy towel on the floor. (The actual robe hanging on the back of the door, with its belt tightly wound round itself to form the initial *K* for "Kate"—the hotel prided itself on these small, personal touches—had quite frankly been too much of an effort to unwind, and who needed the complimentary slippers when the carpet was so soft?) The smiley faces she had childishly finger-drawn in the fogged-up mirror had produced clear tears of condensation that now ran in a downward trail. They led directly to the brown envelope by the sink. She'd dumped it there when she'd run in this morning. She flicked off the steam machine, tore open the envelope, and, carefully clutching the clear plastic folder within so the contents didn't slide out from the open-ended bottom, she stepped gingerly into the bath and prepared to find out what secrets lay within.

Patty Patrice's face had been pretty but unremarkable pre-op: soft brown curls cropped closely to her face, big brown eyes, a beaming smile, and the ubiquitous sparkling white straight teeth made to sing out "God Bless America!" But even with the tap splashes on the photograph which had etched unsightly blue moles on Patty's features as the photographic paper dissolved, nothing could prepare her for the photograph that followed.

Exhibit 2, Patty Patrice's face postsurgery was Patty . . . after some horrendous burn incident, surely? She had looked in her late twenties before; now she looked in her late forties. Her skin was stretched, pulling tightly around her eyes, and where it was tanned and freckly before, afterward it was red and rough, with a sore-looking shine, like a sucked boiled sweet. Her nose had a strange curve upward, her nostrils flared like a monkey's yet conjoined in a sharp point at the tip. Her lips were puffy, swollen, and enlarged. Patty Patrice's transformation was remarkable, but for all the wrong reasons.

Exhibit 3 was a collection of letters, all, it had to be presumed, unanswered, from Patty Patrice to JK3, expressing dissatisfaction with the successive procedures. Exhibit 4 was an invoice from JK3 for the sum of fifty-seven thousand dollars for work undertaken so far, with the notice that if his bill was not paid by the end of the month, he would take her to court. Exhibit 5 was a letter from Patty Patrice's insurers saying they were sorry, but due to the work on her face being "of self-inflicted origin" they would be unable to refer her to any plastic surgeon for correctional aesthetic work, whether it was related to sinus problems or not. Exhibit 6 was some kind of diary, or letter, to no one in particular, or perhaps to Kate herself, she wasn't sure, offering an account of her experiences. She rested her head on the edge of the ceramic bath. It felt cold on the back of her neck. She drew a deep breath, and started to read:

My name is Patty Patrice; I am 33 years old and I am a freak.

I have come to accept this, have had to accept this, because my face has been so damaged that I no longer care to show it in public. I knew I was a freak when only days after the bandages came off, my friend's little girl, Jacintha, who I have babysat for since the day she was born, screamed in horror

*when she saw me. And when I lost my job as the receptionist
at a seniors day care center because some of the old folks complained about the way I looked . . . I couldn't pretend I was
normal anymore. I was a freak.*

*I wasn't always like this. I was a normal girl. Okay, so I
grew up in this strange city, where vanity and values are
warped, and age is distorted so that it doesn't exist, doesn't
happen . . . but I'm digressing—these things I only know
about now, I didn't see what was going on back then.*

*I was born here, in Beverly Hills. I know it's hard to be-
lieve that anyone could come from a normal family around
here, where all the rich people live, but normal people can
live here, they do live here. I went to the high school, got
good grades, my folks worked: my mom was a school admin-
istrator, and my dad was as a doctor. I was good-looking,
pretty I suppose. I was approached while I was still at school
to do some modeling, I had a good figure, I worked out some,
you know. I did some commercials for TV, made a ton of
money, well, not major league, but enough to pay my way
through college.*

*Just when I was leaving college, I met Renton Hertz. He
was nice back then, and we got along all right, so when he
asked me to marry him, I didn't see why not. That makes it
sound like I didn't consider it properly, but I did. Renton
had money, so I didn't need to work. His dad was in con-
struction, owned a big firm, Renton worked with him. He
didn't want to have kids just yet. I didn't wonder why at the
time, I just busied myself around the house and took on some
volunteer work. I've always liked helping others—my therapist says I am a "people pleaser." Well, maybe, but what's
wrong with spreading a little happiness?*

*Renton believed in spreading a little happiness, too. Un-
fortunately he was more concerned with spreading it to his*

dad's personal assistant, Marylou Abbott. He was nice enough with the divorce, gave me some money to compensate for our nine years together, and also to get me on my feet, get me started in something, seeing as I'd never worked, and now that I wasn't anyone's little homemaker anymore, I might need to.

It's funny to think back now, but it was Marylou who first gave me the idea to get the work done on my face. She was younger than me, a nice girl, pretty, I could see why Renton had wanted her. I figured that I could do with some of that, cheer myself up a little, fix things, little things, that had always annoyed me. My parents were dead against it. My dad, being a doctor, thought there was no point in inflicting myself with anything that might . . . well, he didn't want me to take risks, I suppose, unnecessary risks. But to me, they were necessary, and I wasn't taking risks, I was going to the best surgeon in town.

When I met John Kingsley III it was on Marylou's recommendation. She confided in me after her relations with Renton came to an abrupt halt that JK had fixed her nose for her. Well, I had always hated my nose. I wanted a cute, buttony nose like hers. I had the money still from the divorce, the alimony, and I'd saved it, for what I hadn't known. I had a nice job at the seniors day care, I didn't have a big house loan or anything, as my parents had taken care of that for me. I could afford to live a little.

When I first met him, he was charm itself. I needed the attention, I suppose (my therapist says, "Suppose? There's no doubt you needed the attention!"). He had this way of holding my hands so warmly, I swear I could have melted! I feel kinda silly now, admitting that, but he'd pull me in from across the other side of the table, as if he was frustrated that the table was in the way, he wanted to hold me so much!

Now I look back and I think, how stupid of me not to realize that this didn't make him a good surgeon! It just made him a charmer, and that of course is what his business is all about.

Well, of course I fell for him hook, line, sinker. He had these eyes, you see . . . blue, cheeky, and I couldn't resist that. And once, he gave me a camellia, which he said he'd got up as dawn was rising to pick just for me. No one had done that for me before. I guess no one ever will now, the way I look.

He suggested I have not one, but several procedures. I didn't think I looked that bad, really I'd only wanted my nose tweaked a little, but he said, "Think about it this way, gorgeous girl, if you get it all done now, you'll save money, because you'll only need one anesthetic. Also, I'm busy next month, I have a big Vogue *shoot to prepare for."*

It's crazy, I know, but I figured if he was being interviewed for those big, glossy magazines, he must be good at his job. I trusted him. I signed up for a chemical peel to rejuvenate my skin and get rid of deep wrinkles (he said they were caused by stress due to my breakup with Renton, and that no man should be allowed to treat me that way again). The nose job, we'd already discussed. But then he also said a mini face-lift would help with the bags around my eyes, and I could see what he meant. And while he was at it, as I was getting so much work done, he'd throw in some collagen for my lips for free. I'd have a celebrity pout!

I can't begin to tell you about the pain. When I woke up, I felt as if I had a vice clamped around my head, and in a way, I did. They'd bandaged me up so tightly that I couldn't see anything at first. Eventually one of the nurses peeled away one layer of bandages. It was horrendous. It wasn't like a nose anymore, it was like a bloodied parsnip end crookedly fixed on my face. It looked as if there was no flesh, just cartilage. They said not to worry, it always looked like that at this stage, and I didn't worry, I just didn't look in any mirrors, but then they said my skin had gone septic after the peel, probably because they'd done that first, and then operated on my nose and maybe my skin was more sensitive than most. It seemed like so much to be doing at once, but JK said it was to save me money, to put my interests first. But then it went septic around where the stitches of the face-lift were, by my ears, and I had this stuff seeping everywhere. It makes me sick to think of it now. I couldn't believe it, but I still thought everything would turn out all right because this was the surgeon to the stars! They sent me home, but it was bleeding and not just blood, but this sticky, yellow stuff everywhere. I called them up, and the nurse said not to worry, it was normal, and by the way, had they told me about the bruising, which would be black for at least three weeks. My face throbbed all the time, over and over. I had headaches, it was terrible. I couldn't wait three weeks, I just couldn't. Finally my dad came to see me and he just flipped. He got me into the emergency room and they couldn't believe what they saw. "Who did this?" they said, but I couldn't tell them, just couldn't. . . . I don't know why, but I think I still believed that it would turn out okay. My cheeks look drawn now all the time, because they've lost the natural plumpness most people have.

The hospital repaired the damage, stopped the infections from getting worse, but I had to return to JK3 to get the surgery repaired. I know this sounds crazy, but I figured it had to be just bad luck, or some kind of allergic reaction to something. My dad was mad at me. "How can you do this? Look what he's done to you!" But I had to go, some kind of hold he had over me, I guess.

He cried when he saw me again. Actually cried. "Oh, gorgeous girl, we'll make this better, I promise!" But then he made me wait four months before the next appointment. He said it was to let the swelling go down, let my parsnip nose settle, my stitches stop oozing pus and blood, because even though they'd been removed, I still needed bandages in that area, which my local hospital had to change every week.

I went back, but he wasn't there, he was in the operating theater, they said. "I'll wait," but they didn't listen, they were closing up, and if I didn't go, they'd call security on me. I was finally angry. At last I could see what I should have seen months before. This man wasn't interested in me anymore, never really had been, he'd just wanted my money. Now I was just an embarrassment to him, and he wanted me out of his life, and out of his surgery, as quickly as possible.

I can't even sue him. I've tried, believe me, but when you get on the Internet and check out the surgery stories, there are loads of women like me, sad cases, with sad faces and they've found it—almost all of them—impossible to sue their surgeons.

Then he sent me a bill. For ten times the amount he originally quoted me. He said, in the short letter attached, that it was more than the original amount he'd quoted because of things he hadn't anticipated. I called to ask, "Like what things?" but the nurses just said, "Oh, you know, you came back more than most to get your dressings changed, and you had an additional consultation, and then there were all the phone calls." They made me feel like I'd been nothing but a nuisance, but I guess they had to charge me—if they hadn't, it would have looked like JK knew he'd been in the wrong, and I could have had a case. I don't know.

I have given up any chance of restoring myself to anything resembling, closely or otherwise, normality. I have neither the funds, the faith, nor the energy. I am a freak of circumstance, not nature; of so-called medical science; of medical

*ineptitude; of vanity, my reality. The only way I can live
with myself is by knowing that if I can alert other women to
the dangers of the society in which we live, then I will have
achieved something.*

*The saddest thing is that my parents won't even see me
anymore. They can't, I make them too sad. My dad is so upset with what I did, so angry with me for ruining my face.
They help me out with money, and to be fair, even Renton
helps me out with bills, although he needn't do that anymore,
I got my payoff. He's back with Marylou now, they seem
happy enough. I don't blame him, I don't blame anyone except myself and JK3. And now that I'm out of his life, he can
forget me and move on. I can never move on. Not really. I
am a freak.*

Kate put the file down by the side of the bath and stared at
the dripping tap. She couldn't bring herself to stretch forward
and turn it off properly and she couldn't turn it off with her
feet. They were leaden. The only thing that moved was the
tears that were silently pouring down her cheeks, those same
cheeks that JK3 had derided for their flatness. She was crying
for Patty, this woman she'd never met, never known, but who
had been through this . . . torture! She was crying for herself,
for the close escape she'd had in almost being sucked into this
hideous, evil world where nothing was enough if it made you
look good. How many other Pattys were there out there? How
many JK3s? Why were women continuously falling for these
empty promises? She was crying for humanity, for what it could
do in a supposedly civilized, educated, democratic world, all to
make a quick buck here, a few thousand there, never mind that
some poor sucker won't dare to look at herself in a mirror again,
will probably never have a relationship, never have children,
won't be able to hold down a job in public. . . . When would life

begin again for Patty? Kate looked again at the first photo of her. There was something endearingly hopeful, energetic, so happy about her big round eyes. And that was the true tragedy. Of all the features of Patty's that had disappeared in the second picture, it was the sparkle in her eyes that was most shockingly conspicuous by its absence. Patty, the old Patty, was gone. She was never coming back.

And then just as quickly as the tears had come, they stopped, and her head felt clear. The fog of hangover lifted, the heady rush of L.A. vanished, and the weight of responsibility drew down on her. Patty Patrice was her wake-up call, the alarm bell she hadn't heard ringing as she'd accepted *Darling*'s plastic surgery supplement assignment with scarcely a glance over her shoulder to see if her scruples were listening. Patty Patrice was her call to arms, a weighty responsibility turning into the challenge she'd been waiting for. Patty Patrice was also her future as a journalist. Because how else could she reconcile any conscience—political, social, moral, or otherwise—with the somewhat flighty, haphazard, and facile nature of her chosen career path?

Questions rapidly flashed into her mind. Why hadn't Patty sued? Surely everyone here sued? Why was Aurelie helping her? She was bound to lose her job over this; what was more astonishing was that she should want to keep her job at all. She needed to call Patty, to find out more, to see what he'd done to her with her own eyes. There was no question she wouldn't write up her story. Patty had a right to be heard, and *Darling*'s readers had that same right to be informed. Would Alexis go for it? As the entire basis of the plastic surgery supplement, no. As one informed warning on how far wrong surgery could go? Possibly. But would it really carry the same weight if it was only one strand of the supplement? How much stronger, fresher the supplement would be if it was somehow broader than just about surgery. Kate's alcohol-addled brain started to see it taking shape, unfold before her eyes with each drip of the tap.

The cover: a naked female form, beautiful, natural. The cover line: WHY SURGERY IS YESTERDAY'S NEWS. No, too random, too alienating for readers, who, after all, would be expecting something in favor of surgery. She'd come back to that—maybe Tania back in Maidstone could help her out with some suggestions, although the girls in the subs department at *Darling* magazine seemed pretty hot with titles, too. The main feature would have to be Patty Patrice's story, an interview with her, a warning on how surgery could go wrong. There could be another story on how to look ten years younger without resorting to surgery. Nature versus Nurture. Nurture Nature. That kind of thing. It had been done before, but not in this context: a positive, antisurgery article in a supplement devoted to helping women—oh, God, she could feel a cliché coming—help themselves. The final feature could be something on how celebrity culture was fueling unhealthy physical goals, causing us to pander to vanity, narcissism, self-obsession. She would start by looking at Hollywood, the spiritual home of plastic surgery, beginning with how the studios influenced the starlets to look a certain way. Taking her neatly back to Lolly's original feature idea: the history of plastic surgery in Hollywood. Luxury, celebrity, entertainment. Well, there were elements of each of Alexis's requirements in that lineup. Alexis would have to go for it. Oh, yes, the alarm bells would be ringing, all right.

The phone by her head, dripping with condensation from the hot bath, startled her to attention. She pressed the receiver to her damp face.

"Hello?"

"Kate. Or should I call you Cinderella?" Shit! JK3. How on

earth should she play him now? He didn't know, shouldn't know that he was some kind of Antichrist to her. "Kate? You still there?"

"I'm in the bath." A wistful sigh at the other end of the phone told her this was too much information.

"I'd join you only I'm in the garden." Funny how only yesterday, he'd sounded sexy, charming; now she visualized him in leafy foliage surrounded by lizards, himself the king of all reptiles.

"Picking camellias?" She hadn't meant for it to sound sarcastic, but it had.

"Waiting by the fountain, where I last saw you. At least you're not still in my powder room."

It was annoying how in spite of all the things she'd read he'd done, at his mention of the fountain, her good manners prevailed. "JK, I'm really, really sorry."

She tried to stand up to get out of the bath but the lead from the phone wasn't long enough. The phone dropped back underwater. By the time she'd found a towel that wasn't a facecloth or big enough to make a double bed with, he'd gone. Let him think she'd hung up on him. This was just the beginning. She had to get organized anyway. The shoot tomorrow! Her interviews! And most importantly she had to track down Patty Patrice and the mysterious Aurelie.

She looked at herself naked in the mirror and felt lucky to be whole, unscarred, unhurt by any surgeon's empty promises.

The doorbell rang. Why didn't Mercedes just barge in like she had before?

Clutching her towel and wearing her old-lady bath hat, she opened the door to find Clarissa looking at her as if she was a lazy slob for still being in a towel at 11:00 a.m.

"Good morning," she said, managing a grimace of a smile. "You have a casting at twelve midday, an interview at three, another at five, then a beauty editors' dinner for the plastic surgery conference the day after tomorrow. Oh, and a facial in the spa at six. And Alexis called. Twice. And there's this package for you."

She handed over a white box. She wasn't expecting anything.

"Thank you, Clarissa. Obviously we have a lot to talk about. Can you meet me in the lobby in half an hour?"

Still clutching her towel around her, Kate closed the door. Time to get Clarissa onside. She moved over to the bed, now invitingly made up. Funny how just half an hour ago she'd wanted nothing more than to sleep, deeply, forgetfully; now she wanted to change the world, fight Patty's battles and those of every other woman who'd been through these ghastly experiences. She could no more sleep than she could wonder about what to wear.

She opened the box, peeling back the tape gently, trying not to tear the off-white Japanese paper finish, which was irresistibly pretty. She'd like to save the box, wrap some present in it. It had a lid like a cake box's, with precise folds forming a hinge-like motion as she raised the lid.

There was an off-white flower inside.

A camellia.

Calmly, she picked up the box and carried it over to the desk by the window. She dropped it into the bin.

twelve

A car pulled up to the stoplight. The female driver looked like Heather Locklear. She had a platinum blonde bob, wispy fringe. She checked her reflection in the dashboard mirror then pulled off in her black Range Rover as the lights changed to green. Almost immediately the lights changed back. Another woman pulled up in a black Range Rover. She looked like Heather Locklear, platinum bob, wispy fringe. . . .

Kate was sitting in the hotel café counting L.A. sheep: watching identical blondes of a certain age drive past. They all looked perfect, the blow-dry just so, the nipped-in jacket, the jeans, but they all looked the same. Creepily so.

Clarissa interrupted her daydream. "I've canceled your casting, one of your interviews, and the facial and arranged a car to take you to Patty Patrice's house at five. It'll pick you back up at seven, so you'll be in time for the beauty editors' dinner at eight. Are you sure you don't want me to come with you to the interview?" She pushed a lump of mozzarella around in a slurry of balsamic, like a round white pebble at the bottom of a peat-filled river. Clarissa's dietary requirements seemed to defy Atkins or the Zone or any other new fad diet.

"No. Thanks, but I'll be fine," said Kate. She reached across for the saccharin that would apparently knock off two dress sizes with a simple click, remembering Trisha Hillmory's Splenda habit. All that—Maidstone—seemed so long ago, now. She would call her mother today, must do, it had been mean to be so aloof but she hadn't meant to, if that counted.

"Do you—I mean, have you ever wanted to look like—these women?" Kate gestured toward a mother and daughter pair who were strolling toward the café. The mother had the Rodeo classic blow-dry—a little lift at the roots, then straight, then curved inward at the ends; the daughter, a more tousled, jaggedy cut. They had identical figures. Lean, tall, wearing low-cut jeans that hugged tiny, bunlike buttocks. Mini tees, one in pink, one in lime, rose a couple of inches above diamanté-studded belts to reveal flat, tanned stomachs. In spite of being so thin, ample breasts stood to attention above the lace-trimmed scoop of their tops, like full moons rising over the froth of surf at Santa Monica. Silver necklaces jiggled, as if fighting to claim occupancy of the cavernous fold between the breasts. Tortoise-shell sunglasses, taking up what remained of their faces besides the button nose and glossy, plump lips, perfectly matched blonde and copper highlights.

Clarissa sighed. "It's an L.A. thing."

They had planned the next few days meticulously, starting with the rescheduled casting. After lunch a stream of pale, rather plain-looking girls had presented themselves before Kate, then shown photographs that seemed to bear no resemblance to their real selves. She flicked through each plastic-coated portfolio, seeing page after page of long Pantene hair, skin that screamed "it was worth it," lashes that "maybe were Maybelline." The working title for the story they were shooting was "In Search of Natural Beauty" because that was the look—Alexis had argued on the phone—that most women wanted. Looking at the women on Rodeo Drive, Kate seriously doubted this. They didn't want "natural" at all—they wanted "artificial," surely? What was natural about collagen-plumped lips, brows that looked so surprised they said, "*You're* dating George Clooney?" and breasts that stood rock-hard at attention? It was funny how the question What's beauty? had returned to haunt her with a vengeance. She had thrown it out to Alexis in one of their very first conversations in the hope that some definition of her job would come back to her; instead Alexis had seized upon it as a defining moment in the direction of the magazine. Now she had to take the cause and run with it. Yet, here she was, dancing in the shadows of the beautiful people, and she didn't want to look like them at all, didn't want their answer to "What's beauty?" any more than they wanted hers.

*   *   *

"How's it going anyway?" Alexis had asked in a postlunch phone update. Kate had been economical with the truth, thanks to some timely advice from Clarissa. She had shown her the letter from Patty Patrice. Clarissa was visibly shocked and had enthusiastically gone for the story, but not without warning Kate about the considerable dangers that lay ahead.

"If you don't mind me saying," she had ventured, "maybe you should write it first, I mean, don't tell Alexis. She might not get it."

"What's not to get?" asked Kate. Quite how anyone could fail to be moved by such a story was beyond her. Alexis was clearly a woman of intelligence, and *Darling* was a women's magazine—this story was perfect for it, something that would shake its readers from their turpitudinous reverie, would give them something more important to think about than whether they should go for black nail polish or white; Manolo Blahniks or Jimmy Choos.

"Well . . . first off, there's the question of the advertisers," said Clarissa. She sipped from her glass of sparkling mineral water. San Pellegrino, ice on the side, lime not lemon.

"What have they got to do with it?"

Clarissa's water snorted out of one nostril.

"What have they got to do with it? Are you . . . ?!" She checked herself, dabbing at her nose with a folded damask napkin. A waiter rushed up to replace it.

"Nuts, I believe you wanted to say." Kate laughed, although she wasn't sure if her response should be so casual or amused, for what was ostensibly such a disrespectful comment.

"Didn't anyone ever tell you about the advertisers?" Clarissa continued. "You know, those people who pay our salaries?" She pushed her thick-rimmed black sunglasses onto her head. She looked worried, concerned even; quite why, Kate had no idea.

"Nouvelle Maison Editions pays our salaries, doesn't it?" said Kate, quietly, realizing as soon as the words tumbled out of her mouth that this answer was not the right one.

Clarissa sighed. "Look. Maybe magazines work differently in the UK, but here advertisers rule! Sure, we pretend they don't. We talk about freedom of the press, in the same breath that we talk about democracy and the American dream, but . . . it's just not like that." Her voice rose to a muted shriek.

"Well, of course I know magazines aren't all about freedom and democracy, but they're still independent; we can still write about Patty Patrice, can't we? Oh, God, maybe I need to talk to Alexis." Kate reached for her cellular. Was Clarissa being patronizing?

"I wouldn't if I were you," said Clarissa, in a friendly rather than threatening tone of voice. Kate put the phone down obediently. Clarissa elaborated. "I guess it's different where you're from. . . . See this?" She lifted up a burgundy leather handbag. The strap was plaited, and a leather key fob with a silver plate engraved with the name "Clarissa" hung from it. "This bag was hand stitched. They made ten of them like this. Oh, sure, there are thousands of others like this, but they don't have the hand stitching, and they certainly don't have the key fob."

"It's . . . er . . . a lovely bag. A wonderful bag. Um . . . well done. For having the bag."

Clarissa stared at her impatiently.

"I got this bag for free. Its retail value is in excess of two thousand dollars. See these shoes?" She uncrossed her legs, sticking out her left foot for Kate to examine. "Snakeskin. Real. Gold insole. Stiletto. Eight hundred fifty dollars. They'd look tacky if I was wearing them with anything other than this plain black shift dress. Fifteen hundred and seventy-five dollars, by the way. But I knew that when I picked out the dress and the shoes and didn't have to pay for them."

"You stole them?" Clarissa really did have hidden depths.

"No! They were gifts! All of them! The shoes, the bag, the dress—even my skin, which everyone keeps telling me is perfect—it wouldn't look like this without free treatments from my derm and a facial once a week. I can't afford all of this on my salary, and they know that. But they can!"

"Who's 'they'?" asked Kate.

"The advertisers, the publicity people, the guys in marketing who want us to write about their stuff. To sing their praises. To tell it not like it is, but how it could be!"

"But you don't . . . I mean, you stay independent, right? I mean, they don't tell you what to write, do they?"

Clarissa sighed again. Kate felt like an idiot.

"Oh, you really don't know, do you? Sure, it starts innocuously enough. They want to tell you about their new supermoist lipstick. And the best way to tell you is by showing you a DVD presentation, over lunch at your favorite restaurant. You pick out the caviar, have a glass of champagne, because it's on them, right? And then you notice that the portable DVD player is made from a superlight titanium casing, it's the latest on the market, and guess what? It's engraved with your name. A little present from them, because they're fans of your work. Next thing you know, the publisher's sitting in your office, asking how much coverage you are going to give that same new supermoist lipstick, because the company that makes it is considering taking out a double-page spread in the April issue to the tune of seventy thousand dollars. Oh, I thought I'd do a bit on the news page, you say, really happy you've got the DVD player, and the lipstick's not so bad either. That's not enough, she says. Wouldn't it be great to have a feature on how products are so multifunctional these days? How the two-in-one concept has revolutionized our everyday lives? How a lipstick can give color, plump up the lips, and moisturize at the same time? I mean, wouldn't *Darling*'s readers really like that? she says. And you say, well, yes, I guess so, thinking about your DVD player and how much it would have cost you if you'd bought it. And perhaps the two-in-one concept really has revolutionized our everyday lives, and besides, those people from the lipstick company have called your assistant three times this week and it would get them off your back. And so you write it. A whole page. And no one really knows, but the publisher's really happy, and the editor doesn't give a damn, she's so wrapped up in where she's going to get her next free outfit from. And so, sure, Nouvelle Maison Editions pays your salary, but they wouldn't be paying that without the money from the advertisers, and the advertisers wouldn't advertise without the articles they get from you about their supermoist lipstick, would they now? So do you get it?"

It was a blazing hot day but even though they were outside where the air-conditioning couldn't reach them, Kate suddenly felt a chill running through her. The hairs on her arms stood up, her back tingled. So this was what it was all about. People weren't being nice to her, weren't being generous. She'd thought she was a success, popular, winning friends, influencing people. She'd thought she was doing a good job, all the while eking out the good and the bad from the downright ugly. Damn it, she had done a good job, hadn't she? None of the pieces she'd written so far had been about anything she hadn't truly believed in, hadn't researched to the nth degree. But now she had to face a truth so ugly it couldn't be concealed with something flesh-toned, high in pigment particles, yet still supermoisturizing. The truth was, the beauty business was an ugly business.

"I see."

Clarissa sat back, folding her arms across her chest. For the first time since meeting her, Kate was impressed that she could be this impassioned about her work, this aware of a situation that needed rectifying. She'd assumed her various disgruntlements were a bad case of job envy, her excess of attitude about being majorly pissed off that, with Kate as head of the department, she would have to leave the magazine in order to get ahead, or stay put and remain subordinate to this English interloper. She had been wrong, judged her unfairly: Clarissa hated her job because, like Kate, she found it hard to compromise when it came to ethics. All that remained was for Clarissa to open up to Kate, to talk about the principles they clearly shared, and the two could be colleagues, friends, battle the same battles.

"You know Clarissa, I'm shocked, I'll admit, because you're

right, things aren't the same, er . . . where I'm from, or maybe they are and I've just been burying my head in the sand." (They hadn't experienced the same pressure at *Maidstone Bazaar*, unless you counted the free balloons that came with the sunbed vouchers for the Larkfield Leisure Centre.) "But what I don't understand is, if you hate it so much, how come you work in this world?"

"Hate it?!" said Clarissa. She giggled. "No, no, no! I don't hate it! I *love* it!"

Kate couldn't conceal the look of horror on her face. Here was someone who blatantly exploited her work, her readers, for what exactly? A pair of snakeskin shoes and a handbag? She took a sip of sparkling water, at a loss for words.

"You don't understand," said Clarissa, this time sounding genuinely concerned for the shock she'd caused Kate. "I'm not like you. I'm not even like . . . Cynthia. I'm not doing this job because I like writing." As if realizing she'd almost done herself out of her job she added hastily, "I mean, I do . . . and I can do it. . . ."

She paused, waiting for Kate to give her the affirmation she needed.

"Yes, of course you can, I mean, you're very good," said Kate.

"But . . . I'm doing it because, well, what else is a girl to do?"

"Well, you could . . ." Kate could think of any number of things a girl could do besides writing articles about supermoist two-in-one lipsticks. She could get a job for Amnesty International, something Kate herself had once considered. Or at Greenpeace, Kate's first big charitable love. Both would pay decent salaries, though likely not as big as the salary at *Darling*. She could do some voluntary work—she had heard they needed people at the charity clothing shop, to style the clothes and present them in a more saleable way. Clarissa would be good at that. She was just about to suggest these options when she realized that Clarissa couldn't do any of these things. Not really.

"I mean, sure there are things I could do, but none of them would give me perks like these." She gestured to her shoes again. "Look, I'm, I don't mean to be rude or anything, but I'm from a different world to you and Cynthia. I'm here because . . . well, because my dad knew someone who knew someone. I get a small allowance. Small, note, hence I still need the free shoes. I'm meant to be finding a husband. Some nice hedge fund guy, with a house in East Hampton. Or Amagansett. Or maybe even Southampton, in a pinch. I guess then my real work will begin. Charity fund-raising, art lunches, you know. And then all this will come in useful somehow; it'll be like training."

Kate was appalled. She couldn't believe what Clarissa was saying. She fumbled with her napkin. "Is that what you want?"

"I guess so."

They sat in silence, the waiter arriving and noisily clearing away the plates as if to compensate for the sudden gloom that had descended upon them. Kate did not know what to say. She was stunned. This was worse than an arranged marriage. What kind of parents brought a girl up to be this afraid of life, this ignorant of the possibilities? And why? So she could kill time until Mr. Financially Right came along? Clarissa was bright, but what she was saying now was that she had lazily accepted this to be her fate, because she couldn't be bothered to do anything else. Kate wasn't convinced she was as happy about that as she was pretending to be.

"Well . . . good for you." It wasn't what she meant, but what else could she say? A sudden breeze playfully tickled the corners of the waxed paper menu, as if daring them to order a dessert.

"So, the advertisers won't like me writing about Patty Patrice because she doesn't fit in with the sell on plastic surgery, does she?"

"Uh-huh. Patty Patrice doesn't fit in with anything."

So that was it then. She couldn't do the story. Alexis wouldn't like it. JK would sue. The aesthetic surgery clinic that was paying a fortune to encourage women to take minimal-risk procedures in the pursuit of turning the clock back would pull its sponsorship. She would be fired.

But if she didn't write it, what would happen to Patty? Patty wasn't like Clarissa. She didn't have a rich daddy to bail her out, fix the things that had gone wrong, and there was no Mr. Right about to come along anytime soon. Patty needed Kate. The full horror of the immense responsibility she had taken on hit her: without Kate, Patty was lost.

Unless . . . what if she could do this a different way? Expose the dangers. Be responsible. *Darling*'s readers would thank her for that, wouldn't they?

As if reading her mind, Clarissa leaned forward conspiratorially and whispered:

"Of course, you could still do the story. I mean, it's a risk 'n' all, but Patty sounds pretty convincing. And a newspaper would probably run it on the back of *Darling* covering it—you know, the people in the *Darling* media offices would sell the story on to, say, the *New York Times* or even the *L.A. Times*, or both. It could be a pretty big story, maybe even TV coverage if it blew up. It's rare for a magazine to explode a story like that, turn the beauty industry on its head. Alexis loves publicity, you know. Just loves it. It's a career-maker, that kind of story."

"I don't know," said Kate, suddenly overwhelmed by the dilemma that faced her. Five minutes ago it had all been so clear: do Patty, tell the world, expose a liar, tell the truth. Now there was more on the line. Her job, for starters. To not do the story at all was the ultimate sellout, the surrender of any values she'd once held dear. But hadn't she already sold out? She'd been suckered into that very same world of beauty by the salary and the thought of escaping Brian Palmers and *Maidstone Bazaar*, leaving her hometown, even leaving her mother. She'd taken a job for the money, and the escape route it had offered. Her beliefs, ethics, morals, call them what you will, had been about her old world, not this one. About the ozone layer thinning, about the ice caps thawing, about the lack of a cohesive recycling campaign by Maidstone Borough Council. But were these two worlds so separate? It was only now that she was forced to make some kind of stand on plastic surgery, a stand she'd managed to put off by writing about its Hollywood history, that she realized what her campaigns to save the world were all about in the first place. That same world she was busy trying to save was good for nothing if it didn't care about the people who inhabited it. People like Patty who had been sold a dream only to wake up to a nightmare. People who searched for beauty only to end up looking ugly. Being ugly.

"Here's what I'll do," she said, drawing a deep breath, aware as her heart quickened that she was on the brink of making a decision that was as fundamental to her sense of who she was and where she was from as it was to Patty's future.

"I'll write it. I'll write it so well Alexis will have to run it. But I won't tell her that's what I'm doing until it's done. It's a risk, but I'll take it."

Clarissa smiled and sat back in her wicker chair. "I think you're doing the right thing."

Kate smiled back. "I think I am, too. Thanks."

thirteen

The rain had threatened to fall all afternoon, and now here it was, pelting down from purple, blackened clouds the color of unpolished plums. Purple rain, like the Prince song. They were Patty's tears; the only break in their unforgiving rhythm a thunderbolt of lightning. A message from Zeus, raining flash floods down on JK. Here, take that! And that! His camellias would be ruined. It thudded persistently on the windscreen, like the sound of applause as the film credits ran: Zeus played by Kirk Douglas, JK by Owen Wilson, Patty Patrice by Kim Basinger. Who would play the part of Kate Miller? She'd been in L.A. too long.

She shivered on the backseat of the car taking her to Patty's house. The camel leather upholstery touched the backs of her legs and left them cold. She pulled down over her knees her weather-inappropriate floral print cotton dress. The air-conditioning lifted the soft, downy hairs on her shins where she was due for another wax. She remembered how her mother used to bundle her up on her lap when she was about five. She'd stroke her smooth knees and marvel at her skinny little legs, while Kate watched *Mr. Benn*, the only TV program she was allowed apart from *Blue Peter*, that all-time classic of kids' TV shows. She sniffled. Oh, shit, not a cold coming on, the last thing she needed! Outside, L.A. passed her by, the off-white houses and steel gray roofs of La Cienega looking shabby and dull without the blessing of the sun to plant its magic halo. The sea, gray and unappealing, like a faded English seaside town on a February day; the damp mugginess of the air exuding an end-of-the-world feel, the aftermath of a nuclear fallout. It was all a sham after all—the low-roofed buildings that had looked so appealing in the magic of the sunshine now looked like film-set fakes; the sea was cold and unyielding; the beauty so transient. The L.A. that had greeted her a few days ago was shallow, diffident, closed.

*   *   *

After lunch Clarissa had gone back to her hotel room to make the final arrangements for tomorrow's shoot. The makeup artist needed to be confirmed, as did the hairstylist and manicure and pedicure people. The right backdrop needed to be ordered, the photographer's budgets had to be checked. Kate had been happy to let her get on with these things.

She had instead met Harold Epps, a plastic surgeon now in his nineties, for tea by the hotel's rooftop pool. Harry, or, strictly speaking, Professor Harold Bernstein Epps, was one of the oldest living plastic surgeons in L.A., an irregular but welcome fixture on the UCLA lecture circuit, distinguished not just by the longevity of his career, but also by the techniques he had pioneered with some of America's most famous surgeons. Rumor had it, he had given Marilyn Monroe cheek implants; but no one knew for certain. It might have been a chin tuck.

Or it might have been another surgeon, Dickinson-Smith, who might have given her a nose job. Either way, Alexis had been impressed she had managed to lure Epps out of his retirement for *Darling*, and even more so when Cynthia had unearthed a recent interview with him in the *New York Times*. Epps had been scathing about the latest round of reality TV shows taking housewives with low self-esteem and turning them into wannabe supermodels. It wasn't something that would have happened in his day. ("Fabulous!" Alexis had gushed. "He's controversial. Glad the history story's coming along.")

It wasn't, though, not really. Coming along. More like running away, slipping through her fingers. In spite of their relaxed setting at a corner table, away from the waterside loungers, Harry was not forthcoming on the history of plastic surgery in Hollywood. He wore an immaculately pressed beige linen suit, with an open-neck pale yellow Cuban-style shirt and a Panama hat. He shuffled into his seat and ordered an English tea—to make Kate feel at home, he said. And that was his only attempt at lighthearted banter. Frequent lulls in the conversation caused by his alternately masticating the fluffy white scones, then staring at the two tanned, toned actresses on the other side of the pool only exacerbated his natural reticence. He wasn't so much ogling the girls as watching their poolside performance with benign amusement. Each of their movements seemed to be considered, geared toward the suited men on the other side, who must have been important agents, producers, directors, somebodies. They smoothed sunscreen with long lascivious strokes over each other's backs then dived into the pool, flicking their hair back like girls in shampoo commercials. Beads of oil on skin sparkled like dewdrops as the water splashed off their bodies. Kate covered her Dictaphone with a napkin and tried not to scowl.

After an hour with Harry, she was an authority on Los Angeles architecture, surgical techniques of the 1940s, but still wasn't getting very far on the subject of Hollywood history. A more targeted approach was called for.

KATE MILLER: Do you think Hollywood was more "innocent" back then or was every starlet up for a surgery makeover?

HARRY EPPS: Innocent, my ass! Sorry, but you really do have the wrong idea there. Sure, things were different then, but my, they'd been operating on thousands since the '30s—and that was before my time, I might add. There was one surgeon . . . who was (*pause to marvel at diving ladies, about seven seconds*) . . . radical. They used to say he could do breast implants in fifteen minutes! Mind you, he also had a reputation for not bothering to mop up the bleeding, so the floor was filled with blood. (*Pause to spread more strawberry jam on scone, about twenty seconds.*) I heard he was somewhat . . . ruthless.

MILLER: And who did he operate on? (*Give me some names!*)

EPPS: Oh, I couldn't reveal names. No surgeon would do that. It wouldn't be right to say . . . but they were prominent . . . prominent.

MILLER: Well, what about later? During the '50s, for example. Were starlets under pressure from the studios to undergo some kind of physical transformation? (*Give me some names!*)

EPPS: I don't know. I avoided the Hollywood scene. It's just not my temperament. To wit, I would come home and mention to my wife and say, "Oh, So-and-So was in the office," and she'd say, "Well, don't you know who that is?" and I'd say, "No, who was it?"

MILLER: And who was the "So-and-So" she mentioned? Was it Marilyn Monroe by any chance?

EPPS: I can't say. (*Finishes last mouthful of scone—plate empty.*)

So that was that. Their surgery secrets would go to the grave. It was down to Patty Patrice to bring some color, some excitement—a goddamn story—for the supplement.

The car pulled up to a block of sandy-colored flats eight or so stories high. They looked nice enough, but a quick glance at the balconies and the kids' bicycles, the washing hung out to dry, and the odd dried-up geranium in a pot left her in no doubt these were low-rental apartments, not some playboy's penthouse.

The rain stopped. The black clouds were illuminated by a sudden burst of light. There was a freshness in the air, the sulphuric smell of water on a hot, dusty road. Sounds became crisp again, the passing sirens of cop cars, kids' voices playing in the gardens to the side of the flats, the rolling whir of skateboards clunking off pavements. As long as the sun was here, so was optimism, hope, life.

"I'll wait here for you, madam," said the driver, an older driver than JK's Chuck, someone who probably didn't moonlight as a theater assistant, but seemed with his straight back and clean-shaven, open face to have chosen this as his life's work. He held the door open for her and she stepped out, her flat golden pumps soaking up a puddle. She had chosen her outfit with care—a button-down shirt dress with a jolly floral print, something she hoped would be interpreted as friendly, trustworthy, nonthreatening. She looked back into the car to check she hadn't left her Dictaphone behind, or that her cellular hadn't fallen out. She clutched her handbag under her arm, smiled at her driver, and headed for the front door.

The entrance hall was dark, flanked by four doors and a concrete stairwell. Patty was on the fourth floor. The stair light flickered on and off, plunging the stairs in and out of sporadic darkness. At the third step she became aware of someone standing behind her, watching.

"Who's that?" she said. Her hand moved down toward her phone in her bag, hoping the perpetrator wouldn't think she was reaching for a gun, fire at her, kill her dead. She'd been watching too many of those American cop shows late at night in her hotel.

Aurelie was leaning against the wall, in a manner that was less nonchalant, more about concealment. She eased herself up straight, took a white muslin cloth from her handbag and wiped her hands, then dusted down her beige trousers and pale pink jacket. It was only then that she explained what she'd been doing hiding behind the stairwell doors.

"I didn't mean to frighten you, but I had to be sure."

"Sure of what?" said Kate. Her three steps' advantage made her momentarily taller, but the shrillness of her voice revealed how frightened she had been. Her chin jutted forward.

Aurelie moved to the first step. "That you weren't coming with anyone. JK, for example. He's been talking about you all day at the clinic. You are his new obsession."

In another world, that would have been exciting news, resulting in girlish giggles with her and Lise. Now, knowing what she knew, it made her feel physically sick. An obsession. Her hand gripped the banister; she felt her shoulders crumple.

"It's okay," Aurelie said. "He can't touch you. You're a journalist, remember? It's only patients he can touch." She touched Kate's arm; their eyes met. There was a softness in her expression, her eyes were wet and moist, welling up for an instant and then gone, the hardness returned. "Come on. Patty's waiting for you."

* * *

Sunnyside Residences had been built in the 1960s by an architect whose dream was "to make every hour a golden hour." Privately funded, the idea of drenching each home in daylight wasn't practicable in a city where temperatures reached eighty degrees in February. People wanted shade, blinds that kept the heat of the sun away from salads, ice lollies, Coke Zeros. The private, high-income tenants, the playboys and models, never moved in. The landlords lowered the rents; young families and old couples arrived and, after enduring inadequate air-conditioning and the hottest summer on record, were delighted when a block of flats went up next door, shielding them ever more from the white gold of the sun.

You couldn't keep the sun out all together, though. Each apartment had a small, glass-roofed balcony, which you could get to via French doors in the living room. They called it the sunroom. Kate had noticed from the street an elderly couple, sitting like cats on a heat-drenched wall, lazily enjoying the warmth in the wake of the rain without moving from their wicker chairs.

Apartment 44B, Patty Patrice's apartment, she had also seen from the street, without knowing it was hers. Patty's flat had the unusual distinction of having a black sunroom. From the outside it had looked as if black paint had been painted directly onto the glass, transforming the joyful sunroom into a bunker. Where the paint had peeled off in patches, she had caught glimpses of a curtain, thick and woolen, dark. She had thought it was a storage unit, or a communal utility room.

It was to this room that Aurelie now steered her. Dark and airless like a cellar, her eyes blinked as they adjusted. She moved blindly inward, a couple more meters, Aurelie behind her all the way. She couldn't see a thing. Her breathing quickened, her gold pumps edged their way gingerly. She felt a hand on her shoulder, and jumped, but it was only Aurelie. Her shoulder relaxed under her protection, welcomed the guidance.

It was hot. Her upper lip glistened; she wiped it with the back of her hand, grateful that the one consolation for the darkness was that no one would see. Why wouldn't they switch a bloody light on?

"Here. Sit down. Let me help you." Aurelie showed her the way to an armchair. Her eyes, waking up gradually to the shadows, confirmed the shredded threads of the worn-away chair arms that her fingers had brushed as she sat down.

Hot like an old people's home.

Aurelie was crouching by the side of the chair; she took her hand. "It has to be like this. Dark," she said. "I'm sorry, it must be kinda weird for you. I'm used to it now. I forget what it's like for others. Not that there've been any others for a while."

Kate breathed in. She felt nervous. She could not find her handbag, nor her precious Dictaphone. She felt sweaty where her cotton bra rubbed her rib cage. Where was Patty? The panic rose in her throat; she felt as if she was choking.

"It's so hot in here! Aurelie, I don't know if I can . . ." She had been about to say she couldn't stand it, would have to go, her driver was waiting, anything to cut her rising claustrophobia dead in its tracks and get out of here, but Aurelie was there to calm her down once again.

"It's her circulation," she explained. "She's not the same as she was when she wrote the letter. You'll see."

And at once, the door opened again, allowing a glimmer of light to silhouette the newcomer.

fourteen

"Kate Miller. Pleasure to meet you." The woman who stood in the doorway was about five foot four, smaller than Kate. Her voice was soft, wavering. It was as if she had rehearsed this introduction many times, never quite believing she would say it, could say it.

The heat and the dark were suddenly forgotten. Kate tried to stand up from her chair, only to be yanked back down by Aurelie.

"Sit!" she hissed. So that was why she'd been holding her hand—not to keep her calm, nor to give her confidence in the dark, but to hold her back, keep her away from Patty herself. What was she playing at?

"It's okay," said Patty, falteringly. "She can come closer, but slowly."

Kate shook her hand, trying to get away from Aurelie. "I just want to say hello. I'm sorry, but can we turn a light on? I mean, it's a bit silly, isn't it, sitting in the dark like this. After all, I'm here to—"

"Shh!" Aurelie commanded.

Kate had had enough. She'd gone along with this so far, but what were they trying to hide? She could make out in the dim light of the doorway the upturned nose, the reddened, almost raw skin. She could see its texture, rough, uneven, almost lunar with its scratchy surface. She'd seen this all before, in the photos.

"Patty," she began, "look, I'm just not good in the dark." Maybe she was being selfish, but this was just ridiculous. How was she supposed to interview a victim of plastic surgery when she couldn't even see her?

"Sit down," said Aurelie. "Now!"

Aurelie had been alternately threatening, then kind, but always suspicious, never trusting. Now she was being downright rude. Enough was enough.

"All right, that's it," said Kate, turning round to the hunched-up Aurelie still crouching by the arm of the chair. "I'm going. I will not be spoken to like this, however . . . unfortunate . . . your friend is."

She stood up again. Aurelie yanked her back down.

"Enough! Please!" implored Patty, her voice rising to a shouted whisper. They were quieted, like two kids fighting in the back of a car. "Turn the light on."

"You sure?" said Aurelie. "I really don't think that's a good idea."

"Turn it on!"

She let go of Kate's sleeve and walked to the door. The light flooded the room. Kate's eyes studied her face and for a split second as she again compared what she saw now with the photos she had seen earlier, there was a comforting silence. It wasn't as bad as in the pictures. The face, still a mess, but softer looking, less red. The nose job had settled slightly, although there was still scarring around the edges. She couldn't see much else as Patty was wearing a white blouse, and . . .

"Oh! Your arms! Wh-what happened?"

Now she understood why they wanted to keep the lights off. A crisscross of cuts from her forearms to her hands were in the process of healing, livid and red, not fresh, but weeks old, she guessed. A bandage was wrapped tightly and professionally around her left wrist. She drew a sharp intake of breath as she realized. Patty had tried to kill herself?

"I'm so sorry, the light! I'm so sorry, so sorry . . . how completely insensitive of me!"

Patty moved her right hand over her left wrist, trying to mask the bandages, a futile endeavor as they were far too broad to hide with just the width of her slight hand. She looked away from Kate as she spoke. "I didn't want you to know. Thought you might decide not to write about me, might think I was, I don't know, crazy or something."

Aurelie dimmed the light.

"No! No, of course not." Kate stood up abruptly, gestured to her chair. "Sit down, please, how rude of me, you're standing there, and I'm just looking—and—oh, God, when did it happen?" "It" somehow made Patty's suicide attempt passive. When had she slashed her wrists, tried to kill herself, end it all? There were many ways to describe the act, but in this dank, dark greenhouse, they were all too close, too intense. She had never wanted to get out of anywhere this badly.

Patty walked slowly over to the other chair and sat down. She had known where the furniture was, hadn't needed to be guided there, was used to the darkness, liked life with the lights off.

Quietly, she said, "It was a cry for help, that's what my therapist says." She took a sip of water from a small table to the side of the chair. She put the glass down and looked at Kate, taking in the dress, the gold pumps. She didn't seem embarrassed to be checking her out in this way, all the while avoiding eye contact, as if it was her due to make sure this young journalist was worth her story. "So, I cried for help, and you came along." She smiled. A thin, weak smile, the corners of the mouth barely lifting. "Now what do you need?"

"Details," said Kate, her calm restored by the matter-of-fact manner in which Patty had discussed and dismissed her suicide as something that was disconnected from their current business. It was better that way.

For the next hour and a half, she fired off questions: dates, names, the duration of the operations, the cost, who had assisted JK, his manner, if she had signed forms, if there were any witnesses who could corroborate her story.

Witnesses. Yes, of course there were. Aurelie. She had been helpfully fetching papers, herbal tea for Patty, coffee for Kate, seemingly happy in her role as ally, confidante, assistant, but now she stood in the doorway, tray in hand, and looked serious.

"I'll help, of course I will. But not now. I'm more useful to you where I am, working with him. When you're ready, when the article is published."

It seemed like a good plan. Kate could have happily continued—perhaps "happily" was the wrong word here, as she found the whole situation incredibly distressing—were it not for her mobile ringing. Clarissa warned her she had a dinner to attend in one hour, and her hair and makeup people were waiting. Hair and makeup people? It seemed so wrong to be leaving Patty to have dinner with a bunch of beauty editors, to be getting her hair and makeup done. She made her excuses and left, promising to call in a few days when she had written the article.

In the car on the way back to the hotel she gazed out of the window, taking nothing in, writing in her head all the time. Occasionally she jotted ideas down in her notebook. It was raining again. Thunder shook the skies like rockets in a war-torn city in another land. Danger was always somewhere else, she mused. And when it was under your nose, very often you'd pretend you couldn't see it.

fifteen

"So right now, I find that by eating three grapefruits before three p.m., then eating only protein for the rest of the day, I'm never hungry, and I look great!" The woman speaking to Kate on her right was, it transpired, the publicity agent for a new brand of health foods. Diana Alterus had signed a contract promising to keep her weight down to the ultimate in desirable dress sizes, a size zero, otherwise she would be fired. How could they sell a slimming bar, her clients could argue, if their representative was anything less than perfect?

"Of course, you might get osteoporosis, bowel cancer, or several other deadly diseases as you get older, but who cares!" retorted the woman on Kate's left, Vivienne Fox, a beauty reporter from one of the TV networks with her own TV program from backstage at the fashion shows.

Kate laughed. She was the only one who got the joke. The thirty or so other women who sat round the table, of varying ages, but with minuscule dress sizes and perfectly blow-dried hair in common, carried on talking to one another.

"Did you go to the Nova perfume launch?" said one within earshot.

"No, I sent my assistant."

"You got away with that? Wow! I had a three-line whip to go! Publisher went nuts when I said my workload was intense and I had two other launches at the same time. Honestly, I feel like some beauty queen, wheeled out on parade to attend these things. Just send me the goddamn perfume!" She waved the waiter away as he presented a plate of delicious-looking zucchini fritters to accompany her organic salmon.

"Well, it was a big mistake, my not going. They pulled the ads—or threatened to. Our ad team is still in negotiations, but it's tough out there! Smells like crap anyway."

"Hey, did you get that titanium-plated DVD player from Biocorp?"

"To tell me how to use their new skin care range? Yeah, it's great, isn't it?"

"The skin care?"

"No! The DVD player. Mine had my name engraved on it."

"By the way, who's doing your Botox? I just did an article on Dr. Bagshclinkoff—you know, the Russian one?—and the bastard's gone on holiday, and I'm desperate for a touch-up!"

And on it went. Kate had been chugging along, feeling like she could almost pass herself off as a beauty director, thanks to the consistency of the work she'd been handing in. But this was something different. What did she have in common with any of these women?

"Tedious, isn't it?" said Vivienne Fox, on her left, slugging back a glass of champagne as a waiter hovered by her side ready to refill it. "Imagine how I feel, I've been doing it for nearly twenty years!"

Kate gasped. The woman didn't look more than thirty-five. Even to Kate's uninitiated eye, she was more East Coast than West Coast, with a honey brown sleek chin-length bob, smooth skin, and a wrap dress. The only giveaway to her age was a slightly crepey neck and weathered hands. She would never have been able to spot that a few months ago.

"Yes, I know. Don't look that old. But believe me, honey, it's like the picture of Dorian Gray round here, and you should see the hideous secrets in my attic! Oh, they suck you in—quite literally sometimes, ha! Must use that! You get everything for free, and you forget what brought you here in the first place. It's a very seductive job, believe me! Now, you look like a new one, are you?"

"I'm very new. Well, not that new as a journalist, but as a beauty director, very new."

Vivienne removed her glasses and looked closely at her face.

"Hmm . . . let's see. No signs of dishonesty or corruption around the eyes. Mouth beginning to show the benefits of a good lip-plumping cream . . . I can smell a discreet, industry insider perfume, something like . . . Fracas, possibly even an original before they tampered with it. I'd say you've been doing it a couple of months, with a head start on most thanks to extra enthusiasm and a commitment to hard work!" She laughed, affectionately. Kate laughed, too.

"How did you get into it?" asked Kate.

"Now you're really making the illustrious career of a beauty editor sound like a program for alcoholics!" laughed the woman. "It was different back then. You know, a launch was a big deal. Perfumes were rare, exquisite things, not knocked off in a couple of months by the marketing team of some big beauty corporation, looking to fill a gap at Christmas. Yves Saint Laurent and Opium. Coco Chanel and Chanel No. 5. These were great perfumes, created by great designers, and their great 'noses'!

Not that I was around back then, dinosaur I might be. And there wasn't this big plastic surgery industry, for sure. No Botox. No surgeons. No celebrities—ugh! The bane of our lives!"

She stopped to refill her glass.

"No phone calls from readers asking where they could get their noses to look like Michelle Pfeiffer's! And it was an honor to write about these things; you didn't do it for the gifts or the clothes."

She took another slug of champagne. The waiter hovered.

"But now I'm sounding bitter, and I don't mean to be. It can still be a great job, you know, it's what you make of it. I love the spontaneity of being in TV, anything can happen, you still feel like—you know—a reporter! What story are you working on right now?"

"Well . . ." Should she trust her? She'd been talking to her for five minutes, if that, but the champagne was sending warm, friendly vibrations through her body, telling her that it was time she had a friend in the business, that it wasn't good to be on her own, and maybe she needed a confidante, someone to run her stories by, like Lianne or Tania from *Maidstone Bazaar*. As someone who had poured so much energy into her work, it wasn't the social friends Kate was missing—the ridiculous sex stories from Lise, or even the recent rubbish from Jean-Paul, cute as his accent was—but the work colleagues that were lacking. Working on a story that was either a potential career-wrecker or a potential career-maker with nothing but her own judgment for company was a solitary affair. She had tried to share the story with Clarissa when she'd got back, but hadn't felt able to discuss it. Everything was running late and Clarissa had had to dismiss the hairdresser and makeup artist who had been waiting to get to work on her. Kate had only had time to change her dress and rush out to the dinner. L.A. was too small a world; Vivienne might know someone who knew JK, and she couldn't afford to let Patty's secret be exposed via gossip. But she did seem different, she was warm, funny, kind. . . .

"I'm working on a story about—"

"Oh, hold on, looks like you'll have to tell me another time." Vivienne nudged her gently as a suited PR fellow with a square jaw and bright white teeth announced politely yet forcefully:

"Ladies, raise your glasses for our speaker of the evening . . ."

The women stood up, giggling, the champagne softening any inquisitive journalistic urges in readiness for a pleasant talk from . . .

". . . the eminent aesthetic surgeon . . . John Kingsley the Third!"

And there he was. It was only last night that she'd seen him, but it might as well have been years ago, for all that had happened in the last twenty-four hours. JK3 was still tall, blond, handsome, with a naughty glint in his eye and an impeccable dress sense, but she couldn't have seen through him more clearly had she put him on an operating table and opened him up. She wanted to walk out, but she had to be cool, couldn't draw attention to herself, let alone betray her insider's knowledge or betray Patty. If she just sat here quietly, she was sure she could get through the speech, the dinner, without having to talk to him, although he might have checked the guest list and seen that she was here.

"Kate Miller, are you here?" he shouted triumphantly, with a flick of his blond hair. Oh, God. She smiled weakly, just as the suited PR who had introduced him came rushing over and thrust a microphone under her mouth.

"Er, yes." What the hell was he up to now?

"Speak up," whispered the PR.

"Yes!" The microphone screeched as her mouth practically swallowed it.

"Ladies, beauty queens that you all are, tonight I am dedi-cating my speech, this little talk, to the inspirational Kate Miller!"

How could he, the little shit? What could he possibly talk about? Her throwing up in the fountain? Running away in the middle of the night? This couldn't be happening! But it was. Vivienne Fox suddenly jumped up, clicked her fingers, and had two men Kate hadn't even noticed before hurry over from the side of the room with TV cameras. A bright light was turned on her. She could hear a whirring as the cameras started roll-ing. Oh, my Gaad, as Clarissa would say.

"Okay, so some of you won't know who Kate Miller is . . . but I know you all know who I am, and let me just say this now: don't worry, tonight's little talk is going to be just that—little, short, and to the point—because I have one very focused mes-sage for you! Let me start by saying that after years in this pro-fession, I still have a reputation for enhancing the natural beauty of women and empowering them. Empowerment through beauty has always been my life's work! In much the same way as Michelangelo would craft pure beauty from a slab of rock, I craft pure beauty from a slab of flesh. I sometimes see myself as perfecting what God didn't have time to finish. Well, he's a busy man these days!"

There were muffled laughs from the audience; sadly, it seemed to come without so much as a trace of irony. She assumed a stiff pose, which she hoped would come across as one of general composure.

"But yesterday, a cute, really cute English girl came to inter-view me from *Darling* magazine, and can I just say"—everyone turned once more to look at Kate, who, had she been able to gaze back instead of staring transfixed ahead of her, would have noticed that some of the gazes were tinged with more than a hint of jealousy—"this is what beauty is all about!" To her horror the audience started laughing. "No, I'm serious! I mean, look around you! We've all started to look the same, and we surgeons and you beauty editors need to take some responsibility for all that! Look at the blow-dries, the Botox—and sure, I know *none* of you here have it!" (He chuckled.) "But look! We're all so goddamn perfect these days. But actually what makes us different anymore? What sets us apart? Kate's got that look—she doesn't have the perfectly spaced cheekbones, the cutesy upturned nose, the don't-kill-me-I'm-Bambi wide eyes! She doesn't even have the blow-dry, or the inflatable bosoms! Don't get me wrong, I'm not knocking my work, or your work, I'm just saying, I think we're on the tip of a new trend here, and let me tell you, it's the way my work is heading. I think this season it's all about . . . *imperfect perfect*!"

Everyone started clapping. From nowhere a music system blasted out the instantly recognizable voices of Prince and Sheena Easton singing "U Got the Look." A curtain was raised to reveal a board with images of Kate. There was her sitting in the waiting room at JK3's; her pacing about in his office; her on the phone to Lise, laughing; even her in the powder room fixing her hair at JK's party! Somehow he had managed to take pictures of her via his security cameras!

JK3 stepped down from his podium and started walking around to Kate, who was still speechless in total horror. For the first time since she'd arrived in the States, Kate understood the meaning of an expression she'd regularly heard bandied about in New York: "Only in L.A." But before she could even process her thoughts, things began to move rapidly around her. Beauty editors, those same women who had been casually trading gossip over the champagne, sprang into action and gathered around her, notebooks and Dictaphones drawn like pistols in the Wild West. Vivienne, the woman on her left, beckoned to the cameras to turn to her, and, after counting herself in, started reporting, her whole persona transformed from cynical inebriated hack to tireless professional, now speaking into the cameras with seamless, champagneless, ease.

"It took one young Englishwoman, the new beauty director from *Darling* magazine, to shock the entire fashion and beauty industry of the United States, according to the top surgeon to the stars, John Kingsley the Third," she began. "And she's here with me now! Kate Miller, what do you have to say to JK3's announcement, a surprise I'm sure, at this beauty editors' dinner in honor of Face-Off, the international plastic surgery convention here in L.A.?"

Kate couldn't speak. She tried, but nothing came out, although she could feel some movement in her face as her cheeks glowed steadily redder. It didn't seem to matter; Vivienne spoke for her:

"This new beauty reporter has only been in New York and Los Angeles for a few weeks, but already she's made a big impression. JK3 loves her look because it's different, natural, somehow bringing a touch of reality to a world that's become a little too perfect. Some might say that telling a beauty editor she's less than perfect—JK3 singled Kate out for not having the Botox or blow-dries that dominate our world—might be perceived as a backward compliment, but in this beauty-obsessed industry, it seems the editors are taking his comments the only way they know best: at face value. Kate Miller could be the best thing to hit America. This is Vivienne Fox, for CNN's *Backstage and Beautiful*."

Vivienne smiled, pleased with her performance.

"Kate, thanks! That was great!" She turned to the camera crew. "Make sure you get some shots of JK3 and of the other editors, then we'll file it for the breakfast show. How do you feel about being the new look of America, Kate?"

"I'm sure she feels just fine, don't you, Kate?!" said JK3, who now stood beside her and clinched her shoulders with his arm. He was wearing a rock-starry cocktail ring, she noticed. A garnet the size of a chestnut: it alone would probably pay for Patty's face to be corrected.

A blow-dried, Botoxed beauty editor jostled by her shoulder. "Kate, do you mind if I have a quick word? Clover Bute, from *FashionWeek International*."

"I . . . don't really have anything—"

"To say?" said JK. "Hey, shy girl, I meant every word, you know. Ask Aurelie, she'll tell you. I've been going on about you all day to anyone who'll listen!"

"Is this a romantic as well as a professional association?" asked Clover Bute from *FashionWeek International*, notebook at the ready.

"Puh-lease!" said JK. "I never mix the two! Kate's my muse, aren't you, Kate?"

"I . . ." She couldn't speak. What could she say? Suddenly the room felt unbearably hot. She could see thirty little gold-padded chairs dancing in circles as thirty skinny blow-dries thrust their Dictaphones forward. She felt JK's arm circle her waist tightly as her knees, then the rest of her body, gave way.

sixteen

"So how is our imperfect perfect today?" It was Alexis on the phone. It hadn't stopped ringing all morning; even from the relative fortress of the photographic studio Kate had not been immune from the attention. There were some callers Clarissa could fend off, but some—such as Alexis, and a very persistent Jean-Paul—that she couldn't. Clarissa herself had pronounced the incident—with a wry smile—highly amusing, and said that with the right marketing, Kate might be on to something.

"What do you mean?" asked Kate, looking more like imperfect-imperfect today. She hadn't slept well, and had been woken up at 6:00 a.m. by Clarissa, informing her that she was on CNN if she'd like to turn her TV on now. Sure enough, once she'd blazed her way through the hundreds of channels on offer via her remote control, there was Vivienne Fox, JK3, and herself. They looked the consummate media professionals they were; she on the other hand looked confused and at times sullen, then, when she realized the cameras were on her, bordering on insane.

"Y'know, your own cosmetics line, a chat show, your autobiography, well, that's what I'd do if I was in your position anyway."

"Oh, for fuck's sake."

"No, really. You have no idea! Honest to God, the PR from last night—by the way, she's thrilled with the publicity you've generated for the conference, did you see those flowers she sent you? She told me that as soon as JK3 had finished talking about you, the powder rooms were bursting with all these beauty editors scrunching up their hair in an effort to make it look less, y'know, perfect!"

She started emptying a huge black bag with hundreds of flesh-colored G-strings onto an ironing board.

Kate couldn't help but smile to herself. What a weird world this was. Yet why not! Maybe JK did have a point after all. She'd been thinking herself before—on Rodeo Drive—how everyone here did look the same. Maybe she was a breath of fresh air, as one report had described her. Even Alexis seemed pleased.

"Well done, Kate, not easy, but you pulled it off. Very clever move," she had said, as if Kate had engineered the whole CNN report herself. "And can I just say, it'll do wonders for the surgery supplement. Advertising is looking into pulling it forward by a couple of issues. Might as well capitalize on the publicity. Do you understand what that means, Kate?! It's phenomenal, never happened before. It means you're upstaging Fashion!"

"That's great, Alexis! Really great." She hadn't a clue what she was talking about but as long as Alexis was happy . . .

"Of course it means I need your copy in, like, yesterday.

Cynthia's got you on the flight home tomorrow morning. You can e-mail me the copy tonight."

She was gone.

The studio was a cavern of white, so bright that any specks of dust were transformed into fairy dust floating through the occasional sunbeams that lasered their way from window to floor. There wasn't much furniture. A couple of low-slung sofas slouched insouciantly in the corner like a pair of baggy bottomed jeans on some L.A. dude. A long white lacquer table was laid with fruit, bottles of mineral water, and discarded lattes. At the other end of the cavern was a dressing room. Mirrors with blue daylight bulbs interspersed with bright white lightbulbs caught everyone's passing moods, except the model's. Her expressionless face didn't seem to be doing moods this season, but then, Kate figured, she wasn't being paid for smiles until the camera was on, so why should she?

The point of the shoot, Kate had briefed the team upon arriving at eight this morning, was to convey the idea that natural is best. This was met with a look of blank incredulity, as, argued the hairstylist, everyone knew that natural was far from best. Whoever did well through looking natural?

"Actually, that's not true," butted in Clarissa. "Did you see CNN this morning?"

"Thank you, Clarissa, I'll handle this now," said Kate. "So, obviously I'll be saying that we can all make our natural selves look a little better thanks to the use of hair products and makeup—she nodded generously in the direction of the respective artistes at this point"—"but for now, we have a girl who is incredibly beautiful, naturally, and I'd like to shoot her with as little as possible on."

There was a pause from the team, with a lot of shifting about from foot to foot and staring at the floor. A muffled laugh came from her left.

"I mean, she will be naked, so no, she won't have any clothes on, but I don't want too much hair and makeup. What's so funny about that?"

Following Alexis's change of schedule Kate had decided she would leave everyone to get on with it, and attend the plastic surgery conference for an hour or so before returning to the shoot to check all was going well. Her copy would just have to be written tonight. Strangely she wasn't worried about that. She'd written most of the article in her head anyway. Since seeing Patty yesterday so much had happened, yet it had all been so unimportant and superficial in comparison with the main story. She hadn't slept well because her mind had been buzzing with thoughts and ideas. Chance conversations among the beauty editors before everything had kicked off with JK3; snippets overheard in elevators; sitting out by the pool with Harold Epps . . . all these things, all her unconscious thoughts, were being processed somehow in her subconscious. She knew what would happen as soon as she sat down to write. A blank screen would confront her in all its sterility. But soon the words would appear on the page, and Patty's hopeless story would eventually take flight. Besides, any previous concerns that Alexis might not approve her story had been swept away in the flood of publicity following JK's speech last night. As Clarissa had helpfully pointed out this morning, she could pretty much write whatever she wanted now, Alexis would love it!

She had called Patty first thing this morning to talk to her about the CNN piece. It had been a wise precaution. Patty had been unable to speak, choked with tears, her sobs pregnant with accusations of betrayal and how-could-she's. JK3's muse! It had taken a full ten minutes of Kate calming her down and reassuring her that JK's hijacking of Kate's "look" was nothing but a PR stunt, guaranteed to get him news coverage for the big plastic surgery conference today, and had nothing to do with her. Eventually Aurelie had come on the phone, and seemed relieved to hear that Kate was writing the story to-night. She knew what JK was like; she'd calm Patty down, but in the meantime, all this upset and emotion couldn't be good for her nerves. True to form, Aurelie's parting gift was a veiled threat: Kate had to write the story soon, or they'd take it else-where. Aurelie couldn't keep Patty from harming herself for long, especially not with this latest development.

A phone call to JK3 had followed. Strangely, his declaration to the world, avowing himself to be a devoted follower of Kate's "natural" beauty, had had a twofold effect on Kate. Instead of finding it all repulsive, she did in fact feel empowered. Knowing that he found her if not attractive (it was he who had publicly decried any romantic associations, after all) then some kind of beautiful gave her a strange, new feeling of confidence. Was it because he was a man? Partly, and that worried her. It didn't fit in with her beliefs that a woman should feel good about the way she looked without searching for male praise, for some kind of physical evaluation. But if she could just set those tricky little beliefs aside for one instance, then . . . wow! Here was someone who had previously transformed women into one version of beauty, saying that she was better looking than all of them! She was sure it was all cobblers, but it gave her such a feeling of power! He was right—beauty was empowerment—whichever way you dressed it, up or down. Of course, she could also see that had she not had the inside knowledge of Patty's story, she could easily be taken in by his charm. Vanity was a great de-ceiver. But this accolade of his gave her neither the will to flirt nor the self-doubt to fear him and what he stood for anymore. It was her against him, pure and simple. She was the defender of Patty Patrice, and he could call her whatever he wanted, but he was only adding fuel to his funeral pyre.

He was as charming as ever this morning, but she wasn't having any of it. Politely, distantly, she made an appointment to meet him straight after the plastic surgery convention. Just a few more questions, she promised. And vain as he was, he agreed.

She had one more call to make: Jean-Paul Suchet. He'd left several messages, and had been nothing but consistent in his efforts to redeem himself following their last night out before she'd been assigned to L.A. She would finish her copy tonight, fly back tomorrow, and he could take her out the following night. After all, she was becoming accustomed to all this romantic attention. Starting to like it, even. There was that accent of his to consider. And as long as it didn't interfere with her career, which it surely wouldn't, why not? Jean-Paul would be given a second chance.

seventeen

Face-Off was the most distinguished gathering of aesthetic plastic surgeons worldwide, boasted the billboard outside the historic medical center of Los Angeles University. It was certainly popular. Outside, on the steps leading up to the monumental building, film crews gathered, hoping to be the first to report the latest in cosmetic surgery techniques to a world desperate for a miracle transformation. Queues of delegates, mostly male, all wearing gray suits, filed their way up and round the building to a wall of ten or so security-screened entrance points.

Inside, the building seemed to relax into its more historic self. Gone were the officious-looking media guides, handing out press packs in branded carrier bags to journalists. Instead, most of the action seemed to take place in a high-ceilinged wood-paneled hall, flanked with TV screens. It wasn't appealing viewing. Filling each screen to gargantuan proportions were various aspects of red and bloodied noses. Scalpels pulled them upward, outward, a slit here, a cut there. Oil paintings of distinguished men in surgery looked down as a new generation of gray-suited individuals watched the screens avidly. Tissue was snipped away. A brochure offered other how-to DVDs: *Rhinoplasty: The Boxy Tip*, fifty-one minutes; *Saddling Following Septoplasty*, fifty-five minutes. Posters advertised different types of facial peels. A table was laid with several silicone implants, willing passersby to see how real they felt, encouraging them to pick them up and hold them. Kate gave one a squeeze. It felt worlds apart from her own breasts. This was more like some executive stress-relieving toy. Inserted into some willing, nubile blonde, it probably was.

There were coffee machines everywhere. You could tell the surgeons apart from the salespeople. The salespeople all had improbably orange tans, which irked her. She knew there were much better ones on the market. You'd think that working in the beauty industry, they might have bothered to get that right. The surgeons, on the other hand, had tans that looked natural, but improbably smooth foreheads. She'd heard—possibly from Vivienne Fox, but she couldn't be sure—they did each other's Botox.

A gong sounded. The main event, the "Face-Off" between three of the world's leading surgeons, was about to begin.

She filed through to the adjoining theater and took a seat. Strangely she couldn't see any of the beauty editors from last night. On her right was a Japanese-looking man in a gray suit. He had strange-looking eyes, which, after further observation, she realized had been surgically enhanced to appear rounder and more Western-looking. On her left was a rather sweaty, slightly overweight forty-something man. He looked like a salesman. She imagined him driving round anonymous towns in the Midwest, a suitcase full of silicone breast samples, visiting clinic after clinic. It had to be more interesting than selling double-glazing, she supposed.

The glossy brochure lying on each seat described Face-Off as being only in its fourth year, yet already the prestigious convention had attracted worldwide interest thanks to its distinguished board of members, all surgeons with hundreds of years of experience between them. It was dedicated to reestablishing the profession as being serious, in spite of the increasing entertainment value attached to cosmetic surgery, thanks to TV programs performing lunch-hour makeovers. The brochure's editor, one Dr. Val Baker, wanted to assure those attending the conference that promoting the serious, safe side of surgery was the only way ahead. Dr. Val Baker blamed the media for promoting the gimmicky, celebrity surgeons, whose standards many in the profession knew to be below par, and being less interested in the exciting new techniques developed by its pioneers.

Mea culpa, thought Kate to herself. Another moan at the press. Oh, well. A hush descended as the beauty editors suddenly appeared, ushered in like a group of well-dressed flight attendants to the front two rows of the audience. Kate sank down farther into her seat. After last night's performance the last thing she wanted was to join them, although it amused her to notice that a few of them seemed to have neglected to brush their hair this morning, and a couple were definitely not wearing makeup. Imperfect perfect. She giggled quietly to herself. The sweaty man jostled his elbow next to hers, until she elbowed it back over the armrest.

It wasn't long before the real hush came. Face-Off was about to begin. The three speakers, a Brazilian surgeon, Feliz Paracato, and two Americans, one of whom was JK, walked slowly and seriously onto the stage. The audience clapped, some stood up, somewhat melodramatically, Kate thought, then silence fell again as the three took their seats toward the front of the stage. A glamorous yet frail elderly woman wearing a long Oscar-style frock tottered onstage, and the crowd's clapping grew even louder.

"Oh, my, I thought she died years ago!" said the man to Kate's left, working up a sweat as his hands met over and over.

"Who is she?" said Kate.

"Mary Powell . . . the ex-president's wife! She's awesome!"

Quite what Mary Powell was doing in a place like this, Kate had no idea. It looked like Mary Powell didn't have much of an idea either, as she struggled to read an Autocue introducing the three speakers.

"Oh, dear . . . she's got the disease . . . ," said the man sadly.

"What disease?"

He turned to look at her, as if taking in the full scale of her combined youth and ignorance.

"Aging!"

So aging was a disease. She'd heard it before, at the antiaging skin care launches, but she wasn't expecting to hear it so casually bandied about. As if it was anything other than a handy little sound bite. Of course now that it had worked its way into common parlance, albeit at a rarefied gathering like this one, it was only a matter of time before everyone would be talking about getting old as if it was an illness. There would be vaccinations against it, maybe even colonies where sufferers could live in splendid isolation, for fear of passing it on to others. Fund-raising benefits to support those who couldn't afford antiaging creams and face-lifts. If there weren't already.

More clapping. Mary Powell hobbled off, supported by two skinny girls with big breasts and huge grins, as if the audience needed a reminder of the disparities between youth and old age.

The music started up. Quite whose bright idea it was to play "The Eye of the Tiger" to announce the American surgeon Ben Kingdom's work on eye lifts, Kate could only guess (Dr. Val Baker, whose editorial in the Face-Off brochure had so aptly spoken out against cosmetic surgery as entertainment?). Ben Kingdom was in his sixties, and retiring next year (cue: applause); he hailed from New York (cue: applause); and he couldn't reveal his list of famous clients, but you only had to tune in to Letterman each week to see a roster of A-listers who didn't seem to be getting any older (cue: applause/laughter). He was now going to demonstrate his pioneering technique with the eyes, which meant that surgeons could now perform an eye lift that would last longer than ever before, in half the time!

"Is this legal?" Kate couldn't help asking out loud. The sweaty man picked up on her concern. He looked confused.

"Not legal enough! It's awesome, isn't it? You know they called it Face-Off after that new procedure they can do . . . the one where they reconstruct a patient's face by grafting someone else's face onto the original? One day I reckon they'll do it live onstage."

A patient was wheeled on. Much to Kate's relief, it was announced that she was under anesthetic. Large screens came down from the ceiling midway through the audience so that observers wouldn't miss any of the details. The skin around the patient's eye was opened up by a theater assistant, while Ben Kingdom was dressed by six women wearing white tight-fitting trouser suits, all of whom looked like models. He emerged from behind a curtain in his green operating outfit, monogrammed with his initials in diamanté. He walked casually over to the horizontal patient, as if he was taking a walk in the park. To be fair, she figured, it probably was as easy for him as taking the proverbial walk. A man of his standing in "the profession," as she was learning to call it, couldn't possibly be awed by a little thing like an eye lift before an audience of hundreds, could he? Sure enough, before "The Eye of the Tiger" had finished, so had his work. She hadn't counted the number of choruses exactly, so they could have cheated and stuck another couple or so on, but it was impressive nonetheless. Like a victor in a boxing ring, Ben Kingdom raised his arms in the air and smiled.

Next up was the Brazilian. A whole host of possible song titles started to play in Kate's head. ZZ Top's "She's Got Legs." "I like big butts" from "Baby Got Back" (but who remembers Sir Mix-a-Lot anymore?) Oh! "Our Lips Are Sealed" by the Go-Go's! Kate had to force herself back into the here and now, before her thoughts wandered in the direction of a similar musical talent she shared with JK, discovered the night of the better-forgotten peach Bellinis. To his credit, the Brazilian, who was joined by twenty identical-looking blondes in tight white suits, as if to upstage Ben Kingdom's coterie, opted for Chopin's Second Prelude for what turned out to be a breast lift, using a new meshlike bra that was inserted over the patient's own breasts. The sweaty man didn't like this.

"No silicone? That sucks," he muttered, folding his arms.

The sight of two mounds of bloodied flesh and tissue on a giant screen was making Kate queasy. She tried to see where JK was onstage, but the lights were spotlighting Paracato and his two domes of quivering breasts. There was no escape. She looked at the floor and waited for the clapping to start. When it came, it was to celebrate his outfit: a green jumpsuit revealing a trim belly, doubtless the work of some other surgeon, an "in" joke. He was a born showman. Before he took over from where the theater assistant had left off, he kissed his assistants and, standing in a circle with their hands resting on each other's shoulders, he led them in a muttered prayer.

"You know he insists on working on each of his assistants

first? Wants them all to have the Paracato look," said the sweaty man next to her.

"That's just weird," said Kate, although she was beyond being shocked now. It was over in a few minutes. She looked back up from the floor just in time to see him taking a bow, having his brow wiped by one of the assistants.

She had been dreading JK's appearance, following his surprise revelation yesterday evening at the beauty editors' dinner. She had been trying to second-guess his presentation with Clarissa. Would he call Kate up onto the stage and reveal a photo display of yet more pictures she hadn't been aware had been taken in the first place? Clarissa had sniggered he should get Patty up onstage, show the world just how far he was prepared to take the new imperfect perfect. Kate would have laughed at this, she was so relieved to have made progress with Clarissa on the joke front, but it really wasn't appropriate. Poor Patty. If only she had foreseen this that day she'd first gone to see him.

"This guy's great . . . ," said sweaty man, tapping at the picture of JK in the Face-Off brochure.

"Oh, yes?" Kate pretended not to know who he was talking about, and pulled her hair over her face, hiding just in case.

The audience stood up, clapping wildly. A standing ovation? For a man who had butchered a woman's face and didn't seem to care? It was wrong, but she stood up with the others, not wanting to draw attention to herself. He was wearing a theater-green suit, but the color was all it had in common with the usual operating garb. His was like something from Tom Ford, Richard James, Balenciaga, worn with a tie a couple of shades darker and matching green shoes. It was ridiculous, yet, and it annoyed her to admit it, it worked somehow.

"Such a cool dude," murmured sweaty man appreciatively.

Aurelie stood to one side of the stage—at least he hadn't

traded her in for a fleet of white-suited models. She looked neither happy nor unhappy to be there: a perfect study of assistant's complacency.

JK spoke into a microphone affixed to his lapel. He smiled, that infectious, charming smile Kate knew so well.

"I hope you don't mind," he began, "but there's no music. I want you to be with me every step of the way and"—he laughed—"I don't want the music to come between us."

The audience laughed with him. They loved him, the bunch of sycophants, thought Kate. Images once again flashed up onto the screens, but this time, instead of being carved-up faces, what appeared was footage of celebrities with not quite perfect faces. A-list actors and actresses with wrong noses, craggy faces, sagging jowls, all still beautiful people, but you got his point—you loved them in spite of, even because of, their imperfections. They were characterful, larger than life, familiar, warm people you felt you knew somehow. Much to her relief, she wasn't among them.

The whispering started among the crowd. What was he going to do? Take some model and mess up her nose? Only JK could pull off a stunt like that, you just knew he would! They hushed again, awestruck.

"Now, I hope I'm not doing myself out of a job here . . . but, ladies"—he nodded in the direction of the beauty editors, who smiled smugly—"and gentlemen, I really feel like I'm on to something big here, as some of you may have seen this morning on CNN." He grinned.

"Here's a model, pretty perfect, not just any model, a young twentysomething friend of a friend who volunteered to attend today's convention."

He walked over to the shrouded figure lying flat on the gurney and took hold of the scalpel Aurelie was passing to him. A "before" picture of a pretty girl flashed up onto the screen.

"Belle Sarandon. In just a few minutes, her face will be altered. Irrevocably. She's pretty perfect now, but I'm going to make her . . . imperfect perfect!"

Kate couldn't believe this was happening. Surely he wasn't going to . . . he couldn't do that to her! Mess up her face deliberately? To look like what? Some freak's idea of what was in fashion—her?! This had to be unethical, illegal, immoral—not that anyone seemed to care about ethics or morals here! It was disgusting. She couldn't just stand by and watch, article or no article.

She stood up and pushed her way past the sweaty man, rushing toward the exit. She wasn't about to be complicit to his act of cosmetic vandalism. She felt sick.

*   *   *

Out in the corridor, she sought sanctuary in the ladies' loos. She stared at herself in the mirror, remembering a time not so long ago when she had stared at her reflection in Brian Palmers's office, wondering who she might become given the chance. It all seemed so far away, was so far away. Now she was caught up in something she didn't understand, and seemed to be the only one who didn't understand. She hadn't changed so much. A few streaks in her hair, but otherwise, nothing much else. She was still Kate. So how had the rest of the world gone so crazy? She splashed water on her face, drowning her tears of frustration. It just wasn't right!

Aurelie appeared in the doorway and, in the brief opening of the door, she heard the filing past of the crowd, excited talk among men who rarely got excited, signaling the end of the Face-Off.

"He's done," said Aurelie, coolly. "You can go and meet him now." She looked resigned to all that had happened. Yet another stage performance for her, this was nothing new.

"Was it . . . a success?" asked Kate, wiping her face with a tissue.

"Depends what you call a success," she said, turning away to avoid the sudden opening of one of the loo doors behind Kate. Aurelie disappeared, just as a blonde woman in a white suit came out, one of Paracato's assistants. She washed her hands in the sink, professionally, as if she'd just done an operation. From a pocket in her suit she pulled out a spicy-pink lip pencil and shaded in her lips. She ran her fingers through her hair, studying her reflection in the mirror, all the while maintaining a hint of a smile. She nodded at Kate and left.

Kate stared once more into the mirror. It was still Kate staring back at her. Still the girl in Brian Palmers's office who had tried to fix her hair up to make herself look more like . . . what exactly? One of the beauty editors she was now trying not to be?

eighteen

She was ready to write. Six bottles of Diet Coke and two packets of Wrigley's Juicy Fruit lay on the desk before her. The Flaming Lips played softly on iTunes, the volume switched to just below the halfway mark—not too intrusive to write, but loud enough to keep her awake. The hardest part had been persuading the bellboy to move her desk—clear the lamps, letter racks, and hotel directories and reposition the bleached wood desk away from and at a right angle to the window in a nod to something Lise had told her about feng shui, and all your ideas flying out of the window. He'd wanted to call Housekeeping, but from previous experience Kate knew that could take ages. She didn't have ages. The Diet Coke had been the next hardest thing to find, as they only had Coke Zero, but they got there in the end. Someone in the kitchen with the same Diet Coke obsession had apparently been stashing it away secretly in case Coca-Cola were about to render it obsolete in the face of their new hero diet drink. The final touch was a packet of Marlboro Lights, still in their cellophane, waiting like some postorgasmic reward for when she'd finished her masterpiece. She hadn't smoked for a while, but it was comforting to know she had backup.

Her bag was packed, just in case she had to work right through the night. She knew she didn't need them anymore, but she couldn't resist scooping up the free toiletries and depositing them in a laundry bag. The bath cap and shoe shine kit might also come in useful, although she couldn't remember when she had last shined her shoes, but with winter coming up, who knew, there might be knee-length boots to polish.

There was one last thing to do. She sat on the bed, kicked off her shoes, and picked up the small notepad and pen by the phone. She hit Play on the answerphone.

"Message one, received today at nine a.m." Then Lise's voice: *"Hi, doll, it's me. Haven't heard from you in a couple of days, wanted to check you're okay. Can you call me? Am away at the weekend, need to tell you all about it. It's important, so call me!"*

Dirty weekend with Steve. Kate hit Erase.

"Message two, received today at nine fifteen a.m." Her mum: *"Hello, Kate, it's Mum here. Can you call me, please? All's well, but need to talk to you."*

Well, they could wait. They obviously hadn't heard about the CNN thing. Probably better that way—what would Lise have made of it? She pressed hard with the biro on the pad in a circular motion, but it wasn't giving up any ink.

"Message three, received today at five p.m." His voice: *"Hi, Kate Miller. It's JK. Where are you, gorgeous girl? I was expecting to meet you after today's little show—did you like it? Your assistant tells me you're off tomorrow but that I will be seeing you soon. Great news. Call me!"*

Erase. Erase. Erase.

Kate shivered. Every time he'd called her at the studio she'd seen his number come up and had passed the phone over to Clarissa.

"Tell him I'm sorry about this afternoon, but we were shooting and, er . . . there was a panic at the studio," she'd said, and Clarissa, annoyed that her efficiency was being slandered in this way, nonetheless dutifully got rid of him.

There had been no panic at the studio. When she'd returned, still shaken from the conference, Blondie's "Heart of Glass" was pumping out from somewhere, the camera was whirring and clicking, and the photographer was making approving noises. Everyone was entirely absorbed in what was happening in the corner of the white cavern; no one looked up as she entered the room. She dropped her bag on the floor and walked over to see what they were looking at.

Her name was Petruschka. It was funny how Kate hadn't even registered her name before, but here she was coiled in the white cavern, naked except for a gold anklet with the word PERFECT engraved on it (that had been Clarissa's idea; Kate thought it was a little tasteless, but hadn't wanted to shoot her enthusiasm down as it was such a rare occurrence). Kate was mesmerized.

She'd seen women naked before, of course she had. Lise was always taking her clothes off at any given opportunity. Charlie, the ex-boyfriend, had even had a collection of what he called "soft" pornography. When Kate had forced an argument with him and issued an ultimatum—the mags or her—her mum had tried to explain. "Well, to be honest, darling, you should be grateful that's all it is," her mum had said. The women in the mags had been appealing, even she could see that, but not exactly beautiful, rather more like the girl behind the counter at Boots, or Lise even. They looked like they had that bobbly rough skin on their thighs and bottoms, this being the age before "exfoliation" was popular.

Petruschka naked was another thing altogether. She lay slightly on one side, her shoulders square to the camera. Her skin was a honey-colored bronze, the quintessential shade of Californian that all the fake-tan companies tried to emulate. Her hips were womanly, curving round between waist and legs in the shape of a ripe peach. The makeup artist had applied some kind of sheen effect to her shins and thighs, so that her skin took on a golden translucence, but Kate got the feeling it was probably like that naturally anyway. Her legs were long, neither too skinny nor too muscly, but moving ever so slightly in synchronicity with the photographer's utterances. An ankle would lift up now, a knee would bend upward, only by a millimeter or so, but just enough to tense a muscle or relax into a new pose. Her stomach was tight, her tummy button an "inny"; a mane of blonde-brown hair in glossy waves skimmed her shoulders; her mouth opened and closed as her eyes narrowed and widened, her audience captive to her now seemingly ever-changing moods. Her breasts . . .

Her breasts. Kate blushed as she took them in, drank them in with her eyes. She almost had to look away; it couldn't be right to feel like this when looking at another female, could it? She had to be professional, had to look, but it was embarrassing, and yet how stupid to feel embarrassed. Petruschka's breasts were full, evenly tanned, upturned, moving naturally when she moved. Occasionally the model would bring her hand up to conceal them, her eyes looking coy and teasingly at the camera. Kate blushed again. They were evenly spaced, with a natural cleavage that wasn't forced or too deep, just . . . comfortable? Comfort did come into it, because you wanted to touch them, wanted to feel how soft, how responsive . . . would the nipples spring to attention the way they were now with the fan softly blowing on her? Oh, lucky, lucky girl, imagine what life would be like with a pair of breasts like that? What you could do with breasts like Petruschka's!

"You okay?" asked Clarissa. The team was staring at her. The photographer held his camera to one side, waiting for her to get on with whatever she'd arrived to do. Petruschka looked mildly irritated at having been interrupted, but kept her pose.

"Oh, God, yes!" she said. "I mean, they look great. I mean, *you* look great. You look great, Petrusch . . . ka, is it? Sorry . . . yes, well done, everyone, well done!"

"Can you guys get me some water?" asked Petruschka, causing everyone to rush to the kitchen at once.

"Sure. Keep your pose, honey," said Davide. "Jenny, can we have a little more powder in the cleavage, some of that gold stuff?"

Jenny, the makeup artist, picked up a black-lidded tub of powder from a tall stool to her side and selected a brush with a generous head of soft satiny hair from a roll-up brush case. She looked for Clarissa, then, seeing Kate, turned and smiled at her.

"Sorry, could you help me? I just need someone to hold this for a second."

Kate followed Jenny onto the set until she was only a couple of feet away from Petruschka's cleavage. Jenny handed her the powder, unscrewing the lid, then dipped her brush into it. She shook the excess off on her hand, then, without a hint of the embarrassment that had overcome Kate, she dusted it carefully in minute strokes down the center of Petruschka's breastbone. Kate looked sheepishly at the floor, willing her to finish. Close-up, they were even better. She suddenly understood why men were so obsessed with breasts. Some men, anyway.

Petruschka sipped her water; Jenny and Kate backed off the

set. Davide beckoned to Kate, holding out some Polaroids for her to approve. He stepped away from the set, turning his back to Petruschka.

"Okay, she's a little bit heavy on the thighs," he whispered, "but we can retouch that out. Otherwise, not bad, huh?"

Kate couldn't see any heaviness anywhere, but she was in too much of a daze to contradict him. The picture was beautiful. Shot in black and white, it gave Petruschka's irresolutely sex-charged physique a graceful subtlety. Artfully placed shadows protected her nudity with a cloak of sensuality. Kate pulled her shoulders up straight, suddenly aware she was slouching, and tried to look professional, like she'd been on thousands of shoots before with naked women. It happened all the time.

"It's great." She nodded.

"It's a wrap!"

Petruschka jumped up and wrapped a large white toweling robe around her just as the makeup artist asked her to be careful not to get any makeup on it. Too late. She grabbed her bag from an assistant, who had been holding it patiently in case the model needed something while shooting, pulled out a packet of cigarettes, and retreated to the dressing room, her brow furrowed with annoyance. The magic was gone.

Packing the unworn G-strings back into the black bag, Clarissa turned to Kate and asked, "So, like, how come you didn't meet JK after the show, anyway?"

"I . . . er . . . couldn't." She looked away. It was too raw to go into now. She busied herself with the G-strings. Petruschka's breasts had been a welcome distraction from the mutilations she had witnessed earlier.

"Oh." Clarissa shrugged her shoulders and grabbed the G-strings back from Kate, flinging them back into the bag. "By the way, your flight to Rio? You need to be at the airport at ten a.m. tomorrow."

"Rio? JFK, you mean," Kate said, gathering up her handbag and hoisting it over one shoulder. She was finding it increasingly hard to fill it with enough stuff to bulk it out and give it the requisite fullness without leaving it so full that she couldn't find anything.

Clarissa stopped packing the G-strings, put her hand to her head.

"Oh, my Gaad, I'm sorry, I forgot to tell you. Professor Paracato invited you to his eco-spa just outside Rio and I thought you'd want a break after all this, so I said, sure thing, and now you're not heading back home until Sunday. Don't worry about Alexis, I cleared it with her already."

"What?!"

"Is that okay?"

nineteen

From: KateMiller@darling.com
To: AlexisDeVere@darling.com

Dear Alexis,
Please find to follow the main feature for the plastic surgery
supplement. It's not what you thought you were getting, and I
realize I am taking a risk by presenting you with something so
different. But I think it's extremely important as I hope you will
agree when you read it. I know you will understand when I say:
there is no truth in beauty, but there are a lot of lies. This may not
be the article our readers were expecting to find in *Darling*'s
plastic surgery supplement; but if it is a reporter's duty to expose
and write, as Graham Greene once wrote, then it is my duty now
to give you the unexpected and delve as close to the truth as I
can, however uncomfortable that might make people feel. What

started off as an article about the history of cosmetic surgery in Hollywood has morphed into something quite different. To not tell the true story would be a failure in my duty as a reporter.

I look forward to your feedback,

Kind regards, Kate Miller

P.S.: Final feature lineup as follows:
1. When Plastic Is Not So Fantastic, by Kate Miller (copy follows below)
2. Nature and Nurture, by Kate Miller. Copy should be in by Wednesday latest. The shoot went well today—you should have some great visuals!
3. The Mystery of Marilyn's Cheekbones: The Secrecy of Surgery for Starlets in Hollywood, by Kate Miller. Copy to follow—am having difficulties with getting anyone to talk about this. I would like to swap with:
3. (alternative story): Ten Top Surgeons in Manhattan, by Clarissa.
Or 3. (alternative story): Something on new procedures currently popular in South America, by Cynthia.

Can we discuss on my return?

Kate Miller/Darling/When Plastic Is Not So Fantastic

You'll find her tucked away on the tenth floor of a sheltered housing project, or in the folds of a loving family, returning to live with them though well in her thirties or forties and otherwise independent. She is the woman whose social life is conducted through the message boards on plastic surgery websites; she doesn't have a job because physically she scares away the customers. She lives in hope that someday, the man responsible for her heartache, her bitterness, her vapid anger, will be brought to justice. In truly angry moments she even hopes he will suffer the same kind of physical damage he put her through. The forgotten victim, not seen since a whole host of shows celebrating this "art form" took over our TV channels, it is hard to remember she was once a vibrant, warm, compassionate woman, someone like you or me. She is anonymous in our society. She is a victim of plastic surgery.

She may be anonymous but she is far from alone. As a society, we are generally uncomfortable with the idea that mistakes could be made with such serious consequences; however, search for "plastic surgery mistakes" on Google and over 1.4 million entries pop up. The American Society for Aesthetic Plastic Surgeons reports that 11.5 million of us underwent surgical and nonsurgical procedures last year, an increase of 446 percent over the previous decade (figures from 2006). But the same benchmarking organization doesn't hold statistics for cases where the patients aren't satisfied.

The thought of it going wrong doesn't fit in with our vision of plastic surgery as being safe or acceptable now that the final taboos and secret surgeries of the rich and famous are being exposed on a daily basis, often with the tacit approval of the stars themselves, in magazines like Us *or* Star.

But is it more affordable, when the consequences of getting it wrong are so physically, emotionally, and financially expensive? Patty Patrice is one of those women secreted away from the rest of the world in the hope that she will be ever more forgotten. Now, the 33-year-old says of her treatment at the hands of Hollywood's hottest surgeon to the stars, John Kingsley III, "He claims he did this to save me costs, but look what it went on to cost me!"

Her story began in 2006, when shortly after going through

a painful divorce, she opted to have her nose neatened by Kingsley. "We met in his offices, and I was completely taken in by his charm. I guess I was vulnerable, after my divorce, so I let him persuade me to have not one, but several procedures at once." John Kingsley III argued this would save her money on operating costs; in hindsight it was a reckless decision that ended up costing her far more than just money. A facial peel, mini face-lift, and eye lift were all recommended, in addition to the original nose job request. "He promised me he'd make me look like a celebrity," she says, tears welling in her eyes as she recalls the painful journey to her present unenviable situation today. More than just a new look, Patty hoped this would bring her a new self-confidence, and possibly even a new life.

Plastic surgeons will be the first to tell you to be realistic about what surgery can achieve; that it won't change your life. But Kingsley's failure to predict the disaster that befell Patty's face far surpassed any promises he made. Seeing pictures of Patty before and after her operations, it is hard to believe she was operated on by the same surgeon who has appeared on nationwide TV shows like Radical Redux. *In addition, Kingsley has since gone on to win acclaim for his radical, if somewhat tasteless, demonstration at the recent Face-Off convention, attended by the world's most notable surgeons.*

It is impossible not to be moved when you meet Patty for the first time. Short and petite, your perception of her vulnerability is intensified by the knowledge of what she has been through. To add insult to her very real injuries (her skin is still red-raw; her nose, barely cartilege; her eyes, a strange shape with echoes of Michael Jackson about them), JK3, as he likes to call himself, recently issued her with a bill for $57,000, with a promise to sue if it goes unpaid. Patty's life is ruined. She lives on welfare and the kindness of friends.

We meet on a thundery Los Angeles day in August, when

humid temperatures outside demand air-conditioning inside. Yet Patty's apartment is beyond hot, kept this way because she has circulatory problems as a result of the surgery. Beads of perspiration appear on my forehead. The stuffy, clammy air makes the five minutes or so waiting for Patty to appear extremely uncomfortable. She keeps the lights down low because she's embarrassed about the way she looks; embarrassed by the bandages on her wrists where she attempted to kill herself.

"Of course I'm aware of the stares, the whispering I get if I go out. So I don't go out anymore. You don't have to nowadays if you have friends, or the Internet."

JK3 has denied any responsibility and refuses to correct his "work." His world couldn't be more different from Patty's, with a huge home in Bel-Air from which he regularly throws lavish parties for his celebrity friends. But perhaps he's just another in a long list of surgeons who has capitalized on Hollywood's fragile relationships with actors and actresses in order to make a quick buck and achieve fame. When I met him in his office he coyly refused to name any of the celebrities he has worked on, yet was keen to show a potential client a glossy magazine cover featuring six of the world's skinniest actresses, all of whom owe their physique to him.

Kingsley is not the first to market himself by trading on celebrity associations. In 1923 when Ziegfeld Follies star Fanny Brice had her nose job, her surgeon, Henry Junius Schireson, was just starting out on his career. Overnight, thanks to her new nose, he became one of the most famous plastic surgeons in the United States, even though in later years he was to be primarily known as a "quack." Like Schireson, Kingsley has traded on his celebrity associations, with a Vogue *cover here, a makeover TV show there. It's no exaggeration to say the man has single-handedly taken Hollywood by storm thanks to his charm and charisma. But although he undoubtedly reserves his skill and professionalism for these clients, for more "normal" patients such as Patty, perhaps the temptation to allow ego to overtake and let him play God steps in. JK3 talks, without a trace of irony, about "finishing God's work" and happily compares himself with Michelangelo.*

He is not the only surgeon with a God complex. Surgeons in Los Angeles, and, to a lesser extent, throughout the rest of the world have achieved the celebrity status that rivals their Hollywood clients. On the one hand, conventions like Face-Off decry the "exhibitionism" of TV makeover shows, yet on the other hand, they encourage distinguished surgeons (including Kingsley) to appear onstage and perform live mutilations [Legal Dept—Please check "mutilations" RE libel laws?] *before a packed audience.*

So where does all this hypocrisy leave Patty? "I have strength, and I actually do believe I am doing something positive for women by speaking out," she tells me. "Being raised here in L.A. I've seen a lot of things that are ugly, people who value the dollar more than anything else in life. But knowing there are people out there who believe in what I'm doing . . . I feel this is important."

It would be far more convenient to believe in the safety and sanctity of cosmetic surgery and its wrinkle-free, ageless promises. But perhaps now is the time for us all to look in the mirror and kiss it good-bye once and for all. Say no to vanity, and yes to safety and a clone-free future. Say yes to a future where it's okay to say no to the surgeon's knife. Say no to conforming with Botox and Restylane; say yes to seeing yourself age gracefully, beautifully, originally, and the way God intended you to. Above all else, say no to surgery for Patty's sake, and for every woman like Patty. Because there is no truth in beauty.

rio de janeiro

beauty note:

Sundress by Moschino. Handbag, big enough to work as overnight bag, by Chloé. (Note: Are Havaianas thongs too five years
ago? Only they're a tenth of the price in the airport shop.) *Complexion:* Crème de La Mer The Mist facial spritz, hydrated with
Prescriptives Super Flight Cream. *Eyes:* Red Eye eyedrops by Rite
Aid. YSL False Lashes Mascara. *Lips:* Baume de Rose By Terry.

twenty

Of course it wasn't okay. Clarissa knew it wasn't okay. Rio de Janeiro was one thing when it was a rainy gray old afternoon in Maidstone and your only consolation was the thought that the newsagent's on the corner might still be open on your way home from work and you could buy a Pot Noodle, smuggle it into your bedroom, deluge it with boiling water, and then tell your mum you weren't hungry for supper. Then, Rio de Janeiro might be a welcome diversion, something to dream about, peruse the Internet about, research; marvel at pictures of the Corcovado; worry at the living cheek-by-jowlness of it all, the juxtaposition of extreme poverty next to extreme wealth; wonder whether that film *City of God* wasn't in fact set in São Paulo; be amazed by the universality of the Brazilian bikini wax, a trend popularized by two Brazilian sisters who had lived in New York for years.

Rio de Janeiro when you were in a hurry to head back to

New York, to meet your editor and present her with possibly the biggest story of the magazine's history, a story that could quite possibly make your career, and bring someone else to justice . . . well, that was another thing altogether. Plus, she'd been booked into some plastic surgeon's paradise, an "eco-spa" island off the coast, with no, repeat *no*, time to look round the city itself, which was a complete anathema. Why, oh, why, hadn't Clarissa asked her first?

So here she was, flying down to Rio at the invitation of one of the world's most distinguished surgeons (weren't they all?), Feliz Paracato, the man at the Face-Off exhibition who had carved up a couple of breasts as casually as if it was just another Sunday turkey roast. Clarissa maintained she thought Kate might have wanted a break, and so when the surgeon had called her that day in the studio she hadn't thought twice about it. Obviously. Hadn't thought, period. There was no point screaming at her. They were friends now, remember. Better get on with it.

Clarissa had done some research for her. She'd found out a few things about the eco-spa, well, three precisely: (1) there were five endangered pigs, (2) a couple of parrots also lived there, and (3) all the island's electricity came from solar energy. None of this in Kate's eyes made it any more than what it really was: a plastic surgeon's holiday home; a tax-deductible way of entertaining beauty editors looking for a cheap break in return for five hundred words of copy on one of the world's leading cosmetic pros. She had a good mind to give him his five hundred words of copy—in *Green Issues* magazine, exposing him for being an eco-phony.

The plane landed. As she sped in the limo through the outskirts of the city on her way to the marina it was impossible not to be moved by the sights and sounds of Rio. Her eyes followed the snaking path of the viaducts, twisting their way down gently sloping hills, gushing out water into the sea. Clustered around them were the infamous favelas, ghetto housing built from improbably stacked hunks of wood, cardboard, bits of cars, old wooden doors. Some had bricked-up sides, roads, shops. On the other side of the valley large condominiums, wider roads, white-painted houses stuck out of the lush forest. Security gates, swimming pools, schools with American flags flying happily next to the Brazilian flag. All of this was watched over by the beatific gaze of the Corcovado, stretching out his arms to welcome all and sundry, rich or poor, to the most magnificent city in the world.

The marina, where Paracato's boat was moored while waiting to take her to the island, was fringed with palms, like the beaches she could see as soon as they were out at sea, the lifeblood of the city, the spiritual connection of its inhabitants regardless of their financial circumstances. All worshipped at the altar of the beach, Kate realized, hence the obsession with the body beautiful. Cosmetic surgery was a cultural thing here, more than in any other city in the world, it was a need, to be fulfilled just as any other need: hunger, sex, drugs. But did that make it okay? Or did that not make it worse?

Two crew members welcomed her on board the yacht, which looked like a giant gym shoe. Her mum would have called it a gin palace. One of the men had a glass of champagne for her, another was carrying her bags onto the boat. A third, the skipper, hurried down from the top deck to explain the trip was only a matter of a few hours long, and that she should make herself comfortable. Would she prefer nut roast or vegan pasta for lunch? Every so often he'd shout out the names of places they passed: Niemeyer's Niterói Contemporary Art Museum, a fishing village, the Sugarloaf Mountain. It was all a bit surreal. She was on a yacht, in Rio, heading out to who knows where, the rocking motion of the boat lulling her into a reverie, a soporific gazing out to sea she lacked the power to resist. She would be hanging out with one of the world's most distinguished (there it was again) plastic surgeons, and this was . . . work? She tried not to think too much about Duran Duran, but she knew that if Lise was here the two of them would be up at the prow right now, hair blowing in the wind, shouting out the words to "Rio."

*   *   *

Paracato might have created some of the world's most beautiful women (and this she found a dubious statement in itself), but he was certainly not the world's most beautiful man. Short, tanned, and wrinkly. Not a looker. He stood waiting for her on the jetty with six women, young, nubile, blonde, all with short white nurse's outfits. She recognized them from the Face-Off convention. Or at least, she thought she recognized them, but she couldn't be sure because they all looked the same, anyway. For all she knew, these could be completely different ones.

"Welcome to my home," he said, a big smile beaming from his walnut face.

"Hi," said Kate, not so much wearily as with a resigned "what now?"

The girls gave a little cheery wave in singsong voices.

"You must be tired. Would you like a swim? Or shall we tour the island? I have a Jeep here and a driver all ready. . . . Or would you like to see your room? I hope you will be happy here, I so wanted you to see this place, and I have heard so many amazing things about you. My, but you are beautiful!"

She shot him a withering look. He was about 110 years older than her.

He didn't seem to notice. "You will be company for me," he

said, walking up the hilly path with her to a group of white domed houses, early 70s Brazilian architecture at its best.

"Come on!" He put his arm through hers and jauntily walked her into the biggest dome-shaped house, which had a huge plasma screen facing one wall, a wicker bar, hanging wicker chairs, and uncomfortable-looking white concrete sofas that seemed to spring straight out of the floor. The walls were covered with paintings and etchings with signatures that even she knew were worth something: Picasso, Chagall, Dalí. A white grand piano was festooned with framed pictures of himself. Here he was with Gina Lollobrigida; there with Sophia Loren; another with Shirley Bassey. There he was skiing, medals around his neck; another showed him diving from a high board. One framed picture, a group shot, showed him with his family. It was signed: Annie Liebowitz. Closer inspection revealed it had first appeared as a *Vanity Fair* cover.

"What do you do on this island?" she asked as another glass of champagne was thrust into her hand.

"Oh, you know . . . party!" he chckled. "My family comes sometimes, we hang out, I get my friends over. A lot of people have stayed here you know . . . pop stars! And I've had all the supermodels here."

"For work?"

"Oh, naughty girl!" he said playfully. "As if I'd tell you that! They are my friends!"

"And of course, there are your nurses to keep you company." She took off her cotton jacket, aware of his eyes scrutinizing her upper arms. "What?"

"I like women to have a bit of flesh. Everyone's so thin these days," he said, pinching her arms.

"I can't believe you just said that!"

He laughed and patted her bottom.

"I can't believe you just did that!"

"Ah, come on! Relax. Let's have some fun together, Kate, no?" He had a glint in his eye that unnerved her.

"Professor Paracato, I really don't think that's a good idea. I mean, you have a wife, and I have . . . I have . . . my work to think about, and I . . ."

He looked surprised.

"I only meant to go for a swim!" Then he made as if to grab her by the waist. Ugh! Why did men always hone in on the fat bits? She pried his arm off and exited the room, walking as quickly as she could without turning her steps into a run.

He could move fast for a geriatric plastic surgeon. She started running up the hill as he shouted after her, "But if there are other ways you want to relax Kate . . . ?"

At the top of the hill was the pool. It was a perfect square of blue-yellow green, with verdant grass flush to its edges. She wondered how they kept it trimmed so immaculately without getting loads of cut grass in the pool. Paracato arrived behind her, breathless, still laughing.

"Come on . . . let's have a swim together!"

"I'd really rather not," she said, primly. This was a nightmare. Here she was on an island off the coast of Rio, with a lecherous old man trying to get her naked and naughty and in a swimming pool.

"Well, at least let's sit down," he said, trying to catch his breath, "and have a drink together, huh?"

A white-suited man who looked like Nick Nack arrived as if from nowhere, with a silver tray and four caipirinhas.

"Ah! Just the man I wanted to see!" Paracato grinned broadly.

She looked at him and suddenly caught a glimpse of the fun-loving playboy he must have once been. She wondered if he wasn't entirely joking when he said he wanted company. It was clear his wife and kids hadn't been here for ages—there was no evidence of any kind of domesticity; rather, it was one big Bond-style playboy fantasy, which, at his age, was more than a little sad.

"Okay, then," she sighed, sitting down on a lounger.

He sat beside her, still smiling, then downed two of the four caipirinhas in quick succession.

"The glasses are so small these days, no?" He settled himself, yawning. "You know I was only teasing you before. We Brazilian men, love to show women how much we appreciate their beauty. I hope I didn't upset you when I said that about being a little . . . larger."

"No . . . no," she said, not knowing what to talk about now that they were both "relaxing." "Besides, I'm sure you've got a handy suction-thingy to swoosh it all out with," she laughed.

"A microcannula? Don't be silly, I'm off duty. You must think I'm very superficial, but you know . . ."

Not another insecure plastic surgeon.

"I make a lot of people very happy."

And yourself very rich, she thought to herself.

"Everyone likes to look their best," he yawned again. "Even animals lick themselves clean."

"I know."

"And I've reached the age now where, quite frankly, I don't view women as creatures to be perfected, to be operated on."

"I'm sure we're all very grateful for that." She nodded.

There was an awkward pause.

"Professor . . ."

"Please, call me Feliz." He downed another caipirinha and slumped back in the lounger. She noticed his eyes were closing; he was fighting the need to fall asleep. She felt the sun burning into her bones and it felt good. She knew she should reach into her bag for her Sisley Sunleya Age Minimizing Sun

Protection SPF 15, but frankly she couldn't be bothered. It was so hot, she wondered if she could slip quietly into the water without him noticing. She undressed down to her bra and knickers and eased herself slowly into the water, thankful his eyes were still closed. The water was deliciously cool. She glided from one side to the other, frightened to splash or make too much noise in case the old tortoise woke. There was a corner of the pool that looked onto a clearing, where the trees were less dense. The view of the sea, its azure depths tinged with white frothy crescents farther out on the horizon, was exquisite. She noticed another boat had moored at the jetty alongside the one she had arrived on. Maybe he did just want her to relax, she mused, turning with her back to the view now, her arms, her flabby arms, outstretched on the limestone pool surround. She rescued a beetle drowning in the overflow, flicking him out onto the side so he could dry out. The pool, the yacht, all of this . . . she had heard of Brazilian generosity, their relaxed, warm attitude to life. You only had to think of the Carnival—life was one big party. She climbed out of the water and wrapped herself in a towel from a pile stacked neatly to the side. The professor's eyes opened half an inch. He patted, languidly, the lounger next to him, and gingerly she sat down.

"Professor, why did you ask me here?"

"What do you mean?" he said.

"Why did you invite me?"

He sighed, still fighting sleep. The caipirinhas had taken their toll. "Oh . . . well, I didn't, my dear. My PA told me you wanted to visit, to perhaps do a big story on the eco-island, and my work, and on your friend's work, well, our friend's work . . . and don't you ever relax, silly English girl?"

Kate sat bolt upright.

"What friend?" She was suddenly on fire.

"He'll be here in a minute." His eyes closed again; he rolled over on his side with his back to her.

Kate prodded his back, between the shoulder blades.

"What friend?" she repeated.

"John . . . John Kingsley the Third!" he said, before passing out.

"What?!" She felt she was going to explode, the heat rising from her stomach to her throat, her body shaking. So he'd arranged it all. Not Clarissa. Set her up, so that he could . . . what exactly? What was the point? She scooped up her clothes in one arm, grabbed her bag, slipped on her sandals, and started to walk briskly down the hill. Her feet were still wet and the thong between her toes was rubbing. She quickened her pace, her shoes clacking noisily. She had to get off the island, had to leave now. The bastard! He could be here at any minute! Why couldn't he leave her alone? Why make her fly all the way to Rio, and leave her stranded on some island?

She was about halfway down the hill on the way to the jetty when he called out her name. "Kate!"

She could see his blond hair, see him waving frantically. He must have arrived on that second boat. He ran up the hill toward her, a huge grin breaking out, a camel-colored canvas weekend bag slung over his shoulder, bashing against his right hip, until he was only a few feet away. He slowed down into a brisk stride, still smiling.

She waited until he was close enough to get the full force of her rage before shrieking: "How could you?!"

He took a step backward, astonished. "I—Kate—I—"

"How could you get me here under false pretenses? Why?" She broke down in tears. Suddenly the fragility of her position terrified her.

Kate ran down the hill, clutching her towel and her bag, clenching her toes around the thong of her shoes so they wouldn't fall off as she gained speed. And then her toes slid so far forward in her thongs that they crumpled up anyway, unable to brake quickly enough to prevent her from coming thudding down on her knees. The sandy path stung her broken skin.

Quick as a flash, JK was by her side helping her up.

"Leave me alone!"

"Shh!" he said, finger over his mouth as he gently patted her knee with a clean handkerchief. Trust him to have a clean one on hand, probably pressed with camellia flower water, she thought to herself, grateful nonetheless.

"Sit—just for a second, I promise," he said, holding her hand and pulling her down on the grass to the side of the path. "You'll still get the boat."

The fall had knocked her breath away, so she did as she was told, gripping her towel firmly around her and tucking her good leg under the other so that the grass didn't irritate her knee.

"Now, you listen to me. There are two good reasons why I pushed to get you here—and I'm sorry if you didn't want to come. The first is that you and I began a journey, a professional journey that we never completed. You said you wanted a final interview, and, call me an egotistical maniac, but I was more than happy to oblige and tell you about the important work I do here. Then your assistant said you would be thrilled to have a break. So I thought, Paracato is always a good host, and I believed you might like to *see* my work instead of my just telling you."

"But you should have asked me first!" What work here? What was he talking about?

"Shh!" he said again, tipping bottled water onto a handkerchief and pressing it gently over her knee. "I did ask you. I asked Clarissa to ask you, and she said she'd spoken to you and you had said, quote unquote, 'brilliant.' I would never have just assumed—"

"Clarissa! I don't believe it!"

"And my second reason . . . well, I wasn't sure you'd really understood my Imperfect Perfect demo at the Face-Off convention. I don't know, but you kinda disappeared on me, and everyone else seemed to think . . ." He reached into his bag for a Band-Aid, and started peeling off the paper backing and sticking it over her graze. "Actually, I didn't care what everyone else thought, I wanted to know what you thought. You're the only one around here honest enough, or interested enough, to properly care about what you write, and your opinion really mattered to me."

"You w-wanted my opinion?" How dare he? Get her all this way just to fish for compliments. When, knowing what she knew, there was no way she could ever give him praise.

"Look, I don't know how to say this . . . but . . . there aren't many people in my life that I can trust, that I can ask about stuff like that."

She didn't know what to say. Didn't understand what he was saying. What he wanted from her. She stood up, calmly, and hobbled with as much dignity as she could while still in her bra and knickers, clutching the towel, down the hill, JK walking beside her. They were silent now, as if he knew there wasn't much point in saying more.

"Stop a second," he said, seeing her struggle with her towel, bag, and underwear combination. "Give me that." He gestured to the towel, then looked politely away, over his shoulder, holding it up to shield her while she got dressed.

"Don't you dare look." She glowered at him, pulling on her dress then limping on down the hill.

They arrived at the boat in silence. She threw her bag on then reached out to the skipper with her other hand as she walked up the small gangplank.

"Take me back, now," she commanded the skipper, her voice choked with cold emotion. "Good-bye, JK."

"Kate!" JK stood on the jetty, as if about to jump on board, but she thrust out the palm of her hand squarely toward him, warning him away.

"Don't even think about it!" The tears disappeared, and anger brought strength to her voice.

The engines started.

He looked humbled all of a sudden. She had a distance from him now, enough to see him clearly as if for the first time. He was wearing jean shorts and a white T-shirt. He had brown arms, she noticed, muscly; tanned, tight calves.

"Kate, I don't understand . . . why?"

"You're lucky I'm not suing for kidnap!" she shouted back. The skipper and the crew stood poised on the jetty, ready to cast off, all eyes following their drama intently, yet with a servile discretion, pretending not to be.

"But how could I know? Listen, ever since that night at the party when you disappeared—"

"I'm not your Cinderella!" she shouted angrily.

"Okay . . . okay . . . but if I didn't grab my chance, how could I see you again? What would have become of us?"

"Us? . . . Us?! Are you kidding?!"

He seemed hurt. Exasperated. He sighed. "Look . . . I lied . . . when at the beauty editors' thing, someone asked if there was a romantic connection between us. Whatever I said, I don't remember exactly now, but I do remember I denied it. I said I never mixed business with pleasure, or something . . . something dumb like that."

"But there isn't a romantic connection!" Kate looked horrified.

"But there is, Kate."

Her stomach churned. She was thrilled at the thought that

there might be something between them; yet she was simultaneously repulsed by him, angry at all he had done, angry with herself for feeling anything for him beyond revulsion. She had to remember the truth, the real JK only she seemed to know about.

"Okay, I've heard it all, let's go." She motioned to the men.

JK put one foot on the gangplank. "No! Not yet! I'll let you go, but just hear me out!"

Kate folded her arms and glared at him.

"I wanted to bring you here not because I'm madly in love with you or because I want to spend the rest of my life with you, or anything daft like that. I'm not that superficial. But that night at the party, before you threw up—"

"Thank you for reminding me!"

From nowhere a cheap plastic beach ball suddenly bounced into the water, interrupting them. They both stared at it, surprised. Its bright blue, yellow, and red stripes looked out of place next to the sleek adults-only yacht.

"*Meu!*" came a voice from the top of the hill. "*Meu!*" Three children stood at the top of the hill waving, trying to get someone to fish out the ball for them. "*Por favor . . . Pare! . . . Por favor!*"

One of the crew leaned over the side to try to fish the ball out of the water.

"Paracato has kids here?" asked Kate. His grandkids? Great-grandkids?

"No." JK smiled. "That's why I wanted you here. I haven't given anyone this story yet." He waved his hand proudly toward the children. "My patients."

Kate was in shock. He operated on kids? JK operated on children?

The ball scurried along the crests of the waves, blown out to sea by a sudden gust.

"Eu não posso pegar isso! Desculpa!" shouted the crew member back up to the kids. He turned to Kate, shrugged his shoulders. "It's okay. They will buy them a new one!"

"You operate on . . . children?"

JK was too busy pulling off his T-shirt and kicking off his shoes to answer. He dived from the jetty, cutting through the water in a few strokes until he was at the ball, shouting jubilantly up to the children on the hill, something in Portuguese she didn't understand. He passed the ball up to one of the crew, then hauled himself back up on the jetty. The vertebrae on his brown back stuck out as his shoulders rounded over, pulling himself up on his forearms. He shook the water off his hair like a big Labrador and bounded onto the boat.

"You operate on children!" Kate felt her eyes welling up again, in anger.

He was a liar. And a butcher. Who ruined physically perfect women, and now children. He should be behind bars, but instead he was flaunting it, willing her to write about it.

"Oh, Kate . . . Kate!" He ignored her hostility, tugging her down next to him on the wooden seat nearest to the gangplank. His skin smelled of seawater, and something else, something delicious like watermelon or cucumber, the scent of summer. She wished they could bottle that, turn it into a perfume, sweet-salty-sexy. The saltwater dried before her eyes, forming tiny white rivulets on the down of his smooth chestnut brown skin.

She shivered, hugging herself for comfort. She could see the children on the hilltop, reunited with their ball. Their innocent play made the reason for their presence all the more unsettling.

"What could possibly be wrong with a child's face? How could you operate on them?"

He looked perplexed.

"What do you mean? Oh! I see!" He raised his eyes heaven-ward, bemused. "You think I . . . ? No, Kate, no. These kids are seriously flawed, Kate. Harelips. Jug ears. Things that in the States we'd have corrected pretty much at birth, but here they don't have the money. Paracato used to do it. He set up an operating theater here so they could spend their recovery in paradise. Now that he's older, he asked me to help out a little, keep it going. I did some training with him; he trusts me. It's no big deal. But I needed you to write about it to help raise money for some of the costs."

"You mean you don't . . ."

"Do boob jobs on twelve-year-olds? Not my thing. Nose jobs for seven-year-olds . . . there are probably surgeons out there who would do that, but . . . not me." He looked annoyed. "You know what, Kate? Maybe you could stop seeing me as this—I don't know . . . some kind of butcher."

He got up to go.

The sun was disappearing rapidly behind the hilly island as the gangplank was finally pulled up and the crew pushed off from the shore. The purple mountains in the near distance were silhouetted layer upon layer, like the cardboard backdrops of a puppet theater.

JK stopped on the jetty and looked at her once more. He sighed deeply.

"Look, the third thing I wanted to say. Or the fourth. I can't remember. There were a few."

The boat was chugging out now, the engine and the waves making a din.

"What?"

He shouted, "It's just that . . . I'd like to be laughing again with you. Playing Name That Tune with you. Like we did. I haven't done that in so long, not with anyone."

"I can't hear you!"

"I want to laugh with you!"

Kate couldn't believe what she was hearing. She wanted to hear more, but Patty Patrice's face, that face in the sweltering hot apartment back in L.A., was there before her. She could see the weird shiny texture of her skin, taut and pained, gleaming.

The engine jerked the boat forward suddenly. They were off.

"Well . . . I don't want to laugh with you."

"What?"

She shouted back; she couldn't hold her rage in anymore. *"I know what happened, JK! I know what you did!"*

"What do you mean?" He looked concerned, confused.

"Patty Patrice!"

He was gobsmacked. He dropped his hands to his sides, defeated. As if he knew that all the good work for children in the world couldn't make amends. The game was up.

new york

beauty note:

Jeans by True Religion. Top by Kate Moss for Topshop (sent as a free gift to press, sell on eBay?). *Eyes:* Red Eye eyedrops by Rite Aid, concealed underneath with YSL Touche Eclat (shade 3) and Secret Brightening Powder by Laura Mercier. *Complexion:* Revived with Estée Lauder Advanced Night Repair Protective Recovery Complex, enhanced with Estée Lauder DayWear Plus Multi Protection Tinted Moisturizer SPF 15. *Eyes:* Bobbi Brown No Smudge Mascara in black. *Lips:* Lipstick Queen Oxymoron lipstick in Minor Crisis.

twenty-one

Jean-Paul met her off the plane at JFK, so she knew he must be keen. Clarissa had forwarded him her new flight details (at least that was something she'd done right) and he'd rearranged everything around her. Not that artists probably had such tight schedules that they couldn't cancel a coffee or get up a little earlier once in a while, she figured.

No one had ever met her at an airport before. Not that she'd been to that many, the past few days, weeks, excepting.

"Leesen to the noise, Kate!" he said. She'd forgotten how French his accent was. A fleet of police cars screeched past the cab rank. "Did you forget how great this city is?"

"No, I didn't." She hadn't, either. It was good to be back in New York, her home away from home. She'd scarcely spent any time here, but now she was back, it felt like the only place she'd ever had roots. After all the craziness of L.A., and then Rio, it felt somehow safe.

Her real roots were in the meantime trying to reclaim her: messages were piling up on her mobile from Lise and her mum. She would call them later. After this evening with Jean-Paul.

Strangely, JK hadn't called. She had half expected him to call, to try to engage her in a debate about Patty Patrice. He'd obviously given up. Finally. Well, good. She had been foolish to confront him with the knowledge that she knew about Patty. What if he caused repercussions for Patty and Aurelie? Should she say something to them? But then she had convinced herself that he wouldn't say anything; perhaps he didn't even know to what she was referring. If she called him, or Aurelie for that matter, and brought up the subject of Patty, that would give the game away, make it all worse. Better to leave it ambiguous like this. His not calling her spoke louder than ever of his guilt in the matter. Children or no children. She remembered his scent as she'd sat next to him on the boat yesterday. Wet, then hot. His warm brown body, soft skin rubbing next to her bare arms. She tried not to think about him, or Rio, anymore.

The early evening light didn't glow gold like it did in L.A., but the pinkish orange that descended on the skyscrapers before her as their taxi sped into Manhattan more than sufficed. Compared with the sprawl of L.A., she felt almost as if she knew where she was going, as the grid of avenues reaching out north and south fell obligingly into rectangles with east-west cross streets. It was somewhat mathematical, but at least the billboards and shops all served as landmarks when the street numbers turned into a maze.

"Kate . . . I 'ope you don't mind, but we leaf your bags at my flat, and 'ead straight out, okay? There is something I want to show you."

"Thanks, Jean-Paul. And by the way, they say 'apartment' over here, I believe."

She didn't know how to speak to him beyond the trivial. If this was a date, then how was she supposed to behave, and why was she on it in the first place? She felt awkward around Jean-Paul. She felt like she was using him. He'd irritated her before she'd left for L.A., with his chauvinism, lack of loyalty to Alexis, and inept Frenchness. But somehow, she'd always known that a pack of Marlboro Lights wasn't going to be enough of a reward when she'd finished writing the Patty feature. And she certainly needed some cheering up, some de-Rio-ing after her hideous experiences there.

She wondered what Alexis would think of the Patty story. In the end, it hadn't been too difficult a story to write, even though she'd had to do it with Rio looming in the morning. She would have liked to have written more—to encourage women to seek their empowerment elsewhere, away from how they were physically perceived by others or by how they perceived their beauty themselves—but she'd drawn the line. It would have been hypocritical, seeing as she had enjoyed her five minutes of feeling beautiful courtesy of JK's "imperfect perfect" nonsense. Besides, feeling beautiful, that was okay, wasn't it? A good thing. Most of all, she'd wanted to really nail JK. She wondered, now that her article had been sent merrily to Alexis: had she been vitriolic enough? After Rio and the parrot 'n' pig island, she felt she couldn't be vitriolic enough. She would have to get it all double-checked with *Darling*'s legal department, of course. She didn't want a lawsuit on her hands. But she'd seen Patty's letters, the documentation; she had a witness. Aurelie had promised her more should it ever come to court. She was pretty sure of where she stood on that front.

The comfortable grid system disappeared, and their cab moved into a rough network of awkward crossings. The streets were lined with trees springing up at regular intervals through the pavement. Sidewalks. Small boutiques, tiny cafés, and tall old redbrick apartments that looked almost English.

"Where are we now?" she asked Jean-Paul.

"Greenwich Village," he said. "You 'aven't bin 'ere before?"

"You know what? I haven't been anywhere."

She hadn't really. Meatpacking District. Her office in Central Park South. The airport. The Russian baths and the charity shop. She wouldn't be writing any guidebooks just yet.

"Ah . . . zat's what I thought," said Jean-Paul. "Don' worry, we change all that. What have I to show you tonight?"

"I don't know . . . what?" She dreaded to think what.

"New York!" he said triumphantly.

*   *   *

A nd he did.

They started with Jean-Paul's all-time favorite record shop. Or so he said, until further questioning revealed it was his friend's favorite record shop, but that he knew Kate liked records and so he'd pretended for her sake. She was touched.

Fat Beats was situated on the second floor somewhere along Sixth Avenue not far from his apartment.

"Okay, so we take twenty dollars each. I buy you something. You buy me something. That way . . . we get to know each other better." He peeled off a gray-green note from a wad in his back jeans pocket and handed it over to her.

Hadn't they tried getting to know each other already? She seemed to remember it had ended with her storming out of a bar in the early hours of the morning. Tom Waits and his marmalade thighs.

She knew of only one French rapper. MC Solaar was indisputably cool, but even Jean-Paul would know about him. The only French rapper who was ever any good, he'd have his entire back catalog ready to whip out to refute any accusations about how crap French rap music is. She looked over her shoulder to the racks of records near the window. He was fingering through them, his head nodding seriously to the beat of the Beastie Boys track that the three sales assistants were playing from a record player on the counter. Each of their faces resembled the finals in some facial hairdressing contest, their beards and mustaches etched into numbers and symbols as if a graffiti artist had been let loose on a bear with a pair of clippers.

"Excuse me." She played on her English accent. "Do you have any Plastic Bertrand?"

"The Belgian guy?" one asked. "'Ça Plane pour Moi'? Circa 1970 . . .'78?" He disappeared into the back room and emerged beaming. "Hey, guys!" he shouted in the direction of his hirsute companions. "I thought we were never gonna get rid of this!" Much laughter.

Kate looked him squarely in the eyes. "Do you do gift wrap?" she asked, tersely.

❊ ❊ ❊

Next on their sightseeing trip was a narrow house, still in Greenwich Village. "I know you like writing . . . it's your job . . . ," began Jean-Paul, looking up at the building, which was indistinct apart from its thinness. "But did you know that 'ere originated the expression"—he paused, as if concentrating on each word, like a joker anxious he was going to forget the punch line—"'burning ze candle at both ends'?"

"What do you mean?"

"I mean," he said triumphantly, "there was a lady 'oo lived 'ere. A poet, I believe. Edna St. Vincent Millay. She said it first. 'Burn-ing ze can-dle at both ends.'"

"Gosh, your English is good. I could never say that in French!" There hadn't been much call for languages at *Maidstone Bazaar*.

She was touched he seemed to have put so much thought into trying to please and titillate her. "But did she say it here?"

"What do you mean?"

"Well, she was a poet, and she lived here. But did she say it while she lived here? Or did she say it while she lived somewhere else?"

"I don't bloody know, as you say in England!" He looked grumpy.

She laughed.

"You said 'bloody.' You're more English than the English!"

He laughed back.

*   *   *

They only just made it to the Brooklyn Museum of Art, fortunate that the museum was open late tonight. The glass entrance, imposing yet friendly, sat comfortably within the older frame of the nineteenth-century building.

"I prefer this museum to the Metropolitan," explained Jean-Paul. "It's smaller, more, you know, personal." He squeezed her hand gently. It would have been rude not to squeeze it back.

"I don't know much about art," she said. "I really don't."

"I guessed . . . that night I met you. Don't worry. It doesn't matter. It's better, in fact. You come to it with no preconceived ideas. Only a knowledge of—"

"What I like and don't like? I don't know much about art but I know what I like?" She laughed. The joke got lost somewhere in translation, but he laughed anyway.

"Come!" He grasped her hand again and led her into a vast room filled with bright white stone sculptures. Naked forms sat passionately entwined with one another, gracefully waiting for more strangers to file around them, never tiring of their admiring glances.

"Rodin." He sighed. "Look at zis one . . . so beautiful, zis figure. You see, stone is such a perfect material for the human form. It gives shape, sensuality, it's not flat like a picture, you want to touch it, the porosity of the stone it is crafted from makes it seem some'ow receptive, you want to reach out. . . ." He leaned closer, stretching his fingers toward the statue.

"She is pretty fit, yes," said Kate, looking round her anxiously as two security guards eased themselves up from their chairs by the door and slowly made their way toward Jean-Paul, observing him closely.

"I don't think you should touch her, though. That might be seen as sculptural harassment, *non?*"

* * *

"What do you find attractive in a man?" asked Jean-Paul. Only a Frenchman could ask such a direct, loaded question, she figured. They were sitting in a Brooklyn café by the waterfront, somewhere underneath the Manhattan Bridge Overpass. They'd opted for brunch, even though it was dark now, and were wolfing down eggs Benedict in a little café along the East River, with views across the water toward Manhattan. Kate stirred two sugars into her caffe latte, while Jean-Paul looked on, his surprise at her sweet tooth conveyed with the merest raising of an eyebrow.

"A brain is always useful," she said. "I don't know . . . what do you find attractive in a man?"

"Oh . . . you're not serious." He pouted playfully. It was impressive the way he managed to drop his lower lip in a sulky manner and yet still look resolutely heterosexual. "I was just trying to talk, you know, about Rodin, about his ability to present both men and women, and make them appealing to both sexes. I find it interesting, *non?*"

"Oh, I see."

"But since you ask, I like men who are . . ." He paused, sucking his froth-covered spoon noisily before laying it down by his coffee cup. Its bottom was submerged in a shallow pool of milky coffee that had spilled in the saucer. "Older. Who have character in their faces. Broad shoulders. Long feet with a second toe that's longer than the first. A little gray 'air at the temples. Bags under the eyes like, like Serge Gainsbourg's! Maybe a slight hook in the nose."

"You haven't thought about this much then, have you?" Kate laughed.

"It's 'ow I'd like to be when I'm old," he explained.

A tug moved past them, horn blaring. The dark evening sky was deepening into black, and the lights were getting brighter by the second. The view was breathtakingly pretty, like a stage set just for them. He was French, she was British, two outsiders looking into Manhattan. L.A. didn't have that kind of magic. As for Maidstone . . .

"Gosh, that view," she said.

"I know. And you know, I 'ave bin 'ere a while now, and I never get tired of it. Never never never."

They gazed in silence.

"So . . . 'ow you'd like to be when you're old, Kate?"

She'd never really thought about it. She wasn't sure how she'd like to be now, let alone years down the line. How old was old, anyway? If forty was the new thirty, and so on right up to eighty being the new seventy, who knew what lay in store for her?

"I'd like . . . well, physically, I'd like to be fit. I think I'm going to dye my hair once it starts going gray. And I hope that when I get to my midfifties, you know, menopausal or what-ever, I'd like to be a bit plumper, with a big chest my grand-children can rest their heads on when we're watching *Blue Peter*, or whatever's on TV for kids then."

"Ah . . . *Blue Peter* . . . I remember zat."

"They had it in France?"

"Oh, you know . . . zey get everything zere. My parents were Anglophiles. All our 'olidays were in Britain in fact. Anyway . . . are you 'appy the way you look now?" For a second she thought this was a quick jibe at her marmalade thighs confession, then she decided to let the doubts go. The glimmer of suspicion vanished from her face. She relaxed.

"You know, I thought I was, and then . . ."

"Then what?"

"Well, I don't know, here it's so different. In England, you can do well at your job, it doesn't matter so much how you look. Well, it does, but you know, not at my job, I suppose."

"What was your job?"

"I was a reporter on a local magazine."

"And now?"

"Well, now, I don't know. One minute I'm struggling to fit in the requisite number of blow-dries per day, and the next minute I'm on national TV being hailed as some kind of role model by some idiot plastic surgeon for looking messy and unkempt!"

"He didn't say messy, Kate, 'e said 'imperfect perfect.'"

"You saw it?"

"Everyone saw it! But I think you're pretty perfect-perfect myself."

"You smooth talker!" She frowned a little, but the corners of her mouth turned upward. Now that she thought about it, there was something she would like to be different about the way she looked. She could only have realized it now, as she stared out over the river at the lights, aware once again of all the different opportunities that seemed to have landed at her feet in the last two months or so, like some blessed gift from heaven, from her dad perhaps. She often thought of him when confronted with stars, or lights, or a sense of things greater than herself.

"You know what, Jean-Paul?" she said, taking a sip from her Bloody Mary. "I've never told anyone this, I think because I've never known myself, but I've always been slightly embarrassed about the way I look." She smiled nervously at him. "I mean, is it okay to like makeup, to dye your hair, to worry about putting on weight? Doesn't all that stuff make you vacuous somehow, stupid even? And the other day in L.A., I realized, or maybe I didn't realize it then, maybe I'm only realizing it now . . ."

"Go on." He rested his chin on his hand, elbow on the table.

"Well, there was this model. And at first, I thought, wow, she looks amazing! Maybe I'm gay. Then I realized, no, of course I'm not, I fancy men, and then I knew—just now in fact, when you asked me about how I like to look. I knew what it was that was bothering me!"

"What?" He laughed and took her hand in his.

"I'd like to have bosoms like hers! Isn't that weird? I mean, there I am writing an article about how not to get plastic surgery, and actually, I'd like to have bosoms like the model's!"

"It's not really something to worry about, *non*?" Jean-Paul took her other hand, clasped both of them in his, and smiled. "You know some surgeons now . . . you could get them if you wanted to."

"Oh, no!"

"Why not? You dye your 'air, you go to a gym, what's the big deal?"

Kate slurped on her Bloody Mary and frowned a "No way!" back at him.

"Okay, maybe not . . . surgery is not for you, but say, when you get old. Okay, you look like you told me, with dyed hair and big bosoms, but in your 'eart, 'ow do you want to be? I mean, emotionally?"

She thought for a second, looking out over the East River. "I don't want to be alone. Do you?"

"Not really, no."

A couple strolled past, pushing a pram. Late to be out with a baby. All the girls Kate knew in Maidstone with kids were bathing and bed-timing bang on 6:00 p.m. The pram was made from some kind of lightweight tubular steel; it glided past, smooth and streamlined, the man steering.

"What about Alexis, Jean-Paul?" Seeing the woman with the pram, wondering about growing old with no one, these things had made her think of her boss. She couldn't imagine her with anyone, now or when she was older. She couldn't put her finger on why, exactly, just that feeling that devoting all her energy to work, something she'd always believed in herself . . . maybe it wasn't good for one's old age?

"What about 'er?" he said with not so much arrogance as curiosity, perplexed as to why Kate could be asking about her.

"Well, are you seeing her?"

"No. We went out a couple of times. Ages ago. I was joking that night. . . . But you know, Alexis I actually 'ave a lot of respect for. There are many things about 'er. . . ."

"Like what?"

"Well, she 'as a boyfriend, a poet. Frederick Wallner. She goes to a poetry club every Tuesday night. But you can't tell anyone at work, eh?"

"Why not?"

"She's embarrassed. She thinks they will laugh at 'er if it's not something to do with fashion, or you know . . . a shop opening."

"And Frederick? How does she keep him a secret?"

"No. It's 'im who keeps 'er a secret. It's not a good look for a poet, a serious academic to go out with someone who works on, you know, women's magazines. Zat's why she has, you know, the moostache. She thinks it makes 'er look clever."

They laughed. It was impossible to understand how someone so cool in her world could be so uncool in another, or vice
versa.

When he laughed, she noticed Jean-Paul wasn't far off from
his description of how he wanted to look when he was old, his
face full of character, his smile pushing up the Serge Gainsbourg bags under his eyes. His hair was even a little bit gray at
the temples. She wouldn't mind if he kissed her right now. She
wondered if he knew.

*   *   *

A party. Jean-Paul wanted to drop by at a friend's house in
SoHo. Portia London was an art dealer who was having a
gathering of twenty or so of her closest friends.

"Five minutes, I promise. I want you to see . . . I don't
know . . . people."

They had to tap in a security code to gain access to the lift.
It took Jean-Paul five attempts to remember it. They giggled as
they entered the lift, then got out on the wrong floor and had
to walk down a flight of stairs. Outside Portia's apartment was
a rail where her guests had put their coats. Jean-Paul hung his
up, then tried on a couple of others. A Hermès biker jacket
("That's just wrong!" said Kate) and a denim vintage Gucci
that was way too small.

The apartment was midway up a tower block, with a corner
view. Inside, it was small, minimalist, with nothing but a couple of paintings on the wall, an open fireplace, and cream
leather sofas, the kind that you could join up in fifty different
configurations and end up with either a bed, or a sofa with a
footrest, or a big table to put magazines on, but still not be
comfortable for a TV dinner. A waiter passed drinks round
self-consciously. In spite of managing to contain such a large

sofa, the flat wasn't much bigger than Kate's bedroom in Maidstone.

"Portia, 'oo did this painting?" asked Jean-Paul to their hostess, a woman so thin her cheeks were concave. She was wearing a tight black dress. Her matching black bob cut harshly into her face.

She smiled enthusiastically and sat down beside them, stroking Kate's legs. Kate prayed they weren't too stubbly. "Oh, darling, I'm so glad you asked. Miraval Esposito! I bought it in Mexico City—isn't it joyous? He's dead already, but he's going to be sooooo big in a couple of years!"

She moved on.

Jean-Paul looked at Kate apologetically. She burst out laughing.

"I promised, five minutes only. Let's go. I keep my promises."

∗　∗　∗

At the top of the Empire State Building they gazed at the view.

"Oh, my God, it's just like *Sleepless in Seattle*! What was that film it was based on? You know, the black-and-white one, where she can't get up from her chair because she's been knocked over in an accident, and he doesn't realize, at least I think he does but only right at the end, and—oh, you must know the one?"

"I know, I think I know. . . . It will come to me." He looked around anxiously at the small crowd in the bar. "It's not too cheesy for you? Being here, you know, with tourists?"

"I love tourists!" She did. It was wonderful to be doing nothing, hanging out with normal people, not thinking about work, or Patty, or anything like that. Every so often she'd see a helicopter swooping past on some night tour. She felt as if they were all in it together somehow, all celebrating the delights this incredible city had to offer.

"Will you kiss me, Kate?"

He leaned forward and gently kissed her lips. She felt that same feeling she'd felt recently with JK3; like the drunken warmth of alcohol spreading through her veins, only better, so much better than any Bacardi Breezer, drowning her whole body in a seminauseous state of delirium, not wanting to come up for air.

Jean-Paul broke off suddenly and looked into her eyes. The city lights glittered in the reflection of the glass behind him:

"An Affair to Remember."

"What? Well, yes, obviously, I hope so . . . what a lovely thing to say!"

"The movie, Kate!"

"Oh! Thank you!" She laughed. She put her arms round him impetuously. "Let's go dancing!"

"Where?" He wasn't expecting the tourist to be taking charge of the itinerary.

"My place."

twenty-two

"I don't know where to start." Alexis was sitting at her desk, her chin resting on her hands. For once she wasn't trying to edit copy while she was talking. It was a sunny day. The light streaming in from the window behind her spotlit the pages of white paper, neatly printed out in a pile, that sat squarely before her. Kate's copy.

For a split second Kate wondered whether Alexis had somehow found out about her night out with Jean-Paul. What if he'd been lying, and she still had the hots for him? Now that she knew him—well, she didn't know him, but she felt since last night she had a much better idea—it was hard to put those two together in the first place. Maybe it had been a career move on his part: get a glowing review of one of his shows in return for a couple of dinners, maybe more, with the editor? If that was why, or how, then at least he now had some respect for Alexis, and in that sense something good had come out of their

association. She certainly couldn't imagine him being with
Alexis the way he had been with her. Dancing naked in her
apartment to Plastic Bertrand's "Ça Plane pour Moi." Falling
into bed to Bill Wyman's "Je Suis un Rock Star." She couldn't
believe he'd picked out that record for her. She giggled in-
wardly, tried to concentrate on the matter—seemingly a serious matter—at hand.

Judging by the somber look on Alexis's face, it looked like
she'd have to make some copy changes. That was inevitable.
Changes were good. But what?

"If there's a problem with some of the language," she started,
cautiously, "I think I used the word 'mutilations,' for example,
which might be a bit strong, but I'm sure we could get it
checked over with the legal department."

Alexis motioned her to stop talking.

Kate didn't know what to say anyway. She hadn't been expecting this. It had come from her heart, all of it, and somehow she'd thought that Alexis would have appreciated her
honesty, her candor, her openness.

Alexis sighed, her hand over her mouth. She looked worried.

"Kate . . . Kate."

"Yes?"

"I appointed you to write about beauty. To give our readers,
well . . . something different, yes, but something they wanted
to read about. Now, I have issues with what you have written,
serious issues, which"—she reached over for a cigarette, lit it
with her lighter, and inhaled deeply—"which go beyond the
subject matter, and I'll tell you about those in a minute. Those
issues alone mean this article can never be printed."

Kate felt anger, frustration rising like a tide.

"What? Alexis, you don't understand! There's a woman's life
at stake here!"

Alexis motioned her to be silent. The way she scowled told Kate she meant business. "Shut up and listen!" she snapped.

No one had ever spoken to Kate like that before. Not Brian Palmers, not her mother, not anyone. It was unacceptable.

"Alexis, I really don't think you should—"

"Shut up and listen!" Alexis shouted at her, animatedly. From outside the glass wall of her office, Kate could feel the entire office looking up.

Alexis stood up, put both hands on the desk, and leaned over to Kate. Up this close, Kate could see the open pores around her nose, the lines in her forehead. Her lips were dry. Anger aged her.

"Do you even realize what you've done?" She wasn't shouting now, but speaking quietly, rapidly, furiously, in a way that was even more frightening than when she had been shouting. "I mean, do you, Kate? Kate, we are not here to save the world! You are not a reporter! And this is not some feminist magazine!"

Kate sat, stunned. Of course she was a reporter, and weren't all women's magazines feminist magazines, if one went with the definition of feminism that advocated equal rights for all women? What was she talking about?

Alexis picked up Kate's copy and threw it in the bin. Kate drew a sharp intake of breath.

"And don't patronize me just because I'm a fucking American!" she shouted.

"I'm sorry?" Kate really didn't know what she was talking about.

"Quoting Graham Greene to me, like I've never read a book before. Well, you know what, Kate, he also said, in that very same novel, *The Quiet American*, I believe, that the biggest mistake a reporter can make is to become '*engagé*'—you know what that means? Engaged! Involved! I might add the words 'bigoted,' 'subjective' . . . these are all the things that sprang to mind when I read your copy."

She really didn't like it then.

"Besides which, how dare you change an assignment without telling me about it first! How dare you!"

True, there was that, but Clarissa had been so sure. . . .

Alexis reached down into the bin and pulled the copy out again. She whacked it with the back of her hand.

"And another thing . . . you write about 'egos' and 'God complexes.' Does it not occur to you that most men and women who have any degree of talent—politicians, poets, actors, and yes . . . little upstart journalists who think they know better than anyone else—that they have egos, too? That it's these same egos that allow them to develop and nurture that talent? What kind of a dumb argument is that?"

She paced around to Kate's side of the desk and whacked the copy down before her.

"And another thing, did it ever occur to you that this supplement is sponsored by the very people—plastic surgeons—you are attacking? How did you think you were going to get past that one? Do you think they really want to save the world, too?"

"I'm really sorry. Clarissa did mention there might be a problem there. . . ."

"Shh! I'm not done yet!" She picked up a remote control on her desk, pointed it at the neat flat-screen TV to the side of her desk, and hit Play.

"Above all, Kate, this is the real reason I'm so . . . pissed!" She moved back to her desk and sat down, head in hands again. She looked up at her and said, calmly, "I take it you didn't see the news this morning?"

What was going on? Alexis began to shake, as the screen came to life, black lines fizzling quickly into a clear picture.

Vivienne Fox's tidy bob and huge smile came on-screen. A yellow strap line blazed her CNN name and file, with a "Live from Los Angeles" banner along the bottom of the TV screen. She appeared to be standing in the entrance of JK3's clinic, though there was no sign of him.

"Well, Roger, it's been a great victory today for one of Los Angeles's best-loved plastic surgeons. Very exciting, but in the early hours of this morning, two women were arrested for a number of charges, all connected with the surgeon to the stars, John Kingsley the Third."

The camera cut to an image of JK, laughing outside the Face-Off convention, then switched back quickly to a shot of a tower block of flats that looked suspiciously like Patty's. It was dawn, the sky a sleepy gray-white with yellow undertones. Lights flashed like those same thunderbolts of lightning Kate had seen before, only this time they were coming from a cluster of police cars gathered near the front of the building.

"Patty Patrice and Aurelie Spencer have been charged with offenses under the California State libel laws. It appears the two were approaching journalists with claims that the surgeon had damaged the face of Patty Patrice. An ex-girlfriend of Kingsley's, Ms. Patrice had been sending images of herself to selected journalists made up to look as if her face had been ruined by John Kingsley's surgery. Her mission? To ruin the reputation of Dr. Kingsley. . . ."

Vivienne must have been fooled. They'd all been fooled. There was no way you could do that with makeup!

As if anticipating the viewer's disbelief, the camera cut to an image of Patty, scarred and damaged, then showed police ripping off a latex mask from her face to reveal the "before" picture of Patty, like a Scooby-Doo episode now come to life. Suddenly, the camera was showing Aurelie, looking fierce, angry, and unrepentant as police cuffed her and walked her over to a van.

"Her lover, Aurelie Spencer, was able to act as Patty's accomplice thanks to her position as John Kingsley's personal assistant. In a plot that sounds like something from a John Grisham novel, the two had planned to ruin the surgeon's reputation in revenge for perceived slights to Ms. Patrice during his monthlong romance with her. A hoax like this could have cost the surgeon millions in loss of earnings, especially as the pair had planned to disappear just as soon as any articles were published, making it virtually impossible for John Kingsley to defend his reputation in a court of law. The surgeon said today, from the island retreat of Brazilian supersurgeon Professor Paracato, that he was relieved and grateful to the FBI for putting an end to these plans before they'd managed to do any damage, and that he hoped Ms. Patrice and Ms. Spencer would seek psychiatric help for their various problems. . . ."

The camera cut to JK, who was kicking around the same blue, red, and yellow ball he'd rescued previously, with the three children she'd seen on the top of the hill. He jokingly wiped the sweat from his brow, then spoke into the camera.

"Yes, I'd like to thank the FBI for cracking this heinous and very hurtful campaign against my character, and to say how relieved I am that the two women in question are in custody. That's all I have to say, I'm afraid, apart from, let's keep America beautiful! Oh . . . one last thing, I'd like to thank those beauty editors who were approached, but had the faith in me, and the respect for the law, to report these individuals before they could really do some damage. Ladies, you rock!" He smiled graciously, then the cameras cut back to Vivienne.

She smiled adoringly as if basking in his image.

"Well, there he goes, Hollywood's favorite surgeon, and can I just say, Roger, it really is a welcome relief that he's been saved from this most vicious plot. He's on that island to do charity surgery, restoring the faces of impoverished Brazilian children to some degree of normalcy, helping them reintegrate into society and

*move on from the taunts and teasing that has ruined their child-
hoods so far."*

"That sounds like a pretty worthwhile thing to do, Vivienne."

*"Oh, yes. And, Roger, you should know that Dr. Kingsley has also
single-handedly pioneered a new look called 'imperfect perfect,'
which looks set to change the way America considers its plastic
surgery."*

"Could you tell me about that, Vivienne?"

*"Yes, Roger, it started when John Kingsley the Third met a
young English reporter, Kate Miller, the beauty director for* Darling *magazine, and was inspired so much by her natural, fresh
look, he decided to put into practice a whole new approach to plastic surgery. He calls it 'imperfect perfect' but you and I might call
it 'less is more.' Basically, he's against everyone looking the same,
from the Botox to the blow-dries to the one-look-fits-all surgery
being offered all over town. His recent demonstration at Face-Off,
the international plastic surgery convention here in Los Angeles,
astounded fans and is expected to revolutionize the approach of
many surgeons around the world. Basically, Roger, he took a pretty
girl and refused to operate on her, except to remove a precancerous
mole on her face."*

*"Well, thank you, Vivienne, and as they say, 'Only in L.A.!'
Now in the studio . . ."*

Alexis switched the video off with the remote control, then
looked into Kate's eyes.

"Facts, Kate. Facts."

It was Kate's turn to start shaking. The hairs on her arms were
standing up; she felt a chill run down her spine. Patty and Aurelie were conartists! She was next on their list; just another sucker
they were trying to mislead. They'd got farther down the line
with her than any others. And if this had all happened a few
weeks ago, her copy would have been filed, approved, ready to be
printed out and fall into the laps of hundreds and thousands of

240   Kathleen Baird-Murray

Americans, all eager to believe in the downfall of another hero, another vanity case. Newspapers would have picked up on it, the TV news, it would have gone around the world! And it didn't matter that JK was innocent; no one would have cared once the initial story was out, and if he'd sued them, his reputation would have been ruined for the years and months it would take for the case to come to trial. His work on those children would have been finished immediately—they wouldn't let him anywhere near children, even ones in dire need of his help.

She'd got him all wrong. All of him. Not just Patty, but the "mutilation" of the Face-Off model as well. She'd been so determined to "out" him, to out surgery itself, as corrupt, dishonest, unethical, that she'd taken shortcuts, failed to see what he was really doing, failed to see that he could no more harm a pretty face than he could make one from scratch. Despite all his showmanship, his flamboyance, his charm, he was really the good guy in all this, the consummate professional. It was she who was the unprofessional one. She who had allowed ego to overtake and let her feel she was breaking news, fighting battles, on to something that would really make her career. She felt numb. She hadn't even given him a chance to . . .

"You didn't even interview him, Kate," said Alexis. She was calm now, sad even. "You didn't even give him a chance to talk about it, to defend himself. There you were, on an island with him, witnessing his work firsthand . . . you didn't pause for a second to think you might be wrong?"

A tear rolled down Kate's cheek. She sniffed. Alexis passed her a tissue.

"You talk of being a reporter, but that's not reporting, is it?"

"Alexis, I'm sorry, I really am. I don't know how I could have been so stupid to have been sucked into all this." She blew her nose. "But they were so . . . I mean, I saw her! She had cuts all over her wrists, her face was a wreck, I saw it!"

Alexis sighed.

"Listen, they were a couple of pros. Sick, twisted, yes, but clever. The only way you could have guessed was by touching her skin, and being English, and polite . . . they knew you would never do that, would you? Don't you see, Kate, they picked you because you were gullible, new to the game, not like those other, more experienced beauty hacks who spotted what they were up to straightaway!"

"But I read the documents. . . ." That was the mortifying bit. That she'd labeled those other beauty editors as little more than bimbos—more interested in where they were getting their next free Botox shot from—when all the while they were more professional than her.

"It's easy to fake a document. Listen, I'm mad at you, but I'll get over it."

Kate knew she would have to do some serious damage control. Write something else. Apologize to JK—did he even know how close she'd come to exposing him for something he hadn't done? He did seem to genuinely like her—and look how she'd treated him in return! It was too awful to think about. At least she had the natural beauty story shot and finished.

"Did you like the other story?" she ventured timidly. "About natural beauty?"

"Oh, God, Kate . . . I don't know how to tell you this, but we can't run those pictures of Petruschka." Alexis sighed and retrieved three photos of the model resting on the top of her in-tray. She looked them over, with neither admiration nor disdain. "At least, not with this story."

"I'm sorry? Was it too explicit? I mean, I know you're not allowed to sunbathe topless in this country, but I would have thought . . ." Kate sniffed.

Alexis looked at her wearily. "Everyone, Kate—*everyone*—in

this industry knows that Petruschka had her breasts done last
year. JK did them. You can't run a story about natural beauty
and feature a model with fake breasts. It just isn't done."

"Oh, no!" Kate cried. She couldn't believe this was happening to her! Why hadn't Clarissa said anything? Why hadn't the
makeup artist or the hairdresser? And then she remembered—
in their own way, they had. They'd looked away, looked per-
turbed when she'd told them that natural looked best, explained the model would be photographed nude. She hadn't
been receptive to any kind of debate, hadn't even looked for
problems, she'd been so determined to get on with the story.
And she'd trusted Clarissa's choice. Clarissa.

"Oh, God, I've messed up so badly. . . . I'm so sorry, Alexis,
I really am!" She couldn't hold back the tears any longer. She
didn't care that the entire office outside Alexis's glass walls was
probably watching, or that Clarissa was probably fully aware
her downfall was happening so spectacularly right now.

Alexis looked embarrassed at her sobs. She bit her lip
thoughtfully, pushed the cigarettes across the desk like some
kind of peace gesture. Kate continued to cry, couldn't even
bring herself to smoke. Alexis went to tidy up the photographs
of Petruschka, arranging them back in a pile on the in-tray.
Eventually, when it became apparent Kate's sobs were not about
to relent, she got up, walked around to the front of the desk,
and leaned against it. She held Kate's hand.

"Now listen. You're young, you have some things to learn.
I'm angry at myself as much as I am at you. I gave you way too
much responsibility, and you weren't ready for it. Simple as
that."

Kate gulped. She wasn't ready to have her hand held by her
boss. She wriggled her hand out of Alexis's so that she could
wipe her nose with the tissue, now embarrassingly reduced to a
screwed-up ball of soggy disintegrated matter. She wondered

whether it was polite to wriggle your hand back under your editor's when it had just clasped a snotty tissue.

Alexis continued, "I guess that I . . . well, let's just say I hired you because I thought that as an experienced beauty director, with the training of *Harper's Bazaar* behind you, you could handle stuff. . . . I guess not. That's okay, we can work on things, your ideas are good."

"*Maidstone Bazaar*," Kate corrected her.

"Your writing is sharp, Kate, and you musn't let this—I'm sorry? What did you say?" Alexis frowned, confused.

"*Maidstone Bazaar*," said Kate. "And I wasn't the beauty director, I was a reporter."

The color drained from Alexis's face, like a chameleon falling from a leaf to the white sands below. She took a deep breath and stared at Kate, as if frozen in shock, and repeated, "*Harper's Bazaar*."

Kate knew, with the utmost clarity, that something awful would happen as soon as she uttered the next two words; that she could circumvent her fate by using any two other words, or no words at all; that she didn't fully understand why the next two words would have such an earth-shattering effect; but that ultimately she was powerless to change anything and had no choice but to be honest and answer the only way she knew how.

"*Maidstone Bazaar*."

twenty-three

"Lizbet!" shouted Alexis. A hush fell over the office. Everyone looked up and stared, then when they realized Alexis had flung open her door and was now looking at them, fell back to hurriedly typing, crouched over their computers as if the more uncomfortable or bowed they looked, the more convincing it would seem.

It seemed to take an age for Lizbet to traverse the office from the water fountain where she'd been chatting with Clarissa and enter Alexis's domain; but in her twenty or so steps, Kate felt her journalistic life flash before her, her pulse racing uncomfortably, before the final moments of her career disappeared in a puff of smoke before her. What was going on? She hadn't done anything wrong, had she? She'd been offered the job; true, it had come a little out of the blue, but things happened like that in the fast-paced world of magazines, didn't they? *Harper's Bazaar* was another magazine. She knew of it, of course, but surely they couldn't have been so stupid as to muddle the two up, could they?

Sensing Alexis's anger, Lizbet stood in the office, her face composed, waiting patiently for whatever wrath was about to fall, looking as if she'd been in this position a few times before. Alexis stood behind her desk; Kate stayed in the chair, looking like a small child in a headmistress's office, waiting for her parents to arrive before they could have a big dressing-down.

"Tell us, Kate," said Alexis, staring directly at Lizbet, whether because she was too angry to look at Kate or too angry with Lizbet to remove her gaze, she didn't know.

"I'm sorry . . . tell you what exactly? I don't really understand what's going on!" She sobbed again, clutching at the snotty tissue, looking anxiously for a scrap that wasn't already soaked through with her tears.

"Tell me what you just fucking told me!" The swearing was another bad sign. Until today, she'd never heard Alexis swear before. Even Lizbet looked shocked now.

"Um . . . *Maidstone Bazaar?*"

"*Maidstone Bazaar—Maidstone Bazaar—MAIDSTONE Bazaar*! What the hell is going on here!" shouted Alexis. "Since when did *Darling* magazine hire its beauty director from some magazine no one's ever even heard of?!"

It seemed a little harsh. *Maidstone Bazaar* wasn't a bad magazine. It had won awards, been featured in the UK *Press Gazette* a couple of times, the bible for the press industry. Kate's Trisha piece had even been picked up by one of the nationals, which had used it to reveal her split with that orange man—Tania had e-mailed her the other day. So what if it was local? She'd left it behind now, proved that she could do the job, hadn't she? Except for the surgery story cock-up. And the "natural is best" story on the model with fake tits. Kate looked awkwardly at her tissue again.

Lizbet spluttered, "I did what you—what you told me to!"

"No, you fucking didn't!" Alexis shouted. "I told you to find me Kate Miller, *the* Kate Miller, from British *Harper's Bazaar*, beauty director of some ten years' or so standing, friends with Gustav, Lisette—*the* Kate Miller." She turned and looked at Kate disparagingly. "Not—not—this!"

Kate started making an unattractive whooping noise, something akin to hyperventilation or a small baby crying. She was about as far removed from the Kate who had confidently pulled off the big surgery story as she would ever be; a million miles away from the Kate who had frolicked in bed with France's finest artist only a few hours ago. She was a sniveling wreck.

"I'm sorry . . . I don't understand how I could . . ." Lizbet started crying, too, although Kate managed to observe from somewhere under the tears that were falling, the snotty tissue, and her bedraggled hair, that Lizbet's tears were the tears of contagion, the tears you cried because someone else—in this case, her—was crying, suffused with a fair amount of fear and panic as to what the eventual outcome of this would be.

On the other side of the glass, the office had stopped pretending to be working and whispering, and was now openly staring aghast.

"I couldn't find the number, I remember now. . . ." said Lizbet. Alexis looked daggers at her. "So I called international directory inquiries . . . and they gave me the number."

Alexis and Kate looked at her, waiting for more.

"Well, when I called, she answered, 'Kate Miller . . . *Bazaar*,' so I . . ."

Alexis sighed and sat down.

Lizbet looked at Kate apologetically. Kate handed her the last corner of her tissue.

"So," she whimpered, "what you're saying is . . . you didn't really want me here at all?"

"Kate, I'm sorry, I . . ." Alexis looked in despair at her, then turned her back on them both and stared out of the window. Kate's eyes followed her stare, beseeching something to happen; a winged messenger from the East to burst through and make everything all right again. Instead she saw the leaves on the trees in Central Park beginning to turn a yellowy brown. She wondered whether she would be here to see fall, the famous fall; when the old would shift to make way for the new, like some gentle exfoliating process, a little microdermabrasion. Her instincts had been right. She was a mistake. And now look where her vanity had got her. She had allowed herself to believe that she might be special, might be one of the beautiful people.

Alexis turned around again to face Lizbet and Kate. She was calm.

"Lizbet, you'd better call Elizabeth Geary in Personnel. Get her to come down. We need to sort this out." Lizbet left the room, sniffling like a wounded dog.

"What do I do?" Kate looked forlornly at her.

"I don't know," said Alexis.

twenty-four

They had put her on gardening leave. She had had to ask Elizabeth Geary, the nice woman from Personnel, what that meant exactly. Gardening leave, it transpired, was what happened when they weren't exactly pleased with you, but they weren't exactly cross with you either. It was every journalist's dream: a holiday, with pay, until they made up their minds how they were going to get themselves out of this mess you'd got them into. In her case, they felt so bad, they'd even booked her onto the first flight back to London, with the proviso that she finish her rewrite of the surgery story in the week that she was away. It didn't seem like much of a holiday, but she was so shell-shocked she would have taken whatever they offered, anything to not have it end, to not have a one-way ticket.

And so here she was, at the airport, sitting in the lounge with the common people, even though her business-class seat entitled her to unlimited CNN and tartan-wrapper shortbread biscuits in the club-class room over to the right. Here it felt more at home, more real, and she badly needed a dose of reality to make up for her big taste of the great pretend. Her bags had been waiting for her at the office when she'd arrived. Well before her meeting with Alexis, she'd had Cynthia organize a car to pick them up from the porter in Jean-Paul's block. She'd gone straight from the office to the airport. As much as she'd been tempted to swing by Jean-Paul's to say good-bye, she couldn't cope with seeing anyone, not even him. The only person she wanted to see now was . . . no. That was well and truly over. He would never talk to her now.

She felt like a failure. She felt like a failure for feeling like a failure. Why was she giving up already? They'd said gardening leave, not redundancy, and Elizabeth Geary had categorically refused to accept that Kate could have been in any way responsible for what had happened. Even Alexis had defended Kate's reputation, had extolled the virtues of the work she'd done prior to Surgerygate. (Thankfully they hadn't talked much about Surgerygate itself, for which she had done several things wrong. It was hard to think of anything she'd done right.) But with regard to actually hiring her, Alexis had gone through the correct hiring procedures, read the interview with Trisha, commented on its originality. So once again, it came down to those two little words: *Maidstone Bazaar*. Did they have to matter quite so much?

There were no free chairs, so she positioned her bottom uncomfortably on a broad, ribbed radiator, with her back against one of the vast windows that overlooked the airplanes. The glass felt cold on her shoulders. The sun, that same sun that looked so different in Maidstone, Los Angeles, Rio, and now New York, was setting a pale orange, casting a soft glow over the mishmash of faces gathered before her, easing their features. Earlier, she'd steered past the McDonald's outlet and, in a bid of defiance against global branding, gone for a more upmarket kind of café with a name she'd never heard of for her comfort-food take-away. Her noble gesture had backfired. The plate of nachos and cheese now before her had quickly settled into something re-sembling a plate of vomit. She pushed the unbiodegradable polystyrene container under the radiator, and left it sulking there, praying it would be cleared up before the heating was turned back on.

What a mess. What a mess it all was, with no feasible means of being corrected. All these other travelers looked blissfully removed from messes of any sort. Families, fraternity groups on mass vacations, businesspeople tapping away furiously at their laptops; all innocent of the calamities that had tipped over into Kate's life. Free of all charges, their faces were calm, guiltless, going on with their daily business, oblivious to the turmoil in hers. She scrutinized them, weighed them up. They made her think about beauty and what a strange, indefinable thing it indeed was. What was beauty? Genes, luck, and face creams, and not necessarily in that order.

From her position on the radiator she was in the perfect van-tage point to see all mankind, God's big melting pot, in its various beautiful and ugly guises. Couples, singles, middle ages, young ages. What was it that made everyone so different? A sense of humor or a cute button nose and sparkling blue eyes? Kate had only lived in this strange new beautiful world for a few months—weeks—but what if this was the world you grew up in? Plastic surgery couldn't really buy beauty, just im-provements. It couldn't give you confidence, that innate sense of being that those who were born with beauty, true beauty, seemed to have. Or could it?

Lise was beautiful. Not in the conventional sense. There was much about Lise that was beautiful in a cheesy way—the breasts, the hair, the smile, the big eyes. If Kate were being really cruel, she would say that Lise's beauty had a certain blow-up doll quality about it. But it worked. Lise was beautiful because she was the complete package: fun-loving, hilarious, outrageous, sexy. Lise couldn't be anything other than beautiful. Kate had tried calling her back but she was nowhere to be found. Nor was her mother. She was missing them, for the first time in ages. Perhaps even the first time ever.

According to JK, she was beautiful, too. She still didn't really understand why, but perhaps, like Lise, it was the sum of the parts that made her whole, the fact that she was different from the Barbie dolls in his world, the fact that she could still get drunk and throw up in a fountain or forget to book a blow-dry every once in a while. She remembered writing a story about the great perfumes of the world, one of her few main features in the short time she'd been at *Darling*. Some perfumer, a "nose," had said that it was the dirt in the sea of purity that made a perfume truly beautiful, the putrid-smelling civet among the delicate roses or sensual jasmines. Was it this that made her beautiful? The imperfect in her perfect? Except in her own case, her ratio of perfect to imperfect was more likely to be rigged the other way round: a drop of perfect in a sea of imperfect.

She wasn't brave enough to call JK yet. Didn't know what to say, beyond "sorry." She had wanted to believe he was in the wrong because she hated what he did for a living. Alexis was right: it didn't get much more bigoted than that. He'd actually been sweet with her, sent her a flower, made her feel special. Of course he'd done that to Patty, too, at some point; even if her story had been a complete lie, he must have done that to her while courting her, before it all went wrong. But sending girls flowers hardly made him a monster, did it? And hadn't he championed Kate's "look," accepted that the cloned style of plastic surgery that seemed to prevail in America, in the world, perhaps needed to change, to be more subtle? His eyes. She'd liked his eyes. She remembered how she'd felt before she'd got that note from Aurelie. Alcohol had something to do with it. But she could blame it on the peach Bellinis, the sunshine, the moonlight, the good times, even the boogie, but she knew that wasn't all it was. He had followed her down to the island! She . . . missed him. She pulled out her cell phone. Stared at it. Went to dial his number . . . no. Not yet. She couldn't.

There was, too, the question of Clarissa. The whole time she'd trusted her, thought she'd won her round, got her on-side, the girl was in fact scheming away, trying to get her revenge. Now, perhaps that was a little strong, perhaps Clarissa's master plan wasn't a conscious attempt to wreck her career, but there was definitely something a little fishy going on. She must have known about Petruschka's breasts being fake! And she had been so insistent that Alexis would love the publicity that went with the surgery story. She had been a fool to trust her, a fool to let her fly her to Brazil, getting her out of the way for when the JK story broke. She wondered what Clarissa was doing now, pictured her moving herself back into Kate's desk. But she couldn't blame it all on Clarissa. Had to blame herself for most of it, for all of it. She'd broken some fairly preliminary rules. Not validating her sources, not clearing the job with her editor, not checking her facts! She'd never been so haphazard about a story before! What had happened to her?

She still couldn't believe Petruschka's breasts were fakes.

It was only when she was on the plane that she allowed herself to think about Jean-Paul. What was all that about? He was her respite to all the drama of the last twenty-four hours, her knight in shining armor, her distraction from the mental torture she was inflicting upon herself. She liked him, that was obvious. There was chemistry, an attraction that went beyond insults about cellulite in midnight bars, that transcended previous dalliances with one's boss. But there was something else. Something that had nothing to do with Jean-Paul. She would never have been so daring before; never have asked a man home to dance naked into the early hours; never have taken his hand and led him gently into bed, then once in that bed have made all the moves, dancing around his body long after the music had stopped; never have woken up, kissed him good-bye, jokingly stolen his bottle of Eau Sauvage from his bag and spritzed it all over herself, to carry his smell with her for the rest of the day.

What had given her that extra self-confidence, that self-assuredness? Being an English girl abroad, where no one knew her, where she could reinvent her personality, her sexual personality, certainly went some way to explaining this new daring. Feeling successful, being blissfully ignorant still that she'd messed up big-time on the surgery story definitely helped.

But as much as she hated to admit it to herself, she knew what the difference was, the real difference between Kate *before* and Kate *after*. More than knowing that Jean-Paul found her attractive, she found her thoughts returning to another's face, a face that flashed into her mind every so often, bringing with it feelings she didn't know how to handle. Guilt, restlessness, anxiety, even remorse, and the supreme confidence that came with knowing *he* found her beautiful. If she was to be honest, really honest with herself? All those feelings about Jean-Paul were because she couldn't be with JK. All those things she had done with Jean-Paul were things she had wanted to do with JK. That probably wasn't very nice of her. But it was exciting.

maidstone

beauty note:

Model wears Virgin Upper Class freebie pyjamas; Christian Lou-
boutin leopard open-toe stilettos. *Complexion:* Model's own.
Eyes: Model's own. *Fragrance:* Dior Eau Sauvage pour Homme.

twenty-five

S he could hardly be blamed for hoping that once at home, in the bosom of her diminutive family, she might be offered a little comfort. But as she turned the key in the door and walked into the house, it quickly became apparent that this was not to be the case. After a long taxi ride home—extravagant, but what the hell—she'd hoped to find her mum and a plate of veggie shepherd's pie waiting for her. Instead she found the house strangely quiet, despite her telephoning Darleen to tell her when she'd be back. It was, frankly, almost disobedient of her to be so absent in her daughter's hour of need.

"Mum!" she shouted into the hallway, dropping her bags by her feet. Darleen must have pulled up the carpet on the floor. In its place were shiny parquet wooden tiles, crisscrossing their way down to the kitchen. Was that a bang coming from upstairs? Something being dropped in her mum's bedroom? She

rubbed her eyes. Tired. She hadn't slept a wink on the flight despite the business-class comforts she was becoming frighteningly used to, just when they were most in danger of being taken away. She took her shoes off. She'd flown in her stilettos. With cabs to and from airports, she didn't need trainers anymore. Round toes, leopard print, they had suffered a little from the journey, the pile ruffling up at the heels and toes.

"Mum!" Just in case. Was that laughter? She stopped dead in her tracks, frowned, raising her head up in the direction that she'd thought she'd heard the noise. Nothing.

In the absence of a plate of veggie shepherd's pie, she opted for the next best thing. Two slices of thick-cut Mother's Pride white bread, the kind with no nutritional values attached to it whatsoever. They popped out of the toaster, a joyful salute to her return, their welcoming warmth dissolving the butter into a silky yellow pool that dribbled on her chin in a tender caress. Delicious. She looked out onto the green garden beyond the kitchen sink. There was a new birdhouse, she noticed, a heart-shaped one made with twigs, nailed into the sycamore tree in the corner near the back fence. She used to like climbing that tree. She remembered getting her jeans all dirty and her mum getting all cross. Someone had trailed what looked like a honeysuckle plant around its trunk. The lawn was mown short, the borders clipped neatly, the brown soil making a sharp knife edge to frame the border of lime-pink hydrangeas, her mum's favorite flowers.

She fiddled with the tag of the tea bag, pulling the string away until it dangled over the edge of the mug, toast in the other hand. A splash of milk. Two sugars. A cookbook lay next to the toaster, open at a recipe for Oriental Tofu, Onion, and Mushroom Kebabs. By the time the tea was ready, she needed more toast. It was only when she turned around to wedge two more thick white slices of doughy bread into the toaster that she saw him.

"Morris?!"

The gardener was standing in the doorway, naked. He had a fat belly, skinny legs, and his body was pale in contrast with his sun-battered face. She would have screamed, but for the fact that he looked more frightened than she did. When he turned to run away, she noticed his buttock cheeks were disproportionately small to his beer-barreled torso. They jiggled as he ran. His back was hairy.

"I'm sorry, love!" he shouted, panicked, as he disappeared back down the hallway, then ran up the stairs, his hands clasped to his member, even though the damage had already been done.

Kate shook with laughter. She could hear Morris thudding up the stairs, a door opening and slamming shut, then general chatter and confusion, muffled, indistinct, before the door opened and new footsteps came running in her direction. Her tea sloshed over the edge of the mug as she laughed again, so she sat down at the table with the last remaining scrap of toast. Jet lag had taken the edge off any fear she might have expected to feel at finding the gardener naked in the kitchen. Either Morris was some pervert who took great pleasure in wandering around naked in her house when he was supposed to be outside mowing the lawn, or . . .

"Hello, love, didn't expect you back so soon!" It was her mum now who was standing in the doorway, looking surprisingly fetching in a rose-embellished toweling robe, her hair disheveled in a way that no hair product could have delivered. Her cheeks were glowing, this time not through any broken capillaries or excess of blusher, but excitedly, blissfully. Her lips were a just-bitten red, the kind of red that only happened when you'd had the life kissed out of them. She didn't seem to care that her robe was open to the waist, tied just enough to prevent her bosoms popping out, but not enough to hide from Kate her full, comely figure. Her mum was looking, for a fiftysomething or however old she was . . . her mum was looking, well, hot.

"Mum!" She stood for a second, taking her in. She wanted to tell her how well she was looking, to ask her what the hell the naked gardener was doing, even though it was pretty obvious. She wanted to be calm, cool, collected, tell her about her troubles, ask if she'd been well, talk about the weather. None of these topics of conversation came out of her mouth. Instead, she stood up clumsily, sent her tea flying over the table, pushed the chair out, and scrambled to get to her, to fling her arms around her, to burst into tears.

She tried to wipe them away quickly, tried to be the Kate she thought she was, the strong, silent, independent Kate, who'd taken on a top job in New York, hobnobbed with the rich, famous, and surgically enhanced, gone underground in a bid to unearth a huge US scandal (even if it had all been a hoax). She tried to shrug off the tears, like she'd shrugged off all that was Maidstone: the boredom, the bus to work, Trisha Hillmory, even her mum (her mum!), Lise, Tania, Brian, all of them. Instead, she sniffled against her mum's shoulders, and her tears disappeared into a dozen red toweling roses.

"It's okay, darling . . . you're home now . . . it'll be all right," said her mum. Darleen rubbed her back, like she'd done when Kate was a baby, a toddler, a child, a teenager. It was a smooth, gentle, yet firm stroke, different to any beauty therapist's massage or any boyfriend's caress.

"It's good to have you back, love, we've missed you. Shall we have another cup of tea? Morris came down to make me one, but he's a little . . . shy!" With her head on her shoulder, Kate could just open her eyes enough to see past the fronds of

Darleen's brown hair, and beyond into the garden. A sparrow flew into the new nest.

She lifted her head up, looked into her mum's eyes. Her mum and Morris! How long had that been going on for? She burst out laughing. Her mum giggled back, hugging her until she thought her ribs would crack.

* * *

"I didn't want to tell you, because I wasn't sure at first," said Darleen, speaking softly over her cup of tea, raising her eyes toward the bedroom upstairs in deference to Morris's feelings. "I mean, the truth is, I've been seeing him for some time. But I wasn't ready to, you know, commit. He's nice, though. More intelligent than I had him down for . . . well, you know, being a gardener. He knows about plants obviously, but I thought, if he's digging up gardens, it must be because he's academically, well, you know . . . challenged."

She flicked the hair out of her eyes. You'd pay a lot of money for a blow-dry as ruffled and tussled as that. Her mum had never confided in her like this about anything before. Maybe there hadn't been that much to confide.

"Mum, honestly . . . don't be such a snob! You're not exactly Lady Chatterley! Gardening—it doesn't mean he's an idiot! You can make a lot now as a landscape gardener."

"Oh, he won't do that. He's happy doing what he does, he doesn't need a career or anything silly like that. He speaks Latin! Can you believe it? Knows all the plant names. And he's been looking after me while you've been away."

"I can see . . . ," said Kate, marveling at how wrinkle-free her mum's face was looking. She looked years younger. It was quite extraordinary.

"He's retiled the bathroom for me, isn't that nice? We went down to Homebase—oh, it was ever so funny, Kate, I wish you'd seen us, like some old married couple arguing in the aisles about turquoise mosaics or these new, shiny ones—opal . . . opalescent, that's what they were! Very pretty, though, I think you'll love it."

"Oh, Mum, that's lovely for you. I'm pleased."

"And did you see the hall? All that time, those lovely wooden tiles right under the carpet, can you believe it?"

Kate nodded approvingly.

"I knew you'd like him, love." Darleen looked relieved. They sat silently for a second, sipping their tea at the same time, nestling back into an easy mother-daughter telepathy.

"He's moved in, Kate, do you mind?"

She didn't. She was happy for her mum. It was funny how if she hadn't been away, hadn't been through everything she'd been through, she might have felt differently, might have found it harder to understand how her mum could want to move the gardener of all people into their home. But she didn't mind. Not at all. It actually made her feel happy to know that her mum had someone in her life, finally, after all these years of solitude, with nothing but the odd (really odd) boyfriend to keep her company. She imagined Morris coming with his bags—a couple of suitcases?—and the two of them unpacking together, moving his things in among Darleen's easy-iron blouses and lambswool sweaters like a couple of young lovers. Maybe they used her room as a spare room now, kept his junk there, if he had any.

She reached across the table, covered in the same red plastic gingham cloth they'd had since her childhood, and held her mum's hands. It was a movement that reminded her of JK3 and their first meeting, that interview, where he'd pulled her across the table so dramatically it had cut into her stomach, as if trying to make his mark on her.

"Mum . . . I love you," she said quietly. She couldn't remember the last time she'd told her that.

"I know, love. Me, too."

She looked into Darleen's eyes, big watery pools of love, laughter, and everything that had guided Kate through life so far, that had been a constant for her. She knew it was normal not to appreciate your mum, but it was only at this moment that she understood what she'd missed out on by ignoring her for so long, forgetting she was there for her. Love was doing amazing things for Darleen, evidently. Her skin glowed, her mouth lacked those tired, vertical lines that seemed to pull her face downward, she'd lost that grumpy scowl between her brows. . . .

"Mum." Kate let go of her hands and pulled backward.

"Yes, love?"

Kate pulled her shoulders up straight, staring hard at her mum's face. Something in the way her face moved went way beyond what love could do.

"You've had Botox, haven't you!"

Darleen smiled broadly. Nothing else moved, bar her mouth.

"Yes!" she laughed. "It's great, isn't it?"

Kate couldn't believe she'd done it. Hadn't Kate told her not to? That it would wreck her system, lie in it like a cancer waiting to sprout; that there were side effects just waiting to happen—sure, not the first time, but perhaps the second, third, or fourth time as the addiction spread, as her every six-month habit gripped her in a vise, giving her an ageless future, one in which she would never know, always wonder how she would have looked had she not rubbed it all away with some dirty little needle. She could get eyelid drooping! Head-aches that would leave her bedridden or give her double vision! Some people even worried that a lifetime of Botox could result in a future of Alzheimer's!

"Mum! Botox is a poison. Don't you know that?" She said it

gently, but her concern was written all over her furrowed brow.

"And penicillin's a fungus! My derm told me Botox is only harmful when it's undiluted and in really big doses, and you know they don't give it like that to people for wrinkles." She laughed, patting her face as if to check the Botox was still there.

"Yes, but we eat fungus, certain types anyway, that's a different kettle of fish altogether." She wasn't prepared for her mum of all people to be an expert; and besides, how was it that she suddenly had a "derm"?

"Darling . . . look at me," said her mum, this time taking the initiative to reach across the table and hold Kate's hands. "I'm happy," she said. "For the first time in ages, I feel like I'm living. You know what? When I think about it, really, it's the first time since *he* died that I'm happy!" Her eyes misted up; a tear fell from one, silently down her cheek. Kate reached up to Darleen's face to wipe it away with her finger. "It's not the Botox that makes me happy, I know that. But I feel good about life. I want to live it."

She was right of course. What made Kate think she could judge her, tell her off? What did she know about what it was like to be fiftysomething and single, to feel her spirits sink like damp squibs on an autumn night as one by one the knights in shining armor rode on past, heads turned in the other direction, to where the fireworks were lighting up the sky in a blaze of younger, brighter glory? Besides, Darleen was an adult, wasn't she? Capable of making her own life choices. With access to the same caveats and advice that Kate had, thanks to the Internet, and the sudden omnipresence, even in Maidstone, of "derms." And Kate couldn't argue with her; she looked good.

"Mum, you do what you have to do," she said, smiling gently

at her. They lifted their hands away from each other and took another sip of tea. "But not too often, right? Please. You never know what the long-term side effects will be."

"Oh, don't worry. I don't want one of those weird, frozen faces, like that newscaster woman you did once. Trisha. Have you seen her lately? My derm says she'd never have given her that much!"

"How did you know she'd had Botox?"

"Oh, everyone knows!" She took another sip of her tea. "She left a message for you, by the way."

"Oh." She didn't know what was weirder: Trisha Hillmory calling her, or her mum having had Botox.

Morris padded into the kitchen. He had on a checkered lumberjack-style cotton shirt and a pair of faded blue denims, the kind old men wear, with a thick brown belt with a silver buckle. The whole ensemble made him look like a cuddly country-and-western singer, now retired.

"Hello, Kate," he said, smiling awkwardly at her. "Good to have you home. Sorry about before. . . ."

They put their mugs down, and Darleen stood up, in a way that was almost respectful, his entrance propelling her subconsciously toward him.

"Cup of tea, sweetheart?" she said. It was the first time Kate had ever heard her mum call anyone sweetheart.

He nodded and looked for a chair to sit down on. They'd only ever had two chairs in the kitchen; the other four had got in the way and now stood like guards around the edge of the unused dining room next door, spares for any surprise guests.

"Here, Morris, take mine," said Kate, getting up abruptly.

He looked surprised, touched even.

"Oh, no, love. Wouldn't dream of it. Not after your long journey." He smiled again, still awkwardly, then his face turned more serious.

"Did you tell her, Darleen?" Kate noticed that he almost whispered her name, as if it was precious to him. She liked that. He would take care of her mum. Cherish her.

"About us, dear? Oh, yes!" Darleen moved over to him and put her arm around his waist.

"No, love. That's not what I meant." He looked into her eyes, his voice fell until it was barely audible, then his eyes turned to meet Kate's. "Lise."

twenty-six

L ise had breast cancer. Steve had discovered a lump in her right breast, the size of a small pebble, and insisted she go straight to the hospital for tests. She'd been frightened to go, terrified, something inside her warning against the dangers of discovery. She'd been desperate to let Kate know, but desperate at the same time to protect her. And she wanted to tell her herself. No one else was allowed to, they could only urge her to contact Lise, if they got the chance. With Kate dashing around here, there, and everywhere, that had been impossible. So two weeks or so ago, Lise had had her right breast removed, and after a short spell in the hospital, she was now recuperating at home until the surgeons decided what the next course of action was.

They drove in silence round to Lise's flat, Morris at the wheel, Darleen beside him, Kate in the back. She had cried the instant her mum had broken the news to her, felt panic rising furiously and steadily until she was at the point she found herself now: numb.

She should have listened more. Lise had tried a few times, told her she had something important to say. Kate could have called her back. She shouldn't have dismissed her so readily, so self-importantly, assumed she was so busy shagging Steve that nothing else was happening in her life. All the while Kate had been racing round America, concerning herself with trivial, dumb, stupid, beauty things (plastic surgery, for God's sake!), tumors had been trying to take over Lise's beautiful, fit body, sending messages from one cell to the next, taking her over, spinning her mind out of control and sending her into some sad, black hole. Kate should have been there for that.

She gazed out of the window at street after street of suburban bliss. Lights, flickering TV screens, cars parked in driveways; she envied the normality of these warm, inviting homes where people didn't appear to suffer illnesses that threatened to take them away from each other.

Lise was lying in bed propped up by enough downy pillows to feather several flocks of geese. She smiled as soon as she saw Kate and went to lift her arms to welcome her, but before she'd raised them very high, she had to rest them back on the pillows.

"Hopeless! But I've got Tenzin coming round in a few weeks, the martial arts guy from the gym. He's going to get the strength back in my arms and shoulders really soon, he promises!"

She looked the same. Not exactly the same. Her blonde hair looked dull at the roots, as if it needed a wash. She was wearing one of Steve's shirts. Kate could just see the traces of a cotton camisole where before there would have been a push-up bra, her smooth décolleté on show. She wondered what it would look like now, underneath. Dreaded to think.

"Lise . . . I'm . . . I'm so . . ."

"Don't even say it!" They looked at each other, Kate sitting on her bed as close as she could get to Lise without squashing her. Their eyes welled up. Seeeing each other trying so hard not to cry made them giggle.

"Don't!" said Lise. "It hurts!" She clutched her chest. That made them laugh even more.

Steve rushed over to the bed and took Lise's hand.

"Take it easy, babe, it's not that funny!" He looked at Kate, smiled at her, but his eyes were sad. "Go easy on her with those jokes!" He let go of Lise's hand. "I'll get some takeaway for everyone, shall I? Couple of pizzas suit everyone?" He nodded his head toward the door, and Morris and Darleen obediently took their cue.

"We'll come and help you, love. The car's out the front," said Darleen. They had stayed standing near the door, jackets still on. Kate was suddenly aware how small Lise's studio was. Steve grabbed his wallet and keys from the sink area of the kitchenette, and they filed out.

There was silence for a minute, the kind of comfortable silence shared only by friends and lovers, while they looked at each other, as if taking in everything that had happened.

"He's living with me now," said Lise, her face suddenly glowing like a small child's opening her presents on Christmas Day. "Left his wife. For me, can you believe it?" Kate was impressed and shocked at the same time. She tried not to look upset, but all those children Steve had! She fought the urge to judge once again, but it concerned her, even though she knew Lise was sick and needed Steve, probably even more than the wife did right now.

"Look, I know you don't like him," Lise continued. "But it's not like you think it is. Well, some of it is." She twisted a ring on her finger, her old ruby ring, looked down at her nails. They were painted impeccably, a dark red.

"It was pretty awful for him. He found out all sorts of stuff. His wife had been cheating on him with someone who used to work at his bank! You know, I never really asked him about his marriage. All that time we were dating, I just assumed . . . well, that it wasn't my business. That it wasn't right to pry. But actually, he was really unhappy."

"His wife didn't understand him?" asked Kate, the cheek returning to her smile.

"No, not like that. Well, I suppose that was what I was expecting, which is why I didn't ask." Her eyes looked downward. She fiddled with the ridged hem of the duvet cover as if it fascinated her. "He's been amazing, Kate. I couldn't have done it without him."

She hadn't said it to hurt Kate, but it hammered their disconnection home. Kate was no more the confidante, the best friend. She'd been replaced by Steve. And that was fine. The way it had to be. But she wished she could have been a better number two, if nothing else.

Lise gripped Kate's hand tightly.

"I'm . . . I'm so glad to have you here. It's been awful, Kate, really awful." A tear fell down her cheek, the right cheek. It led to that right breast, now mutilated, amputated, gone.

Kate reached over to hug her. It was an awkward embrace, physically constrained by the fear of hurting Lise. Their cheeks touched, they held each other fondly, didn't let go for what seemed like ages.

"How are you feeling?" It was a pretty stupid question in the circumstances, but Kate really did want to know.

"Oh . . . pretty bad!" She gulped. "If I'm to be honest." She sighed, looked away from Kate, fiddled with the duvet cover again. A shadow passed over her face; the brightness was gone. "The worst bit was when the doctor"—she gulped again—"he cut my bandages off. He left the room so I could see what it looked like . . . where they'd removed it. It was just . . ." She couldn't finish her sentence. Tears poured down her face, she couldn't hold them back. Kate held her closely, carefully, gently. She kissed her forehead and cried softly. She held her in her arms and rocked her gently from side to side. "It was so frightening!"

"Look, I'm here now. I can stay longer if you want. Whatever you have to—I mean, if you have to have chemo or radiation or whatever . . ."

Lise raised one finger to her mouth, gently silencing Kate.

"It's okay, really. They are fairly positive I won't need it," she said. When her smile returned, it was the practiced smile of those who knew they had to put on a brave face when explaining this next bit. "They think my chances are good, very good, and that they've cut out the little buggers. And they reckon I can have a boob job, imagine that! A boob job free on the National Health Service! I'm thinking blow it all up, go big, DD, or maybe EE cup, what do you reckon?" Her laughter suddenly changed midsentence to a bitter sobbing. She could hide her pain from her work colleagues, even her family, but not from Steve, mused Kate, nor from herself. She hugged her as close as she dared.

"I shouldn't cry about it, it's so stupid!" she said. "But I liked them! I know I've got my life, I should be grateful, but how can I be grateful when I look like this!" Kate let her talk. She could feel where the bandage stopped and started under Steve's shirt, feel her chest moving in and out as she sobbed, feel where one mound protruded, and where one didn't.

"Steve"—Lise sniffled—"Steve . . . says . . . it'll be okay. We'll be okay. But what if he's wrong? And what if, you know, what if Steve goes off me? I'm damaged goods now, aren't I?"

"Lise, Steve's right," said Kate. "He's not going to go off you. It'll be okay." But what if it wasn't? She didn't know if it would be okay, nor who, right now, could make that promise.

She noticed a picture by the side of the bed. It was a Polaroid of Lise, naked from the waist up. She wasn't smiling, and she wasn't posing sexily for the camera, just lying on the bed, staring into the lens, her expression composed more than defiant.

"We took that just before I went in," she said, her eyes following Kate's gaze.

*   *   *

The rest of Kate's week in Maidstone disappeared in a controlled blur of rest, and concern over Lise's rehabilitation. Steve took advantage of her presence to put in a few days at the bank and spend some much-needed time with his kids. Kate moved into Lise's flat, spending her days running errands for her or just hanging out; and the nights curled up in her bed with her. It wasn't that Lise needed someone with her all day long—she was as fiercely independent as ever and desperate to get her fitness back. But the two enjoyed hanging out together. Their time now was suddenly precious, limited by Kate's ominous return, limited more ominously still by Lise's brush with death. Kate entertained Lise with stories, of drunken parties with handsome surgeons, or nights out in Brooklyn with her French artist. She left out the work dramas. There was no point. She knew Lise would be upset for her, and she wanted to spare her any unnecessary stress.

The day before she was due to leave, she announced out loud, to no one in particular, "I'm not going back."

They'd been watching movies. Lise had given Kate a strict brief on what to get from Blockbuster, after Kate had unwittingly dug out an old Danny Huston movie in which the hero died an untimely, painful death from cancer. Only comedy films were allowed from now on. She'd chosen *Zoolander*, and they'd laughed their way until the middle bit, where Lise complained her ribs were hurting and she needed to pee, and could

Kate make her a cup of tea? Like a hypnotist's trigger, the flick of the kettle switch reminded Kate of the time she'd called Lise from JK's office. The stress of knowing she had unresolved business with JK, and with Jean-Paul, but mostly with Alexis, coupled with the horror of what she'd missed with Lise, by not being there for her, filled her with dread. Her stomach felt tight, like she'd felt before starting school each term.

"What did you say?" said Lise, emerging from the bathroom. She'd complained the worst bit about the surgery was the constipation as a result of the anesthetic, so they'd given her pills. These seemed to make things worse. Her trips to the bathroom were more frequent, coupled with long descriptions, information Kate really didn't need to know but accepted as being important to take Lise's mind off other more pressing aches and pains.

"Nothing," said Kate.

"Rubbish," said Lise. "You said you weren't going back. That's something." She settled tentatively on the bed. Usually it was folded up into a sofa bed by day, but they hadn't bothered. They preferred to sit in track bottoms, Lise still with her many pillows around her.

"You have to go back, you know." She munched on a Dorito. It broke in pieces, crumbs flying into the bed. Kate would have to do a big sweep later.

"You have to go back. Number one, it's your job, and that's what you've always wanted, whatever problems you're having with your editor."

"How did you—?" Kate interrupted.

"Never mind how I know, I just know. You're a professional; I'm not, but you are. You can figure out the office politics—you're smart like that."

Her mum must have told her.

"Two, you have a boyfriend. Maybe two boyfriends! I mean,

how long did it take you to learn how much fun life can be?!
And three, if I can just continue for a minute, assuming you're
worried about me, don't be. I can worry enough about me.
And I'll be fine . . . shh!" Kate went to interrupt, but Lise was
on a roll. "I've got Steve, and New York is just a short flight
away; if you need to come back, I'll call, I promise! And I don't
think you will need to. So don't even think about it. It's decided."

Kate placed the mug of tea by Lise's bedside and walked
around to the other side with her mug. There wasn't much
point arguing. She knew Lise was right. The irony was that Lise
had always known how much fun life could be. It was Kate
who hadn't. If cancer was supposed to make you rethink your
life, then they'd booked it in with the wrong patient. It was
Kate who had to learn how to live, had started to do just that.
She had to go back. She had to resolve her business with JK,
hand in her article to Alexis. There was no other way.

twenty-seven

Later that same day, Kate returned home to pack. This time as she opened the door, she heard a familiar voice talking to her mum. She instantly recognized the saccharine sweet, somewhat patronizing, and insincere tone as belonging to none other than Trisha Hillmory.

What now?

She couldn't have been here long. A whiff of Thierry Mugler's Angel lingered in the hallway. Sweet, cloying, poisonous, and instantly identifiable, whether you were among thousands in a shopping center or cast adrift on an ocean.

She eavesdropped for a second as she approached the kitchen.

"Oh, I have missed her," Darleen was saying, "but I'm so proud of her, going out there on her own like that. I'd never have been as adventurous at her age."

"Really?" said Trisha. "I'm sure you would!" They laughed, inappropriately, or so Kate thought. How could Trisha have known how adventurous her mum was or wasn't at Kate's age? Idiot woman.

No putting it off. She noticed her mum had moved some of the dining room chairs back in.

"Trisha!" Kate announced, standing tall in the doorway. She'd left the track bottoms at Lise's and was wearing a pair of skinny black jeans, with an asymmetric black top. It hung loosely, artistically, over one shoulder, while the other side clung below her arm, giving a gentle silhouette where bosoms, even nonexistent ones, were only subtly alluded to. Her wedge boots had a round toe. Lise had gone around the edge of her eyes with a black kohl eye pencil. She liked to think the final result was a cross between a French fashion editor and Chrissie Hynde from the Pretenders.

"It's so great to see you!" That was one thing that working in a magazine had taught her: how to gush a greeting. No one seemed to care if it sounded insincere. The point was that it was made, with enthusiasm, however real or fake. She topped it off with a couple of expertly applied air kisses. Darleen looked at her doubtfully; Trisha was clearly impressed.

"Wow! Look at you!"

Kate smiled at her, but it was a halfhearted smile. She didn't know how she felt about seeing Trisha in her kitchen with her mum. She put her hand up to her cheek, as if to feel the graze where Trisha's shoe had fallen, the incident that had started off this whole thing in the first place. Trisha had slept her way to the top, then dumped the man who'd put her there. She was a clever girl; she hadn't needed to do that. Kate might have notched up a couple of glaring errors recently, but at least she had never done that.

"So, what brings you here, Trish?"

Trisha beamed, that same beam she'd seen a million times at the end of each news item, announcing the serious story with a humorous twist, the "and finally" moment where the viewer could relax and think that all was well with the world because a family of ducks had held up the traffic in Tokyo for an hour, or a cat had survived the spin cycle of a washing machine.

"Well, in a funny way, I owe it all to you, Kate!"

She hadn't expected gratitude from Trisha of all people.

"Well, not all to you. Obviously years of experience, my qualifications, my unique personality—coupled with my sense of fun, which gives me the confidence needed to appear on reality TV shows, and thus gain popular appeal and notoriety—has a lot to do with it too, but . . ." She hammered out each word slowly and earnestly, then giggled, nervously. That wasn't like her. Kate realized with some degree of satisfaction that Trisha was actually nervous around her.

"Well, as I was saying," she continued, "things have changed in the last couple of months or so, since you wrote that story about me. That awful man I was seeing, Donald Truckell, well, I started seeing the director-general of the BBC and Donald didn't like that so he outed me to one of the Sundays. Can you believe it? I mean, nobody knew, and what harm did it do?"

Darleen's eyes looked as if they were about to pop out of her face. It was a relief to see that she could still make such expressions. Kate wondered if the Botox was preventing them from popping out altogether.

"But all's well that ends well. The dog had to resign. His bitch of a wife kicked up such a fuss, such a shame! Anyway, they gave me a new job, anchorwoman for BBC World News, so now I'm, well . . . worldwide, which is great." A sudden wave of anger flashed across her face before the screen returned to normal. "Oh, all right, being taken off national news and put to that late-night news show that people only see in hotels might be perceived by some to be a somewhat lateral career move, but it could have been worse! People watch me all over the world, can you believe that?"

Kate stared at her blankly.

"And, well, obviously, I saw your story on CNN. It's fantastic, Kate, a real rags-to-riches type of piece, and as a Maidstone girl, I really think you owe it to your community to let yourself be interviewed by me for tomorrow morning's show. So that's why I'm here!"

"Rags to riches?"

"I want the exclusive, Kate. We'll send a car to take you to our London studios, and"—she said London as if Kate had never set foot out of town before—"and obviously there's a fee to cover your expenses. The interview shouldn't take more than an hour. And it's great exposure!"

"A fee?" Suddenly she had an idea, a way to make this work for herself. "How much?"

"Five thousand pounds. We don't usually pay anything, but . . . I'm funding this one myself." Trisha assumed a puppy dog pose, her eyes widened, and for a split second Kate thought they were actually welling with tears. "Please, Kate, I really need this break!"

"Trisha, I'm wary of the press." She sat down on the third chair and motioned to Trisha to sit down, too. She hastily did as she was told, smoothing out the creases in her dogstooth check jacket. It looked cheap; the buttons were a nasty black plastic. Perhaps doing the graveyard shifts at the BBC was taking its toll. Her hairstyle had changed subtly, with more wings around her face, and her eyebrows were arched and rigid, as if she was surprised, permanently. "You know how it is, Trisha. By the way, I've never known, am I calling you Trish, or Trisha?"

"Oh, whatever you prefer!" Trisha smiled, enthusiastic, needy.

"You see, in my experience," continued Kate, "they'll promise you anything, promise you a bleeding trip to the Bahamas, a Balenciaga, anything to get their story." Trisha looked pained. She fidgeted uncomfortably.

"So we'll do it my way. Make it ten grand. Cash on the day, please. And I want the car to take me straight on to Heathrow in time for my flight. Okay?"

"Oh, that's just great! Thank you so much!" Trisha jumped up from her seat and clapped her hands gleefully. Darleen looked at her with a worried expression on her face. Even she could see the woman was unhinged.

"I'm sorry, but I have to go now. Call me to let me know what time the car's coming, won't you?" Kate stood up, shook Trisha's hand, and left the room. She walked upstairs to her bedroom.

She could hear her mum showing Trisha out.

"Well, that went well, didn't it?" Darleen said, politely, patiently holding the front door open. She was wearing a pair of gold mules and a Juicy Couture look-alike tracksuit. Kate realized her mum had taken the week off to spend with her. In the circumstances, she'd been very understanding about hardly having seen her. She knew Lise would have to take priority for now.

"Oh, yes, I'm so, so happy. We'll look after her tomorrow, Mrs. Miller, or can I call you Darleen? Do you think Kate will be donating the money to a charity?"

"I haven't the foggiest, dear."

The front door clicked shut.

Kate looked around her bedroom, aware that soon she would be leaving it again, that the room that had for so long been her sanctuary, her den, was no longer needed. Posters on the walls—of the Greenpeace ship *Rainbow Warrior*, a Flaming Lips tour that she'd never managed to afford tickets for, Bowie's

Ziggy Stardust album cover—spoke volumes to her of another lifetime. There was a brown wicker chair in the corner, upright, stiff-looking, that Darleen had half attempted to restore following a few stints at an evening course in basket weaving and wickerwork. It was this chair that Kate pulled out now, dragging it in front of her desk. Piles of unopened mail sat on the right; bank statements she'd not bothered asking to be sent on, knowing her salary was to be paid into her new American account; a couple of good luck cards from Tania and Lianne at the office. Briefly she thought of them, wondered when she'd see them next. Hopefully not too long. But was that correct? Did she really hope it wouldn't be too long, or was that just some platitude people said to not feel so bad about not missing others? She opened each one, her fingers bluntly shuffling through the fold at the top of the envelope.

Don't forget us! wrote Tania. *Because we won't forget you!*

She had forgotten them. Hadn't made any effort to keep in touch, and had barely thought of them. They'd been there for her. Working at *Maidstone Bazaar* hadn't been awe-inspiring, the offices were by definition parochial, the work sometimes ridiculous, but it hadn't been such an awful place, had it? The people were nice, lovely, brilliant. Even Brian had his good points.

She sat down, reached for the phone. All was clear in her head now.

There was work to be done.

twenty-eight

It was interesting, Kate mused as she stood by the window of her bedroom looking out onto the street, how little sleep one needed when the fires of adrenaline burned so vehemently inside. The brown light of dawn was starting to push away the blackness from the streets, easing the eye gently into another day. It was 5:00 a.m. She'd seen the whole night through, been its companion from dusk until dawn as she sat by her laptop, made calls, found answers to questions she needed answering from the Internet, and even handwrote cards to Tania and Lianne at her old office. Everything was set. She could hear her mum downstairs making cups of tea, three. She'd filled her in on what she planned to do, and Darleen had stared at her flabbergasted, shocked at her daughter's sudden confidence in transatlantic travel arrangements.

The car would be here in thirty minutes, just enough time to do a quick reread of the most important article she had ever

written in her life. Funny that; she'd thought her original article, the one that had got her into all this trouble in the first
place, about Patty, was the most important article. But this
one, this one had to do a lot of things, answer a lot of questions, explain a lot of truths, and, most importantly, answer
questions of her own.

"Some Kind of Beautiful" she'd called it. Which it was. An
essay about the rights and wrongs of plastic surgery, and
whether that was still a question worth asking today. She found
herself coming back time after time to that very definition of
beauty that Alexis had challenged her with way back when.
She hadn't been able to answer that question then; was she any
closer to answering now? What was beauty?

As if searching for answers, she looked into the mirror,
studying her reflection as she had all those months ago when
she'd first got the call from Alexis. Her views had changed,
even her looks had changed, but was she was still searching
for answers, or did she have them, somewhere inside? She sat
down at her desk again, looking at the article. So . . . what
was beauty?

For Trisha Hillmory and every other insecure woman in
the world, it was about conforming to a look, an idyll of
beauty that they would never in their own eyes achieve. For
her mum, it was about being in love, having great sex with
someone who loved her. It was about enjoying her face, defy-
ing age in a spirited, life-affirming way. For Jean-Paul, it was
about his art, about creating something that made him stand
out from the crowd. For the children who JK worked with, for
the children Paracato had worked with, it was about getting
through life without being teased, hurt. Self-preservation. For
JK himself it was about taking pride in his work, beauty as a
means to an end.

For Lise, beauty was life itself.

And for Kate?

She pulled down a photo album from a dusty shelf above the desk. When you were an only child, the pictures tended to be all of one person. You. There she was, gawky, funny, cute, as a child. Her nose was a button nose, her tummy, even then, a little potbellied. She wondered if JK would have found her beautiful then. She knew the answer to that one. He loved children. Three pages on, there she was a few years older, tiny breasts forming lumps in her T-shirt, breasts she'd been embarrassed about, breasts that had grown into only slightly bigger lumps in her T-shirt that she was still embarrassed about. Would she have them surgically enhanced if she could? Like Petruschka's? Maybe not now . . . but maybe one day?

She was still in the skinny black jeans she'd worn all day. She looked cool, she thought to herself, if not beautiful, then, a woman finally in charge of her look, not afraid of it anymore.

Her eyes scanned down the page of her finished article. Paragraph three. She'd reflected on Naomi Wolf's polemic "The Beauty Myth." Published in 1991. Had she been too controversial in suggesting that it was time to move on from this position? That in the early '90s, being a feminist just as surgery was gaining popularity was understandably a frightening time for women. She'd wanted to interview her on the subject but hadn't had time. But she couldn't help thinking that yes, women had moved on since then, and what was the difference between highlights, makeup, a decent moisturizer, and what we did now in the name of beauty—having a few little injections every so often to preserve our youth?

Had Kate's views changed that much since she had arrived in New York? She still didn't feel comfortable with surgery, or injectables. She knew Botox wasn't for her. She was convinced they still didn't know enough about it. And besides, if coffee was a toxin, something you weren't supposed to drink because toxins might lead to cancer, what the hell was Botox? But Botox was right for some women, making them feel confident, happy about their looks and their lives, in the same way that her skinny black jeans made Kate feel now. The one thing that told her was that she didn't have the right to judge. So, she didn't care if she grew into some ancient craggy rock of a woman. But some women did care, did worry, and okay, sometimes, often in fact, they took it too far, but who was to say what other demons they faced in their lives?

She opened up her laptop one more time. There was something else she needed to add. Something about Lise. She felt her eyes filling with tears and as they rolled down her face, she started to type furiously. Fury was a force to be reckoned with, she thought to herself, and it really was fury she was feeling. Why had cancer happened to Lise? Why?

The paragraph fit neatly at the end, after the bit about bad-looking surgery and women looking like Barbie dolls. It needed this ending, needed something personal. After all, what was more personal than cosmetic surgery?

She wrote:

What I realized as I saw my friend Lise and her bandaged chest, what I appreciated for the first time as my mother looked at me without scowling, is that it's me, and those women like me, who have become narrow-minded bigots.

Was that too harsh? Not really. She continued:

Lise and my mum have shown me that life is for living. Now. It's bigger than the rights and wrongs, the blacks and whites of whether or not surgery is ethically, morally, or feministically speaking good or bad. Who are we to say that one person's suffering is better or worse than another's? That the woman who has always hated her nose is no more or less a person than the woman who wants facial reconstruction following a car crash?

She stood up again, looked out of the window. Her neighbor's cat prowled around the bottom of their oak tree, chasing after a bird, then gave up, sat down, and started licking itself. Like Paracato had said, even animals lick themselves clean. Even animals take a pride in their appearance.

The last sentence. It came. Like it always did when she needed it most.

The whole point about beauty, the answer to the question "What is beauty?" is this: beauty is life itself. So if it makes you feel better, do it.

Kate shut her computer down. Satisfied. She took one last look around her little room and gathered her bags to take them downstairs, her precious laptop clutched under one arm. Her eyes were red, but it was nothing she couldn't fix with a couple of eyedrops and some YSL Touche Eclat in the shadowy hollows underneath.

"Kate, love!" her mum shouted up the stairs in a loud whisper.

"Coming!" She patted her hand over her handbag, confirming her passport was in there. She'd made her bed, filed her mail. She dragged her bag down the stairs, the wheels leaving tracks in the carpet which her mum would no doubt gratefully vacuum away later in the day, glad to have the chance to be a mum again.

"You all set, darling?" said Darleen. She hugged her. "No more thoughts as to when you'll be back?" She held her arms and looked hopefully into Kate's eyes. She looked so happy, so fulfilled, even though Kate knew she was sad at her departure.

"No, Mum, can't say yet. But I'll let you know. Maybe you and Morris could . . . well, I'll let you know." She knew exactly when she'd be back, but it depended on a few important things falling into place.

Darleen picked up her mug of tea from the counter. KATE was emblazoned on it in bold red letters. It had been the mug she'd used at *Maidstone Bazaar*, a Christmas party gift from Brian, who'd had a fit of generosity after a circulation increase.

"Love, I don't want you to think . . ." Darleen looked worried. "I mean, I know Morris is living here now, but your room is still your room. I'm—we're expecting you back."

"I know. Thanks, Mum."

The doorbell rang. You never got to drink those last-minute cups of tea, she thought to herself. You knew you'd never get to drink them, but you still made them, still ceremoniously poured them: the good-bye mug.

twenty-nine

It was simple enough. She would look into the camera with the red bulb on the top, and keep her eyes fixed on that camera, until the light moved to another camera, when she would move her eyes to look in that one instead. The problem was that in practice, when Trisha was actually speaking to her, it felt rude and strange to be looking at a red bulb instead of at Trisha. She was aware her eyes were dancing nervously between Trisha and the camera, Wimbledon-spectator style. They'd stuck a wire with a mike up her front which clipped onto the lapel of her black silk shirt and caused the lapel to hang down loosely like some wilted flower with a too-big head. Her trousers, which had looked fine when she'd put them on before the mirror this morning, stretched uncomfortably tightly over her thighs now that she was seated upright and uptight on the sofa.

This was Trisha's territory. She could see the woman positively dazzle now that she had the cameras, the lights, the makeup, the hair, the Chanel-style suit. She had bounced into the greenroom and pressed an envelope into her hand, bulging with what could only be cash.

"Kate, I'm so grateful. Honestly, it's a big deal . . . you don't know how much—"

"Thanks." Kate smoothly put the money into the large leather handbag studded with hardware at her feet. It was spent already, in her head, down to the last penny. She waited until Trisha had left the room, then, when no one was looking, reached back into the bag, peeled off a grand in notes, and folded them neatly into her trouser pocket. She rummaged again in her bag and pulled out a small piece of paper, folded, and tucked that in her pocket, too.

Once on set, she felt hot and sweaty, her palms doing their own thing, cold and sweaty. Suddenly they were starting. Music, cheery, with a news-heavy bass adding a little drama to the day-time tones, piped them on board, then the numbers appeared on the monitor, counting them in . . . . three . . . two . . . one—

TRISHA HILLMORY: Hello. Today I am thrilled to have with me in the studio the girl who's been causing a sensation in the States with her new approach to beauty, and an old personal friend of mine, Kate Miller.

KATE MILLER: (*Oh, Trisha. You'll never learn, will you?*) Hello.

TRISHA: So, Kate, would you like to tell us what's been happening Stateside? A report on CNN last week—can we show that to the viewers?—revealed that you have in fact been inspiring plastic surgeons to completely change their outlook on aesthetic surgery today.

KATE: Trisha, that's something of an exaggeration. One surgeon, John Kingsley the Third, said at a—

TRISHA: (*she held up a hand to silence Kate*) Great. (*she turned to the camera*) That's great, we're going now to the CNN report that first brought this to our attention. . . .

Kate used the video playback opportunity to slick back the flicky bit of hair that kept tickling her eyebrows, thanks to the hairdresser attacking her in the dressing room with a pair of overzealous straightening irons. A fluffy, tapping noise blared out loudly as her fingers grazed the mike, until the soundman came rushing over and crossly readjusted it. As the report ended, Trisha resumed.

TRISHA: Now, of course, Kate, you were, before you went to the States, something of a rookie reporter, weren't you? Working on a local paper.

KATE: Yes, that's right, Trish. *Maidstone Bazaar.* We have a circulation of—

TRISHA: And I gather it was thanks to an interview with me, during which you allowed me to painfully air the story of my breakup with media guru Donald Truckell, that you landed a prime job in New York, am I right?

KATE: No. It was more to do with the fact that the lazy PA to the editor over there didn't check her facts.

TRISHA: (*laughter*) Oh! You're just the funniest! But seriously, what was it like, moving first to New York, then going to Los Angeles and being thrown into this strange world where beauty really is paramount, and at any cost.

KATE: (*Is that the best you can do, Trisha?*) It was great. Really great. And that's what I want to clear up, if I may, Trisha.

TRISHA: Clear up?

KATE: Yes, you see, I got it all wrong.

TRISHA: (*laughter, this time nervous*) Well, let's see, you ended up on prime-time TV on the biggest national news channel in America. How could that be wrong?

KATE: No, not that bit. Well, actually that had nothing really to do with me, more to do with JK.

Trisha looked confused. For once she appeared to be actually listening. For a moment, Kate was aware that the eyes of the studio, the camera people, the sound guys, the hair and makeup people standing patiently in the wings . . . the same eyes that had been on her since she'd sat on the sofa were now on her in a different way, as if sensing one of those intense moments in television when something might be said that actually meant something. An air of expectation hung heavily around them.

TRISHA: Go on, Kate.

KATE: It's not as simple as it seems.

TRISHA: What do you mean, Kate?

KATE: I arrived in L.A. determined to hate what I was going to find. That's not easy for me to say, because as a journalist, I'm supposed to be objective.

TRISHA: Inexperienced journalist, perhaps?

KATE: (*Thanks, Trish.*) Possibly. Yes, definitely. But even setting that aside, as a human being, I came already prepared to hate, to dislike, to frown upon whatever it was I was going to find, before I found it.

TRISHA: Plastic surgery, you mean? But most of us would agree that plastic surgery is all right for celebrities, but for normal people, surely it's wrong?

KATE: Look at it another way. I mean, you've had Botox—sorry, I know you won't thank me for saying that, but it's true. You dye your hair. . . .

Trisha looked around frantically as if trying to call Security. Kate, unphased, continued.

KATE: I don't know, you probably go to a gym, do Pilates, who knows, who cares? The point is, we all do something to make ourselves look better. We all need to do that. It's human nature. And now that science, medicine rather, can offer us real ways of looking good, who are we to judge those who want cosmetic surgery, or even those who operate on others?

TRISHA: I don't understand, are you saying that you think surgery is a good thing?

KATE: I'm saying it's not for me to judge. And that's where I went wrong. I judged. I was ready to believe in the malicious machinations of a woman who was truly bonkers, who had plotted against the one surgeon who was genuinely extolling the virtues of a newer, natural approach to surgery. Why would I believe her over him? Because in my head already, I'd figured out that surgery was bad; she must therefore be good. Life's not that simple.

TRISHA: You're referring of course to the libellous claims of his ex-girlfriend, Patty Patrice.

KATE: Well, ironically, Patty Patrice was the one who changed the way I thought about surgery. Inadvertently.

TRISHA: So it's thanks to Patty that you now think surgery is a good thing, basically?

KATE: It's an "okay" thing. Don't get me wrong—it can be awful. I've seen faces on women that are so far removed from natural that I wonder what they were thinking of, what their surgeons were thinking of. And of course, there comes a point where self-esteem is elevated to such a degree it becomes plain old vanity, and that's not good for the soul. But I've also seen breasts on a model that defy anyone to identify them as fakes.

TRISHA: Are you thinking of any celebrities in particular who
have done this?

KATE: I wouldn't want to say. They're happy with the way they
look. But there are other uses for cosmetic surgery, which go
beyond having a bumpy nose straightened out or a few
wrinkles smoothed away. Breast reconstruction after a mas-
tectomy, for example. Or cases where a person's self-esteem
has been so eroded over the years by a lack of confidence in
the way they look, that it can really change their lives.
What's wrong with that?

TRISHA: And you feel that you got this surgeon . . . (*she looked
down at her notes to check his name*) John Kingsley the
Third—that you got him wrong.

KATE: Very wrong. He's not judgmental. He takes everyone at
face value. He spends a lot of his free time working in Brazil,
looking after children who are born with deformed faces but
whose families are so poor they can't afford to fix them. It's
not something he ever publicizes—in fact, I know he only
wanted to talk to me at all because the hospital was in need
of more funds—but I think it's important that people
understand that some surgeons get a bad rap they don't
deserve. He was nothing but gracious to me, the whole time
I was there. Sure, like all surgeons, he can be a bit, you
know, ostentatious, rock-starry. But for me to arrive and
judge him like that . . . I was prepared to write about him in
a way that would have ruined his career, and all for my own
hang-ups about the way I look, hang-ups about the way I
think others should look. And that's not right, Trisha.

Trisha looked blankly at Kate. She had no idea what to follow this confessional with. She had been expecting to talk in a
loose, friendly way about what beauty meant to the beholder.
She had a line earmarked to throw in at an appropriate opening,

about beauty coming from within, which she was particularly proud of.

TRISHA: And presumably, what is right, Kate, is his claiming that you are a role model for today's look?

KATE: Well, I think what JK means is that there is a culture among women to look overgroomed, overperfect, if there's such a thing. You know, the perfect blow-dry, manicure, the wrinkle-free complexion, the straight nose . . . (*She realized as she was talking that this was in fact the very look Trisha was sporting.*) Even supremely beautiful women keep messing around with themselves, getting face-lifts, Botox, chemical peels, fillers, fixers, neck lifts, lipo, tummy tucks, things that we don't need, in pursuit of an ideal that the more steps they take toward it, the further away they are from reaching it. But at some stage as an adult you have to face up to aging. And JK's argument is that a little more of a natural approach is not only healthier, but it makes you look younger, more beautiful, too.

TRISHA: In other words: beauty comes from within. (*She smiled, triumphantly.*) Well, thanks very much, Kate, I think this chat has been very illuminating.

KATE: Thank you. Actually, if I could just say one more thing, quickly, Trisha, I want to say sorry, to JK. Sorry for being so quick to judge. Sorry for . . . everything. (*Trisha looked embarrassed. She laughed it off.*)

TRISHA: Of course! That's just great! Well, thank you, Kate Miller. And now we're going to the news desk for an update on all that's happening in the world today.

The music started up again and the red light moved to a camera in another part of the studio, where a news presenter Kate vaguely recognized as being on the *News at Ten* until he'd been caught having an affair with a call girl, started talking about another bomb scare in Israel. Trisha turned to face Kate and looked at her, a worried expression filling her eyes.

"Well . . . that was interesting. I have something to ask you about all that. . . ."

"What? And by the way, thanks." She stood up, ready to follow the assistant who was suddenly by her side to take her back to the greenroom.

Trisha tugged at Kate's sleeve like a pet Chihuahua looking for its mistress. "Do you think—I mean, obviously with your new experience—do you think I am looking a bit, you know, too *perfect*?"

* * *

There was a neon-lit corridor linking the set with the greenroom, filled with framed pictures of Trisha Hillmory and the male newscaster she'd just seen. The assistant, in his late twenties, walked slightly ahead of her, turning every so often to make light conversation.

"I saw the show—it was good what you were saying. You came across very honestly, I suppose. We don't get much of that."

Kate didn't need the small talk. She had a plane to catch, things on her mind. She reached into her pocket for the thousand pounds she'd stuffed there earlier, then stopped under a picture of Trisha with a former prime minister, now retired. She supposed in the old days, before the affair, it would have been a picture of Trisha with the current prime minister. She almost felt sorry for her.

The assistant walked on a couple more paces before realizing she had stopped.

"Can I trust you?" she asked him.

"Well, of course. What can I do for you?" He looked surprised.

"I want you to get a copy of the show that we just did. A video of it, or whatever format it's on, I don't know the terminology, I'm sorry . . . I want you to get it as quickly as possible to someone. In America. Here's his address. I've given you e-mail, phone numbers, everything, but it has to be with him by the end of today. Do you understand?"

He was taken aback by the authority in her voice.

"Well, I don't know how easy that's going to be, but I'll look into it for you, certainly."

Kate pressed the notes into his hand.

"A grand. I want you to do more than just look into it. He has to get it today, okay? Oh, and this note needs to go with it. If you have to type it and send it in an e-mail, you can do that, but it has to get there."

She handed him the piece of paper. The assistant restrained himself from counting the money, but was evidently thrilled by the bulky weight of the notes that now greased his palms.

"No problem. In fact, now that I think of it, I'm pretty sure we've got a bird up at eleven to send another piece over to L.A.—I'll stick it on the end of the feed."

"Bird?"

"It's a satellite," he said.

"Of course," said Kate. "Good."

new york

beauty note:

Dress: 3.1 Philip Lim. *Body Oil:* Aromatherapy Associates Renew Rose. *Hair:* Ruffles smoothed with Kérastase Vernis Nutri-Sculpt Ultra-Shine Top Coat for Dry, Sensitized Hair. *Eyes:* Shu Uemura Liquid Eyeliner in black. *Lips:* Estée Lauder Re-Nutriv Sun Supreme Lip Balm SPF 15. *Fragrance:* Solange Azagury-Partridge's Stoned. *Nails:* $10 manicure at Think Pink (West 58TH St. location).

thirty

"I'm sorry."

She seemed to have done a lot of apologizing lately.

She was at Jean-Paul's apartment in Greenwich Village, standing at the door with her bag in tow, aware that she hadn't so much as called him since she'd left him under the sheets. It was early evening. She'd slept all night on the flight from London to New York, her first proper night's sleep in what seemed like ages. She had one last evening with Jean-Paul, and then who knew what tomorrow would bring.

He looked at her, a flash of reproach clouding his face for a second. Then he grabbed her, hugged her, and kissed her in the doorway. She felt the buckle on the shoulder strap of her bag dig into her shoulder uncomfortably as he pressed his body against hers, but she wasn't about to pull away. Everything else about the embrace was spot-on. The bones of his pelvis jutted into her; she pressed her thigh against his legs as his hand gripped her bottom. He pulled her into his home, their lips still locked, and tightened his arms around her, walking, guiding her to the sofa. It was only when he pushed her gently down on the wide, brown leather cushions that he allowed her to draw breath.

"You should be sorry!" he laughed. "But then . . . I didn't call either, so I'm sorry, too."

He kissed her again, but this time she pushed him away, hand on his chest. He looked at her face, taking it all in, surprised.

"What?"

"I've got a few things to tell you." She looked seriously at him, but it was impossible to keep a straight face. The corners of his mouth kept wrinkling upward; his eyes were smiling brightly.

"I—I'm going to quit my job and move back to Maidstone," she said. It was the first time she'd told anyone, and it felt good to hear the words thud out, to bring them to life and make them real.

Jean-Paul looked at her blankly.

"It's a bloody joke, right?"

She could see how it might look. He didn't even know the ins and outs of the debacle at *Darling*. He must think she was giving up on a career, a new home, possibly even a new relationship.

He knelt on the sofa, body erect, poised to pounce like a tiger. His hair flopped over his face. She sat upright and smoothed it away from his eyes. Their faces were close to each other's now, but the expressions were different. She looked as if her mind was made up; she had a determined, measured air about her. His eyes were taking it all in, before the words were spoken, as if the pennies were dropping: Kate was going back to England, and that meant the end of Kate and Jean-Paul before it had even begun. From outside she could hear the familiar noise of cop cars. She pictured the yellow cabs, the tall buildings that continued to impress her, the busyness of people rushing about, the blue sky blessing their productiveness somehow, where in England it seemed always gray.

But she had made her decision. She knew it was the right thing to do, in spite of Lise's protests. She didn't know whether she'd be back in New York ever, but she'd had adventures, she would take with her happy memories, life-enriching experiences, and if there was one thing she'd learned from what had happened to Lise, life was all about living. Her friend needed her—she would never have said so herself, naturally, but for a while at least, it was time for Lise. To throw herself back into this crazy world of looks and looking, Kate needed to be able to immerse herself totally, and this, for now at least, was out of the question. Jean-Paul or no Jean-Paul.

"Lots of things have happened since I last saw you." She attempted to explain, holding his hands.

"You don't need to explain," he said. "Look, Kate, it's okay. What we have—had—it's been so much fun, a magical time, really. And it's not that I don't care that you're going, because I do, of course I do. But we 'ad fun, and if it's meant to—"

"Shh! Don't say it," she said. She had a strange sensation, a feeling that she might actually cry, but it wasn't from a sense of loss about what was to happen to Jean-Paul and Kate. It wasn't self-pity either. More the sense that she was on the brink of realizing and enacting changes that would shape who she was going to be in the future, her very being. It was frightening to be so in control after the last few crazy months of flitting from story to story, city to city, living on the adrenaline rush. She knew, Jean-Paul knew, theirs was not a big dream about love. It was a fun fling, on a balmy, perfect evening in New York. They were honest with each other, and that was worth more

than any empty protestations about how much they loved and
needed each other. Because they didn't. Not really. They would
be friends, she hoped, e-mail buddies, and maybe they'd see
each other again, maybe they'd pick up where they left off, but
the timing was all wrong for now. And that was just the way it
was. She didn't mind; neither did he. It was perfect.

And if she was to be honest with herself, she knew she had
feelings, ones she hadn't even begun to deal with yet, for another, her Mr. Imperfect Perfect, who right now was hopefully
watching a tape of her apologizing profusely on TV. What
would he think of her now?

"Come . . . we 'ave one more night together? Let's do some
of your crazy naked dancing!"

And so they did. And more than dancing. For most of the
night, in bed, out of bed, in the shower even, the stereo on full
blast with all their favorite tunes, until they collapsed, dozily,
into each other's arms to sleep off what remained of the night.

"Fuck, that was great!" he said, lying back like a sated lion.

"Yup!" She sighed.

Kate sat up suddenly. Something was wrong. She couldn't
put her finger on it, but he'd sounded so different this time,
so . . . so . . . He had said it with a perfect English accent.

"Say that again!"

"Fuck! That was . . . great?" They looked at each other. He
paused, didn't know what to say all of a sudden.

And then she realized. The "flat" instead of "apartment," the
"bloody hells," the "brilliants," the "lovelys" and the "nices."
The growing up watching *Blue Peter*. The preferring *EastEnders*
to *Coronation Street*. The Anglophile parents!

"You're English, aren't you!?" She pulled the sheets over her
breasts, immediately on the defensive, her face incredulous.
She grabbed a pillow and started whacking him over the head
with it, aggressively.

"You're bloody English!!! All the time, you were putting on that ridiculous, cheesy, camp Maurice Chevalier accent, and what was all that about?"

He raised his hands to protect himself from the volley of goose-feathered blows raining down upon him.

"Kate . . . Kate! Let me explain, please. . . ."

She stopped for a second.

"Sure thing, Jean-Paul, or do I call you John? Plain old John? Only I haven't . . . finished . . . beating . . . you . . . up yet! I can't believe it!"

She punctuated each word with a pillow thump, then lay on the bed, fists clenched by her head, facedown into a pillow. "I can't believe you!!" She was shouting now, her voice tailing off into giggles of sheer incredulity. It was a situation so bizarre she didn't know whether she should laugh or be angry.

He stroked her hair gingerly, like a cat tentatively stretching a paw out into the pouring rain, but she pushed him away.

"Look, Kate . . . I—I—I came here fifteen years ago, and no one cared. It was full of English artists, American artists, trying to make a name for themselves. So I put on this accent. My mum was half French, so I knew how to do it. . . . I guess it's not strictly a lie, as that makes me a quarter French."

"It is a lie, Jean-Paul, of course it's a fucking lie! And I'm English, and you lied to me! Me! I feel like such a fucking idiot!"

Jean-Paul straddled her, tried to turn her around to face him, but she wouldn't budge. "Kate. Kate! But what could I do? Once I started, it was impossible to stop. And I couldn't risk you telling Alexis or whoever."

It was odd to hear her Frenchman talking so much like an Englishman. Could an accent really make such a huge difference to a career?

She wriggled round finally, and lay on her back glaring at

him sulkily. "And did it? Did it make such a difference to your fucking career?!"

He looked directly in her eyes; his voice was soft, serious.

"Well, yes. That was the weird thing. It worked. I tell you, once people thought I was different, they looked at me in a special way. People like Alexis treated me like some exotic specimen, actually looked at my art as opposed to judging me as yet another pretentious young artist with aspirations above his station."

"Oh, and that makes it all right, does it? You know what? You know what, Jean-Paul?"

That was the problem. She couldn't think of "what." His was an odd kind of lie, because it wasn't as if he owed her any kind of loyalty or honesty. She supposed it wasn't so different from the world she inhabited, the world of beauty, where you judged and were judged by appearances always. This was no more of a lie than getting highlights, she supposed, or having a face-lift. So it made better economical sense to be French? Well, why not? It was all too much to take on board. Kate rolled over with her back to him. She needed to get some sleep. Tomorrow she had to go to the office, and then fly back home. It made her feel exhausted just thinking about it. She wondered how Lise was getting on. She wondered whether Steve was curled up in bed beside her, or fetching her mugs of tea. She knew he would be. She hadn't told Lise what she was planning on doing. She would be giving up a lot here. A job—if it hadn't already given up on her. Her own apartment. An imposter. But maybe, she would be gaining something else. Someone else. Someone not bloody John Paul from . . . England!

"Jean-Paul!" She rolled over angrily to face him. "I'm really pissed off with you!"

She hadn't noticed that he'd leaned in closer to her, so that now she was within an inch of him, their noses almost touching.

Such impropriety when she was trying so hard to be angry, distant, made her laugh. He laughed, too, and seized the opportunity to embrace her once more.

"I'm sorry," he said. "I would have told you, honest."

"You so wouldn't!" she said.

They held each other fondly, like good friends and old lovers. She knew she would keep in touch with him. She wasn't sure how often, or when, or how much she would value his friendship, but she would.

The light started to eke its way in through the slatted wooden blinds. Kate flung her arm over his chest and nuzzled her head until it was comfortably ensconced in the crook of his arm. She fell asleep.

* * *

In the morning she awoke with a start. She had so much to do. She had to pack up her apartment and head to *Darling*'s offices. But Jean-Paul was having none of it. He had prepared her a tray of breakfast: a pile of pancakes with butter, sugar, and wedges of lemon and a mug of steaming tea. His face was animated; he had something to tell her.

"Hello, love."

She had forgotten he was now English. It was disconcerting. "Oh, God," she said, then rolled away, face back into the pillow.

He was dressed already, wearing jeans and a gray cashmere V-neck sweater.

"Listen, I've had a brilliant idea." Brilliant. It wasn't just a bad dream then. He carefully handed her the mug of tea.

"Go on then, what?" It was definitely a good thing she was going back to England. Let him sort out his identity crisis by himself.

"I'm going to open up this flat." There it was again. "Flat" not "apartment." "I'm going to make it into an installation, an artwork." He looked energized about something, but she was none the wiser as to what he was talking about.

"I've been thinking about it all night. I've been drawing how it's going to look, and it's going to be amazing!" He beamed, a grin stretching from ear to ear like a Cheshire cat. Of course, now that he was English he would know exactly where Cheshire was.

"Okay . . . but I'm still not getting it," she said, grumpily.

"Don't you see? All my assumed Frenchness, living another life, another persona! That's my real artwork!" he said. "Never mind my paintings, which will now become the paintings of someone else, the paintings of Jean-Paul Suchet. . . . *This* artwork will be amazing! Imagine, over fifteen years of living as someone else, as an imaginary being. If that isn't art, what is? And this flat will be my testimony to it all, the witness to how we fabricate our lives, go through them pretending to be someone else, never quite facing up to who we might be, or who we could be."

Kate sat up and stared at him. He really was crazy.

"Kate, I'm on to something big here. I know it. Julian Schnabel will love it. Nan Goldin will be crazy about it—it's so like the work she did with the rock-and-roll AIDS portraits, about life itself as art form. And you know, there was that guy a couple of years ago, won the Beck's Futures prize? Jamie someone. Did something called . . . It'll come back to me!" He rubbed his hands backward and forward over his hair. "I've got it! *Lustfaust!* How ace is that? Jamie Shovlin! That was his name. Genius! Re-created all this memorabilia and fanzine stuff about a band that had never existed. Put it in little glass boxes, amazing stuff! Talk about lightness of being! I could take things from this apartment, put them in glass vitrines, and exhibit them as fragments from Jean-Paul Suchet's life! Portrait of the

Artist. Hang his paintings, again, Jean-Paul, the artist, all the while asking, 'Who is Jean-Paul? Is he real?' It's about appropriating an identity, and I've gone further than anyone, I've done it, lived it, been it, for over fifteen years! Genius!"

She had lost him to his art. And that was no bad thing. She'd never really had him to lose him, nor he, her.

*   *   *

A couple of hours later, she stood again by the door, this time to say good-bye.

"So what do I call you? I don't even know your name," she said.

"John Sutch," he said, grinning. "From now on I'm plain old John Sutch. From Croydon."

Kate gave him one last kiss, then stood back and looked at him.

"John Sutch from Croydon? It was a pleasure to meet you."

thirty-one

Eleven a.m. By the time Kate arrived through the great swing doors at the entrance to Nouvelle Maison Editions, they had calmed down from their whirling dervish rush hour of a few hours ago to a more sedate waltz. The doors were like guards to this monstrous building, threatening in some ways, with its lumpy, gray gargoyles on the roof, and its clean, empirical, Art Deco lines everywhere else, but in spite of these stony-walled attributes it had never seemed frightening to her. Gargoyles made her think of the Hunchback of Notre Dame. The Disney version. And Art Deco was Edward and Mrs. Simpson, wasn't it? Quite what the two styles were doing together she didn't know. She entered the building and drew a deep breath, marveling at how Manhattan's most attractive people always seemed to be assembled in the lobby area, waiting for who or for what she never knew, but at least ten model types, clean-cut young men, and smartly groomed twentysomethings seemed to be hovering there now.

She remembered the first time she had swung through these doors. She had been full of confidence, bravado, enthusiasm for whatever challenges lay before her. She'd known no one! Back then, she'd asked to see Alexis, and had actually had to look her surname up in her diary, momentarily forgetting the name of her new boss in her unique state of jet-lagged disorientation. She was not sure she could do that now, again. Start over in a strange city. She cringed at the thought of her cheap outfits, which she'd hoped to pass off as . . . she hadn't even known the names of the labels she was aping.

Cynthia met her outside the lift. She looked apprehensive, awkward.

"Hi," she said, staring at her for an instant before air-kissing her cheeks. "I'm—I'm sorry it all . . ." Her words petered out. Kate could have tried to fill them in with something appropriate but she didn't know what to suggest beyond "went wrong" and then again, what had gone wrong? She wanted to tell Cynthia that she planned to resign; wanted to encourage her, praise her for her work, which had improved infinitely since she'd arrived. But to do that would imply that she knew she was leaving, and she couldn't tell Cynthia before she'd told Alexis.

"How have you been anyway?" she asked Cynthia. They hadn't had a proper chat for ages. She'd been in L.A., then barely caught her breath in New York before going back to Maidstone.

"Oh, you know. Fine. Actually not fine. Since you asked, my parents are insisting I return home and get a proper job, you know, one with a half-decent salary in a law firm or something. So, I'm stalling!"

"Gosh, I'm sorry about that." She was sorry, too. Cynthia had shown potential, had ideas, and with the right training and experience could develop as a writer. There was an awkward silence. If they had been in the lift still, this would have been the bit when they would have looked up at the ceiling or straight ahead at the door, in order to avoid conversation or even eye contact. They walked toward Alexis's office, eyes bowed to the floor, straight ahead, around, anywhere except at each other.

"Oh, and Jane-Louise is pregnant."

"She is? That's brilliant!" She wondered if they even employed pregnant people here.

Cynthia delivered her final volley:

"And Tony in the canteen has put his choc-lattes up to four dollars, can you believe it?"

*　　*　　*

Alexis sprang up from behind her desk like an overexcited golden retriever, shaking her glossy, blow-dried mane extravagantly. Had it been that soft and flouncy before? Her facial hair had been bleached away, or waxed, or electrolysized off, if that was even a word. And for all that she could still air-kiss like a pro, Kate thought she could detect more than a hint of genuine warmth as she hugged her.

"Kate, darling. It's good to have you back."

She sat down, avoiding the other seat, the one where she'd sat for their last, hideous meeting. She sat in quiet confidence, expectantly, as a hushed formality descended.

Alexis brandished a few sheets of paper, triumphantly. She sighed.

"It's a great story, Kate. I knew you had it in you. And it'll go in the issue as planned." She beamed. "I think it's the kind of piece that will get picked up by the papers, too, syndicated. Of course, it's far less sensational than that other one, but, my . . . so much more real! It will strike a chord with lots of women, I have to say, it struck a chord with me. I'm really pleased you pulled it off. There was a lot of pressure from us for you to do so, but you did it."

She put the copy down to the right, and picked up her brown leather notebook, with the gilded edges, the one she used for daily notes and meetings.

"I've had a busy week, one way and another," she continued, "but it's been productive, and I think you'll be pleased with the outcome. After you left, Elizabeth Geary proposed a solution to our problems, which I am in agreement with. Obviously we couldn't risk word getting out about this mistake of Lizbet's, so we had to make discreet inquiries about the other Kate Miller at *Harper's Bazaar*. She's a nice enough girl, Kate, but she's not you, and I'm convinced that my instincts about you—well, obviously it's confusing now as to whether my instincts were about you or about someone I thought was you—but anyway, it turns out that she is on maternity leave right now, which is a huge relief as it means we don't have to offer her any job. Elizabeth has pointed out that we really need to help you a little more, and so with this in mind we're setting in place a series of training controls that will help you. Getting you to go on shoots more, that kind of thing. And then there's—"

"Alexis, there's something I need to tell you."

"I don't want your apologies, Kate, I really don't. I needed you to understand, not to apologize. They're quite different things, you know. And I have something to tell you, too." She took a sip from a glass of water. It was a pretty, pale pink glass, with an uneven, handmade quality to its edges that refracted the light so that the surface of the water shimmered delicately, in a diamond pattern. If only they could get that effect on an eyeshadow, Kate thought to herself. Perhaps a little silver metallic shot through it, worn with maybe a black kohl eyeliner to rock it up.

"Kate, you're a natural at this. I know you've made mistakes, but I think we should have given you more structure to work within at first. When I look back at what you have achieved, which was remarkable anyway, I might add, bar those last few incidents . . . it is incredible to think that you pulled it from nowhere. From out of a hat, you might say. I know you've had some training, and newspapers, even local ones, are not a bad place to start. But to do what you've done—make the transition, and manage staff—well, it can't have been easy. And now that we both know where we stand, now I know you're not from the place I thought you're from . . ." She coughed, a small, fractious cough, as if in memory of the pain of last week's discovery.

"I can't do it, Alexis," said Kate.

Alexis looked up at her, surprised.

"What do you mean?"

Kate drew a deep breath. "I'm sorry, but I have to resign. My friend's got cancer." She'd been fine up to now, but the act of telling someone else about Lise was making her feel emotional once more. "I need to be with her. I mean, I think she'll be okay, they've done the operation, everything, but it's not right, my being here. I need to be a support to her, need to be doing something to make up for the fact that—" She couldn't say any more. She felt the tears, another outpouring about to come on. Again! She couldn't cry any more tears, could she? What was wrong with her?

Alexis stood up to face the windows for a second, then turned around to look at Kate.

"I—I don't understand. No one has ever . . ."

"I'm really sorry, Alexis, but I have to get back to Maidstone. Tomorrow. I mean, I'm flying back tonight. I have plans. And I need to follow through, with Lise. Look, it's been fun, really fun here—"

She looked around her, taking it all in. She saw the view once more from Alexis's windows, the big, wide green of Central Park, with its trees, now wearing their big bright early autumn leaves. People walked briskly, their bare arms cloaked in a host of lightweight but warm jackets from Banana Republic, the Gap, Club Monaco, Target, all made in factories in far-flung places like Portugal, Mexico, India, China. When she turned her chair slightly, she could see the office behind her: Jane-Louise and Cynthia at the water fountain; faces huddling over computers; chatting, hardworking beings enjoying their work. There was a camaraderie, a professionalism, a slickness about this office that she would never find in Maidstone. The art department was a proper art department. Mario Testino, world-famous photographer, was sitting perched on the edge of the desk of the art director, laughing, and it was no big deal! The subs station was surrounded by thick volumes of reference works, dictionaries, thesauruses, just like the Department of Factual Verification in Jay McInerney's *Bright Lights, Big City*! Tracy was returning with a trayful of Starbucks coffees, no doubt in protest at the hike in prices at Tony's canteen. They had a man called Tracy working here!

Alexis looked at her, as if reading her thoughts.

"Let me tell you something, Kate. It's sink or swim here. And you've swum. More than any of us, you came from nowhere. I don't mean to be horrible about small towns—but in this world they count as nowhere. It's a well-kept secret that people who do well in this business come from small towns. Or Texas. Now, I know what you're thinking, you can't be yourself, you can't support your friends and family, and hold down a job like this. But you're wrong, Kate. You can keep your own life."

From a drawer she pulled out a picture of herself, next to a man.

"I haven't shown anyone this, but this is my fiancé. Frederick Wallner. He's a poet. We got engaged last week! I'm marrying a poet! And thank God I can get rid of the damn facial hair at last!" She made a strange little "whoopee!" type of noise, and then composed herself quickly, continuing, "I do my job, but I keep my life, too. I go to poetry readings, imagine that! You're hungry for work, and that's no bad thing. I used to be like that. Am like that. It's very American in a way. You're a writer at heart. You won't be doing this job forever, but for now, I see someone who's come so far, she can't stop. Look at how you've helped Cynthia blossom. Her copy's improved no end! And your ideas are rich and vibrant. You inspired our leading plastic surgeon! Sparked a national craze! And so, you dress a bit differently now than when you first came, you've gotten rid of those crazy highlights, but what I love about you, and people like you, is that you're no clone. If I'd wanted a clone, I'd have employed . . . I don't know, Kate Miller from *Harper's Bazaar*!"

Kate wiped her nose on her sleeve. Didn't Tom Ford come from Texas?

"Does your friend . . . does she actually want you to move back to Maidstone?"

Kate thought hard. Of course, she knew Lise had said she shouldn't come back, but what if she hadn't meant that? She needed to make up for everything she hadn't done, somehow, some way. She needed to spend the time now that she hadn't spent before. They would have fun together, nights out, as soon as Lise recovered. She would help Lise and Steve move in somewhere bigger together, watch them be happy together. She would be there for Lise as she . . . as she what?

"She hasn't insisted on it; quite the reverse," Kate said.

Alexis paused to look closely at Kate's face. She could see the pain behind the brave-face smiles.

"You need to be there for her. As much for yourself as for her," said Alexis, "but, and I know this will sound like a platitude now, you need to remember you're no good to her unless you're happy and fulfilled in your own life. You can't put your life on hold for her. Or for anyone. Do what you can for her. Spend some time with her. Let her believe that life goes on. She needs to know that right now. Then come back."

Kate looked at her. In just that short time of working with her, she suddenly felt that she had found a true ally, a mentor, somebody on her side. Alexis was giving her a dream ticket—the ticket of the open door. She could go back to Maidstone, look after Lise, and see how things went!

"Kate, there's something else I need to run by you." Alexis frowned, turning again to face the window. "I'm not happy with the way Clarissa's working out. Sloppy copy. Too many 'appointments' in work time—where, God only knows." She faced Kate. A broad smile spread slowly across her face.

"I was thinking about firing her, and promoting Cynthia. What do you think?"

london

beauty note:

Dress: Zac Posen mini. Matching underwear (just in case) by Agent Provocateur. Shoes: Roger Vivier. *Stomach*: Cream for emergency tummy firming, Bliss Love Handler. *Complexion:* SheerinO'kho First Class Flight moisturizer boosted after visit to airplane toilets (that light!) with Chanel Beauté Initial Spray Serum, enhanced with Estée Lauder DayWear Plus Multi Protection Tinted Moisturizer SPF 15. *Eyes:* Revlon Bedroom Eyes eyeliner and Benefit BADgal Lash mascara in black. *Cheeks:* Nars blush in Orgasm. *Lips:* Lipstick Queen lipstick in Nude Sinner. *Fragrance:* Jean Patou, Joy.

thirty-two

I t was all going according to plan, or at least, her plane had landed on time. Flying economy hadn't been so bad. Especially with the guilt-fueled business-class upgrade Lizbet had arranged, as soon as she'd heard Kate was insisting on flying back on her own terms and not on the company's credit card. She'd left it open-ended with Alexis, grateful to have discovered yet another new professional term she'd been unfamiliar with up until now. "Sabbatical" was added to the lexicon along with last week's newcomer, "gardening leave." A sabbatical was almost as good as gardening leave—you didn't get the big salary, but then neither did you get the pressure of the shadow of alleged bad behavior hanging over you. You could take a month off, six, a year in some cases, then come back and start where you left off. She hadn't told Lise yet. She had plenty more to tell Lise.

She collected her baggage from the carousel and made her

way through Customs. Lizbet had graciously agreed to send the rest of her stuff over, as soon as she'd made up her mind, so she'd been able to keep her same overnight bag and leave the rest behind. They would continue to pay the rent on her flat until the end of the month and the next, so there was no hurry to pack up her effects. She'd called Jean-Paul, or John Sutch, as he was now known, but he'd cut her short, something about a meeting with Jay Jopling, as he was thinking about targeting the London art world. He'd been charming about it, but she understood. No decisions. No commitments, for either of them, at least for the short term. It more than suited her.

As she rounded the bend into Arrivals, the usual coterie of white name placards and, no doubt, misspelled names met her. She wondered how JK was feeling right now, how he would feel when he saw her face eventually. She remembered how nice it had been that one time in New York when Jean-Paul, correction, John Sutch had been at the airport for her. She watched a twentysomething woman with two kids heave one of her suitcases back on the trolley, as it tried to roll wonkily away.

She felt so excited she had to force herself to walk slowly, calmly. In the newsagent's opposite, the front pages screamed out headlines that had ceased meaning anything to her recently, but for now, for the short term at least, would start to mean things again. She picked up a copy of the *Sun* and a copy of the *Guardian* and paid for them at the till, even though she knew she wouldn't have the level of concentration required to get through even the headlines of the broadsheet. She wasn't going to try to work out time differences anymore. Two flights. Three flights? In the last week or so. Too much.

Over at Starbucks, she ordered a latte with a shot of caramel and sat down at the bar-style round table nearest to the entrance.

If he was coming at all, he would be here in the next fifteen minutes.

She hadn't made much of a contingency plan. What if her flight had been late? What if his flight was late? But he had her number, she supposed, so he could always call if he needed to.

She flicked through the *Sun*. Keeley, the topless model on page 3, was hoping the soldiers in Afghanistan would restore order to the country soon so that women there could return to their jobs and schools.

She felt . . . what did she feel? Nervous, most definitely. It didn't matter too much if it all went wrong, but if it all went right, how much better would that be? But most of all, she felt loved. She felt blessed. She felt blessed that Alexis had given her chances and opportunities she had only dreamed of, and that when she'd messed up, she'd been given more. She felt she'd discovered her family and friends again, fallen in love with them again, in a way that this time around she knew they would be there for her no matter what. She felt that in John Sutch, she'd found she could have fun in a way that was not about her career, fun like women her age were meant to have. She felt benevolent toward Trish, who, after all, was just Trish at the end of the day, and who would always be the same and (it had to be said) who had given her plenty of money—ten grand!—to help her carry out the next stage of her plan. She felt happy to see her mum blossom and move in a direction she would never have envisaged for her had she not gone to New York. And with JK she felt . . .

"Hey, gorgeous girl, is this seat taken?" An American accent, from behind her, an accent that made her rocket out of her seat and turn around, all pistons firing.

"You came!"

John Kingsley III stood in front of her. Tall, handsome, blond. With the squiffy nose she'd come to find attractive. She jumped up and hugged him impetuously, before realizing that she'd never actually hugged him before. She didn't know how

322 Kathleen Baird-Murray

to behave, now that he was the goody and not the baddy she'd had him down as. She pulled her arms off him quickly and stood up straight, trying to look composed.

"How could I refuse?" He laughed. It was no good. She had to touch him again. She grabbed his hands and pulled at him to sit down.

"I'm so, so grateful, and I'm so sorry. You saw the tape of the TV show, then. Oh, you must have done, otherwise I guess you wouldn't be here, so you know that I'm sorry, don't you, really sorry, and I'm so grateful that you're here, I really am!"

"Kate . . . please . . . it's okay."

"I almost forgot, I've got the money for it, you know! I'm not expecting you to do this for free or anything!" She pulled up her handbag from the floor and went to find her purse, which had disappeared somewhere in the voids of linings, rivets, key fobs, and other handbag paraphernalia.

"Kate . . . Kate . . . you're not going to insult me by offering money, are you?"

"Well, I—" She stopped fumbling and looked into his eyes. "I found out how much you would normally charge for a boob job, sorry, I mean a breast reconstruction, and then I . . ." She noticed a frown starting to form on his face, coupled with a smile.

"Look, it's sweet of you; but if it makes you feel better, give my fee, or even what you can, to the children's charity."

"All right!"

"Well, let's go then! I hope you don't mind, I booked a driver already to take us to . . . Maidfair?"

"It's Maid*stone*! County town of Kent, you know! My hometown, so don't knock it!"

"As if."

He put his arm through hers and raised his other hand toward a gray-capped man standing by the entrance to Starbucks, who strode over efficiently and picked up their bags.

People stared at them. Kate realized the whole point of L.A. gorgeousness was to transport it elsewhere, show it off in gray, rain-soaked London, where just one drop shimmered like the truest Hollywood star.

"Come on then! Let's go meet your friend Lise, shall we?"

She halted abruptly, and looked directly at him, then said, gravely, "I haven't told her yet."

"You haven't? Well, that's okay, it'll be a surprise. I guess quite a big surprise." He narrowed his eyes a little, working it all out. "And don't worry, if it's not, you know, medically convenient, I can come back and do it another time. The important thing is I get to meet her, you know."

"Thanks, JK." Kate couldn't help herself from squeezing his hand. She was relieved beyond belief that he had accepted her olive branch, risen to the challenge. He'd been a good man, all that time, with a good skill. She thought of how much Lise would love him; how happy she'd be when she found out he was there to create breasts for her that would do justice to the beauty of her own natural original ones.

"Oh, and you may have to persuade her those big inflatable ones are no longer in fashion."

"You're the boss."

They got into the car. He gripped her hand tightly. Surgeon's fingers, she smiled to herself. The driver started the engine and pulled off, another car quickly taking their precious parking spot.

"By the way . . . did I tell you how gorgeous you look on TV?"

Kate blushed. The car entered a tunnel. As their eyes adjusted in the darkness he reached over and gently placed a strand of her hair behind her ear that had fallen over her mouth. His fingers brushed over her lips.

She sighed. "No, you didn't. But we have a good couple of hours' journey ahead of us."